One
Shoe
Off

SUE MERRELL

Jordan Daily News Mysteries:
Great News Town (2011)
One Shoe Off (2012)
Full Moon Friday (Coming 2014)

Also by Sue Merrell:
Laughing for a Living (2010)
http://suemerrellbooks.com

DEDICATION

This book is dedicated to all the journalists I worked with in my 40-year career. Their unflinching devotion to truth and fairness has inspired me throughout my life and sets the bar for my fictional friends at the *Jordan Daily News*

.

ACKNOWLEDGMENTS

First of all, I want to remember Molly Zelko, the 47-year-old editor of the *Spectator* weekly newspaper, whose disappearance from Joliet, Ill., on September 26, 1957, was the inspiration for my fictional character, Zelda Machinko. I'd also like to thank the late John Whiteside, and his friend and co-writer Lonny Cain, who investigated her disappearance in 1978 for a series of stories in the Joliet Herald-News.

I want to thank the talented team that worked with me on *One Shoe Off* including my writing coaches Roe Van Fossen and Martha Robach, my editor Jane Haradine, my graphic designer Ryan Wallace and all my first readers in Peninsula Writers.

I especially want to thank the fans who entered the Cussin' Contest and suggested some of creative curse words Duke uses in *One Shoe Off*. Winners, who will receive a free copy of the book, include Michele Aversa, Pam Barr, Cerise Fuhrman, Donna Huldin, Susan Maciak, Crissy Meek, Will Swanson, Kristen Talaga, Angela Wallace, Sandy Workman and Kate Zuidema. Keep on cussin'—creatively.

Jordan Daily News Staff

Becky Judd, 29, tall, thin black reporter

Dick Stone, Sports editor

Duke (Ormand Dukakis), 41, reporter, columnist and alcoholic

Hammond Reginald, managing editor

Helen, the receptionist

Hoss, 49, hefty copy-desk chief

Josie Braun, 35, petite city editor nicknamed Peter Pan

Mack Stanton, 63, distinguished perfectionist photographer

Maggie, 69, veteran reporter can't use a computer but knows everyone in town

Nick, 28, baseball-loving, heart-breakingly handsome assistant city editor

Page (Stanley Pageniewski), quiet, giant photographer

Rest of the characters

Abe Hendrix, owner of Hendrix Hardware

Alphonse Baker, Chicago attorney in the 1950s

Ben Davis, farmer died in *Great News Town* leaving property to Becky Judd

Bill and Chuck, Zach's assistants

Blaine Avril, construction worker found murdered near sewer project

Bob Wise, Cade County Administrator

Brittany Miller, young widow of Scotty Miller, dating Nick Davidson

Carolyn Cantrell, Tom's mother

Christopher Sheffield, Maggie's son who is a medical missionary

Connie Davis, U.S. Senator from Illinois

Daniel Pasternak, former Jordan detective who investigated Zelda Machinko

Earl Smith (Smitty), construction worker who digs up bones

Elsie, clerk for Jordan Police Department

Francis "Buster" Boardman, union leader and reputed gangster in 1950s

Fred Wheeler, Justice Department agent investigating the sewer project

George Sheffield, Maggie's policeman husband, deceased

Gary, nursing assistant at Herkimer

Herbert Flatt, beefy worker on sewer construction project

Irwin MacDonald, *Spectator* paper boy

Jackie Peters, second-shift clerk at St. Mary's Hospital

Jennifer Dukakis, 16, daughter of Duke and Sharon

Joe Humboldt, site manager for state forensic team

Katherine Sheffield, Maggie's daughter, Hollywood screenwriter

Kevin Walsh, 8, son of Josie Braun and Kurt Walsh

Kurt Walsh, Josie's ex-husband, works for Downtown Development board

Letha Albright, meter maid who discovers body

Linda Cantrell, Tom's sister who has Down Syndrome

Margaret, secretary for T&T Construction

Mitch, gum tester at Pop-O gum factory

Paul, tour guide at Pop-O gum factory

Pearl Zaenger, 1950s tipster to something buried under street

Polly, Josie's neighbor, mother of Timmy

Richard Hamilton, personnel manager at Anderson Construction in Michigan

Ron Baylor, beefy worker on sewer construction project

Roy Hatch, Mayor of Jordan

Rudy Randolph, owner of Ranch Rudy day-care center

Sharon Dukakis, Duke's wife, a teacher

Sid Collins, gas station owner killed in the 1950s

Terry Tate, owner of T&T Construction, contractors for the sewer project

Timmy, Kevin's best friend

Tom Cantrell, homicide detective for Jordan City Police

William Stiles, Illinois legislator

Zach Teasdale, Cade County Coroner and wealthy businessman

Zelda Machinko, *Spectator* editor who disappeared in 1956

Chapter 1

A siren.

The faint metallic whine was barely audible above the muffled voices on the police scanner at the *Jordan Daily News*. The scanner sat on a bright-orange metal credenza behind the desk of city editor Josie Braun. She kept it turned low to avoid the incessant chatter, but a siren, picked up when a responding officer keyed his mike, meant an emergency. Josie leaned back in her chair to turn up the volume. Amid the bursts of chatter, she picked up enough to understand an ambulance was headed to Jackson and Pearl, only two blocks from the newspaper office.

It was about ten thirty in the morning, just after the first deadline for the afternoon paper, which served Chicago suburbs. Any minute Josie would receive copies of the first edition, slightly warm and smelling of ink. But there was enough time to investigate the siren and add a story to today's paper before the final deadline at noon.

Like centuries of sailors before her, Josie had been seduced by the siren call. She wouldn't be satisfied with the safety of an adequate first edition. No, she couldn't let the scent of something exciting go unheeded.

She glanced around the room deciding who would be best to send. She could hear reporter Becky Judd and assistant city editor Nick Davidson in the midst of a heated discussion. Nick, whose paper-strewn desk was corralled by a ring of baseball trophies, had hung a *Sports Illustrated* swimsuit calendar on the support beam behind his desk. Whenever Becky looked up from her terminal, Miss May's belly button stared back at her like a sexy Cyclops.

"This is harassment," Becky said, rising to every inch of her regal six-foot height.

Such a drama queen, Josie thought. Becky could find injustice anywhere. It was more than the perspective of a black woman in a white man's world. Becky's heart for the hurting made her a good reporter.

"I'd say it's encouragement," Nick replied with a playful wink.

He was one of those impossibly handsome guys who was used to getting his way by flashing a dimpled smile. But Becky was too much of a feminist to be easily swayed, so Nick switched to First Amendment tactics.

"If you can't have free speech in a newsroom, what's this world coming to?" he said.

Josie didn't want to interrupt such a choice argument for anything as routine as checking out a siren. Her gaze swept past the block of copy editors, busily making last-minute changes to today's front page. She saw a few reporters on phones, then she spotted Maggie Sheffield on the other side of the room.

Gray-haired Maggie was sixty-nine. She had been a reporter at the *Daily News* for more than fifty years and had no plans to retire. Computers baffled her, so she preferred to type her stories on an IBM Selectric. Josie, who was about half Maggie's age, admired the older reporter's handle on the community. Maggie was on a first-name basis with all the cops and judges. She could remember when many were kids.

A deep voice from the neighboring desk interrupted Josie's survey of the room.

"Mule muffins! Is that ambulance headed to the sewer construction site?"

Josie smiled at the latest creative expletive from Ormand "Duke" Dukakis, an investigative reporter and popular columnist. He was Josie's friend and confidant. There had been a brief affair a year ago, and although that was over by mutual agreement, she felt a surge of energy as Duke got up from his desk. He moved a life-size cardboard likeness of himself, a remnant of some advertising campaign, and squeezed behind it to turn up the volume on the scanner.

"Base to 660. Come in, 660. What's your ETA? Over."

Voices alternated with bursts of static. An eerie silence fell over the office as reporters and copy editors, lured by the hypnotic sound, stopped what they were doing.

"660 here. ETA two minutes. Over."

It was a small office, only eight reporters, but several left their desks and wandered over to stare at the scanner as if they could see the story unfold on some imaginary television screen. The copy editors paused to listen, but they were less intrigued than the reporters and remained seated, still busy working on today's paper.

The siren faded as the ambulance arrived on the scene. The chatter changed. Between bursts of static, Josie heard the code "10-79," a call for the medical examiner.

"Sounds like there's been a death at the sewer construction site," Duke said. "Doesn't sound like an accident. Sounds like they just found a body."

Lured by the Pied Piper melody of the police radio, Maggie had made her way across the newsroom and paused at Duke's words. She reached out as if to steady herself on the chest-high stack of Chicago-area newspapers that had accumulated on the edge of Josie's desk. Josie looked up and caught the pleading look in Maggie's eyes before they rolled to a ghastly white. The lids fluttered closed and Maggie sank to the floor, pulling newspapers over her like a blanket.

"Maggie!" Josie screamed and jumped up from her chair. She pushed through the reporters crowded around the police scanner. Becky was at Maggie's side, cradling her head in a pose like Michelangelo's "Pieta." Becky's big brown eyes turned to Josie for answers.

"Don't move her. She might have broken something," Josie said, falling to her knees beside them. "Maggie, can you hear me?"

Maggie didn't respond.

Josie put an ear to Maggie's mouth and heard a reassuring puff of air. She turned to Nick. "Call 911."

"Done," Nick responded, the phone already at his ear. "They want to know if she's having a seizure."

"I don't think so. She's not shaking or foaming at the mouth or anything."

"Is she diabetic?" Nick asked, parroting the 911 operator's questions.

"Hell, I don't know!" Josie shouted. "Just tell them to get over here—now!"

As soon as the words escaped her lips, Josie regretted them. "Dear God," she whispered, "please be with Maggie. Help her through this."

Unspoken was Josie's prayer for herself that somehow she would know what to do. A few minutes ago, getting a story about a dead body was her top priority. Now someone's life was in her hands. She looked up and saw at least a dozen faces looking down at her, expecting her to have answers she simply didn't have.

She waved a protective arm over Maggie. "Step back, give her some air," Josie said, though she was the one feeling like she was suffocating. As the crowd parted, Josie could see that even the copy editors were on their feet now. Everyone loved Maggie. Everyone cared. And nobody knew what to do.

Dick Stone, the sports editor, came running around the partition between the sports department and the newsroom.

"I've had some training in CPR," he said, pushing through the crowd and kneeling down next to Maggie.

"She seems to be breathing," Josie said, backing up to give Dick room as he placed fingers at Maggie's throat to feel for a pulse.

"Water," Dick said, looking up. "Maybe a splash of water will bring her around."

"Here." A small paper cup from the water cooler was thrust through the crowd.

The managing editor, Hammond Reginald, opened the door of his glassed-in office. "What's going on?"

"It's Maggie, she collapsed," one of the copy editors said.

"Well, call an ambulance," Ham said. "And get back to your desks. We've got a paper to put out. You can't help her by standing around."

Dick flicked a little water on Maggie's face and slapped her cheeks.

"Maggie? Can you hear me?"

Maggie's eyelashes fluttered, and then her eyes opened as tiny slits.

"Can you hear me, Maggie? Say something," Josie said, squeezing Maggie's hand.

Maggie remained quiet and still, her eyes barely open.

The siren's wail grew louder and louder until it filled the room with its cry of urgency.

Josie felt a warm hand on her shoulder and looked up at the calm quiet of Duke's face.

"I'll follow up on the body," he whispered. Then he placed a hand on Maggie's forehead, like a parent taking a child's temperature. "Hang in there, old girl."

✻

In the bustle of paramedics coming in and chairs and desks being moved aside to make way for the stretcher, Duke slipped outside and walked briskly down Jackson Street to the cluster of police cars two blocks away. He recognized Letha Albright first. The meter maid was leaning against the front of a squad car. Her hand was over her mouth as if she was about to puke or had already done so.

Beyond the squad car, Duke saw the brown leather jacket of Jordan police detective Tom Cantrell, who was looking into a homemade cap on the back of a small red pickup. The truck was covered with the blue-gray dust that permeated everything since the city had torn up four blocks of Jackson Street for a major sewer project. The huge yellow bulldozers that had made a giant sandbox out of one of Jordan's main streets were strangely still. A couple of uniformed officers were talking with a group of workers on the other side of that impassable gulf. Two others were stringing yellow crime scene tape from the red pickup to a tree to parking meters, pushing onlookers back as they moved. Duke knew the police were too busy to talk to him, so he returned to Letha.

"Are you OK?" He held out the clean white cotton handkerchief he always carried in his pants pocket.

Letha jumped a little at his voice. Her dark eyes, full of fear, looked first at Duke and then at the handkerchief. She lowered a shaky hand from her mouth, took the hanky, and rubbed it across her lips. The fear in her eyes softened a little. She was a stocky black woman in her late twenties, Duke guessed, with a prim navy-blue meter-maid's hat perched on a halo of shiny black curls.

"You found the body?" Duke asked. "That must have been awful for you."

Letha looked over her shoulder at the police officers but said nothing. She dabbed at the corner of one eye with the handkerchief, then looked down at her feet.

"It got on my shoes," she said, her voice barely above a whisper. "I stepped in it. I stepped in the puddle of blood."

4

Her voice cracked at the final word, and tears began rolling down her cheeks. Duke placed a hand on her shoulder. He could understand her horror. Less than a year before, he had found two bodies, one a good friend. But friend or stranger doesn't really matter. Death, especially violent death, reminds each of us how precarious our hold on life can be. Letha's tears released that pent-up fear. She dabbed at her eyes, blew her nose, and took a deep breath. She was ready to talk.

"I put a ticket on the truck first round this morning, about nine. Ever since they tore up Jackson, there's been a parking shortage around here, so I've stepped up my rounds in the area."

Duke knew firsthand about the parking shortage. The visitors' lot on the Jackson Street side of the *Daily News* had been closed by the construction, so ten spots in the employee lot on the Mill Street side had been reserved for guests. The reporters and advertising representatives played musical parking spots every morning.

"When I came back at ten," Letha said, "the truck was still there with no one even bothering to put any money in the meter or take the ticket off the window. Usually people that overstay at least try to feed the meter a couple of times.

"I went back to check the license plate again. It was an out-of-state vehicle, so there wasn't a plate on the front like in Illinois. I wanted to be extra sure I had the number right, because I was beginning to think this might be an abandoned vehicle. Those reports are more complicated 'cause of the towing company and all."

Letha sighed deeply and looked back at the police still hovering around the truck.

"I'll bet the paperwork piles up like dino dandruff," Duke said, and Letha smiled at the image. "What state did you say?"

"Michigan. I figured he probably was one of the construction workers, but they usually pull right into the dirt." She pointed at some trucks and beat-up cars parked at one end of the sewer project. "We can't have them scattered all over creation."

"So then you noticed the blood?"

"Yeah," Letha said, her voice no longer shaky. "Back by the right rear tire. Stepped right in it. I thought it was oil or something. It just looked all dark, black like. Until I tracked it up onto the sidewalk. Then I could see it was reddish. I don't know why, but I bent down and put my finger in it. I thought it was transmission fluid until I touched it."

Letha sighed again and shook her head.

"I figured I'd better not touch anything else, so I called it in on my handheld. When I told them about all the blood coming from the vehicle, they said they were sending an ambulance just in case someone inside was injured."

"Then you never saw the body?"

"Yes, I did. When Tony arrived. Tony Vincenzo was the responding officer. He opened the back of the truck. It wasn't locked. And there was this guy, wrapped up in a bloody tarp. When Tony unrolled it, the guy's face was half blown off." Letha shivered at the recollection.

Exit wounds, Duke thought and made a note on his pad. He stood next to Letha and watched the police taking photographs of the body and the truck. Duke spotted Cantrell, who was turning away from the truck and heading toward the mounds of sand that had once been Jackson Street.

"Excuse me," Duke said, touching Letha's arm, "I need to talk to him."

"Oh, my," Letha said, holding out the damp handkerchief.

"Keep it," Duke said and waded into the sandy sea.

"Hey, Tom, wait up!" Duke shouted.

The police detective had made it about halfway across the street when he heard Duke's call. He paused and turned back. They approached each other like a pair of gunfighters meeting at the OK Corral. Duke was even wearing cowboy boots, the pointed toes and small square heels making distinctive prints in the dirt. But the rest of his clothes, navy-blue slacks and a conservative plaid long-sleeved cotton-polyester shirt, didn't match his Western footwear. Exactly six feet tall with the slightly softened torso of a trim man turning forty, Duke walked with a forward lean as if the noon deadline for the final edition was a stiff wind at his back.

Tom walked with more of a swagger, swinging from side to side as if to some internal melody. Thin and muscular, he was taller and younger—six-foot-two and barely thirty years old. His brown slacks stretched tight over his taut buttocks and thighs. The brown leather jacket he wore winter and summer was unbuttoned. His hands, stuffed in the pockets, pulled the jacket open as he walked, revealing a white shirt and orange paisley tie. He probably was listed as African American on the police department's affirmative-action forms, but his honey-beige skin tone wasn't as dark as a good tan. His black hair was shaped into a military-style flat top. A thin mustache accented the serious set of his mouth.

When the two men were close enough to speak without raising their voices, Tom pulled his left hand from his pocket and glanced at his wrist. "You're getting slower in your old age, Dukey boy. We've been here forty minutes without any reporters getting in the way. I was beginning to worry about you."

"I've been here. I've just been staying out of the way."

"What? You're getting considerate?"

"No, just getting the story from the lady who found the body."

Behind the shield of dark glasses, Tom shot a look at the meter maid still leaning against the patrol car. Duke knew Tom wouldn't like it that she had talked to him, but was too composed to show it. The two men stood almost face-to-face, but their bodies were skewed just a little so they looked past each other, as though, even with sunglasses, looking into each other's eyes might reveal too much.

"Sounds like a mob hit," Duke ventured.

"Mob? Jeez, is that what that nervous broad said?"

"A construction worker, killed execution style, stuffed in a trunk—"

"Trunk? It's a truck, for God's sake."

"Same dif," Duke said, smiling to have gotten a rise from Tom. "You got an ID?"

"You know I can't give that out until we notify next of kin."

"But his driver's license is Michigan? He's with the construction crew?"

Duke was holding his notebook in one hand, his pen poised in the other. It made Tom wary.

"Listen, I don't have anything to say," Tom said, walking away.

"Bullfrog farts," Duke mumbled, following at Tom's heels. "Just give me a statement. I've got to write something in about fifteen minutes to make today's city edition. We'll wait until tomorrow for the full story."

Duke knew his begging gave Tom the feeling of control, but he'd feed Tom's ego if it would loosen his tongue.

"If you guys were smart, you'd send a cute broad like that foxy Becky to ask questions," Tom said, turning back. "Now, I might tell her that we got a white male, DOB 6-6-55, joined the construction crew a week ago, evidently from Michigan."

"Great, I'll see if I can get Becky to follow up," Duke said, making hurried notes in his notebook. "So, he was shot in the head, right? And you're not thinking suicide?"

"Suicide? Damn. He was shot in the back of the head and his hands were bound with electrician's tape. Don't know how he managed to shoot himself and hide the weapon too."

"So it was a mob hit."

"Now listen, Dukakis, there's no organized crime in Cade County. That's a thing of the past."

"Squirrel squat! You and I both know organized crime never really goes away. It changes style. There was plenty of talk when this sewer contract was awarded that it was a bit shady."

"You sound like those paranoid workers over there who are afraid to admit they ever had a beer with this guy. Go ahead. Write your story for today, and leave the shady stuff out of it. Tell Becky I should have an ID to give her by the end of the day. Maybe she'd like to talk about it over dinner."

Chapter 2

A stroke, a massive stroke.

The doctor's words echoed in Josie's head as she pulled into the driveway of Maggie's small brick Tudor. The house, with its exaggerated gable over the entrance, was nestled between two huge trees, a clear indication of the age of the neighborhood.

Maggie's large handbag was sitting on the seat beside Josie. It seemed odd to be here at Maggie's house with Maggie back in St. Mary's Hospital fighting for her life. It could be days before they would know the extent of the damage, the doctor had said. Maggie's daughter, Katherine, who lived in California, was taking the next flight out. In the meantime, Josie knew Maggie's black and white Boston terrier needed to be fed and walked.

As Josie walked up the curved sidewalk, Buttons stuck his head between the drawn drapes. He yipped as she stepped onto the small concrete porch. Josie flicked the silver clasp and opened Maggie's purse. She fished past the worn red wallet, the blue and white cellophane pack of tissues, then averted her eyes so as to not really be snooping in the purse. She let her fingers feel along the bottom for the familiar shape of keys.

Three keys attached to an orange plastic daisy. Just three. The house, the car, and what, her desk at work? It was easy to pick the house key. When Josie inserted the key, she heard Buttons' high-pitched bark just behind the door. A dog owner herself, Josie was ready for the enthusiastic welcome, bending down to be sure the dog didn't escape and yet a little wary that Buttons might bite. He yipped incessantly as Josie slipped in, dangling Maggie's purse over the opening. After several minutes of bouncing around, backing away, and barking, Buttons calmed a little and seemed to listen to Josie's soothing words.

"Your mother is sick, little fella, so she sent me here to feed you." Josie ventured forth a hand. Buttons sniffed at first, then licked her fingers. Josie continued to talk as she lifted the little dog and carried him toward the kitchen.

"It's been years since I visited your mommy," Josie said in a silly dog-talk falsetto. "Must have been when Christopher got his doctorate. There were so many people here, you probably don't remember me. Now, where would your mommy keep the dog food? You want to go outside first? Oh, of course you do."

She stepped out the back door and Buttons leaped out of her arms, barking at birds and then pausing to lift a leg in the grass before chasing after a squirrel that ran up a tree. The scent of fragrant lilacs filled the air. Life seemed so abundant here, so different from the lifeless pallor of Maggie as they wheeled her into the ambulance.

After Buttons' romp outside, Josie found the dog food on a shelf in the pantry, refilled the dish, and replenished the matching water dish. Buttons didn't pause to question where his owner was. He simply started eating. After watching him a few minutes, Josie headed down the hall to Maggie's room. Family photos lining the wall seemed to stare at the intruder, questioning what she was doing here. The bed, not expecting guests, was only half made, a comforter pulled up and smoothed but the pillows still uncovered. A shimmering scarlet nightgown was draped over one.

Josie touched the fabric as if, somehow, it would bring back Maggie. Oh, the pieces of ourselves we leave scattered behind, she thought. Josie opened the closet. She recognized the familiar dresses lined up like thin reflections of Maggie.

This sadness is ridiculous, she thought. Maggie isn't dead, for Pete's sake!

Maggie would wake up soon; she would want a few things. Josie gathered items as if packing for a short vacation. A sweater, a robe, a couple of changes from the underwear drawer, the scarlet nightgown, a sweat suit that looked warm and comfortable. She picked up a few toiletries in the bathroom and added them to the growing pile on the bed.

She needed something to put everything in. A soft-sided bag in a tapestry pattern on the top shelf of the closet caught her eye. Josie stood on tiptoe and reached for it. At five-foot-two, she could barely touch the bag, so she jumped, poked, and pushed until the bag edged out a little over the shelf. She leaped again and grabbed the bag. It slipped down, but brought with it a small hard-sided brown case that fell to the floor with a crash. The case popped open, scattering newspaper clippings all over the carpet.

"Shit! Way to go, clumsy," Josie chided herself.

She tossed the tapestry bag on the bed and then got down on the floor to pick up the clippings. One red shoe, with an open toe and four-inch heel, had landed in the middle of the clippings. It hardly seemed like Maggie's style of footwear, Josie thought, as she picked up the shoe. It was a style from the past, with a thick platform and an accumulation of dust in the folds of the fabric covering.

"I wonder where the other one went," Josie said, scanning the floor and lifting the dust ruffle to look under the bed. Holding the shoe, she looked through the dozen pairs of shoes lined up on the closet floor. There was nothing even faintly like it. Perhaps this was a remnant of Maggie's younger days, Josie thought, as she picked up one of the brown flat-soled Hush Puppies Maggie usually wore. It was much longer. The red shoe, Josie realized, was too small for Maggie.

Must have been Katherine's, Josie thought, tossing the shoe onto the closet floor. The mate, she figured, would show up.

She turned her attention to the clippings, so yellowed and brittle that newsprint confetti surrounded the readable pieces. Reporters keep clippings, lots of clippings. Maggie had been a reporter for more than fifty years, so it wasn't surprising that she would have a suitcase full of yellowed articles on the thicker paper of many years ago.

Still, Josie regretted she had disturbed and damaged them. She started to read, more to piece the torn clippings together than for information.

"*Spectator* Editor Missing," one headline read. The masthead said June 13, 1956. A photo of a woman, identified as Zelda Machinko, smiled at Josie. Photographs taken at happy times never go too well with crime stories, Josie knew, noticing Zelda's carefully coiffed hair and well-painted lips. Buttons came into the room and rushed over to sniff the musty clippings.

"Oh, no you don't," Josie said, shooing the dog away with a sweep of her hand. She gathered several pieces of brittle paper into the case to get them out of his reach. As the pieces fell apart in her hand, Josie resolved to take the case home to work on restoring the damaged clippings. Just before she closed the case, she noticed a clipping with a photo of a man wearing a stylish fedora from the '50s. He was holding a shoe. Josie pushed away a scrap of paper to read the cutline.

"Detective Daniel Pasternak holds a shoe believed to have been worn by Zelda Machinko on the day she disappeared. It was found on the loading dock behind the *Spectator* offices."

Josie pawed through the closet floor and retrieved the red shoe. Though the photo was small and faded, she knew she was holding the shoe in the picture.

Chapter 3

Duke opened the door to Mel's and waited a moment for his eyes to adjust to the darkened room. The sounds of men laughing and pool balls clicking, mixed with the smell of cigarette smoke and stale beer, felt like home. But it scared him. It had been eight months since Duke had had a drink—ever since that day Josie convinced him to admit himself to a detox center. He hadn't thought he had a problem with alcohol; other people thought he did. His wife, Sharon, had left him. Hammond was about to fire him. Then his friend Carl was killed and Josie was almost killed by the same maniac. Duke realized life was too precious to waste on excuses.

At first, he thought he was going to rehab for Josie so she might consider the brief affair they'd had as the beginning of a lifetime together. But as the haze of addiction lifted and the counselor asked him to make amends to the people he had hurt, he realized it was Sharon who really knew him. She had stood by him for so many years. He came out of that clinic determined to win back Sharon's trust. Without alcohol, there seemed to be so many more hours in the day. Jennifer, their sixteen-year-old daughter, was even starting to talk to him again like she used to. Just before he left the office, she had called to say she'd gotten an A on the algebra test they had studied for together the night before. Sharon, however, still watched him suspiciously. They would do things together as a family, but Sharon insisted on keeping her own apartment. A few times she had succumbed to his charms and a good-night kiss had turned into a night of passion, but she always was cool the next morning.

Now he had nothing. Not Sharon. And not Josie, who had returned to treating him like a coworker and friend, with never a mention of that week last summer. And he couldn't even drown his loneliness in a beer.

He wanted a drink every day, but happy hour—that time right after work—was the hardest. He'd made it this long by following the rules—staying away from bars and drinking buddies. But he couldn't live in a bubble forever.

Mel's was just about a block from the sewer construction site where the body had been found. Duke suspected it would be a good place to hear a little of the street buzz. Looking around, he saw several regulars he recognized. He started up a conversation with a group at one end of the bar, and suddenly, Mel, the owner, was standing in front of him.

"Haven't seen you in a while," Mel said.

"Just the man I want to see," Duke said, leaning on the bar. "I was wondering if you knew that guy who got killed. Did he come in here much?"

"Of course," Mel said, wiping the bar with a large white rag. "He usually came in with the rest of them after work. But like I told the police, he was a quiet one. Never caused any trouble. Never saw him put away more than two drinks at a time. What can I get you?"

"Oh, I can't stay," Duke said, licking his parched lips. "Do you remember what he drank?"

"Nah, I didn't know him that well. He was only in a coupla times. Sat with the rest of them, but was kinda by himself, if you know what I mean."

"An outsider?"

"Yeah, I guess you'd say that."

"So, did it look like some of the other guys maybe had it in for him? Was he that different?"

"No, no. Just quiet. You know, you might want to talk to those guys by the pool table. They're part of that sewer project."

Duke had already guessed as much by the yellow hard hat sitting on the bar. He made his way to the other end of the room and introduced himself to a pair who looked like twin linebackers on a football team. One had a deep tan and dark hair. The other was freckled with light reddish hair. But their six-foot-plus height and muscular builds were identical. Both wore white T-shirts and close-cropped hair.

"Are you going to put our names in the paper?" the freckled one asked.

"Well, that depends. Do you want me to put your names in the paper?"

"Yeah, sure. I was one of Scooter's best friends. I'm gonna miss the prick."

"And your name is?"

"Flatt, with two Ts. Herbert Flatt," the man said, craning his neck to be sure Duke wrote it down correctly.

"Don't listen to him, he don't know what he's talking about," the darker man said without looking at Duke.

"Scooter? Was that his name?"

"Well, his name was Blaine. Blaine Avril, but what kinda name is that?" Herbert asked. "Sounds like a fag name. Maybe that's why he never picked up no dames."

"Nah, he was married," the other man said, still not looking up from his beer. "Showed me a picture once of his wife and kid. Ugly baby."

"Excuse me," Duke said, turning to the other man. "You worked with Mr. Avril too?"

"Sure, we all did. What's it to ya?"

"Oh, I'm just trying to get a little color for the obit. You said he showed you a photo of his wife. Did he tell you her name?"

"Nah, we weren't that close."

The second man, who identified himself as Ron Baylor, told Duke the dead man was fairly quiet and lived in a small travel trailer in the campground.

"He was from Michigan?" Duke asked, just for confirmation.

"That's what he said," Ron mumbled and finished his beer.

"You say that like you didn't believe him.".

"Well, there was something screwy there," Ron said, scratching his head. "He didn't sound like them Yoopers. You know, they say 'Eh' all the time like Canadians and talk like they got a stopped-up nose. Hey, Mel, another pitcher."

"Oh, Scooter wasn't from the U.P.," Herbert said. "He said he was from the southern part of Michigan. St. Joe, just a couple hours from here."

"So did you see him last night?"

"Sure, right here," Herbert said, and then turned to his buddy for confirmation. "He was here, wasn't he?"

Ron responded with a shrug as he poured beer into empty glasses, setting one in front of Duke. "Hell, I don't know. I think so. It wasn't my day to watch him."

Duke stared at the glass of beer in front of him, then made a conscious effort to pull his eyes away and look at Herbert, who was guzzling his.

"What did he do?" Duke asked. "Did he have a special skill?"

"Drove a 'dozer, what else?"

"Did he get along with the guys?"

"What are you trying to say?" Herbert thrust his face right into Duke's so Duke could smell his beer breath and look into his bloodshot eyes. "You think one of us wasted him?"

"Walrus whoppers! If I thought you were murderers, would I be drinkin' with you in a bar?" Duke said, raising the full glass of beer. "But it sure would be a dingo-drizzlin' way to get your name in the paper."

"Hell, yes," Herbert said with a hearty laugh and clinked his glass against Duke's. "I like this guy."

"You like everybody, Herbie," said a man approaching with a pool cue. "Who's playin' the winner?"

Herbie took the pool cue and headed toward the table.

"Terry, this here's a reporter," Ron said, introducing the man who had just joined them. "Terry's the one you should be talking to. He owns the company."

"Terry Tate," the man said, shaking Duke's outstretched hand. He was balding and had a firm handshake. His piercing blue eyes looked at Duke suspiciously. "Do you always interview people when they're half-snockered?"

"This isn't an interview, Mr. Tate," Duke said, handing him the full glass of beer and picking up Herbie's almost empty one from the bar. "Just a friendly visit. I was wondering about the man who died."

"We're all wondering about him," Terry said, taking a swig from the glass. "Damn shame."

"I hear his name was Blaine Avril and he was from Michigan. How long has he been working for you?"

13

"A week, ten days. If you want specifics, stop by and see Margaret in the office tomorrow. I'm not really comfortable answering questions in a bar."

"Sure, sure. I've got to go anyway. But could you tell me, is it normal to hire people from out of state like that?

"Why not? They go where the work is," Terry said, refilling his glass from the pitcher. "His references checked out."

"When was the last time you saw him?"

"Last night, I suppose. When he left work."

"And what did you do when he didn't show up this morning?"

"Listen, I don't have time to babysit these men. They don't show up, I don't worry about them. I'm not their mother."

"But didn't it leave you shorthanded? Did you have to call in someone to take his place?"

"We made adjustments. Didn't you say you were leaving?"

"Sure. I'll stop by your office in the morning." Duke placed Herbie's almost-empty glass back on the bar without taking a sip.

"Thanks for the beer," he said and walked out, feeling triumphant. Another day without a drink.

※

It was ten minutes after six when Josie pulled into the lot at Ranch Rudy, the Western-themed day-care center where her eight-year-old son, Kevin, stayed after school. Josie expected Rudy would give her a lecture; he'd often said late parents were his biggest problem.

"They're breaking the trust," he'd say. "There's got to be trust between a parent and child and a child's caregiver. When they hear "Happy Trails" on the boom box, it means round 'em up, pardner, pick up your toys and put them away. But it also tells the kids their parents are coming. That's why they are happy. But if the toys are stowed and the coats are on and Mommy doesn't come, I've got a pretty sad wrangler. Don't let me or your child stop trusting you."

Well, she'd just explain about Maggie. Surely Rudy would understand. Josie had her explanation all ready when she opened the door into the spacious play area. The room was empty. Chairs were upturned on the tables; toys were safely stacked in their bins. There were no happy hugs. No sloppy kisses. No delighted faces looking for approval of the latest artwork. No squeals of "That's mine!" No patient reminders to be nice.

Josie had never seen the room empty or quiet. Had never noticed the Army-green carpet or the ugly amber paint on the walls.

"Rudy? Kevin?"

Josie's voice echoed through the empty playroom, but as she listened for a response, she heard faint voices. She headed down a dark hallway. Off to one side she saw the nap room for the younger children with wall-to-wall cots. On the other side was the nursery, lined with cribs. She poked her head into the laundry room, where sheets and towels were tumbling in a dryer. Then she stepped across the hall into a small dark office, where a radio played low. She turned off the radio. She could still hear voices. She headed down the hall toward the kitchen.

Rudy saw her first. He was stirring batter in a big silver bowl with a wooden spoon. Kevin was seated nearby, licking another wooden spoon.

"Well, there she is, pardner," Rudy said.

Kevin looked up. As soon as he saw his mother, he dropped the spoon on the floor and ran to her. He threw his arms around her waist.

"Hey, Bud, that's no way to treat Mr. Rudy's kitchen," Josie said. "Now, pick up that spoon." Only after the quick remark did Josie realize Kevin had a death grip on her, his head of curly blond hair buried in her side. When she pulled him back, she could see he was starting to cry.

"What is it, honey? Don't you feel well?" Josie's hand went automatically to his forehead, but Kevin, trying to hide his tears from Rudy, tucked his head back into his mother's waist.

Josie looked to Rudy for some explanation, but he only raised his eyebrows. He returned to his work and began filling muffin cups with batter. Josie crouched down and hugged her son.

"What is it? Did something happen?"

"I just want to go home," he whispered.

"Sure, we'll go."

"Don't forget to take that eye of God you made," Rudy said as he continued to fill muffin cups. "Yours turned out very nice."

Kevin looked at him blankly.

"The yarn thing you made yesterday," Rudy said. "I think you left it in my office."

"Why don't you go get it, honey, and I'll wipe up this muffin dough on Mr. Rudy's floor."

Kevin seemed reluctant to leave his mother's side. It was the way he had clung to her right after the divorce, like he was afraid she might leave him the way his father had.

"Go on now so we can go home."

Kevin walked away slowly, watching over his shoulder as Josie ripped off a paper towel, wet it at the sink, and wiped up the spots of muffin batter on the cabinet and floor. She checked to be sure Kevin was out of earshot before she spoke.

"I'm sorry to be so late, I really am. It's just been one of those days at work."

"Maybe it's been one of those days for Kevin," Rudy said, placing the filled muffin tins in the oven. "He's just a kid, you know. He depends on you."

"But I was only ten minutes late."

"Ten minutes is an eternity when you're eight. Long enough to imagine the worst."

Certainly Kevin knew of bad things that could happen. First his father had moved out, and then just last summer Josie was almost killed by a serial killer. He'd seen the story on television even though Josie had tried to hide it from him. Suddenly, Kevin was standing in the doorway, holding up a creation of red and white yarn wrapped around a cross of Popsicle sticks.

"Oh, that's really neat," Josie said, reaching for it. "Where shall we hang it? In the kitchen, maybe?"

Kevin hung his head. It was going to take more than false admiration of his artwork to salve these wounds.

"Tell Rudy 'bye," Josie suggested as she wrapped an arm around her son and steered him toward the exit. "Since it's so late, maybe we'll just pick up a Happy Meal for dinner. Would you like that?"

"But you said Happy Meals don't have good nutrition. You said I need more vegetables."

"Well, once in a while is OK, after a hard day," Josie said as she opened the car door to the backseat. She started to pull Kevin's seat belt around him.

"I can do it," he said, though he lifted his hands and allowed his mother to lock him in.

"You're very special to me, Kevin," Josie said and kissed her son on the forehead. "Don't ever forget that."

By six thirty, Nick was the only one in the newsroom, finishing up some final rewrites on the afternoon's stories. Suddenly the swimsuit calendar that had been hanging on the wall behind him was draped over his head. He looked up from the paper tent to see Becky, an angry black Amazon, standing beside him with her arms crossed.

"I'm not your whore, white boy, and you're not my pimp," she said.

Nick waited, expecting a punch line, but the fury in Becky's eyes told him she wasn't joking.

"What's gotten into you?" he said cautiously, pulling the calendar off his head.

"Oh, don't play coy with me. You set me up. I don't need you setting me up."

"I set you ...What are you talking about?"

"Well, I've got brains and I could see right away what Cantrell had on his mind. You guys think you can just deal with a woman like she's got no brains at all. He acted like I should be grateful. Grateful! He just assumes we've got a date or something."

Becky walked in circles, shaking her clenched fists. It frightened Nick. He'd seen Becky fly off the handle before, but usually she wasn't angry with him.

"Wait a minute," Nick said. "Did Detective Cantrell say something inappropriate? Was he fresh with you?"

"Fresh? That Mamma's Boy don't know anything fresh. He's stale as month-old chewing gum!"

"I don't get this. I thought you said he made an advance."

"Advance? He acted like he was already on second base and assured of home plate. What exactly did you promise him when you sent me over there?"

"Promise?"

"Oh, don't pretend you weren't in on it. Cantrell as much as said so. I'm sitting there at his desk, ready to take notes, and he walks around behind the chair and puts his hands on my shoulders. Can you believe it? Then he says he was expecting me and we can talk about business over dinner." Becky exaggerated the words into melodic smooth talk. "That's when he says, 'The *Daily News* is finally getting smart about doing business.' That's not the kind of business I do and I don't know where you got the idea."

Becky was eye to eye with Nick now, shaking a fist in his face.

He said the only word that might dissuade her. "Duke!"

Becky paused. She wasn't sure why Nick was blaming Duke, but the tactic worked. She pulled back and waited to hear what Nick would say.

"I had no idea. Duke said Cantrell should have an ID on the body by the end of the day. Duke suggested sending you over there. We're getting pretty low on staff with Maggie gone and, well, it sounded like a good idea. I really didn't know."

"You mean Duke set this up?"

"Well, it doesn't sound like him. Maybe Cantrell just got the wrong idea. He does have a bit of an ego."

"Ego! If you pricked him with a pin, he'd disappear. He's nothin' but hot air."

Nick chuckled. "Sounds like you like him more than you want to admit."

"Like him? I detest him!" Becky said, falling into her desk chair.

"But he gave you the ID?"

"He didn't give me anything but a headache."

"That's OK. I'll stop by there on my way in tomorrow. I'll get the ID on this Michigan guy and tell Cantrell to back off."

"I don't need you to fight my fights for me. I was more than clear with Cantrell."

"OK," Nick said, returning the calendar to its spot on the wall. He adjusted it a little and then stood back to be sure it was straight. When he turned to Becky, she simply closed her eyes and shook her head, mumbling something about "Men."

Chapter 4

Zelda, 1953

I'm touchin' up my war paint, if ya know what I mean, when that heavy mahogany door opens and knocks me over the sink like an amorous bull climbing up my backside. The courthouse restroom is barely more than a closet, and I look up from the sink to see that *Daily News* reporter, the pregnant one, big as a buffalo.

"Didn't your mama teach you to knock?"

"Sorry, I need the toilet," she says, twisting one way and then the other trying to figure out the best way to squeeze that basketball belly past me. We dance a bit. I slip in between the partition and the sink as much as I can, and she waltzes around, leading with her bustle so her belly can have the wider berth. "Sorry," she says again as she backs into the stall, "but these days when I have to go, I can't dally."

"Don't let me stop ya. I'm just doin' my face," I say. After she's past, I spread myself out again on the well-lit side of the mirror. It's a good thing I'm wearing my tight navy-blue suit with the slim-as-a-cigarette skirt 'cause I don't think my crinolines would survive the crush. I've seen this gal before, but we never talked. She is new to the court beat and better suited to the society pages, especially now that she looks like a blimp.

"If you're gonna tinkle, better make it snappy," I say loud enough to be heard over the partition. "When Judge Springer calls somebody into his chambers, he doesn't mince words. Court will be back in session faster than a round in the ring with Rocky Marciano."

I get back to my business at the mirror, specifically curling my lashes. If the eyes are the windows to the soul, I want lace curtains on mine. My soul needs a little dressin' up. I fit the clamp over one eye, careful not to break one of my bright-red nails in those too-small finger holes, and squeeze the clamp down. When I look up, she's standin' there, staring at me with her mouth open.

"What's a matter, sweetie? You've never seen a lady curl her eyelashes?"

I turn to her, still holding the clamp on one eyelid. Her reddish hair is short and curly, the same shade as the freckles that cover her face and arms. Pregnancy hangs on her like a bad prank. She looks too innocent to know about sex, even though she isn't a child. She is probably in her thirties, a few years younger than me. But she has about as much worldly savvy as that baby she carries.

"So what's the *Daily News* doing sending a pregnant lady into this den of iniquity?" I ask as I return my eyelash curler to my purse and search for my lipstick. "Shouldn't you be home knitting booties or something? Shows you the *News* doesn't take gangsters very seriously."

To my surprise, little Miss Mommy shoves me aside, reaches her hands under the faucet and turns on the water.

"I'm every bit as serious as you are," she says, hitting the soap dispenser with the heel of her hand and working up a furious lather. "I covered the military training at the Great Lakes Naval Center during the war and went to San Francisco to report on the returning troops, while you were back here in your furs and heels, slinging mud at our war effort."

"Whoa, furs and heels? You think I'm some scatterbrained bimbo just because I'm not wearing maternity clothes and loafers? I'll bet your war experience is limited to following hubby around. Am I right? You're not in any hurry to cover Korea."

Her downcast look tells me I guessed right. Women like her always confuse their accomplishments with their husband's. She might have done some stories for the *Daily News* during World War II, but she got the assignments because that's where her husband was. But I know how hard it is for a woman to make it on her own merits. This little sweetheart could be propping up her swollen feet on the sofa, but she's trying to make sense of the Cade County court system. She needs my encouragement, not my scorn. When I finish slathering on my Ruby Romance lipstick, I hold it out like a peace pipe.

"Listen, honey, I'm not the enemy. A little lipstick will brighten up your face so the fedoras won't think you're about to have that kid every time the judge taps his gavel."

She takes the tube and dabs it on with little blotches no bigger than her freckles. Then she presses her lips together. Applied so sparingly, the color seems several shades lighter. I'm impressed. I know I have a pretty abrasive personality. Usually scare off two or three secretaries a year. But this kid is her own person.

"You got your own style, kiddo. They're always tellin' me I got style, but most of those lamebrains can't see past the 36-24-36. That's OK, I'm not ashamed of how I look. I figured out long ago how to open a door with a smile. But once ya got the door open, it's what's under these brunette tresses that counts. A lady's gotta have brains these days. How'd you end up on the court beat?"

"I told you. I've been writing for the *Daily News* for years," she says softly, handing back my lipstick.

"I know, covering the war and getting in a family way. But court takes special knowledge. Court is the most important beat because it's the last chance at justice. The legislators make the laws, the cops enforce them, but the real power is with the judge. He can cut it up like a Debbie Reynolds paper doll if he wants to."

She chuckles. "It's funny for Zelda Machinko to be talking about justice," she says. "Aren't you the one who writes all those nasty editorials about the cops and the judges and everyone else? Even about our publisher."

I expect a little spunk from her, but this is a low blow.

"Nasty depends on your point of view," I say. "I think the widow and her children would tell you that the gangsters who killed an innocent tailor and burned his business were pretty nasty. And the judge who set them free again? Well, you tell me."

She stands silent a moment, then reaches out her hand.

"I'm Maggie Sheffield," she says, smiling like somebody turned on a light inside her head. "My husband is George Sheffield, the cop who investigated that tailor's murder. He went on and on about how the court had screwed up everything."

"So is that it? You're only covering courts because your husband opened the door? When are you going to go out on your own?"

She looks down again, and I know I am hitting a nerve.

"George may be the reason I got interested in this beat, but I had to overcome a lot of objections to get this assignment. My editor says it better not look like I'm taking the cops' side. He told me just report the judgment and stay neutral."

"Neutral is journalism jargon for ignorance," I say, slamming a hand on the sink. "Of course they don't want you asking questions. Your publisher, Fred Hanson, lives out in one of those fancy new brick ranch houses they built west of town. And you know who lives just down the street? Francis Boardman—Buster Boardman is what his cronies call him. The biggest gangster in town. He supposedly runs a local labor union, but it's just a front for his band of bullies. And when I say so in print—which I do every chance I get—then I'm being nasty."

"I'm sorry, I didn't mean to say you were nasty."

"Oh, that's OK, honey. They don't want you to ask questions because then you might get nasty too. We can look at each other like the enemy, like we're competing for some big scoop in the courtroom. Or we can realize that the real enemy is the guy on trial, and if the judge is too chicken to stomp his face, then it's up to us little ladies."

"The fourth estate," Maggie whispers.

"That's right, kiddo. We got the ultimate power if we're not afraid to use it."

It's time to get back in the courtroom so I tell her to let me go first and follow a few minutes later.

"It wouldn't look good for us to be seen together. Your Mr. Hanson might get worried," I say with a wink. I suggest we meet back at the restroom afterwards in case she has any questions. Legal stuff can be a little tricky until you get used to the lingo.

21

We dance around each other one more time to get the door open. In the tango, she steps on my open toes with her paddleboat loafers. When I lift my foot to inspect the damage, I poke her in the shin with my stiletto heel. We're both hobbling and bumping into each other.

"A shoe like this is a lady's weapon," I say, stroking my injured toe.

"That's a weapon, all right," Maggie agrees, trying to reach over her protruding belly and rub her leg. "Would you actually kick someone on purpose?"

"If I have to. But I call it my weapon because a shoe like this gives my legs a little shape to distract the horny bastards and makes me tall enough to look 'em in the eye."

Chapter 5

The room still was dark when Josie was awakened by the warmth of Kevin crawling into bed beside her. Warm, too warm. Josie's maternal thermometer kicked in, and instantly she was wide awake. She reached a hand to Kevin's forehead. Fever, but not too bad. Probably about 100.

"I don't feel good," Kevin rasped hoarsely.

"You're OK, honey," Josie said reassuringly. "Just go back to sleep. Mommy's here."

He curled up with his back to her, and she pulled the sheet over his bare shoulders. What had he done with his pajamas? Josie noticed he'd been taking them off in the middle of the night lately and sleeping in his underwear. Was he getting too old for super-hero nightwear? Probably he was trying to imitate his father. Kevin had gone through several mysterious stages since Josie and Kurt divorced almost two years earlier. Although Kurt still lived in town, working for the city's Downtown Development board, he seldom took Kevin on weekends anymore. Something always came up. Kevin was lucky if his dad could find time to visit for a few hours a week. Maybe Kevin felt closer to his father when he slept in his underwear like a grown-up.

Josie brushed the damp blond curls on Kevin's forehead. She would let him rest until daylight before checking his temperature with a real thermometer. She watched the digital clock count off the minutes as she thought through how to change her day's schedule. Just before six., she called Nick at home.

"Hey, Kevin's got a fever. I think I should stay with him until we see how he's doing. Can you handle the deadline rush this morning?"

"Well, I was going to stop by the police station," Nick said in a deep early-morning voice. "But I can send Duke over there to get the ID on that body they found."

"I thought Becky was supposed to get that last night."

"It's a long story."

Josie waited, knowing Nick would edit down the long story into the necessary elements.

"Detective Cantrell got a little fresh, I guess."

"What?" Josie spoke a little louder than she had intended. She picked up the phone and walked away from the bed. "I'll call the police chief. Becky doesn't need to put up with that."

"No, let me talk to him," Nick said. "Becky's been awfully touchy lately. Maybe she just misunderstood."

"Well, I don't want something like that to fester. I'll talk to her about it when I get in. I'll decide whether Kevin needs a doctor or a babysitter and try to be in by noon."

"How's Maggie?"

"They didn't know much last night. I'll call over there this morning. When was her daughter supposed to get here?"

"Last night, I think."

"OK, I'll check with the hospital and the house. Sure you don't want me to call the police chief? I can do that from here."

"No. Becky's probably cooled down by now. Just stay home and be a mommy. I can handle things at the office."

Josie smiled. Appointing Nick as her assistant had been a wise choice. She remembered how it was when she first became city editor two years ago. She felt like she had to do everything just to prove she could. Then last year, when she'd almost become one of the victims of a deranged killer, her priorities changed. She felt a tremendous sadness for her friends who had lost their lives, but she also felt invigorated, desperate to enjoy every moment.

Chippie, their golden retriever, was dancing around the foot of the bed, anxious to go out. She'd locked Maggie's dog in the garage, afraid the two might not get along at night. She got up, let both dogs out, and put the teakettle on. It was too early to call the school to tell them Kevin was sick or to ask Polly, her neighbor, if she could babysit. Besides, she wanted to wait a little while to see what other symptoms Kevin might have. She poured hot water over a bag of Constant Comment and inhaled the sweet orange aroma. She paused for a few minutes of silent prayer to thank God for Nick handling things at work so she could keep Kevin her top priority. Even with a sick child and problems at work, it was great to be alive.

The dogs were pawing at the back door.

"Good morning, fellas," Josie whispered as she opened the door. "You're going to have to keep it down today. The master's not feeling well."

Chippie seemed oblivious to her admonitions, bounding into the kitchen full speed, sliding into an open cabinet door and then bouncing back to the refrigerator. His nails clicked on the tile as he danced around, and his tail switched in Josie's face as she tried to measure out a cup of dog food and refill the water dish.

Buttons was more reserved, trying to stay out of the big dog's way. Josie filled a separate dish for him and placed it a good distance away so the two dogs wouldn't fight. When she talked to Katherine, they would decide what to do with the little terrier.

Josie poured more hot water over the tea bag and sipped as she surveyed the old newspaper clippings she had left on the kitchen table the night before. She had put the most fragile ones in plastic bags and arranged the larger, sturdier pieces in chronological order. The oldest clippings, 1953–1956, were written by Zelda in the *Spectator*. Maggie's stories covered five years, starting with Zelda Machinko's disappearance in 1956.

Year after year, Maggie had pursued every angle. Even after the police had given up searching for Zelda, Maggie continued to do stories on the anniversary of the disappearance, talking with every possible witness.

Josie picked up a glossy photo of Zelda that was mixed in among the clippings. The eyes, dark and mischievous, sparkled under severely arched eyebrows, plucked thin as was the style in the fifties. Something about her eyes was oddly familiar, and Josie shuddered off the feeling of recognition.

She unfolded one of the earliest stories and chuckled to see a picture of an unrecognizable downtown street lined with funny little bubble cars from the late forties and early fifties. The *Spectator*, which had gone out of business long ago, had been in a red stone building with scary-looking gargoyles on top. Josie didn't recognize it at first, but she could see the building next door was the old Herkimer Hotel, now called Herkimer House, a retirement home. The red stone building—minus gargoyles—must have been remodeled into the Red Geranium, a restaurant next door to Herkimer House.

The *Daily News* offices used to be downtown as well, across from the courthouse. There was a parking garage there now. The *Daily News* had moved into a brand-new building west of town in the 1970s, about the time a shopping mall was built there and not long after the tractor plant opened on Jackson Street. But in 1956, that whole area was nothing but cornfields. In fact, Josie remembered reading a story not long ago … what was it? Oh, yes. When they started the sewer project. Duke had done a piece about the original paving of Jackson Street and the laying of the sewer line. That also had been in the fifties.

"Mom?"

Josie looked up. Kevin was standing there in nothing but his white Jockey shorts. He looked pale and skinny.

"Honey, aren't you cold?" Josie pulled off her orange terry robe and draped it around Kevin's shoulders.

"My throat hurts," he rasped.

"Well, I've got the perfect thing for that. A little hot tea with lemon and honey."

Josie sat Kevin in a kitchen chair, wrapping her robe around him. She turned the heat on under the teakettle and reached into the kitchen junk drawer where the thermometer usually ended up. Amid pencils, batteries, and half-eaten pretzels, she found the little gray plastic case. Before the teakettle whistled, she washed the thermometer with dish soap, shook it down, and tucked it under Kevin's tongue.

"You've got to keep your mouth closed so the thermometer can work," Josie reminded Kevin. He complied for a few seconds, then his lips parted.

His nose was stuffy. He was breathing through his mouth. The thermometer read 100.6.

"Hey, that's pretty hot. Did you swallow a fire-breathing monster?"

"Mom!" Kevin exclaimed, smiling.

"Here, let me take a look. Say aah." Kevin complied, and Josie used the handle of a spoon to hold his tongue down and a little flashlight from the junk drawer to illuminate the white spots on his throat.

"Yep, there's a fire-breathing monster in there," she said. "We better put the fire out with some tea."

"Monsters hate lemon," Kevin said. He'd heard this routine before.

Josie brought a cup of tea to the table, a little plastic squeeze-bear of honey, and half of a lemon. Kevin doctored his own tea as Josie carefully swept the newspaper clippings out of his way.

"What's that?" Kevin asked.

"An old newspaper."

"It broke, and you're trying to put it back together?"

"Something like that."

While Kevin sipped tea, Josie called the school and then the doctor. She made an appointment for that afternoon. After Kevin was tucked back into his own bed, guarded by Chippie at his feet, Josie called Nick and told him she wouldn't be in until after the doctor's appointment.

"Everything's under control," Nick said.

"Did you get the ID on the body?"

"Duke's down there right now."

"OK. Have him check with authorities in Michigan and find out if this guy has a record or a family or what. Any calls I can make from here?"

"Maggie. Ham was asking about her."

"Yep, that's next on the list."

Josie called the hospital room, and Maggie's daughter, Katherine, answered. A Hollywood screenwriter who'd never taken time to marry, Katherine said her mother was unconscious but stable. Her brother, Christopher, was a medical missionary in Africa. She had gotten word to him, but they were waiting for more information before he tried to return to the States. Their father, George, had died several years earlier from colon cancer.

Josie relayed the update to Ham, the managing editor, who said he would visit Katherine and see if he could be of any help. He'd always been rather fond of Maggie's attractive but willful daughter, and he loved to take charge.

"You just stay home and be a mother today," Ham said with more understanding than Josie expected. "Your son needs you. We'll get by."

❀

A hot shower is like recharging your batteries, Josie thought as she stood under the cleansing stream. Her blond hair was cut in a short pixie style, so she washed it every day and seldom even used a blow dryer. It wasn't hard to imagine why the reporters sometimes called her Peter Pan.

Josie made cinnamon toast and another cup of tea before she sat once again at the kitchen table to read the tale of Zelda Machinko. According to the clippings, Zelda and her newspaper had been making charges of racketeering against someone named Francis "Buster" Boardman. It sounded like the *Spectator* was a bit of a scandal sheet and made lots of claims with little evidence. One story implied the mayor was taking bribes. Another said the superintendent of schools was siphoning money from the transportation budget. Either Jordan was a much more exciting town in the fifties or Zelda had an active imagination.

Zelda had told several people that Boardman had threatened her life.

"If he gets me, I'll kick off one of my shoes as a sign it was him," she had told them.

According to Maggie's stories, Zelda had been working late that June night. The next morning, her secretary found an unfinished editorial in the typewriter and a spilled cup of coffee on the desk. Zelda didn't come in to work that day and didn't keep appointments. Police checked her house, but there was no sign of her. Later, one of the *Spectator*'s delivery truck drivers found one red shoe on the loading dock.

The mystery surrounding her disappearance attracted national attention. Among the clippings were mentions in the *Chicago Tribune* and the *New York Daily News*. Robert Kennedy, brother of the future president, joined the investigation in 1958. As chief counsel to the Senate Select Committee on Improper Activities in Labor and Management, he came to Jordan to look into an informant's claim that Zelda was buried in an orchard.

Josie unfolded more clippings, hoping one would say Zelda had returned or her body had been found. The clips stopped in 1961, so Josie hurriedly jumped to the last stack. Surely, the stories stopped because the mystery was solved. Instead the 1961 stories were mostly about Francis Boardman. His gangland ties were accepted fact by then. There was a federal investigation into the Federation of Hotel and Service Employees he had organized. There were raids on bars he owned and charges of illegal gambling.

Then Josie unfolded a clipping with the most gruesome photo she had ever seen in a newspaper. It was of a 1960 Cadillac, the windshield shattered with bullet holes. Two bloody bodies could be seen inside. Boardman and his wife had been executed in a gangland war.

Josie carefully refolded the clip. She had more questions than answers. Did Boardman have something to do with Zelda's disappearance? What happened to her body? Would there be any closure? If Maggie had been looking for Zelda all these years, why did she give up after Boardman died? And why had she kept the shoe?

Josie picked up the red shoe and examined it as though there was some secret compartment in the sole or the heel. It was covered with a silky fabric. Josie could feel the texture of the fabric's paisley pattern as she ran her fingers over it.

"A lady's weapon," Josie thought, and then wondered where she'd heard that. It was just a shoe, a terribly uncomfortable shoe. She tried it on. It was a little tight and unbelievably pitched. She hastily removed it.

"Zelda, these shoes would have killed you anyway," she mumbled. "But where are you? Where?"

Josie unfolded a clipping from 1958. Not long after Kennedy's unsuccessful dig in an area orchard, a brazen Maggie filed a petition before the city council to have a road dug up. A farmer's widow named Pearl Zaenger told Maggie she had seen someone dump something when the road was being built, about the time Zelda disappeared. She hadn't spoken up earlier because her husband said it would just cause trouble. The council, embarrassed by Kennedy's unsuccessful dig in the orchard, denied the petition.

The clipping included a map of the area Maggie had requested to be dug up—Jackson Street just west of the railroad tracks, near the dirt road to Pearl Zaenger's farm. The dirt road that later became known as Pearl Street. A cold chill ran through Josie's body and she dropped the clipping

Oh, my God, Josie thought. Maybe that's why Maggie had a stroke. When she heard about the body they found at Jackson and Pearl, she thought they had unearthed Zelda.

Chapter 6

Duke had a mischievous grin when he stepped out of the elevator on the second floor of the Jordan police station. Elsie, the gruff black woman behind the horseshoe-shaped counter, was a little suspicious.

"All right, Mr. Dukakis. Stop right there," she said. "What are you up to?"

"No good," Duke said, pulling his hand from behind his back to reveal a bouquet of yellow jonquils.

"Oh, my," Elsie said, her gruffness melting into a smile. "You remembered!"

"Mouse musings! Of course I remembered. Jonquils are your favorite flower, so whenever I see them blooming in my yard, I think of you. Now, seems to me I also remember you've got a white milk-glass vase in the bottom file cabinet that should just about hold these."

"Oh, Mr. Dukakis. You're such a scamp!" She took the flowers, smiling broadly, revealing a matching bouquet of yellowing teeth.

"Scamp is right," said a booming voice from the doorway. "Are you trying to bribe a cop, Dukakis?"

Duke turned. Tom Cantrell was walking toward the desk with a couple of green file folders.

"No way," Duke said. "Elsie's not a cop and it's not bribery unless I'm trying to buy favors. I'm only seeking the favor of her smile."

"He's a gentleman," Elsie said, placing the vase on the counter next to the files Tom had placed there. "All you bums ever give me is more work to do."

"Yeah, Tom, you should thank me for brightening up this dreary place. Didn't they put any windows in this building?" Duke followed Tom into the investigations office, a cluttered arrangement of desks with plainclothes policemen on phones or at computer terminals. It reminded Duke of the newsroom without the newsroom's bright-orange file cabinets. Everything in the police station was washed out and colorless. Beige, only not as bright as beige. Like color was a crime.

Duke took a metal chair in front of a neutral desk that was clear of pictures or personality. "Sounds to me like you need a couple of lessons on dealing with ladies," Duke said with a chuckle.

"What's that supposed to mean?" Tom asked as he fell into the chair across from Duke.

"Well, let's just say your score with Becky isn't as good as your conviction rate."

"I tell you, that Ms. Judd friend of yours is one stuck-up broad. Don't need the hassle."

"Uh, huh," Duke said with a knowing smile. "Now you gotta talk to me. Want me to cross my legs and try to look cute?"

"Impossible."

"So spill. What have you got on the stiff?"

"Sorry, we don't have any more to release than what I already told you."

"Dragon drool! Becky said she didn't even get an ID last night. What's going on?"

"Out of state. Takes time to track down relatives."

"There are phones in Michigan, I hear."

"Listen, Dukakis. I can't tell you anything, OK? Leave it at that."

"Next time I'll bring you flowers if that's what it takes."

Tom looked Duke in the eye for several moments. It wasn't a poker face of false bravado, but a look of concern, regret, hesitation. Duke would rather he would just lie with a smile on his face instead of this sincere my-hands-are-tied frown.

"What's going on?" Duke mouthed silently in case Tom was afraid of being overheard. Instead, Tom lost the look of sincerity and turned brusque and businesslike. He pulled a paper from his file drawer and slid it across the desk.

"White male, twenty-nine, Michigan driver's license … that's all I can give you."

Duke looked at the paper, hoping to see more than what Tom had said. Instead he found a short, formal news release typed on official stationery. The police department rarely issued news releases.

"Gorilla grapefruit!" Duke said, pocketing the paper. "This is ridiculous. I talked with his coworkers last night. I know his name is Blaine Avril and he told them he came over from St. Joseph, which is barely across the line into Michigan."

"You can't use that name."

"Turtle turds. Dozens of people already know who he was. He even told 'em he had a new baby. Showed pictures. Drank Stroh's like a good construction worker, but didn't get wasted. Real friendly. Did his job, no complaints. Listen, I try to cooperate with you guys, don't I? But if you stonewall me, I can get everything I need, with or without you guys."

"It would be better if you didn't identify the victim until we've notified the family," Tom said, closing the file drawer and rising abruptly.

"I have to use the name," Duke said, standing up. "Too many people know. If you guys haven't tracked down the widow yet, then I'm sincerely sorry. But we're identifying the murder victim in today's paper."

Again the two men stood silently reading each other's faces.

"Wait a minute," Duke said. "It's an alias, isn't it?"

"You're so all-fired smart, Mr. Reporter, why don't you ask his drinkin' buddies? Ask the ladies down at the laundromat. Ask anybody you want. You don't need us guys."

❋

Duke left his car in the visitors' lot at the police station and hurried around the corner as fast as he could walk. The police department might confiscate Blaine Avril's employment record, if they hadn't already. Oh, why had he allowed himself that arrogant outburst? Yes, he had other sources, but the police department had always been his best source. He would have to find a way to apologize to Tom before word of his faux pas spread.

Still thinking about his predicament, Duke burst into the offices of T&T Construction. It was the proverbial hole in the wall, a narrow hall in the lower level of Herkimer House. Stepping into the cramped quarters, Duke found himself face-to-face with Zach Teasdale, the nattily dressed coroner. Teasdale was a wealthy businessman. His office was an elected position rather than a profession. He seemed out of place in this room of clutter, outdated furnishings, and peeling paint.

"Oh, Zach, I wasn't expecting to see you this morning," Duke said.

"I'm equally surprised, though I guess I shouldn't be," Teasdale said, with a slow smile and a ready handshake. "We both follow the grim reaper."

"I suppose there will be an inquest?"

"Possibly, although the cause of death seems apparent."

"And the autopsy?"

"I should have something for you by the end of the week," Teasdale responded, with a friendly pat to Duke's shoulder. "Now, if you'll excuse me, I'm late for an appointment."

Teasdale hurried through the door, taking with him the delicious aura of good grooming wrapped in wealth and power. In his absence, the musty odors of dust, mold, and a bit of stale coffee grabbed Duke's attention. How he wished he still had that bouquet of flowers. He could use a good door opener.

"Hi, Margaret. I'm Ormand Dukakis from the *Jordan Daily News*," he said, holding out a card to the blue-haired woman sitting at a wooden desk wedged into the corner.

"Should I know you?" the woman asked.

"I was talking with Mr. Tate last night," Duke responded. "I was asking him about Mr. Avril's background, and he said to see you in the office this morning."

Margaret looked at him blankly, as if processing her options.

"I don't know what I can tell you," she said, pushing back from her desk. "Only met the guy once. The guys on the site would know him better."

"I was hoping to get a look at his application," Duke said, gesturing toward a file cabinet. "I just want to talk with his family. I know the police already informed them, but I'd just like to get a comment. People deserve a chance to speak up for their loved ones, don't you think?"

"Well, I suppose there is a place to list an emergency contact, if that would help you," Margaret said, going to the file cabinet. "I don't know that I can let you look at the application, but if it's got a next of kin on it, I don't see any harm in giving that to you."

She pulled a sheet of paper out of the file, examining it at the open drawer, too far away for Duke to see.

"Yeah, here's the name. A sister, it says."

She laid the paper on her desk, ripped a small square of yellow paper from a pad and wrote the name and phone number.

"A sister? That's odd. The guys said he was married. Had baby pictures," Duke said, stepping up close enough to read over Margaret's shoulder.

"I don't know nothin' about that," Margaret said, handing over the yellow scrap of paper. "This is the only name I've got."

Duke looked at the name on the sheet. It was a Chicago number.

"Didn't he give you a Michigan address? I thought he was from Michigan."

The woman turned the application over. "Yeah, there's a Michigan address."

"I don't suppose you could give me that too, just in case this sister isn't home when we call."

Margaret hesitated.

"It's not like it's an invasion of his privacy," Duke added, "since he's dead."

Margaret took another small yellow sheet and began copying the address. Duke cocked his head to read over her shoulder. He scribbled something on his pad before she turned around and handed him the second slip of paper.

"Is that usual to get workers from out of state on a project like this?" Duke asked.

"Happens."

"Do you have anyone else on this crew from out of state?"

"I don't give them the third degree. We got a few workers came to us from other jobs. This requires people certified on the big movers. Not too many of them standing around Jordan just waiting for us to dig up some pipe."

"Guess not." Duke chuckled. "It's just that it is such a shame, him getting murdered like that. I mean, new in town and all that. You wouldn't think he'd have any enemies here."

"Enemies?" Margaret gasped. "Why, I just figured it was a random robbery. Isn't that what they think? The police don't think it has anything to do with ..." She paused. "Mr. Tate's a good man," she said, puffing out her chest like a defensive mother hen. "All the guys who come in here to the office, they're all good men. Oh, they might drink a bit and get rowdy, but they are hard-working, law-abiding men. Every one of them."

She stuffed the application back in the open file and slammed the drawer for emphasis.

"Is there anything else, Mr ... er, ah ..."

"Dukakis. Listen, Margaret, you've been a great help. You alone in here all day?"

"We have a bookkeeper comes in two afternoons a week, and Mr. Tate is usually here early in the mornings except now with this project and the murder and all."

"Well, it's an awfully tiny place and kinda cramped. Seems a bit stuffy in here."

"You think it's stuffy now, you should be in here in July! I have to listen to those compressors running the air conditioning for the Herkimer. Rattle the teeth out of your head. But it never gets cool in here. All them old people complain too. Things just make noise as far as I can tell."

"Lizard lumps. Maybe the system needs Freon," Duke said.

"Yeah, I was telling Mr. Teasdale that. Thought I'd speak up early. It takes a while for them to get any work done."

"Mr. Teasdale? I thought he was here the same as me, to get information on Blaine Avril."

"Nope, you're the first person who's asked to see that application. Haven't even had a cop in here asking questions. Guess they got all the information they needed down at the site."

"But if Teasdale wasn't here about Avril, why was he here?"

"Oh, he was looking for Terry—Mr. Tate."

"Why did you tell him about the air conditioner? What's his relationship to T&T Construction?"

"You know, I have no idea. He's just the moneyman. If you want something done, you tell him and it happens."

"Is he one of the partners in the company? Is Teasdale the other "T" in T&T Construction?"

"No, silly." Margaret laughed and returned to her chair. "That's for Mr. Tate's son, Michael. He's only sixteen, but Terry expects him to join him in the business."

"So, what about Teasdale? Is he an investor or a client?"

"You sure ask a lot of questions."

"Occupational hazard."

"I don't know," Margaret said with a shrug. "I always thought he owned the Herkimer. That would make him the landlord. But the rent checks go to NBT Trust, whatever that is."

"Puppy puddles! You type up all the contracts and reports, Margaret. If anybody would know how Teasdale is related to the company, you would."

"Like I say, it's always been a bit of a mystery. I've never seen his name on any of the contracts or proposals. His name only shows up one place."

"And that would be …"

"The mailing list. I send him copies of everything."

Deadline has a way of focusing a man's attention. Duke pushed aside questions about the county coroner and forgot for the moment his problems with the local police. He had to do a story on Blaine Avril, and he had to do it quickly.

Looking over Margaret's shoulder, he had copied two pieces of information she probably wouldn't have given him: Avril's Social Security number and the name of his most recent employer. Both might come in handy. But first he called the Chicago number listed for Avril's sister. Disconnected. Somehow, Duke wasn't surprised. Then he tried directory assistance for an Avril phone listing in St. Joseph. None. He called a friend at the courthouse and no criminal record for Blaine Avril with that Social Security number. The Michigan Department of Motor Vehicles showed no driver's license in that name.

Duke pulled out the crumpled release from the police department. "Michigan driver's license," it said. Was the driver's license in a different name? Duke tried all the various spelling combinations he could think of. Blaire Avril, Blane Avril, Blaine April. Blair April. No, he had seen the top of the employee file. The name was typed plain enough, Blaine Avril. And since he was hired to drive the big movers, he must have had a special license for that too. He had to have presented documents in that name—yet those documents must have been forgeries.

The clock was ticking and he wasn't getting any closer to finding out who Blaine Avril was or wasn't.

He flipped his notebook to the name of the most recent employer. Anderson and Sons. Duke wished he'd had enough time to copy down the reference's phone number. Duke remembered Tate saying something about "references checked out." Maybe the road construction business was enough of a fraternity that he would have known of Anderson and Sons by reputation. Duke remembered the Illinois Department of Transportation had once distributed a catalog of road construction vendors. Duke found a copy tucked in among the area phone books behind Josie's desk. At the top of the list was Anderson and Sons in St. Joseph, Michigan. He called immediately.

The woman who answered the phone quickly transferred his call when he said he was trying to verify employment. When a guy named Hamilton answered the phone, Duke took his best shot.

"I'm trying to verify the employment of a heavy machine operator named Blaine Avril."

There was a telling pause.

"Who is this?" the voice asked.

"I'm with the *Jordan Daily News* in Jordan, Illinois, and I'm just trying confirm whether Mr. Avril ever worked there."

"I'm not at liberty to discuss employees with you," Hamilton replied.

"I realize that. I'm not expecting you to tell me about his performance. I just want to confirm whether he worked there or not."

"What did you say your name was?"

"Dukakis. Ormand Dukakis."

"And why are you interested in Blaine Avril?"

"Then you know him?"

"I didn't say that."

"But you repeated his name. It must have struck a bell."

"Listen, I can't talk to you about personnel matters."

"Well, maybe you'd like to know that Mr. Avril is dead."

"Dead?"

The reaction was more than passing curiosity, Duke thought. "Yes, I just wanted to talk to someone who might remember him, might help me to get in touch with his family."

"I can't help you with that."

"Well, could you at least try to get word to them? Ask them to call me."

"Give me your number."

Duke did as requested, buoyed by apparent recognition of the name at this road construction firm. There was a Blaine Avril after all, or at least he had worked before using that name.

Duke didn't have as many facts as he would have liked, but he was on deadline. He had to write as much of a story as he could. He painted a portrait of a hard-working young man, with favorable comments from his coworkers. But the victim's name was carefully couched, "who identified himself as Blaine Avril from St. Joseph, Michigan."

"What is this?" Nick asked.

"Something's fishy," Duke responded and filled Nick in on all the dead ends he had followed.

"Call the paper in St. Joe," Nick suggested.

"I will," Duke said. "And the *Milwaukee Journal.* He's got to show up somewhere. Don't worry. I won't give up, but I knew you needed something before deadline."

Duke returned to his desk and pulled out a yellow legal pad—the thinking pad, he called it. On yellow sheets that wouldn't get confused with his notes from interviews, Duke outlined his thought process. He listed reasons a person might change his name:

Marriage—shouldn't affect a man.

Adoption—shouldn't affect an adult.

To cover a criminal record.

To hide from someone.

To avoid child support? Duke wasn't sure if a simple name change could accomplish this, but it was worth looking into.

Witness-protection program. This was the option Duke liked best. It would be a big story and it jived with what appeared to be an execution.

Duke leaned back and looked at his list. "Bunny beans," he mumbled to himself. "Is that all? Why would I change my name?"

"To become a movie star," he wrote. That led to "To impress somebody," which led to "Because the real name stinks."

Duke was smiling to himself. His list was getting personal. He'd always hated Ormand and was delighted that most people used the nickname he'd picked up in college. But "Ormand" was his official byline, and he got lots of calls for that name. He'd thought about changing it.

"Nickname," Duke added to the list, though Blaine hardly seemed short for anything.

"To get information." Duke had misidentified himself on the phone many times. When he was young and ballsy, he'd pretended to be in the market for a car to write about fraudulent sales techniques.

Could Blaine have been a reporter? "Call *Journal*," Duke wrote. The St. Joe paper couldn't afford to investigate some kind of sewer fraud, but maybe Milwaukee could. He also added *Chicago Tribune* and *Sun-Times* to his list.

Maybe he was a spy for another company. Aha! That could be the answer. Maybe the folks at Anderson and Sons recognized the name because he was spying for them.

Duke caught a flash of hot-pink fabric as Becky strode past his desk and confronted the cardboard cutout version of Duke that stood behind him. Left over from a marketing campaign, the cutout featured a slightly younger, less gray Dukakis, notebook in hand, with a cartoon blurb announcing, "Gotcha covered."

"Got you, Mr. Dukakis," Becky said as she punched the cutout in the nose and knocked it flat on the floor.

"What in the eternal inferno?" Duke asked, jumping to his feet.

"You're next if you don't come up with an explanation fast," Becky said, turning to him.

Duke looked over his shoulder at Nick, who seemed amused that Duke was getting the brunt of Becky's anger.

"Come on," Duke said, catching Becky's elbow with a firm hand. "You look like you need some lunch. I hear you've got a soft spot for the spiced chai over at the Red Geranium."

"Well, you hear wrong. You can't buy me for a cup of tea."

"Then can we talk? I'd like to talk to you about some problems I'm having with a story, and it's always nice and quiet there."

"Quiet because they charge an arm and a leg," Becky snapped.

"I'm buying."

Becky reluctantly got in Duke's turquoise Pontiac Grand Prix, but her stiff body language made it clear he hadn't won any points yet.

"Listen, I'm sorry if Tom Cantrell was a little forward," Duke said as he pulled out of the parking lot and headed toward downtown and the tony Red Geranium.

"Great!" Becky exclaimed. "Nick probably told the whole office."

"I don't think so," Duke said. "He just had to give me some explanation this morning when he asked me to go over there to get the ID you were supposed to get last night."

"Serves you right." Becky looked out the window. "What did you promise Cantrell anyway?"

"Nothing, I swear. Why don't you tell me exactly what happened?"

Becky launched into a word-for-word account of her conversation with the detective from the night before. What he was wearing, how he touched her shoulders, his intimate tone. Duke tried to keep any sign of his amusement from ruining the compassionate concern on his face.

"I'll talk to him. He was out of line," Duke said as he pulled into the parking lot at the Red Geranium. Becky started to open her door.

"Sit tight, I'll get that," Duke said, jumping out and running around the car. Duke was fifteen years older than Becky and old-fashioned enough to still open doors for ladies. She was a bit too independent for such courtesies, but angry enough today to accept his token of respect. Besides, she knew Duke wasn't coming on to her. Everyone in the office knew Duke was trying to patch up his marriage with Sharon. Becky had a lot of respect for that. But that didn't give him any right to try to set her up with some cop. Being a gentleman now was not going to erase the fact that Duke had just assumed Becky would be interested in Tom Cantrell. Chee, the very thought made her skin prickly.

"I just want to be clear," Becky said after they were seated at a corner table covered with a white table cloth. "I don't need you fixing me up with some cop. It demeans me as a reporter."

"And I certainly didn't mean to do that," Duke said. "Nor did Tom. He always speaks of you with respect. He was just saying the other day what a fine job you did on that embezzlement trial."

"He was?"

"Oh, yeah. And that was heavy stuff. I sure didn't understand all that math, but you got right to the heart of the matter."

"I always was good in math."

"See." Duke smiled as the waitress placed their orders on the table. "Tom's not my buddy. But he's a good cop, a smart guy. Back in my drinkin' days, we might have tipped a few, but to me that's all part of doing the job. Cops are people under the uniform. People with kids in school and bills to pay. People with aging parents and hobbies they don't have time for. People just like us. That's all."

"I want to keep everything strictly professional," Becky said, sitting up a little straighter.

"And, you see, that's where we disagree," Duke said, hunkering over his coffee as if he hadn't noticed Becky's rigid posture. "People aren't one-dimensional. Tom's a cop, a professional, but did you know he's got a retarded sister?"

Becky's scowl softened a little.

"Yep, cute kid. She's in her twenties. Lives with his mom, a widow. He supports them. And he plays piano too. Did you know that?"

"No."

"Yeah, one night over at Charlie's Place, the other cops were eggin' him on, and he sits down to play. Well, I couldn't believe it. Jazz. Gospel. Even Chopin. Yeah, he can really play. I'd a never guessed it, I mean he seems so strictly business most of the time. But since that night, every time I look at him I see a piano player, a man with sensitivity and rhythm. Kind of softens the edges, you know what I mean?"

"I guess so."

Duke could see that Becky was beginning to relax a little, so he pushed on.

"So the man noticed that you're not just a good reporter. You've got a pretty face. Can you fault the man for that?"

"Yeah, but he figured I'd be willing to put out just to get information." Becky pulled up rigid again. "I'm not into that game!"

"Bumblebee butter! Of course, you're not," Duke said, raising his hands in protest. "And if that's what it seemed like, no wonder you're out of there. I would be too, not that Tom would ever come on to me."

Becky smiled.

"But it's OK to be friends with sources. What would it hurt to have a drink with the man?"

"I don't like him. He gives me the creeps."

"OK, fair enough. So you don't want to lead him on. That's admirable. But at least give him a chance to apologize for last night. I swear, he didn't mean to give you the wrong impression. He's a good source. You don't want him thinking you're some touchy dame who overreacts to a hand on the shoulder."

"You think I'm overreacting," Becky said, her scowl returning.

"Parrot pennies! You're not listening," Duke said, keeping his tone jovial. "I said that might be the impression you left. That's all. You can smile and be friendly to the guy and just calmly tell him you have other plans for dinner. You can set your boundaries, and he'll respect them. That's OK. But you want to keep that connection open."

"Yeah, I guess you're right."

"Good, maybe we can stop over there after lunch and see if he's got any more details."

"I don't know."

"OK, I'll be straight with you. I need your help. I got a name, but my gut tells me it's not the real name. There's something going on, and Tom won't tell me what it is."

"And you think he'll tell me?"

"Well …" Duke's impish grin said more than his words.

"I told you I won't play that game!" Becky's raised voice attracted attention from the next table, and Duke winced.

"OK, OK. All you need to do is go over there with me. Let him apologize for the misunderstanding last night. Keep that door open."

Becky looked at Duke for a few minutes. "OK," she said finally. "I'll talk to him. But I'm going over there on my own. I'm a grown woman, and I can handle a fresh cop without hurting his precious feelings."

Duke smiled. "More chai?"

※

Tom Cantrell was on the phone when Becky stepped into the investigations office at the Jordan police department. Although she struck up a conversation with one of the other detectives, Tom spotted her immediately and lost all interest in his caller. Becky had a willowy grace and a light, melodic laugh that he found irresistible. Her skin was a dark mahogany color, like a fine polished table. He was so afraid of making a fool of himself over her that he half wanted to disappear rather than face her. But he simply couldn't resist.

She was still chatting with the other officer when Tom finished his call. He tried to pretend to be busy, but he couldn't keep his eyes off her. She was glancing at him too and smiling. Was she signaling him to come over? No, he'd already screwed this up by pushing too hard. He forced himself to read every word of the report in his hand, so he was almost surprised when he looked up and saw her standing at the edge of his desk.

"Got a minute?" she asked and then flashed a smile that took his breath away. He motioned to a chair, but his voice wouldn't work. She lowered herself to the chair as gently as a butterfly alighting on a flower and crossed her long, thin legs, like rubbing antennae together in a mating ritual. Tom swallowed hard. She was silent for a moment, just smiling. Tom didn't trust his voice.

"I'm sorry if I overreacted last night," she said, lowering her lashes shyly.

"Oh, no," Tom said and leaned in closer so they wouldn't be overheard. "I'm the one who should apologize. I didn't mean to come on so strong. I only thought … I mean … jeez, I don't know what I thought. But I didn't mean to be rude or pushy. I just thought maybe we could be friends."

"I don't think it's a good idea," Becky said, leaning in toward the desk so he was almost overcome by her faint floral scent. "We need to do business together. We need to keep a professional respect."

"Respect," Tom repeated and leaned back in his chair to clear his head. "Of course."

Becky smoothed her skirt and sat up like a soldier coming to attention. "I was wondering if you have any more information on the body that was found at the construction site."

"I'm sorry, my hands are tied on this one," Tom said. "As soon as I have something to release, you'll be the first one I call. I promise."

"This is so odd," Becky said, leaning forward again. "What's going on?"

"I told you, my hands are tied."

Becky's eyes met Tom's, and she saw the same sincerity Duke had sensed before.

"I can respect that," she said. "But when there's a murder, people get afraid. They need to know if there's another maniac on the loose like last summer. Do you think it was a robbery? Or someone he knew? Just what angles are you investigating?"

"Well, I can tell you we believe this was an isolated incident. The victim knew his assailants or was known to them. We have no reason to believe the public is in any danger."

"Oh, that helps a lot," Becky said, writing down his words. "Sometimes we get so caught up in little details like name and age that we forget to ask the really important questions."

Now Tom smiled. "And sometimes we forget to give the really important answers."

"Well, I guess that's all for now," Becky said, rising quickly like a lily opening up. Tom remained seated for a second, just taking in her spectacular regal grace. Then he stood awkwardly, knocking off a stack of reports on the side of his desk and sending them showering to the floor. Becky bent over to help him gather them up, and once again he was smitten by her scent.

They stood and she handed him a jumble of papers. "So, you'll call if there's anything new?"

"I'll call." His eyes locked on hers.

"OK, then." She turned and walked toward the door, then returned in three long strides.

"Hey, some of us reporters are going to the Andre Watts concert on Saturday at the university. I thought maybe … well, Duke said you played piano. I thought maybe you would like to join us."

The corners of Tom's mouth turned up a little and quickly grew into a full-fledged smile that seemed to light his cheeks and eyes until his whole face glowed.

"You'd have to put up with a bunch of reporters, I'm afraid," Becky said. "You could bring along some friends from the department so you wouldn't feel outnumbered. Or maybe your mother or sister. Duke told me about … well, I mean it wouldn't be a date or anything, just a casual group of friends."

"I understand," Tom said. "Sounds like fun."

"Yeah." Becky lowered her lashes again as though for a minute she couldn't look at him. "Well, until Saturday, or whenever you call … about the case."

"I'll call," Tom repeated.

Chapter 7

On Thursday, Josie left Kevin in the care of Polly, her neighbor. He was on antibiotics and wasn't running a fever anymore. Although Nick had done a great job during Josie's absence on Wednesday, there was a backlog of mail to read, assignments to make, calls to return. But she managed to get away from the office by four thirty so she could stop by the hospital and see Maggie before going to the monthly Chamber of Commerce cocktail hour. Glad-handing was part of her job as city editor, meeting the newsmakers and letting them meet her.

Maggie had regained consciousness, but only in the medical sense. She lay in her bed with oxygen tubes in her nose, an IV in her arm, and electrodes fastened to her chest. Her eyes fluttered open and closed, but there was no expression on her face.

"Can she hear me or see me?" Josie asked.

"I don't know," Katherine said, patting her mother's hand. "She doesn't respond. But the doctor said it's to be expected. The first forty-eight hours the body is in a protective state. They won't really start assessing the damage until then. But I just talk to her anyway. I've got to believe that on some level, she knows we're here."

"Hi, Maggie. It's me, Josie."

Maggie made no response. She just stared blankly at the ceiling.

Katherine looked at her watch. "Would you mind talking to her for a little while? I need to make some calls, and it's a good time in California to catch people at their desks."

"Sure, I'll tell her all about my day. Nobody ever listens anyway."

Katherine left the room and Josie pulled up a chair. She started jabbering, first about Kevin's fever and Nick taking over the office for a day. Then she told about the problem of getting an identification on the body and Duke's belief that the man was using an alias. Maggie's eyes closed.

Josie scooted a little closer.

"I found the suitcase full of clippings, Maggie, the ones about Zelda Machinko."

Maggie's eyes opened.

"I didn't mean to pry, really. I was trying to pack a suitcase for you, and they just fell out of the closet. I've been reading them. Some great work there. How come you never told me about that story? Too long ago, I guess. But I wanted you to know that I figured that's who you were thinking about when the call came in about a body being found at Jackson and Pearl. You thought it was Zelda, didn't you?"

Maggie's eyes closed.

"It's OK. I'm going to work on it for you. Somehow, we'll figure out what happened to her. I promise."

When Katherine returned, conversation bounced to non-medical topics. Katherine's work on an upcoming movie. Complaints about the new version of Coca-Cola. Speculation about President Reagan's embargo on Nicaragua.

"Buttons is getting along well with Chippie," Josie said. "I was afraid the big dog would hurt him, but Goldens are so patient. Chippie even backs up and lets Buttons eat first."

Josie offered to keep Buttons as long as needed, but neither of them said anything about the fact that Maggie might never be able to take her dog home again.

The meeting room at the Marriott was packed with chattering people when Josie arrived for the Chamber party. She dreaded these events because her ex-husband, Kurt, always was there. In fact, Kurt was the life of the party. As director of the Downtown Development office, he was practically the host. He shook every hand, patted every back, told one story after another, then laughed loudly. By comparison, Josie seemed dull and quiet.

She was thinking just that as she sipped a glass of merlot near one corner of the room. Coroner Zach Teasdale approached. Zach was a small man, barely five-foot-eight, but he carried an aura of wealth and power that made him seem gigantic. He wore a well-cut gray silk suit with a pale gray shirt and burgundy tie. His black hair was neatly trimmed, slightly feathered on the top as if he'd just come from the stylist. When he reached out his hand for Josie to shake, she noticed his nails were as smooth and well manicured as any woman's. It made her feel self-conscious. She could only hope there wasn't newsprint on her hands.

"I wanted to tell you how great the paper's been looking," Zach said. "You've been doing an excellent job there. I can see your touch."

"Thanks, but it kind of has a mind of its own," Josie said.

"Ah, no, I can see a woman's touch," Zach repeated, holding on to Josie's hand. "When Martin was in charge, the front page was all big money and big government. Since you've been there, we've rediscovered the people who make the news. It's actually quite enlightening."

"I don't know—"

"Oh, you think I'm the only one who notices? No, at the meetings I attend, people are talking about it. Not about you, necessarily, because most of them may not see the connection. But I hear them talking about your paper and the stories. You're touching people. You're making a difference."

"Well, thank you again. I don't know what to say."

"Say you're tired of listening to your ex tell another self-serving tale. Say you can't handle another glass of cheap wine. Say you'll join me for dinner at the Red Geranium, and I'll order a bottle from the reserve and show you what merlot should taste like."

Josie was stunned. Zach was rich and handsome and actually interested in her? Josie saw herself as a mother and a city editor, so it amazed her that this man saw a woman. A desirable woman.

"I … I really can't," Josie stammered. "My son is sick. I need to get home. But please, give me a rain check." Josie placed her hand on Zach's arm, caressing the fine silk of his suit.

"How about Saturday?"

"Well, ah … yes. That sounds wonderful."

"It's settled then. Your son. How old?"

"He just turned eight, but he's going on eighteen."

"Of course, precocious. I would expect nothing less. So he's into video games and computers."

"Of course, and the soccer team."

"Really? They start that young? I never was into sports myself. I was afraid I'd get trampled."

"You don't seem afraid of much now," Josie said. As she sipped her wine, she noticed how Zach's dark brown eyes twinkled.

"That's my defense mechanism," he said.

"Knowledge is more important than brute strength."

"Yes, but it's who you know more than what you know."

"I suppose, but as the coroner, sometimes you have to deal with some pretty awful knowledge," Josie said. "I know you see sordid details from autopsies that never make the paper."

Zach seemed to bask in Josie's praise. "The world isn't ready, won't ever be ready, for what I've seen."

"That was a strange case this week, the body at the construction site," Josie said. "There seems to be some conflicting information about the identification. When will you have the autopsy results?"

"Ah, I should have known the conversation would get around to work. It's to be expected, I guess. You only want me for my office."

Josie smiled. Zach's office was his least attractive attribute. "I'm sorry, I shouldn't talk business here."

"No, that's OK, but I'm afraid I can't be much help."

"Oh?"

"Yes, federal agents came and took the body away this afternoon. It's out of my hands."

❀

Josie couldn't make her excuses fast enough.

"Forgive me, Lord, but it wasn't a lie," she prayed as she practically ran through the lobby of the hotel where the Chamber was meeting. "I do have a sick son at home. I do have to get back to him. But if you'd just keep him safe a little longer, I've really got to do this."

She ducked into the little alcove just past the elevators, where she knew she would find a pay phone. She inserted the *Daily News* phone card. She dialed Nick's beeper. She had left her assistant city editor at his desk a couple of hours earlier, but now at six thirty, she wasn't sure where he would be. She figured he'd have his beeper on him.

Actually, the beeper was on the stack of clothes Nick had thrown on his sofa as he prepared dinner for his current love interest, Brittany Miller. Brittany and Nick knew each other from community softball games. She had been married briefly to one of Nick's friends, Scotty Miller, a young sheriff's deputy who was among those killed during the previous summer's murder spree. Since Scotty's death, Nick and Brittany had become closer and in recent weeks they had started dating. Nick had been taking it easy, going slow out of respect for Scotty. But now the relationship was finally escalating into passion. When the beeper sounded, Nick's welcome kiss was heating up into a romantic first course. He wasn't about to be called away.

"Wow, you're so hot, you've set off the smoke alarm," he mumbled between steamy smooches.

"I think it's your beeper," the pigtailed blonde said after the second beep sounded.

"Work," Nick mumbled as he lifted the noisy contraption from the pile of clothes. He dialed the number displayed and Josie picked up the pay phone.

"They've taken the body," she blurted out.

"Hold on. Who? What body?" he said, turning his back to Brittany and trying to talk softly so he wouldn't alarm her.

"The feds and Mr. No Name."

"Wait a minute, you're flying off without me, Peter Pan. The feds took Blaine Avril's body? Why would federal agents be involved in a local murder?"

"I don't know, but Zach just told me the feds took it."

"Zach? As in Teasdale?"

"Can't you keep up? Where are you?"

Nick looked across the room to catch a flash of blond pigtails bobbing around in the kitchen.

"About to eat dinner. Where are you that you've been talking to the coroner?"

"Chamber cocktail party. Oh, shit, here he comes!"

Josie slammed the receiver down and ducked into the corner behind the phone as Zach and a couple of his men headed for an elevator. Zach always had guys around him, like Secret Service following the president. People in Jordan figured they were just the bodyguards that came with wealth. They certainly didn't come with the office of coroner. Most of the time, the guys watched silently from a distance, but as they stopped in front of the elevator, they were joking and laughing like high school boys. Just as Josie started wondering why Zach and his entourage were headed upstairs to a hotel room, the pay phone rang.

"Chuck, I think your wife is calling to check up on you," one of the men joked.

"Yeah, get that and tell whoever answers the party's in room 211," another said.

Josie heard the ding of the elevator arriving and the noisy men disappeared. The phone kept ringing. Josie reached around and picked up the receiver.

"Are you still there?" Nick asked.

"Sorta," Josie said.

"While you were playing hide and seek, I called Duke," Nick continued. "He got all excited about the body being kidnapped by feds. He said the guy probably was in the witness-protection program. Anyway, he will try to confirm as much as he can for tomorrow's paper. It's in good hands."

"Thanks, Nick." Josie put the receiver down and slipped out of the hotel, fearing Zach would reemerge from the elevator at any second. When she reached her red Ford Escort in the parking lot, she got in and just sat there. Nick had taken charge. She didn't need to solve this problem. She could go home to Kevin. So why did she feel the tiniest disappointment?

Duke was in the fourth block of Hudson Street on Jordan's near west side when he spotted Tom Cantrell's city-issued beige Taurus tucked in close to a detached garage. He didn't know the address, but he remembered that Tom lived on Hudson someplace. A few years earlier when Tom had closed on the house, he'd bought a round of drinks for everyone in the bar.

Hudson was one of several tree-lined streets in a quiet older neighborhood. The blocks were square and orderly, as was the style in the fifties and sixties, not like the curving, rambling streets in the subdivisions of the eighties. The homes along Hudson were brick. The cracks in the concrete sidewalks and driveways were like wrinkles on the face of an aging grande dame. The neighborhood was mixed, and a cluster of boys, some black, some white, were shooting baskets in the driveway across the street.

Duke parked in front of Tom's house, which was a yellow brick ranch with geraniums tucked between low-lying bushes. The glass was still in the front storm door; the weather wasn't really warm enough yet for screens. The front door was open. Duke could see the back of Tom's head at the kitchen table, so he knocked on the glass rather than press the doorbell. It seemed friendlier, as if his intrusion might be welcome.

Tom's head spun around, but before he could move from his chair, a short, heavy girl suddenly appeared in the entryway.

"I get it, I get it," she echoed joyously. "Hi. Who are you? Do you want to come in? We're eating supper. I got the last pork chop."

The girl flung open the door and was welcoming Duke when Tom appeared at her side.

"Linda, I've told you never to open the door to strangers. Go back and eat your dinner."

"I could share my pork chop if you want some," Linda said to Duke, undeterred by her brother's reprimand.

"Linda, come in here and clean your plate," a soft, but firm, voice said. "Leave Tommy to handle his business."

Linda tucked her head down and walked back into the kitchen with the tall, thin woman who Duke assumed was their mother.

"Lost?" Tom asked, standing in the entryway with his arms crossed.

"Sort of," Duke said with a smile. "I thought maybe you could point me in the right direction."

"Oh? To where?"

"Wherever they took Blaine Avril."

"Took who? What are you talking about?" Tom looked over his shoulder to see Linda stuff mashed potatoes in her mouth.

"We're going for a walk," Tom announced to his mother.

"Me too!" Linda said through a mouth full of food as she rushed toward the door. "I cleaned my plate."

"No, you help Mom with the dishes, and maybe we can go get some ice cream later," Tom said, turning his sister's shoulders back toward the kitchen.

"Mom, Tommy's going to get us some ice cream," she said.

"Come on," Tom said, pushing Duke out of the doorway. "She won't be distracted for long."

Tom led Duke in long strides down the sidewalk. When they were far enough from the house that they could no longer be seen from the front door, he slowed his pace.

"Now, why are you coming to my home to ask about the construction site murder? I've told you all I can tell you."

"Bushwhacked buffalo chips! You don't know, do you?" Duke said with a smug laugh.

47

Tom twisted his lips to one side but didn't say a word. Duke laughed louder.

"They didn't tell you, did they? Those fleet-footed feds came and got your stiff and never even told you."

"Where are you getting this bullshit?"

"The coroner."

"Teasdale? He gave you a report on the body?"

"Not exactly. He said it was out of his hands. Sounds a lot like you, actually, only he said the feds came and took the body away."

A few expletives escaped Tom's lips.

After they had rounded another corner, Duke said, "OK, so we know Blaine Avril, or whatever his name is, was beamed up by the federal government. My only question is, why? If he was in the witness-protection program, how can it hurt to reveal his identity now?"

"Witness protection? Where do you get this stuff?"

"What else would pull the feds in? Drugs? Terrorism? There's an empty drawer at the morgue. I've got to tell people something."

"Tell them to mind their own business," Tom said, lengthening his strides to leave Duke behind. Duke was shorter and older, but he quickly caught up to the angry cop.

"Listen, I don't blame you for being mad. Some federal agents just came in and ripped off your case and didn't have the decency to tell you. But don't be mad at me. I'm just the messenger.

"I know," Tom said, and slowed his pace. "It's just that I can't help you. I really can't."

"I understand this is something big, and I don't expect you to tell me anything that's going to hamper the investigation or help the bad guys. I just need you to give me some idea of who's in charge now. The federal government is huge. Do I call FBI or INS? Was Avril an illegal immigrant? Is that why his record doesn't show up anywhere? Was he a drug dealer? Do I call DEA? Or is he in witness protection? Just give me an agency to start with."

Tom stopped and looked at Duke, then looked up and down the street.

"There's a guy over at the Justice Department. I still have his card," Tom said, pulling a card out of his pocket and handing it to Duke. "They came in and claimed the case yesterday. That's why I can't talk to you. He won't talk to you either, but there it is. If the body has been taken away, those are the guys who have it."

❅

Within an hour, Duke had confirmed that the body had been removed from the morgue at St. Mary's Hospital. Hospitals are a constant flow of activity—patients coming and going, pills being ordered and dispensed, bodies going out the door for funerals. And for every aspirin, there's a piece of paper in the records department. So Duke just asked Jackie Peters, a second shifter in the records department.

Jackie used to work at the *Daily News*, taking dictation from the freelance writers who covered the school board meetings in neighboring towns. Now she was a medical transcriptionist, an expert in reading doctors' doodles on patient charts and turning them into billable records accepted by insurance. She was alone in the office and eager for company when Duke showed up.

"I don't have anything to do with the morgue," Jackie said with a playful tilt of her head. "But if you're saying somebody picked up a body, they must have had an ambulance or a hearse. It's not exactly something you can tuck in your briefcase or wheel downstairs in a wheelchair and prop up in the back seat."

Jackie laughed heartily at the thought, and Duke couldn't help but get caught up in her offbeat sense of humor. Before long she had the name of the ambulance company in Chicago that had transported the body, the time of departure, and the signature of Fred Wheeler, the same name on the card Tom had given Duke.

It was almost midnight when Duke called Josie.

"Am I waking you?"

"Wouldn't be the first time," she said in a husky bedtime voice "Actually, I just dozed off."

"How's Kevin? I heard he was sick."

"Strep. He seems to get it every spring," she said, sitting up and turning on the light so the conversation wouldn't seem like pillow talk. "What did you find out about the body?"

"Well, it's definitely been hauled off to Chicago, and I've got the name of the federal agent involved. I've just got to wait until morning and hope he calls me back. Say, how'd you manage to get this tip out of Teasdale? The cops didn't even know about it."

"Really? He just brought it up at the Chamber meet-and-greet. I don't think he realized how important it was."

"Don't kid yourself," Duke said. "Teasdale knows how to play every angle. He knows exactly what will get his name in the paper, and he's probably regretting that he won't get much play on this one."

"Oh, he's just being open and honest. Government can use more of that. He's just a little showy because he grew up a millionaire."

"Pigeon paste! I'm thinking the King of Pop-O has more than bubble gum on his shoes. If things ever slow down enough, I'll find out what."

"Don't be silly. He's a charming, educated man whose family made millions in a bubble gum factory. Probably the worst thing he's guilty of is giving everybody tooth decay. I kinda like him."

"What do you mean, kinda like him?"

"Duke, it's late. Can we talk about this in the morning? It sounds like you've got a good start figuring out what happened to the body. Go get 'em, Tiger."

Chapter 8

Zelda

I knew Buster Boardman was crooked the first time I laid eyes on him. He wasn't that different from the mafia types in Chicago when I was growing up. You think Elliott Ness and Al Capone were all about illegal liquor and speakeasies, but that was the fun stuff. Most of it wasn't fun at all.

Every Thursday, these two henchmen would come into my father's butcher shop in their pinstriped suits with white spats covering the tops of their shoes. I didn't understand when I was a kid that my father was paying them just to stay in business, just to be allowed to do honest work. But those spats told me that these guys were something special. They didn't cut meat like Papa, or shovel coal for the furnace, or even sweep up storerooms like me. They couldn't do any kind of honest work and keep their spats clean. I thought they were so handsome. When Mama read me stories about Prince Charming, I imagined a dark Italian man in a pinstriped suit and spats.

One day this car pulls up, a big, fancy limousine with a chauffeur. I thought it was a movie star come to buy my Papa's Polish sausage because everyone said it was the best on Milwaukee Avenue. All these men get out of the car, like maybe six or seven. But one man, he was the boss. You could tell. He not only wore white spats, but he had a white cashmere coat slung over his shoulders. You might as well have put a crown on his head in that neighborhood. I'd never seen such a coat before.

All the men came into Papa's shop in a cluster, like a swarm of black-and-white striped hornets. Customers scattered as if the men really were hornets. Except Papa. He came around the counter to speak with them, and they all went back into Papa's little office and closed the door. It wasn't long before the man in the white coat came out of the office. He pats me on the head and tips his hat at Mama behind the register. One of the other men comes along behind him, the chauffeur I guess, and opens the door for him. Then before he leaves, he turns over the sign on the door so it says Papa's shop is closed.

I could hear noise in the office, like a chair knocked over, but when I go to peek, Mama sends me upstairs to my room. I knew better than to ask Papa about his black eye. A man has his pride. I never saw the men in spats after that. Mama kept us kids upstairs on Thursdays. Sometimes Papa would go down to the shop late at night to work, and Mama would say prayers in front of the little shrine to Our Lady she had upstairs. One Sunday, when Mama and us kids were at church, there was a fire. Papa, the shop, our home—all gone.

The papers said Papa was a gangster. Said he had been helping to dispose of bodies along with the waste from the butcher shop. I never believed it. It was just part of the Elliott Ness scare tactics. Everybody was a gangster in those days.

Why am I telling you this? You want to know about Boardman. Mind if I smoke?

Boardman doesn't wear spats, but he might as well. He works at the hotel, next door to the *Spectator* offices, and I never saw the man get sweaty. I never saw him without his suit coat, even on the hottest day of summer. He is way too cool, that one, like there isn't blood in his veins.

Never trust a man who dresses too well or stays too clean. It ain't natural, and whatever he's up to probably ain't legal. I watch him out the window from my office on the third floor. I watch him come in the morning and leave at night and go in and out several times in between. You know, he's never alone. He's got these men everywhere he goes, like the swarm of hornets that walked into Papa's. So I start watching the men, union organizers they say. Federation of Hotel and Service Employees. All the restaurants, hotels, bars. They're collecting money, just like the spats comin' into Papa's.

Now, don't say I'm imagining things, honey. They may be negotiating for better wages, but I figure if a cleaning lady don't like what she's getting paid, she can just quit and go do something else. Hard workers never have trouble finding jobs. But it's the spats, the dandies who don't want to get their hands dirty who are doing the dirtiest work of all.

I've got to be goin' soon. Got a deadline to meet, so if you don't mind me puttin' on my stockings while I talk ... Where was I? Oh, yeah, figurin' out Boardman. So he builds this big house west of town. Brick mansion, must have five bedrooms at least and a three-car garage. Whoever heard of a three-car garage? Must have cost $50,000. Where does a hotel manager get that kind of money?

So I start watching the Herkimer. It's January, not exactly tourist season. And you know how it is in winter. It's night more than it's day. Well, I notice that the windows on the third floor on up, the hotel rooms, don't have any lights on. Ever. But the parking lot behind the place is full when I leave at night. I stay later and watch later, and cars keep coming, even after midnight. They start thinning out about two a.m., and usually the lot is fairly empty before morning.

Now, if it were still Prohibition, I'd say he was running a speakeasy, wouldn't you? But booze has been legal for twenty years, and it flows freely at the Herkimer and at least a dozen other bars in Jordan.

See, that's the thing. There ain't no money in honest racketeering. His goons can push people around, intimidate, but how much money can a bartender or maid contribute? Certainly not enough to build a house with a three-car garage and keep Buster in pink shirts and white bucks. If gangsters want to make money, they gotta step over the line. They gotta do what's illegal. You look for that line between what people want to do and what the law says they can't do, and that's where you'll find organized crime running the ferryboat to illegal fun.

You mind checkin' if my seams are straight, kiddo? I don't know how they expect a woman to get dressed by herself. There's no way you can see the back of your legs, even in the mirror.

Thanks, gotta go. Deadline.

Huh? You haven't figured it out yet? Gambling. Buster's runnin' a casino in the Herkimer.

Chapter 9

By eight the next morning, Duke was making his third call to the Justice Department and wondering what time agent Fred Wheeler normally got to work. His answer came walking into the newsroom.

"Who's that?" Duke heard Josie say from her nearby desk. He followed her stare to see four men with military haircuts and conservative suits approaching Helen, the receptionist. Two were wearing little hearing-aid radios in their ears.

"Looks like Secret Service," Josie said. "Is the president in town?"

"Justice Department," Duke whispered. "I'll bet that's the guy I'm looking for."

Duke stood up just as Helen turned around and pointed in his direction. He met his guests halfway across the newsroom.

"Mr. Dukakis? Fred Wheeler. You been trying to reach me?"

"Yes, sir," Duke said as he shook Wheeler's hand. "This is really great service. I can't believe you got my messages already."

"It's the modern age." Wheeler glanced around the bustling newsroom. "Is there someplace we can …"

He didn't finish the sentence. Duke nudged him in the direction of a small conference room. Wheeler was about Duke's height, younger and slimmer, with a light brown burr of hair, piercing blue eyes, and a long, sharp nose. At his elbow was a shorter man, with a crown of dark brown hair circling a bald spot and the ashen jaw of a man who never really can look clean shaven. The pair wearing radios and expressionless faces stood by the newsroom door like sentries.

Wheeler strode into the conference room, sat in a chair on the far side of the table, and leaned the chair back on two legs like a teenager.

"So what can I do for you?" he said, as though Duke had invaded his office instead of vice versa. The shorter agent was standing, looking through the glass wall into the newsroom. Duke closed the door and took the chair across from Wheeler.

"Well, I understand you've taken over the investigation of the man who was found murdered Tuesday at Jackson and Pearl," Duke said, pulling a notebook from his pocket and laying it on the table. "I need an ID."

"I believe your paper already gave a name to that body. Didn't I read that in your paper yesterday?" Wheeler was smiling.

Duke could see this wasn't going to be easy. "Well, since it's your case, I didn't want to presume," Duke said, trying to sound as humble as possible without puckering up and planting a smooch on Wheeler's bony butt.

Wheeler chuckled softly but didn't offer any more information.

54

"I know you picked up the body yesterday," Duke said, trying a little firmer approach. "You don't have to tell me what he was doing in Jordan, just—"

"I don't have to tell you anything," Wheeler said, lunging forward as the chair's front two legs came down with a thud. "But what I am going to tell you, for your own good, is that we never had this conversation."

"Well, that's pretty easy, because it hasn't been much of a conversation."

"And you don't have any information about the body being picked up by anyone," Wheeler continued. "As far as you know, he's still in his little drawer at the morgue waiting for next of kin to be notified."

"Listen, a man was found dead in Jordan. A man who worked beside folks from Jordan. A man who drank in the bars with folks from Jordan. They have every right to know what happened to him."

"They'll get over it," Wheeler said, leaning the chair back again.

"I'm trying to respect your authority," Duke said. "I know you've got a job to do, but I do too. Just tell me what you can."

"I told you. We were never here."

"But people have a right to know. If you don't work with me, it may look worse than it is. We'll have to say the Justice Department has assumed the case and refused to comment. People will come up with their own idea of what that means. You don't want that, Mr. Wheeler."

"What I want is no mention of Fred Wheeler or the Justice Department. You got that?"

"I have to tell the people what I know unless you can give me a good reason I shouldn't. What would be compromised by a story in the newspaper at this point? Give me something to work with."

The man standing at the window behind Duke spoke suddenly.

"She's cute, isn't she?" he said. "I mean in an impish, tomboy sort of way."

The second agent had spoken so softly that Duke wasn't sure he heard right. Duke turned to look at him and could see through the glass wall that Josie and Nick were talking in the center of the newsroom.

"It's no wonder they call her Peter Pan. Good nickname for her," the agent continued, turning away from the window and looking at Duke. "I can certainly understand what you see in your boss lady, Mr. Dukakis, but I wonder what your wife would think about your little affair last summer."

Duke started to stand up, but the agent placed a firm hand on his shoulder and pushed him back into the chair.

"And your daughter," the agent said. "They're so idealistic at sixteen. She probably thinks the world of you."

"Yep, girls sure admire their fathers," Wheeler said, leaning forward again as the chair legs returned to the floor. "But she's got a right to know."

"Yes, a right to know," the second agent repeated, his hand still firmly planted on Duke's shoulder.

Duke looked from one smiling agent to the other. He couldn't believe what he was hearing.

"You can't threaten me," Duke said through clenched teeth.

"Oh, of course not," the nameless agent said.

"We couldn't do that," Wheeler added. "We never had this conversation."

Wheeler stood up, but Duke remained tethered to his chair by the weight of understanding. The two agents headed out of the conference room, and Duke noticed that Wheeler nodded politely to Josie as he passed. Then the whole entourage left the newsroom as though the visit never happened.

Josie stepped into the conference room where Duke was still sitting at the table, staring into space.

"So have you got a story for today or not?" she asked.

Duke seemed startled. He answered in a low, defeated tone. "Huh? Oh, no. Nothing for today."

Josie signaled Nick that there would be no late addition. Then she closed the door to the conference room and took the seat across from Duke.

"So what did they have to say for themselves? Who is the dead man? Why did they take him?"

"They didn't say much of anything, really," Duke replied. "They don't want anything in the paper about their involvement."

"Of course they don't," Josie said with a laugh. "But I know you won't let them get away with that. What did they give you?"

"Not much," Duke said, lifting his eyes to look directly at Josie. The pain she saw frightened her.

"What is it? It must be something really awful. Tell me what's going on."

Duke took a deep breath. "How many people do you think know about last summer?"

"Last summer? Why the whole country knows about Malcolm Jones and the murders. It was on CNN, for Pete's sake. This can't possibly be as big as that!"

Duke shook his head. "Not the murders, us. How many people know about us?"

"Oh, my gosh, is that what's got you upset? Did somebody say something? Did somebody tell Sharon?"

"Not yet, at least I don't think so. But somebody sure blabbed." Duke got up from the table and began pacing. "That's the only thing that makes sense. I can't believe—I won't believe—they were spying on us. Us! I mean, we're nobodies. Hippo hash! If they know who everybody is sleeping with ... They just can't be spying on everybody!"

"Who? Who do you think is spying on us?"

"Them. Aren't you listening? The feds! They made it clear, if we put anything in the paper about their involvement in this case, they will tell Sharon about us."

"They threatened you?" Josie jumped up and began pacing behind Duke. "They can't do that. I'll call this Wheeler's boss. Even agents have bosses. Hell, I'll have Ham call him. We'll complain to Senator Davis if we have to. They can't threaten a newspaper, of all things. Wait 'til we—"

Duke raised a hand to Josie's mouth.

"What are you saying? You're going to tell Ham we had an affair? You're going to bring in a senator? We might as well take out a full-page ad! We can't tell anybody and they know it!"

Josie pulled away from Duke's grasp. "But we can't let them get away with this. We can't let them control the freedom of the press."

"Stop being such an idealist," Duke said, falling into a chair. Josie returned to the chair across from him.

"OK, let's think this thing out," Josie said. "We know the man was murdered, we know they took the body. But we still don't have an accurate ID, and we don't know why they're hiding it. But you've got other sources. Keep asking questions. Something will break."

Josie paused and switched to a more caring tone. "And you've got to talk to Sharon."

"I know," Duke said, leaning his head into his hands.

"It's the only way you'll be in control of the situation," Josie said. "Do you want me to go with you?"

"Why? So she can claw your eyes out?"

"We're all adults here. We made a mistake. We're sorry. It won't happen again."

"A mistake, huh?"

"I don't mean it like that," Josie said, reaching a hand out to Duke. "You know I love you deeper and purer than some tawdry affair. I respect and admire you. I want what's best for you, and I think that's mending your family. Isn't that what you want?"

"I don't know what I want. I'm too busy trying to figure out what Sharon wants … what's best for Jennifer … how to keep my boss happy. There are too many women trying to make me into something I'm not. If I could have a coupla beers, I could figure this thing out!"

"Don't go feeling sorry for yourself, mister!"

"I'm not feeling sorry for myself. I just want to live my life without always worrying about hurting other people."

"You don't mean that. Everything you've ever done, every word you've ever written, has been because you care about other people."

Duke stared at Josie, the frustration in his face slowly melting into a smile.

"This respect and admiration stuff is a heavy burden, you know?"

"I know," Josie said, smiling back.

"But I don't think I can tell Sharon about us. It would just stir up a hornet's nest."

"Honesty is the cornerstone of a good relationship."

"You mean if Kurt had come to you and confessed his affairs, you would have forgiven him and you two would still be together?"

"What affairs?" Josie asked, her forehead crinkled in concern.

"See what I mean?" Duke said with a big "gotcha" smile. "You're not even married anymore, and the mere suggestion of an affair has you in a tizzy."

"OK, maybe honesty isn't going to be easy."

"Maybe?"

"We could just forget about the body the feds took," Josie suggested.

"No," Duke said without hesitation.

"I could assign someone else."

"No, I'll keep making inquiries discreetly. Take my chances."

"In the meantime, should we try to find out who told them about us? I hate to think someone in the newsroom is gossiping to federal agents."

"Or they've got something on somebody."

"That's an idea!" Josie exclaimed. "Who might have a skeleton—"

Nick burst into the conference room. "Excuse me, but I thought you'd want to know. The owner of Ranch Rudy day care has been arrested for molesting a child."

Chapter 10

Nick quickly told Josie the facts they had gathered so far. Police had confirmed that day-care center owner Rudy Randolph had been charged with molesting a five-year-old girl in his care. The police said a kindergarten teacher had reported her suspicion to Family Services. A mother who had heard a rumor tried to pick up her child and discovered the facility had been taken over by Family Services.

"What do you mean, taken over?" Josie asked.

"Well, as best we can tell, the other employees have been hauled in for questioning, and the children are being interviewed by social workers. They've got a whole team there. The children can't leave."

"What? They're talking to kids without their parents?"

"Judge Sarenda approved it," Nick said.

Josie checked her watch. It was after nine o'clock. They'd have to hurry to make the ten o'clock deadline for the first edition. But mostly Josie was checking the time to imagine where her son would be.

"Kevin would have caught the bus for school at eight ten," she said, thinking out loud. "He probably doesn't know anything about this."

The look on Nick's face said it wasn't that simple.

"Evidently, the school-age children were picked up at the bus stop by DCFS and taken to their offices downtown. The director said they planned it that way because they wanted to separate them from the younger kids."

Nick's words seemed to suck the air out of Josie's lungs. Kevin had been kidnapped by some know-it-all social agency? Her baby was being questioned, prodded, frightened? Anger rushed in with every breath until Josie's face burned with fury. She barked orders to Nick and the rotund news editor, Hoss, then left the office.

Her mind raced with only one thought: Get to this downtown office, wherever it is, and rescue her child from these monsters. Rushing downtown in her car, this immediate goal seemed doable, so much easier than facing the possibility that Kevin might have been molested or that she, his mother, might have left him in the care of someone capable of something so unthinkable.

Josie thought about Rudy. Could he? Of course not! Rudy was the most angelic man she'd ever met. She'd always marveled at his rapport with the children. He would get down on the floor to play with them, building a tower of wooden blocks. But he could be as strict as an English nanny about each child hanging up his own coat in the morning. And he'd always been like a friend, listening when Josie was going through her divorce, advising when Kevin turned his anger on his playmates. Rudy was more priest than pedophile.

59

That thought so startled Josie that she involuntarily slammed on the brakes and had to pull off the road. She had read about pedophilia in the Catholic Church, but she always thought a priest who would abuse a child would seem different somehow. Was it possible that an abusive priest behaved as respectably as Rudy?

Right there, with traffic whizzing past, Josie bowed her head in prayer. "Please God, don't let it be true."

Pulling back into traffic with a new urgency, Josie wondered if she should have suspected something since Rudy never married. Or had he? Josie knew nothing about what Rudy had done before moving to Jordan. When was that, ten, fifteen years ago? Ranch Rudy had been at the big old farmhouse on the edge of town as long as she could remember. Certainly all of Kevin's eight years. He had started going there as a toddler, only two years old. Visions of her son as an innocent, bright-eyed baby flashed through Josie's mind as she pulled into the parking lot at the sterile-looking white brick building with the small green sign: "Cade County Department of Children and Family Services." Josie stepped into a phone booth at the corner of the building and called Nick. They'd managed to get a quote from the judge, Nick reported, and the story would make all editions.

"Great," Josie said. "For tomorrow, have Becky check Rudy's background. When did he move here, where did he work before? I'm sure he said something about a degree in early childhood development. Find out from where. And check the licensing requirements. They must have to check police records."

Josie hung up the phone, ran up the stairs, and opened the door into chaos. More than a dozen parents—alerted by a word-of-mouth network faster than any official media—were gathered around a reception desk. Everyone was speaking at once.

"I'm calling my lawyer," a tall black father was saying. "You have no right to hold these children."

"If you don't sit down and wait quietly, I'll have to call police," said the woman at the desk.

"I want my baby. Give me my child," wailed a pregnant girl who seemed too young to have a school-age child.

Josie pushed through the mass of noisy parents. "We need to see the director, Shirley Henderson," she said in an authoritative tone. Josie knew the director's name from stories in the *Daily News*, though she couldn't conjure a face to match. "I'm sure she will want to talk to us," Josie added, handing her business card to the receptionist.

"Yeah, call the lady in charge of this fiasco," shouted one of the mothers.

"I just don't understand what's going on," the black man added. "Why can't I see my son?"

Within a few minutes, a tall, dark-haired woman in a light-blue suit stepped into the doorway.

"Now if everyone will just take a seat," the woman said, raising her hands. "I'm Ms. Henderson, director of CCDCFS, and I assure you your children are being well taken care of. An intervention is a standard procedure in potential group situations such as this. We find the children are much more truthful when interviewed before outside sources start introducing false ideas."

Outside sources? Josie thought. She means us. The parents.

"But I don't want somebody asking my Amy questions about sex. She's only seven," a mother said.

"Our clinicians are trained in interview techniques," Henderson replied. "Every effort is being made not to alarm the children. They have been told they are visiting our facility as part of a school field trip. Your children will be released to you as soon as we complete our interviews."

One by one, the parents did as they were told. They signed in, showed two forms of identification, and waited. They were called one at a time into an interview room by a listless white-haired man. Josie hoped he was not one of the "trained clinicians" who had interviewed the children. He gathered basic facts about Kevin's age and how long he had been attending Ranch Rudy as if he were filling in a form about a lost glove. He gave a judgmental "Hmmm" when Josie, in answer to his question, said she had been divorced two years and that Kevin saw his father only "some weekends."

"Any adult males in the home?" he asked.

"No, just Kevin and me and a big golden retriever. I don't suppose he counts," Josie said, hoping a little levity might ease the tension.

"Sleepovers?" the little man continued, never looking up from the form.

"Well, yes, I let him have a couple friends over on his eighth birthday, but they were so noisy, I decided never again."

The man looked up with an impatient sigh. "Not the child," he said. "Do you have any adult males sleep over?"

Josie could feel the fire sneaking into her face. There hadn't been any men since that week last summer with Duke, but this little man had no right to ask about that!

"No," she said, pulling herself a little straighter in the chair. "I'm a good mother. My conduct is not part of this investigation, is it?"

"Just routine," the man said, without changing his tone. "Have you noticed any changes in your son in recent weeks?"

"No," Josie responded, then added, "Well, he stayed home a few days this week because he's been sick."

The man looked up.

"Sick? He didn't want to go to Ranch Rudy? When did this start?"

Josie tried to think back.

"Tuesday. I kept him home Wednesday and Thursday. He was running a fever. He couldn't have just been faking. I took him to the doctor. He said it might be strep throat and put him on antibiotics."

The little man made another of his "Hmmm" sounds. Josie barely heard the rest of his questions. Her mind was flitting back to Tuesday night when she was late to pick up Kevin. When she had found him in the kitchen, alone with Rudy.

Returning to the waiting room, Josie couldn't stop thinking back over the years. How many times had Kevin been alone with Rudy? Had her son ever seemed afraid of Rudy or balked about being left at the Ranch?

"I heard it was a little girl who told on him," whispered a woman in the next chair. Josie recognized her as the mother of two boys, both younger than Kevin. "I think that means our boys should be OK," the woman continued. "If he's into little girls, he probably leaves the boys alone, don't you think?"

Josie shuddered. It sounded like slim consolation. She heard her name called and looked up. Kevin was standing in the doorway, his jacket bunched up under one arm and his backpack dragging on the floor. She jumped up and hugged him fiercely.

"Are you going to take me to school?" he asked. He seemed startled to see her. "I thought we were going to school. I'm missing lunch hour."

Josie looked up at the woman standing beside her son, but it was like trying to read lab results on a technician's face. There was no sign of whether her son had confided some abuse or not.

"Well, I thought you and I would go to lunch together today," Josie said. "Then you can go to school this afternoon, if you want."

Josie helped Kevin with his jacket and ushered him outside.

"OK, what's up?" Kevin asked as he started walking toe-to-heel down the curb, trailing his backpack in the gutter. "Did that killer from last summer attack again?"

"No," Josie said. "Why would you think that?"

"Everybody's acting strange, like something bad happened. And you're picking me up in the middle of the day."

"Well, something bad did happen," Josie said. "A little girl was hurt, and I just wanted to be sure you're OK."

"I'm bored," Kevin said. "This place is dumber than school, and they ask really dumb questions. Can we get a Happy Meal?"

Once Kevin was chowing down on a cheeseburger and fries, Josie felt she had to say something about what had happened.

"So you had a boring morning, huh?"

"Yeah, I guess," Kevin said, opening up his burger to pull off the "gross green stuff" in the form of a dill pickle slice.

"They asked some pretty dumb questions?"

"Oh, all that boring good-touch, bad-touch stuff," Kevin said with a shrug. "Rudy told us all about that stuff when I was a little kid."

"He did?" Josie said faintly, her stomach in knots.

"Yeah, and they talk about it at school," Kevin said, pulling a handful of fries through a puddle of ketchup. "It's so dumb."

"But it's important," Josie said, looking into Kevin's eyes. "No one, even a teacher, should touch you in a way that makes you feel ashamed. You need to tell me if something like that happens."

"Whatever," Kevin said. "Can we go to school now? I want to see Timmy."

❀

Becky stood over Josie's desk like a tall tropical palm offering little shade from the searing sun.

"He does have a police record, but it's not much," she said, flipping the pages in her narrow notebook. "Randolph was arrested twenty years ago when he was a student at the University of Vermont. It was some environmental protest, nuclear power plant stuff. Nothing about child abuse.

"College records show he was a creative writing student. Actually showed some promise. Won a scholarship, some writing awards. Then his wife was killed."

"Wife?" Josie said, with mild surprise.

"Yep," Becky said, thumbing through the pages of her notebook again. "Sarah, oh, sorry, that must have been the daughter."

"Daughter?" Now the surprise was so pronounced in Josie's voice that Becky started reading directly from her notes.

"Theresa Randolph, 24, and infant daughter Sarah, March 13, 1968. Car crash. Icy roads. Here, I have a copy of the story from the Burlington paper. I talked to a reporter there and she looked it up and faxed it to me."

Josie grabbed the paper from Becky's hand and read every word of the story of a long-ago car crash. Why hadn't Rudy ever said anything about losing his wife and daughter? What else did he keep to himself?

"Looks like he dropped out for a while," Becky said. "I didn't find anything else until five years later, when he got the degree in early childhood development. Hmmm, Michigan State University."

"Why did he leave Vermont? Why did he go to Michigan? What other places did he work?"

Becky just shrugged.

"County land records show he bought that old farmhouse in '74, the summer after he graduated from Michigan."

"Well, keep checking," Josie said. "Talk to the other employees. What does DCFS say?"

"Ongoing investigation," Becky replied with another shrug.

That was all they had told the parents too, Josie thought.

"Oh, one more thing," Becky said as she was walking away. "The hospital called. Maggie is conscious. Her daughter had said you'd want to know."

"Oh, my God," Josie mumbled. "I forgot all about Maggie."

"Ham said he was going over there this afternoon," Becky added. "He'll probably bore her back into a coma."

※

Well before the scheduled drop-off at three fifteen, Josie was waiting at the bus stop with the other mothers in the neighborhood. They had heard about Rudy's arrest on the radio and wanted to know if Josie had any more details. She told them as little as possible. She felt oddly embarrassed to have something so ugly touch her family. When the bus arrived, all the children piled off as if nothing unusual had happened. Josie tried to spot any uneasiness in her son, but he came down the bus steps with a scavenged length of yarn looped over Timmy, his best friend.

"Can Timmy come over?" Kevin said before his feet touched the ground. "He's Boba Fett and I just captured him."

"Rrrrrr," Timmy said, clawing at Kevin.

"Why don't you boys come over to our house?" Polly asked. "I just made oatmeal raisin cookies, and Boba Fett looks hungry." Timmy growled again as the bus drove away, and they crossed the street behind it.

"Really, Polly, I'd rather Kevin came home with me tonight," Josie said. "And I've got Oreos."

"Oreos! Oreos!" Kevin chanted. Then the yarn broke, and he ran down the sidewalk chasing his escaped friend.

"Kurt will be by soon to take Kevin for the weekend," Josie said. "I want to talk to him to be sure he's OK with all that happened today."

"He looks OK to me," Polly said.

"I know. That's what worries me. Shouldn't he be, I don't know, upset? Even if he doesn't understand exactly what happened this morning, he knows something's not right. Shouldn't that be bothering him?"

"Never complain about a happy kid," Polly said. "Parent's Bible, chapter one, verse one."

Before the mothers parted, Polly agreed to watch Kevin before school for the next week, until Josie could make other arrangements. Josie never asked if Ranch Rudy would be closed. In her mind, it was strictly off-limits.

The boys played on the patio, close enough that Josie could hear their conversations about some pretend *Star Wars* confrontation. Chippie and

Buttons started chasing each other around the yard. Both dogs seemed to be enjoying this time together.

Josie sat by the sliding glass door to read the brochure the little man at DCFS had handed her: "Talking to your child about abuse." How could they put out a brochure, with colored photos, like this was some everyday occurrence? Shirley Henderson hadn't returned Josie's calls. She'd tried twice to get through to her. No news is good news, Josie told herself. If DCFS suspected Kevin had been abused, they would have told her, wouldn't they?

The doorbell jolted Josie out of her thoughts. The front door was unlocked. Kurt usually walked right in. But sometimes he rang the bell first out of some pseudo-politeness. Josie turned and saw her handsome ex-husband striding into the entryway and tossing his keys onto the hall table as if he still lived there.

"Is he ready?" Kurt said without a hello. "Thought we'd get a Happy Meal and catch an early movie."

"He had McDonald's for lunch," Josie said. "Can't you take him someplace with vegetables?"

"Well, la-di-da," Kurt exclaimed. "If it isn't mother of the year." He stopped in the middle of the dining area off the kitchen. He hung his suit coat over the back of a chair and loosened his tie. Even at the end of a warm day, his shirt looked perfectly pressed without so much as a ring of dampness under the arms. He was smiling calmly, like nothing ever was out of order in his world.

Josie felt an urge to run to him, to have him wrap his arms around her so she could cry. But she remained in her seat on the other side of the table, her son's comforting laughter just outside the sliding glass door.

"We need to talk about something," she said.

Kurt's smile stiffened a little, but not much. He glanced at his watch.

"Well, if this is going to be a long talk, can I get myself a beer? It's been a busy day." Kurt didn't wait for an answer. He opened the fridge and began searching. "A ceramics manufacturer from Detroit was in today. Think they're going to build south of town if I can convince the township board to extend the enterprise zone. Good company. Could be a hundred jobs. Not a bad day's work."

Kurt stood up and looked at Josie. "You don't have any beer."

"Kevin and I are on the wagon."

"I'll try this froufrou hard lemonade." He took a glass bottle out of the refrigerator door. "So what do we need to talk about?" Kurt closed the refrigerator, leaned against the door, and took a long pull of the artificially yellow liquid.

"Rudy Randolph was arrested this morning."

"Oh, I heard about that," Kurt said, gesturing with the bottle. "Darn shame. He always seemed like such a nice guy."

"Kevin spent the morning at DCFS."

"Our Kevin?" Kurt's permanently sunny expression was showing the first sign of clouds.

"They interviewed all the children."

"Oh, that could make an ugly stink," he mumbled.

"Kurt, this is not about some blemish on the perfect development profile you've built for Jordan," Josie said, standing up. She walked toward the kitchen and added in a more hushed tone, "This is about our son."

Kurt looked out the window at the boys climbing over the swing set.

"Looks OK to me," Kurt said, taking another pull from the bottle.

"He may have been abused. May be holding it all in."

"Psychobabble," Kurt said, shaking his head. "We could tell if he was unhappy. Where'd that yippie little dog come from?"

"It's Maggie's."

"You took the dog?"

"Somebody had to."

"Put it in a kennel, for Pete's sake. You don't need another dog."

"Will you listen to me? I want to talk to you about Kevin. Remember what the psychologist said about his obsession with that toy tractor after you left, how he was trying to hold on to you?"

"More psychobabble," Kurt said, finishing the bottle and dropping it in the trash. "You can't believe all that stuff, babe. Believe your eyes. He's a happy kid, a little messy, but all boy."

Josie handed Kurt the brochure. Its sanitized approach to sexual abuse might make sense to perfect-world Kurt.

"Just be on the lookout for some sign that Kevin is suffering," she said. "Bad dreams. Or constipation. Or refusing to use a urinal."

Kurt carefully folded the brochure into thirds without looking at it and tucked it into his pocket.

"We are not going to spend the entire weekend looking for stupid signs," Kurt said. "We're going to take care of this right now."

Kurt strode through the dining area and out the sliding door.

"Daddy! Daddy!" Kevin came running from the swing set and was wrapped in Kurt's outstretched arms.

"Hi, buddy," Kurt said, ruffling his son's hair. "Hey, Timmy. Boy, you're getting big."

"Hello, Mr. Walsh," Timmy said, hanging back shyly by the swing set.

"Listen Timmy, you'll have to go home now. Kevin and I have to leave. But he'll be back Sunday. Why don't you come over then?"

Timmy left reluctantly, but Kevin was too involved in a tickle fight with his father to notice.

"OK, OK, you win," Kurt said, brushing errant blades of grass from his sleeve. "Hey, buddy, I've got a question for you." He draped an arm over

Kevin's shoulder. "That guy who runs the day-care center, Rudy. Is he a pretty nice guy?"

"Kurt!" Josie exclaimed.

"I just want to know," Kurt repeated. "Do you like him?"

"I guess so," Kevin said. "What movie we gonna see?"

"In a minute," Kurt said sternly, pulling Kevin back to face him. "I'm not finished talking to you about this Rudy guy."

"He's silly," Kevin said.

"Yeah, I remember he's pretty silly," Kurt said. "But does he tickle fight as good as me?"

"No." Kevin giggled and rushed in to tickle his father.

"OK, OK," Kurt said, slipping out of his son's grasp. "Does he ever play monster hand?" Kurt raised one arm with exaggerated Frankenstein fingers. Kevin squealed and started to run away. "And does he ever pull your pants down like this," Kurt teased, yanking at Kevin's loose jeans and exposing his bare butt.

"Dad! No fair!" Kevin screamed, recovering quickly and pulling the jeans up as his face turned red.

"Kurt, what are you doing?" Josie ran forward to comfort Kevin, but the boy was on the move.

"I'll get you," Kevin said and laughed, trying to yank at his father's belt from the back. Kurt dodged out of his son's grasp, with college-basketball-player dexterity.

"You can get me next time," Kurt said, punching Kevin's shoulder and wrestling him to the ground. Kevin threw both arms around his father's neck.

"Play horse," Kevin ordered.

"No, not in these clothes," Kurt said, calming Kevin's rambunctious wrestling with a firm hug.

"Now, I know you really like Timmy a lot," Kurt said in a soft, conspiratorial whisper. "But he's a wimp. I bet he'd be afraid of Rudy."

"Naaa," Kevin said. "Rudy's pretty cool. He shows us how to make all kinds of neat stuff."

"Does he know any wrestle games we haven't played?" Kurt asked, looking right into his son's face. Kevin thought for a moment.

"I don't think so, but he made this really neat castle out of Legos, Dad. You should see it. It's got a drawbridge that works and everything."

"Sounds cool," Kurt said, standing up and giving Josie a smug told-you-so grin. "Go get your bag. We got a big weekend ahead. And you don't want to miss the beginning of *Back to the Future*."

Kevin squealed in delight and ran into the house. Kurt draped an arm over Josie's shoulder. "OK, super-mom, does popcorn count as a vegetable? I think we just talked our way right through dinnertime."

Josie hated it when Kurt was right. Especially when his haphazard parenting seemed better than her diligent efforts. But she had to smile watching Kevin and his father still teasing each other as they climbed into Kurt's bright-red Firebird. They shared some sort of male communication that Josie never would understand. All that really mattered was that Kevin seemed unscathed by the day's events. Rudy hadn't abused him. He may not have abused anyone, Josie thought as she sliced cucumbers and onions into a Greek salad. Kevin's recommendation of Rudy as a "cool teacher" only reinforced Josie's gut feeling that Rudy couldn't have done this awful thing.

Chapter 11

After her salad supper, Josie drove to the hospital to see Maggie. She was encouraged to find the ailing reporter sitting up in bed, wearing the pink sweater Josie had packed for her. It seemed to give color to her cheeks and make her seem almost normal. Almost, except for the pulse monitor attached to one finger and the gizmo beside her head with the little green light bouncing across the screen.

"Maggie, you look great," Josie announced as she entered the room.

The patient looked toward her visitor. Her eyes seemed to register recognition, but her face twitched instead of smiling. Katherine, who had been sitting beside the bed with her back to the door, stood and welcomed Josie. She talked enthusiastically about "recovery" and one "good sign" or another, but Josie could see a lot of concern in the young woman's face. The weariness in her eyes revealed her dawning awareness of a very long recovery ahead. Her mother would survive, and she couldn't help but be relieved, but an unspoken fear of something worse than death seemed to fill the silence between her words.

"She's not able to talk yet," Katherine said. "But she does seem to recognize us. Mom, look who's here. It's Josie." Again the face twitched. In some desperate attempt to smile or talk, Maggie emitted a low guttural grunt that sounded like pure frustration. Josie patted Maggie's hand.

"Don't worry about it, Maggie. You're a hundred percent better than yesterday. By tomorrow, who knows what you'll be able to do? Just rest and build your strength. Was Ham here?"

Josie turned to Katherine for an answer. She wasn't surprised to hear that the managing editor had brought the large bouquet of flowers that filled a vase on the bedside table. He'd probably wanted to impress Katherine more than Maggie.

"I don't suppose he brought his wife," Josie asked innocently. When her eyes met Katherine's, they both burst into laughter.

"You don't bring a wife along on a dirty-old-man fantasy," Katherine said.

"I wasn't sure you knew," Josie said.

"Oh, sure. Mom used to tease me about him, didn't you, Mom?"

Josie and Katherine turned to Maggie, but there wasn't so much as a grunt in response. Their laughter stopped.

"How long can you stay?" Josie asked.

"A few more days. I have to go back to California, take care of some things. Then I can return. For a while."

"Don't worry about your mom," Josie said. "We'll see that she has plenty of visitors. Is that OK with you, Maggie?"

The grunt seemed more controlled this time, coming out right on cue.

Josie visited for about forty-five minutes, surprised to learn that Katherine was only three years younger than she was. Maggie was several years older than Josie's mother. Josie realized how fortunate she was that both her parents were in good health. Fortunate not only to enjoy time with them, but to be free to pursue her career without trying to care for a parent hundreds of miles away. As the bond with Katherine grew, Josie told her about her discovery in Maggie's closet.

"Did she ever talk to you about Zelda?" Josie asked. "Maybe you heard her talking to your dad about it?"

Katherine just shrugged. "Mom and Dad had lots of cop friends. They talked about lots of old stories. Yeah, I vaguely remember some talk about the missing editor. It was some sort of old legend, I thought. I never realized Mom knew her personally."

"And there was a shoe, one red shoe. Did she ever show you that?"

Suddenly Maggie let out a mournful groan, a grunt coordinated with a slightly opened mouth. Katherine jumped up and held out a glass of water with a straw. Sipping required more coordination than Maggie could muster.

"You're sure trying to talk, but I don't know what you want," Katherine exclaimed.

Maggie's eyes were fixed on Josie, and she thought she could hear "shoe" in Maggie's repeated moan.

After Josie left the hospital, she drove to Ranch Rudy. The first level was dark, but upstairs, where Rudy lived, several lights were on. Josie pulled in and waited. Should she ring the bell? Rudy must have seen her car lights because she saw him pulling back the drape. He might recognize her car. She couldn't just leave. Josie pulled around to the back, where Rudy parked his car. She rang the buzzer at the delivery entrance. Before long, Rudy opened the door.

"I thought that was you down here," he said, looking around the parking lot. "Is something wrong?"

It seemed like such an understatement.

"Kevin's all right, isn't he?" Rudy asked, still not inviting Josie in.

"Oh, yes, he's fine. I was just checking on you."

"Me? Well, I've survived so far."

There was an awkward silence, and Josie realized she didn't know what to say. Her first instinct was to apologize for even thinking him guilty of abusing a child, but she wasn't sure he wasn't a pedophile.

"Well, you're the first one to actually show your face. I guess I should invite you in," Rudy said, stepping back.

Josie looked into the spotless kitchen where she had discovered Rudy alone with Kevin just a few days before. Sudden uneasiness gripped her.

"I just wanted to be sure you were … OK."

"I've been released from jail on bail, if that's what you're asking," Rudy said, walking into the kitchen and leaving Josie no choice but to follow him. "I understand Family Services went into overload."

"Yes," Josie agreed, closing the door behind her. "It was pretty frightening … for the parents."

"I hope the children weren't alarmed," Rudy said, filling the tea kettle with water and placing it on a burner. "Want some tea?"

Josie hesitated. "Kevin seems fine. A little confused about the questioning, but not upset."

"That's good. Too bad I can't say the same for some parents."

"What do you mean?"

"I've been getting calls. Some don't even identify themselves."

"Oh, that's terrible."

"I wish there was something I could say to ease their minds," Rudy said as the kettle called. He poured two cups of water and set them across from each other at the table. Then he placed a basket of teabags between them. "Help yourself."

Josie fingered the envelopes, though it was her words she was trying to choose.

"It's just so frightening," she said, picking a healthful green tea. "It's hard to know what to do."

"I know. I don't know what to say either. I don't blame them for being worried about their children. And I'm sorry about what happened to little Isabel Edison."

It was the first time Josie had heard the child's name. She sorted through the names and faces in her memories of Ranch Rudy events and tried to remember Isabel. It wasn't a child she knew well. Brown stringy hair, a little chunky. That was the most she could recall.

"I have no explanation why she would tell a story like this. And there must be some physical evidence." Rudy seemed to be thinking out loud instead of talking to Josie. He sipped his tea and stared into space. "Maybe Monday we can get this all sorted out. I'll come up with some sort of handout to give the parents, some guidelines for talking to their children. Maybe I should meet with the staff tomorrow. See if they have any questions."

"My gosh, you're planning to open on Monday?" Josie exclaimed.

"Of course," Rudy said, looking at her. "Why wouldn't I?"

"Well, I thought maybe they had pulled your license. Just during the investigation, I mean."

"The law, unlike parents, believes in innocent until proven guilty," Rudy said, finishing the last of his cup of tea. Josie sipped her tea and remained silent.

"You're not sure about me are you?" Rudy asked.

"I don't know what to think."

Rudy stood up so quickly his chair fell to the floor with a crash. "Kevin's been coming here for most of his life. I should think you'd know me by now."

"I thought I did," Josie said as she stood up. "But then I find out you were married once and had a child. I find out you had this whole other life before you came here."

"Of course I had a life before I came here! Did you think I was born thirty-five with glasses?"

They stood in the kitchen staring at each other, neither willing to offer comfort or further accusation.

Finally, Josie said, "I'm sorry about your wife and daughter."

"It happened a long time ago," Rudy said, picking up the chair. "How did you find out about that?"

"We were just checking your background, for the story."

"Story? There's going to be another story in the paper after that huge splash today?"

"It wasn't huge."

"You checked into my family from seventeen years ago? Did you also check that I had a dog that mysteriously died when I was seven? Or that my parents once got into a fight and the neighbors called police? Wait, I think one of my uncles served time for armed robbery. Or was it burglary? I forget. But if you look back far enough, I'm sure you'll find enough dirt for that gossip sheet." Rudy was storming around the kitchen now, sweeping up the cups into the sink and returning with a red dish towel to mop the rings off the table.

"I'd better go," Josie said, turning toward the door.

Rudy called after her.

"If Family Services accused you of abusing your son, I would testify in your behalf, without hesitation. I thought I could count on you for the same."

Chapter 12

Zelda

I am working on an editorial about Buster Boardman and lose track of time. When I hear a sound and look up, the whole office is dark except for the gooseneck lamp on my desk.

"Is someone there?"

No one answers, but I am sure I see someone walking through the shadows.

"Who is it?"

"It's me, Miss Machinko. Irwin MacDonald."

Just as he says his name, the boy steps into the halo of my lamp so I can make out his face. He's a gangly teen, holding his cap in his hand like he's having an audience with a queen. Am I really that awe-inspiring?

"I'm bringing in my collections for the month."

"Collections are due by five o'clock, before the girls leave."

"I ... I ... I know," Irwin stammers, "but I had to babysit my little sister until Ma got home."

"Well, bring it over here. Let's have a look."

Irwin dumps his pouch on the desk, pennies and nickels skittering off the desk and onto the floor.

"Now wait just a minute," I tell him, not about to put up with such shoddy business from a carrier as old as Irwin. "Count this out. You know how I like it. I want you to sort this into stacks of one dollar."

I cross over to the bookkeeper's desk and get the ledger while Irwin crawls under my desk and corrals the errant coins. I stand back, pouring myself a cup of coffee and enjoying a smoke while he makes neat piles on my desk. He's really not a bad boy, just sloppy. He does the job though. Kids who will take a route and keep it three or four years are hard to find, so I bite my tongue as he counts his piles, stacking coins into dollar portions as I showed him.

I move a little closer to oversee the project. I don't deal much with the books anymore, but it's good to keep a hand in, otherwise the business gets away from you. You gotta remember it's all about these coins. Fifteen cents means another paper on another kitchen table. And if you get too idealistic, just spoutin' about truth and justice, and nobody's reading it, well that's like singing in the shower. What good is it?

I help Irwin count his piles and imagine families at kitchen tables all over town readin' the truth about Buster Boardman. I don't mind the interruption, really, but I'm gruff with Irwin 'cause I want him to do better. To sort his money before he comes in.

"You're a nickel short," I tell him when the tally comes to $25.15. He looks at me uncomprehending.

"Paper's fifteen cents a week, sixty cents a month. $25.15 isn't a multiple of sixty. You should know all the multiples of sixty."

"Yes, ma'am," he says, hanging his head.

"Listen, it's no big deal to me," I tell him. "It just comes out of your half."

I note the total in the ledger, less $12.55 for the carrier. I count out that amount, drop it back in his pouch, and put the rest into the cash box.

"Now if you want to get back under my desk and find that lost nickel while I'm putting the cash box away, that's fine with me," I say, heading back to the bookkeeper's desk with the ledger and locked cash box.

Irwin is not one to let opportunity pass him by. He gets down on his hands and knees, wandering out of the pool of light into the darkened office behind my desk. That's when two men burst into the room.

"What are you doing here? We're closed!" I shout, stepping back to my desk and reaching for the top drawer where I keep my gun. A hand shoots out of the blackness and grabs my arm, spilling the coffee on the desktop. Suddenly the second man steps forward with a red dish towel and starts mopping up the spill.

I pull free and rush into the darkness. I've got to get them away from the kid. The one is chasing me with outstretched monster hands, laughing. I break into the hall where light comes in from the hotel sign. The other one is there. He flicks me with the damp dish towel.

"I thought I could trust you," he keeps repeating. I recognize him. It's Rudy.

I run down the back stairs, Rudy flicking his dish towel at my head.

The overhead door is open onto the loading dock, and I run right into the first man. It's Kurt, tickling me with both hands. I can't squirm away. Rudy throws the towel over my head from behind. I can't see, and Kurt is tickling me and grabbing me and carrying me away. In the last second, I kick off one shoe so they will know.

And from somewhere comes this painful moan, "Shoe!"

Josie awoke panting. A nightmare. The vivid reality disintegrated as the familiar shadows of her bedroom came into focus.

"No," Josie moaned, vainly trying to recapture the images in her dream. She had to write them down before they were gone. She fumbled with the light on her bedside table and pulled out the pad and pencil in the drawer.

Rudy. Kurt. She wrote the names as they came to her. Zelda. Irwin. Donald? Was there a Donald too? Dish towel. Tickle fight. Counting money.

Shoe. She wrote the words as fast as she could, knowing in a moment or two they would be gone from her memory.

As her eyes became accustomed to the light, about all that remained of her dream were the words on the pad. Rudy? Of course he would be in her dream after the events of the day. But she had no good or evil sense of him. Just him standing there with the dish towel, as he was when she left his kitchen.

Kurt. He often appeared in her dreams and nightmares. It had been hard separating her identity from his. In this dream, she was remembering his tickle fight with Kevin. But he wasn't tickling Kevin, he was tickling her.

But it wasn't her, it was Zelda Machinko. She could see Zelda's face with the bright-red painted lips, her dark hair curled around her face, and pearls at her throat. Just like the picture in Maggie's clips. Zelda was talking, telling the story. A narrator. Josie had the feeling Zelda may have invaded her dreams before. She felt like she had met Zelda, knew her, but it had to be her imagination. Josie was just a kid when Zelda disappeared. Still, Josie imagined the offices of the *Spectator*. Upstairs, dark, a hotel sign glowing outside. Was that imagination or memory? She could almost see it.

And the boy with the coins.

Josie looked at her pad. Irwin? Donald? What was the boy's name? It didn't matter. It was only someone she invented, someone she imagined. Josie replaced the pad, turned out the light, and lay back on the pillow. Maybe if she went back to sleep she would see the boy again, and this time she would get his name.

Chapter 13

Josie had been to the new chrome and glass Jordan Public Library many times, trying to nurture a love of reading in her young son. But the township's historical archives were stored in the cramped basement of the former stone library. You could smell the mustiness of history. She had to find Ollie, a bald man with thick dark-rimmed glasses. He would know in an instant if the library had any photos or documents from the old *Spectator*.

At the desk sat a pale girl, barely out of high school, with a wisp of dyed black hair sticking out from her elastic ponytail holder. Josie stood at the desk a minute or two before the girl looked up from the paperback she was reading.

"Uh-huh?" the girl said.

"I'm looking for some information about the *Spectator*."

"Uh-huh," the girl repeated, only this time without the questioning inflection.

"It was one of the local papers back in the fifties."

"Uh-huh."

Did that mean she understood? Did she speak English?

"Is Ollie Stewart here today?" Josie asked, hoping the girl would say "Uh-huh" and point to some office down the hall.

"Nope," the girl said, closing the book and standing up to reveal a strip of bare midriff between a too-short green T-shirt and hip-hugging brown slacks.

"Actually, 1947 to 1958. It was a boom paper after the war," the girl said, tugging half-heartedly on her shirt. "What date are you looking for?"

Josie wasn't sure which surprised her more—a punk rocker in the musty archives of the Jordan Public Library or that the rocker obviously knew something about the long-extinct *Spectator*. Josie recovered her voice quickly.

"I'm not actually looking for copies of the paper. I'm wondering if you have anything else. Old photographs of the building. Business ledgers. Employee lists. Something like that."

"Archives," the girl said, and started walking down a darkened row of shelves filled with cardboard filing boxes.

"Well, are you coming?" she said, tossing the words over her shoulder. By the time Josie caught up to her, the girl was unfolding a short ladder.

"Pictures are on the upper shelves," she said. "This area would be the early 1950s. They are filed by decade, mostly, unless we know the year. Then it will be marked on the back. It should be in this box, if we have any. This is for local businesses."

She carried the box to a little metal table that was under a small window. A shaft of light filtered in, but it was too dark to read the light pencil writing on the backs of the photos. The girl pulled out a few pictures, turned them over, and threw them back into the box.

"I'll get you a lamp," she said and headed back down the darkened aisle.

Josie pulled a stool out from under the table, sat down, and began thumbing through the photos. Before the girl returned, she had found a street shot of the Herkimer Hotel showing about half of the red stone building next door that housed the *Spectator*. The girl returned and plugged in a small desk lamp.

The Herkimer's limestone exterior hadn't changed much. A deep portico or covered walkway ran across the front of the building under a series of arches. Now white rocking chairs are tucked in that area to accommodate the older residents. In the picture, it appeared that small groupings of dark tub chairs were placed on the portico. A tile mural stretched across the second floor, telling a story of Indians and riverboats and prairie farmers. The mural had become a Jordan trademark for brochures and stationery. Above the mural were three floors of windows for the hotel rooms. And on the corner, next to the *Spectator*, was a lighted vertical sign that said "hotel" in big letters. Just like the sign in Josie's dream.

The red granite building next door was much smaller, only three stories tall and maybe a third of the width of the old hotel. Huge gargoyles were perched on the corners of the building, looking like giant red vultures about to attack the street below. Josie was glad the ugly statues had been removed.

She shuffled through pictures of buildings and workers, factories and stores. She had turned over almost every one when she came across one with a cluster of six people gathered around a couple of wooden desks with black manual typewriters. It wasn't hard to pick out Zelda Machinko in the center of the group. She was a striking woman. "*Spectator* Staff, 1950" was written on the back in a lovely cursive hand, but there were no names.

"Is there anything besides photos? Actual records or old ledgers?" Josie asked when the girl stopped by to check on her. "I was hoping maybe something had survived, an old gray ledger about this big." Josie held up her hands as if holding an imaginary ledger a little narrower than a sheet of typing paper. The girl looked at her blankly, and Josie's hands fluttered down to her sides. "No? Well, I didn't think so."

"I think there may be some annual reports," the girl said. "The Chamber of Commerce donated their collection last year."

Josie finished looking through the box of photos by the time the girl returned with half a dozen small booklets, annual reports for the Spectator Publishing Company. The girl returned to her paperback and Josie glanced through the reports. They were boring lists of numbers—circulation, annual budget, number of employees. Someone named Walter Biggs was listed as managing editor and publisher on the 1957 and 1958 reports, but when she went back to the 1956 report, next to the words Managing Editor was the name Zelda R. Machinko.

Josie wondered what Zelda's middle name was. Ruth? Rachel? Rebecca? She made notes in her spiral reporter's notebook. If she were writing a story on the *Spectator*'s demise, the numbers would have been fascinating. The little weekly's circulation dropped from 27,987 to 14,165, almost cut in half, the two years after Zelda disappeared.

But Josie was looking for names and faces. The boy in her dream. She knew it was crazy to think he was a real person, much less that he was a real person who really worked as a paperboy thirty years ago. After all, in the nonsensical way of dreaming, she had transposed current events and people into the dream. She had taken the two men she had fought with that day—her ex-husband and her son's day-care provider—and turned them into the goons who kidnapped Zelda. If the dream was going to show her faces from the past, why not the faces of the real kidnappers? That would be a helpful dream.

But Josie thought the stranger in her dream was the real oddity. Why would her imagination create a paperboy? Was this a kid she had met somewhere and forgotten? Her own paperboy, perhaps? No, a girl delivered Josie's paper, and she never stopped by the house to collect because employee subscriptions were deducted from their checks. Josie tried to conjure up other boys she'd met, perhaps one of the kids who dropped by the sports department. Wasn't it more likely she would find the boy among the people she saw every day rather than in the library's archives?

Josie gathered up some loose photos to return to the box. These were mostly community events—Christmas decorations and summer fairs. Then she spotted an outdoor picnic with a banner "Paperboys' Picnic." It was a photo of more than a hundred boys. Some were posing with canvas bags over the shoulder. Some held the ends of the banner. Most wore swimming trunks and big grins, with chunks of watermelon in their hands.

Attached to the back was a typed cutline probably from an old newsletter: "From 1951 to 1960, Jordan Chamber of Commerce held an annual picnic for the 'young businessmen' who manned paper routes for all three of the city's papers: *Daily News*, *Spectator* and *Herald*." Then, to Josie's surprise, the little typed story listed the names of the paperboys, with an N, S, or H in parentheses to indicate which paper the boy carried. Josie scanned the names, saw a few Donalds and even fewer Irwins. Suddenly her finger stopped.

"Irwin MacDonald (S)"

Josie counted rows and heads until she had figured out which smiling face was Irwin's. It was too tiny to identify. She went up to the front desk and asked for a magnifying glass. The girl looked up from her book and let out a frustrated sigh. She opened the bottom desk drawer and, after a bit of rummaging, emerged with the requested magnifying glass.

Josie held the glass up to the photo and saw exactly what she had expected: the boy in her dream.

❉

"I don't know how he got into my dream, but I didn't make him up. He really exists," Josie said, attacking her Coney dog with a knife and fork. Discovery always sparked her appetite.

"OK, so Irwin MacDonald exists," Duke said, taking a big bite of Coney dog followed closely by a napkin across the lips. "But there's no way he was in your dream, unless you saw his name and photo before. Dreams come from your subconscious. You can't dream something you don't already know."

"But it's happened before. It's Zelda. She speaks to me in my sleep."

"Rooster refuse!"

Josie laughed. "That's a new one. I've never heard you say that before."

"No animal is exempt," Duke said, popping the final third of the Coney dog into his mouth in one gigantic bite.

Josie stared in disbelief. "That was truly amazing. I thought only mythical beasts could swallow their prey whole."

"I may be a mythical beast, but I don't have dead ladies talking to me in my sleep."

"Or live ones, for that matter."

"Position's still open."

Josie and Duke smiled at each other for a long moment. There was no denying the attraction still was there. Josie shouldn't have called him and asked him to meet her for lunch, especially since that Wheeler guy was threatening to tell Sharon about their affair. But Josie was so excited about discovering Irwin, she had to tell someone. And the someone she wanted to tell was Duke. They met at Dog Town, a little café near the office. Duke inhaled two chili dogs, with cheese and onions, before Josie finished dissecting one.

"I'm worried about you," Duke said when he'd finished his second dog. "You had quite a trauma last summer. It's natural you would identify with this missing editor. But to seriously believe she's talking to you … Well, I think you may need counseling."

"Counseling? Oh, for Pete's sake. If I were looking for analysis, I would have called Kurt. He is always ready to tell me what I'm doing wrong."

"Listen to yourself for a minute. You believe a woman who disappeared thirty years ago is visiting you in your sleep, giving you clues. Now tell me that doesn't sound just a little bit crazy."

"And here I thought you'd be as excited as I am."

"Why? Because you've got the name of somebody who used to be a paperboy for Zelda? Dozens of reporters have talked to hundreds of people about Zelda Machinko. Every lead has gone nowhere. If they couldn't find her thirty years ago, you aren't going to find her now."

"Irwin was the last person to see her. I know it in my bones. He knows who got her."

"Crocodile compost! You said yourself your dream faded away so fast you couldn't remember the name, and now you're convinced you remember the face. It doesn't make sense."

"It's him. I know it's him."

"I know, you feel it in your bones or your toes or some such. Didn't you say Kurt was in your dream too and Rudy Randolph?"

"I know it sounds crazy," Josie said, curling into the corner of the booth with her Coke. "So tell me your project is going better. Any luck identifying the dead guy?"

"Funny you should ask," Duke replied, sitting back on his side of the booth with coffee cup in hand. "I was thinking about that name. Blaine Avril. Odd name for an alias. I mean, if you wanted to blend in, wouldn't you pick some John Jones sort of name?"

Josie nodded. She could tell Duke didn't need an answer.

"So I went back over all the ground I'd already covered. The fake Social Security number and stuff. The only thing that worked out halfway well was the reference he gave at that Michigan road construction company. The guy I talked to there didn't admit he knew him, but he seemed to recognize the name. So I was looking at IDOT's construction partners catalog again and guess what?"

Josie nodded again and Duke leaned over the table as if sharing a secret.

"The address of the road construction company is 3811 Blaine Avenue. Get it?"

"Odd coincidence."

"Horse hockey! He was there when he made up the name. He took his alias from the address."

"Sounds plausible."

"Anyway, I was thinking I might drive over there Monday, talk to the guy face-to-face. See what I can get."

"As your boss, I have to ask: What's in it for the paper? Do our readers really care about the identity of this transient? It would be a lot easier to drop it."

"I told you, I'm not backing off."

"Pride goeth before a fall."

"Smug editor speaks with lisp. How's this MacDonald character going to be worth it for the paper?"

"I'm not doing it for a story; I'm doing it for Maggie. To give her some closure. Besides, I'm not driving to Cincinnati to talk to him on company time."

"Cincinnati?"

"Yes, you interrupted me before I got to the end of my story," Josie said. "I was so excited to find the name that I asked the librarian for a phone book so I could see if he still lived here. I was disappointed when he wasn't listed. Then I got to thinking. If he was about fourteen or fifteen when Zelda disappeared in 1956, that puts him in his mid-forties now. Probably has kids in college or moving out. Empty nest. Career high point. Good time to move. So I went to the office where we have phone books going back a few years." Josie flashed a satisfied smile. "Looks like he lived here until three years ago."

"So you went over to his old neighborhood and talked to his former neighbors," Duke said.

"How'd you guess?"

"Reporting procedure 101. And I'll bet some biddy next door gave you his phone number."

"Actually, the biddy gave me a lecture on the new owners who evidently tore out some bushes she liked, but eventually she told me MacDonald got a promotion a few years back and moved into a new condo complex in Cincinnati."

"Phone number?"

"Still tracking that one down, but she told me he worked at Hazelton Manufacturing, so I figure to call them on Monday."

"About Monday—"

"OK, OK. Stay for deadline, and then you can head to Michigan."

"Great. Hey, a bunch of us from the office are going to the Andre Watts concert tonight at the university. Wanna join us?"

"Sorry, I've got plans."

"Oh, a date, huh? Who's the lucky guy?"

"I'd rather not say at this point."

"What's the matter? Is he married?"

Josie stared daggers at Duke. "That was uncalled for."

"You're right. I apologize."

"Speaking of married, have you talked with Sharon?"

"Well, she and Jennifer are going to the concert with me tonight. Things are going pretty well between us. I don't want to upset the apple cart by telling her about last summer. I just don't think it's a good idea to bring it up. If Wheeler tells her, then I'll deal with it."

Chapter 14

Jennifer answered the door waving a piece of paper. "I've been accepted at Stanford, Daddy. California! Sunshine! Freedom! I can't wait! Isn't it great?"

"Yeah, great, baby," Duke said, trying to calm her bouncing enthusiasm so he could get a hug. She reached out her long neck briefly in a semi-hug swipe at affection. She had Duke's thick, dark hair but it had been streaked with blond. Highlights, isn't that what she called it? She still had Duke's dark eyes and heavy brows, though she kept them plucked into graceful arches. She was grinning ear to ear.

"Being accepted to Stanford is quite an honor," Duke said, trying to mirror her smile. "But I thought you were going to community college for the first two years."

"Community ... Oh, Daddy, that's like 'High School II.' Stanford is sweet." Jennifer twirled away on her toes, and Duke noticed for the first time that she was wearing a dress instead of her usual jeans. A green dress, too tight, too short. When had her legs gotten so long? And lovely.

"Sweet?" Duke said with a sigh. "Expensive. Far away. Left-wing, socialist, pinko fags. I can think of a lot of words to describe Stanford, but sweet isn't one of them."

"Oh, Daddy." She giggled and headed to the kitchen. "Mom, Dad's here."

Jennifer's figure was in full bloom now, not the first innocent curves of puberty, but richly rounded breasts stretching the clingy fabric, and soft, swaying hips. My God, she was a woman. And it scared him.

Sharon appeared in the kitchen doorway. Her hair was so short, now that she was working, and that baggy sweater didn't do a thing for her figure. She was wiping her hands on a dish towel.

"Just cleaning up the kitchen," she said. "Did you eat?"

"Yea, I had some dogs earlier," Duke said. "We can get dessert at the concert."

"Can I have nachos?" Jennifer said, joining her mother. She sounded like the little kid Duke remembered, back before highlights, Stanford, and clingy green dresses. It made him smile.

"We'll see," Sharon said, hugging her daughter. Everyone remarked on the resemblance between Sharon and Jennifer: same height, same cheekbones, same heart-shaped face and dazzling smile. Duke was bursting with love for both of them. He wanted to throw his arms around them and hold on for dear life. But he felt like his arms were tied to his sides. He felt like a disobedient puppy that needed to wait for some signal from his master.

"Well, I'll go touch up my lipstick," Sharon said, turning away. Jennifer remained in the doorway, looking at her father. Duke could see that she understood completely, perhaps even better than he did. Jennifer could understand her father's eagerness to be loved again, her mother's reluctance to allow it. Maybe that's why she wanted to go to Stanford, so she wouldn't be torn between them anymore.

"So, how much is this Stanford going to cost me?" Duke said.

"Oh, it's not for sure yet that I'm going," Jennifer said, chewing her lip. "I sent out applications to Northwestern, U of I, Cornell."

"Cornell?"

"Some of my friends go there. Mom said it wouldn't hurt to apply."

"Still planning to study microbiology?"

"For now. I don't have to declare a major for two years."

Sharon emerged from the downstairs bathroom. She had exchanged the sloppy sweater for a smart royal blue shirt and camel blazer that dressed up her jeans. Big gold hoops dangled from her ears.

"Wow, I love those earrings," Duke blurted with genuine enthusiasm.

Sharon smiled. "One of the benefits of wearing my hair shorter. You can see my earrings. Ready to go?"

As soon as they arrived at Lewis University's Fine Arts Center, Jennifer bumped into a girlfriend. The concert was general seating and the plan was to gather in section C. The first to arrive would save seats for others from the *Daily News*. But Jennifer said "the gang," meaning her high school friends, wanted to sit in the balcony. As far as possible from parents was the general idea. Duke didn't say anything when Jennifer walked away. It would give him a little face time with Sharon.

Becky, who had organized the *Daily News* outing, waved to them from the front of the hall. She had grabbed front-row seats.

"Have you ever seen Andre Watts? He's a really emotional performer," Becky explained. "You want to be up close. He doesn't just play piano, he emotes. He talks to the keys. He almost cries sometimes. You've really got to see it."

Sharon and Duke exchanged glances. They weren't big classical music buffs, but they liked socializing with the *Daily News* crowd. It was a safe way to be together. Everyone knew what their marriage was going through. Nobody asked embarrassing questions. It was like the family everyone wants to have.

Several of the coworkers were there, including assistant city editor Nick Davidson and his new girlfriend, Brittany Miller. Nick and Duke were standing in the aisle talking when police detective Tom Cantrell came up with his sister.

"We've got you outnumbered tonight," Nick said, shaking Tom's hand. "We're going to get you in a corner and pummel you with questions."

"I was afraid of that," Tom said with a smile. "That's why I brought my second in command. This is my sister, Linda. These are the bad men I was telling you about, Linda. They are the ones who always give me a headache."

"You said I always give you a headache," Linda responded without missing a beat. Nick and Duke laughed.

"I can see you and I have a lot in common," Duke said, shaking Linda's hand. She had the physical awkwardness common in people with Down syndrome, but she had an eager smile.

"Yeah, it'll keep you busy all night just trying to explain Chopin to Linda," Tom said.

"Is Chopin playing the piano tonight?" Linda asked, and the men laughed again.

"Here, I want you to meet my wife," Duke said, taking Linda's arm. "She's a teacher."

Tom watched as his sister met Sharon and then Brittany, Nick's girlfriend. Everyone was laughing, especially Linda. He was glad he had brought her.

"That must be your sister."

Tom spun around and discovered Becky had come up behind him.

"Did you bring your mother too?"

"No, Mom's just enjoying having a night off without worrying about her kids," Tom said. His cheeks burned and he hoped Becky couldn't see the effect she had on him. "My, don't you look nice tonight." His words sounded trite, scripted. Black man repartee. He wished he could think of something more original.

"I'll bet you've caused your mother lots of worry," Becky said. "I'm glad you could come. Have you seen Watts perform before?"

"Oh, yes. He's my hero. He's the reason I learned to play piano. That and Mom was always on my case."

"Sounds like my kind of woman," Becky said with a laugh.

The lights flashed a warning, and everyone jockeyed for seats. Linda seemed right at home between Sharon and Brittany. Tom and Becky took the last two seats by the aisle.

The performance was every bit as enchanting as Becky had promised. The front-row seats allowed them to follow every agonized expression on the artist's face. But nothing could keep up with his fancy finger work as his hands skipped over the keys like a sorcerer casting a spell.

"It's almost as if he's possessed," Becky said as they stood at the intermission. "It's as if Mendelssohn is trapped in the Steinway and Andre Watts is setting him free."

"Exactly. Music is that way. It's a language without words, and he speaks it very well," Tom said.

Linda came rushing up to them. "Can I play next? I wanna play too."

"No, Linda. We are just listening tonight," Tom said, obviously embarrassed by his sister.

"Can you play piano?" Becky asked.

"Sure. I'm a natural," Linda responded. She moved in close to Becky, standing almost nose to nose. "Who are you? Do you give Tommy headaches too?"

"This is Becky. She works at the newspaper," Tom said, pulling his sister back to a more comfortable spacing. Then he turned to Becky. "Linda likes to play piano with me. Four hands."

"So, can I play, huh? I wanna play. You can play too."

"No, Linda. Do you want some ice cream? Let's go get some ice cream." Tom turned to Becky. "Can I get you something?"

"Just a bottle of water. That would be nice."

Tom started ushering his sister down the aisle.

"Wait up," Duke called. "I promised Jennifer I'd meet her at the nacho stand."

The two men chatted as they walked down the aisle, caught in the crush of people headed out for a break.

"So, what do you think?" Tom asked. He'd left his ubiquitous brown leather jacket over the seat back, and his hands floundered to find a home in his tight pants pockets. He settled for hooking a thumb in each pocket.

"I think you and Becky make a handsome couple. Congratulations on finally getting a date."

"It's not a date. Group thing. Safer."

"Yeah."

"I mean, what do you think of Watts?"

"Well, he's no Billy Joel, but he can play piano," Duke said with a shrug. "Sharon likes it. Romantic. So that's good."

"Yeah, whatever it takes to get lucky, huh?"

"I'm lucky," Linda said, turning around. "I've got Mom and Tommy. That's lucky, isn't it, Tommy?"

"Sure it is," Tom said, patting his sister on the back.

"Yeah, but if Becky hears you talk like that, man, your donkey coach will turn into a pumpkin," Duke said.

Linda laughed. "Yeah, like Cinderella. Then you won't be so lucky."

"You got that right," Tom said, shaking his head. "But I'm not here just to impress Becky. I like the way Watts makes a piano sing. He really gets into it, don't he?"

Duke smiled. Tom could make classical music sound cool.

"Still got your nose in a snit over the feds?" Duke asked.

"We're not going to go there," Tom said, looking down at his shoes.

"Where?" Linda asked. "The restroom? I need the restroom."

"Ah, just a second," Tom said, looking around for a sign as Duke pushed ahead to the concession stand. Jennifer came up to them, bubbling about how cute the pianist was "even in that fancy suit."

"Tuxedo," Duke said. "The man's winning all sorts of awards and degrees and she just notices what he's wearing."

"If he was wearing cutoff jeans, everybody would notice," Tom said. "Depends on your perspective."

"Cutoffs? That would be cool," Jennifer said.

"Yeah, cutoffs are cool when it's hot," Linda said.

Jennifer laughed at the comment, and Duke introduced Linda and her brother.

"Would you mind helping Linda to find the ladies' room?" Duke asked. "I'll get the requested nachos."

"Oh, sure," Jennifer said. "It's right down here, Linda." As the two girls headed off into the crowd, Jennifer stopped to shout back a clarification on her request. "No jalapenos, Dad, and get me a super-size Coke, no ice."

"Super-size? You drinking it or taking a bath?"

"No bath. We're just going pee," Linda called back.

"Oh, no," Tom said, shaking his head as several in the line chuckled.

"She's really a sweet girl, Tom," Duke said. "I'm glad you brought her."

"Oh, I'm glad too, it's just sometimes, you know."

They were silent for a few minutes as they stood in the slow line at the concession stand.

Tom snorted a little laugh. "You were asking earlier if I was upset about the feds. You never saw nobody make a fuss like Teasdale. That man thinks he runs this town and them feds showed him he don't."

"Yeah, I woulda liked to have seen his bubble burst," Duke said. "It doesn't seem like the coroner should hold so much sway."

"He does. It ain't murder until he says so."

"Well, really, it's up to the coroner's inquest."

"Nope, it's Teasdale. He's got the chief and the mayor and everybody else in his pocket. When it comes to homicides, he's the man. If a case don't rub him the right way, he just lets it slide. A transient death like this one, it would have just faded away."

"Really?"

"Yeah. We may never hear what happens now that the feds are workin' it, but at least somebody's on the case."

Chapter 15

Josie didn't have any trouble deciding what to wear on her dinner date with Zach. Her closet was full of neutrals—the beige, camel, khaki, and brown she wore in the office on a daily basis. Quiet classics, she called them. But toward the back was one purple sheath. Purple is for parties, Josie thought when she bought it a few years before. But there hadn't been many parties. Josie slipped into the dress and chose a long floral scarf in shades of lavender and turquoise. She tied the scarf once at the throat with a long tail dangling in front and another falling down her back.

When the doorbell rang, Josie recognized the man on her porch, but she didn't know his name. He was massive, like a football player in a Sunday suit, with mirrored aviator glasses. He offered a friendly smile.

"Evenin', ma'am. Mr. Teasdale sent me to pick you up."

Josie looked out and saw a gold Mercedes in her driveway. A man was standing beside the car. The shaded rear windows concealed any passengers.

"Is he in the car?" she asked.

"He's been unavoidably detained." The man spoke as if he'd rehearsed the phrase on the way to her house. "He'll meet you at the restaurant."

Josie had seen both of these men with Zach, but she felt awkward leaving with strangers. She was angry he was putting her in this position.

"I saw you with Zach the other night at the chamber event, but I didn't catch your name," Josie said, reaching out a hand.

"I'm Chuck," he said, his large hand engulfing hers only briefly, a brush more than a shake. "Shall we go?"

The driver introduced himself as Bill. The pair chatted amiably with Josie on the way to the restaurant even though she was tucked away in the sumptuous leather cocoon of the generous rear seat.

"Do you do this very often, pick up people and take them to meet your boss?" Josie asked, sliding forward to lean on the back of the front seat.

"Whenever needed," Bill said without elaboration.

"It's a varied job," Chuck added. "Answer the phone, walk the dog, take Mom to the beauty shop. Everybody needs a couple of personal assistants. Only difference is Mr. Teasdale can afford it."

When they arrived at the Red Geranium, Josie noted two more "personal assistants" at the bar. Zach was at the rear of the restaurant talking with the owner. He spotted her right away and smiled. She hoped her cool response telegraphed the message that she wasn't impressed by him pawning her off on his football team.

"This way," Chuck said, taking Josie's elbow and ushering her away from the entrance toward a short flight of stairs.

"Where are we going?"

Chuck didn't answer; he simply led her into an elegant private dining room. The walls were covered in scarlet brocade with matching drapes in the fringed Victorian style. A harpist played in one corner and in the other corner, framed in ferns, was a small round table, set for two, with a floor-length white tablecloth. Another table, with short tablecloth, was set for four near the entrance. In the center of the room was a large angel-sculpture fountain trickling water into a basin with rosebuds floating. Josie was speechless.

"There you are," Zach said in a soft voice as he came up from behind her and slipped an arm around her waist in a brief hug. He was just a few inches taller than Josie in heels, and he wore a well-cut navy-blue suit.

"Come on," he said, taking her hand. "I want you to meet Maria."

Zach pulled her over to the harpist, whose lithe fingers rippled over the strings, making it sing in delight.

"Maria, I want you to meet Josie Braun. She's the editor at the *Daily News*. A very important person. You'll want to know this lady."

"A moment, please," Maria said, her fingers continuing to stroke the strings. Her whole body swayed and her eyes closed as she caressed the instrument. When she finished, she sat absolutely still for a moment as if expecting applause, which Josie and Zach supplied.

"Maria is from Venezuela," Zach said. "She's been in this country less than a year. I was in South America for business and heard her play in a restaurant. I knew she had to come here to study at the university."

"I never go to school until Mr. T," Maria said, blushing for her benefactor.

"That sounds like a story," Josie replied. "Is that why you brought me here, Zach? A little publicity?"

"Of course not," he said softly. "I brought you here to share a lovely dinner and get to know you a little better. I brought Maria here tonight because I thought you would like to hear her music. I'll admit it occurred to me she might make a good story for the paper, but I wasn't going to suggest that until after dinner."

Josie laughed. At least Zach was honest about his publicity-hungry side. She wrote Maria's phone number on the back of one of Zach's business cards and promised to have Becky call her. A student recital was planned at the university in June, Zach pointed out, and an interview with Maria would be a good way to advance that concert.

"You want to write the headline too?" Josie snapped.

"I'm sorry. I'm just used to taking control," Zach said.

"So I've noticed."

Maria returned to her harp, and Zach ushered Josie to the dinner table, where candles were glowing, salads were waiting, and a waiter was pouring wine.

"I took the liberty of ordering some Château Haut-Brion. I saw you drinking merlot the other night and wanted you to taste this Bordeaux blend. The palate feels very soft, fairly diffuse in character, with a slightly lighter tannic backbone."

They clinked glasses and fell into an easy conversation. Zach asked about her day, and Josie hesitated to reveal her discovery of Irwin. Even she thought the story sounded too crazy to explain on a first date. But she did mention her visit to the library.

"I was doing some research today and saw an old photograph of this building, back when it housed the *Spectator*."

"Oh, I'll bet you were looking into the Zelda Machinko story. That's the only thing the *Spectator* is known for. I was just a kid then, growing up in Naperville, but my mom used to talk about Zelda. She was quite a character."

"Yes, she disappeared from this very building. I think her office was upstairs somewhere."

At this point, Chuck approached the table and whispered something in Zach's ear. Zach nodded, whispered something back, and Chuck returned to the table by the door, where he was seated with the other three.

"What's with the football team?" Josie asked.

"Excuse me?"

"Chuck the quarterback, consulting the coach. A big play coming up?"

"Oh, that was a phone call. I have business interests all over the world, so sometimes the calls are not during regular business hours. I apologize."

"Wouldn't it be easier to have an office somewhere with a manager to take care of this stuff?"

"I do have an office at the factory, but I'm never there. And that's really only a small portion of my investments—real estate, entertainment, insurance, the funeral home. Not to mention the duties of the coroner's office. I have a whole staff there. I just prefer to have my guys close by wherever I go. They take care of business while I enjoy the pretty lady."

Zach raised his glass again to Josie's. As soon as they replaced the glasses on the table, the omnipresent waiter appeared to refill them. He whisked away the salad plates and served the entrée—grilled salmon, asparagus with hollandaise sauce, and rice timbales.

"Sorry, but your 'guys' don't look like the typical office staff," Josie said between bites of salmon. "They look like bodyguards. Why would a coroner and bubble-gum heir need bodyguards?"

"Gum's a sticky business."

"I guess I asked for that."

"These are my friends, guys I went to high school with or college," Zach said, glancing at the table of assistants. "I'll admit I've always gravitated toward guys I figured could win the fight, if it came to that. Let's face it, I'm a runt."

"You shouldn't be so self-conscious about your height," Josie said. "I'm the shortest person in the newsroom, but I never think of it. When I see a group photo, I'm always surprised that I'm a head shorter than everyone else."

"You think I'm self-conscious?"

"Don't you think surrounding yourself with the testosterone team is over-compensating a bit? You look like some underworld mob lord and his goons."

Zach reared back his head in a hearty laugh, so unlike his usual restrained self.

"Underworld mob lord! Oh, that's too good." He continued laughing until the guards ceased their conversation and looked over at Zach and Josie.

"They're staring at us," Josie whispered. "Should I be worried?"

"Yes, they're sizing you up for cement shoes," Zach whispered back.

Now it was Josie's turn to laugh. When she'd regained her composure, Zack was studying her with a slight smile.

"This is how I thought you'd be," he said. "Bold but compassionate. It's the way I've seen your personality in the *Daily News*. Since you've taken over, the paper reflects the whole community differently. I like it. I like it very much."

Dessert—a chocolate mousse with fresh raspberries—came in elegant crystal champagne flutes. Zach told stories about his trips to South America, unpretentious tales of exotic plants, spicy foods, tantalizing music. He said very little about his business there, and then only in response to Josie's direct questions. He made going to Venezuela sound as routine as visiting Kentucky or Arkansas, ordinary but exciting. He had an enthusiasm for everything, and Josie decided that's why he always sounded like he was selling something.

"Don't you just love fresh raspberries?" he asked suddenly. "You bite into them and they explode with flavor. It's a different kind of sweetness than the wine or the mousse. It tingles the tongue. Do you want some more?"

"Oh, no, I'm fine," Josie said.

"I want more. Where did Peter go?" Zach looked around for the waiter who had been constantly at their side. He had disappeared. One of the "assistants" jumped up and was at the table instead.

"Tell Peter to bring me another flute of raspberries," Zach said. "This dessert just whets my appetite."

Two assistants left the room. Surely it didn't take two to carry a message, but they seemed joined at the hip, doing everything in pairs.

"So tell me about you," Zach said. "Why are you looking into the Zelda Machinko story? Has there been a development?"

"Not really. A friend of mine—you know Maggie Sheffield? She had a stroke, and she's in the hospital."

"Yes, I was sorry to hear that. How's she doing?"

"She's conscious, but she can't talk yet. Years ago, Maggie wrote a lot of stories about Zelda Machinko. I thought maybe, for Maggie's sake, I could check it out again."

"Check it out? I would think most of the people who knew her would be dead or retired by now. Who will you interview?"

"I don't know. We'll see who's still around. I'm trying to soak up the atmosphere of the story. The times and the people. For Maggie."

"Atmosphere, huh?" Zach took the flute of raspberries Peter offered. He plunged his thumb and forefinger into the glass, plucked out a berry and tossed it in his mouth. "Mmmmmm, exquisite. Sure you won't have some?"

Zach fingered a few more berries and tossed them in his mouth one at a time. Then he held one out for Josie. She leaned forward and allowed him to place it on her tongue.

"Just bite into it and let it explode," Zach instructed. "Isn't it divine?"

Josie laughed and wiped a napkin across her lips. "Here you are in a five-star, gourmet restaurant, with items on the menu I can't even pronounce, and you are making a big deal about plain ol' raspberries."

"Sometimes the best things are the simplest. You've just gotta relax and enjoy," Zach said, holding out another berry. Josie took it between her teeth. She held it in her mouth gently for a second, then bit into it and let the flavors develop.

"You're right. They are extraordinary."

"Extraordinary," Zach repeated, tossing two into his mouth. He savored them for a moment and then said, "I've got an idea. Let's go upstairs. Let's see what's left of the *Spectator* offices. Would you like that?"

"Upstairs, tonight? Won't it be awfully dark and scary? What's up there now?"

"I don't know, but if you want atmosphere, that sounds like the place to go."

Josie glanced at the other table. All four were having drinks and laughing. "Will they be going?"

"Do you want them to?"

"No, not really."

"OK, I'll send them home."

Zach snapped his fingers to get their attention, then jerked a thumb toward the door. The men looked at each other, picked up their drinks, and left. Zach stood up, held out a hand to Josie, and said, "Let the adventure begin."

With a guiding hand in the small of her back, Zach directed Josie to the back of the restaurant where the owner, Cecil Barnes, was leaning against the bar.

"We want to look around upstairs. How do we get there?"

Cecil looked confused, but he didn't try to dissuade Zach.

"There are stairs, but they are pretty rickety. I would take the freight elevator, next to the kitchen. We use the third floor to store any extra canned goods that accumulate."

"Is there electricity up there?"

"Yeah, but I'm not sure how many fixtures have working bulbs," Cecil responded. "Wait a sec."

He stepped behind the bar and reached under the counter. "Just in case," he said, handing a large flashlight to Zach.

Zach pushed Josie through the swinging door into the kitchen, which was fairly quiet at this late hour. A couple of men were loading a dishwasher.

"Lo, Mr. Teasdale," one of the men said.

"Hi, guys. Which way to the freight elevator?"

The men looked at each other. One wiped his hands on a dish towel and led the way through a side door to the old loading platform. He reached in a hand and turned on a light. This is where Zelda kicked off a shoe all those years ago. It seemed strange to be here now.

Giant cans of tomato sauce stood along one wall. A huge freight elevator took up most of the space. It was big enough for hauling giant rolls of newsprint to the presses on the ground floor. It probably once lifted pallets full of printed newspapers back to the loading dock. Zach pulled the rope to lift the gate and stepped inside.

"You coming?" he asked. The floor was rough, punched metal, and the walls were wire mesh. Through the holes Josie could see the old bare wood of the elevator shaft, littered with bits of graffiti. Josie read one of the scrawls aloud. "'I kilt a bar.' What is this? Daniel Boone?"

"Some drunk or vagrant," Zach said, laughing.

Light from the loading dock area filled the open elevator, but Josie looked up into the inky darkness of the elevator shaft.

"What's up there?"

"Don't worry. It's not a rope pulley. It's been refitted," Zach said, as he pulled the strap to bring the safety gate back into place. A small electric box, about the size of an aluminum loaf pan, was attached to the frame. Three raised buttons, about the size of thimbles, had been rubbed clear of any writing. Zach pressed one and the elevator lurched into action. Boards and caulking of the past fifty years ran behind the wire mesh screen like an old black-and-white movie. The elevator squeaked to a stop on the third floor.

"The restaurant spans the first two floors," Zach said. "I think the presses used to be below on the ground floor where Cecil put in parking for the employees. Might have been typesetting on the second floor, but the offices were upstairs, on the third floor."

Zach pulled the rope to open the gate again and shone the flashlight ahead on a cluster of boxes and cans. He pulled a string dangling down in the middle of the boxes, and one bare bulb ignited.

The eerie room had a stifling, dusty smell. To the left of the elevator, shafts of moonlight shone through the tall windows and painted ghostly gray stripes across the bare wood floor To the right was a wall of dark so thick that Josie reached out her hand to see if she could touch it.

"What's back there?"

"Not much, I would think," Zach said. "That's where the building butts up against the Herkimer. That's why there aren't any windows over here."

Josie turned back toward the open room. She wandered out of the halo of the bright bulb and into the seductive gray. Each stripe of light seemed to beckon her until she was halfway across the room.

"Where are you going?" Zach called from the oasis of light.

"I don't know," she said. "Wonder what happened to all the desks and file cabinets and linotype machines.

"Probably moved down the street to the *Daily News*. Didn't they buy out the *Spectator*?"

"I don't think so. I think the *Spectator* just closed," Josie said, ambling through a shaft of gray light. She kicked bits of debris with the toe of her shoe. "Offset printing was getting popular then, and they probably couldn't afford the change from hot lead to offset."

"Somebody must have sold the stuff to salvage," Zach said.

Josie stopped at one of the windows and looked down at the street. It was well lit below with street lamps, cars, and the restaurant sign. But there was no neon hotel sign up this high, as in her dream. It must have been torn down years before.

Zach walked across the room, his flashlight beam cutting through the atmosphere of long ago like an express train to the present.

"What are you looking for?" he whispered.

"I don't know," she said without turning to face him.

"Guess we don't really need this," he said, turning off the flashlight and joining Josie at the window. "It's kind of heavy in here, like too much past. It smells dead, as if the air is gone. I like the liveliness outside better."

"Why did you come up here with me?"

"Because you wanted to see it."

"There's really nothing to see. It's not like Zelda would have written a note in the elevator shaft."

"Maybe she did. You want to look?"

Josie laughed. "No, I'm not expecting to find notes or old desks from an office that closed twenty-five years ago. I just want to soak up the atmosphere."

"Like savoring raspberries."

"Yeah, I guess."

Zach stood by her silently for a few minutes, then he put his arm around her. Josie liked the warmth of his arm and leaned into him.

"I wonder what it was like to work at a newspaper in those days," she said. "Back when they typed on manual typewriters, cut the stories apart with scissors to rearrange paragraphs, and glued them back together with rubber cement."

"No way! You're kidding me," Zach said. "Like paper dolls? Who told you that?"

"Maggie. She still does it sometimes. She has this smelly jar of rubber cement on her desk with a brush attached to the lid. It's like some mysterious goo from a science-fiction flick."

Josie noticed a glint on the floor. The moonlight singled out a giant fishhook against the wood. She walked back into the shaft of light and reached out to touch the ghostly shape. She almost expected it to disappear, a figment of her imagination. Instead, she was surprised when her fingers touched cold metal, solid. When she picked it up, the hook resisted, with the unexpected heaviness of a substantial chunk of lead at the base.

"First Daniel Boone, now Captain Hook," Zach said when Josie returned to the window with her prize. "I think we've stepped into Disney World."

"Or *The Twilight Zone*," Josie said, holding the hook to the light for closer examination.

"What is it?" Zach asked, touching the sharpened point.

"I think it's a spike. They used them to stick stories on when they were finished with them so the papers wouldn't fly all over the place."

Zach laughed. "I had no idea working for a newspaper was so playful. It's almost as bad as making gum."

"Would you show me?" Josie said. "I'd love to see how gum is made."

"Tonight?"

"No, some other time, perhaps."

"Perhaps," Zach said, pulling her closer. In the shadows, without the benefit of his expensive suit, polished Italian shoes, and fancy gold watch, he was just a man who liked raspberries. A man who ran million-dollar businesses, but was willing to go on a wild-goose chase with a silly woman for no reason at all.

Josie gave in to his embrace, the heavy, hooked lead spike dangling from one hand as she reached her other arm around his neck. Their bodies fit together like puzzle pieces. Josie didn't even need to stand on tiptoe. Her lips found his like they were snapping into a place they were always meant to be. His kiss was tender, exploring; her response was soft, willing but not too eager. Both could taste the passion and hunger, but they were wary.

Zach's hand slipped off Josie's shoulder and down her arm until his fingers closed over her hand holding the spike.

"Maybe we should resume this sometime when you aren't holding a lethal weapon."

Chapter 16

Zelda

You know the sound of silence? The way a busy room slowly gets quiet when something is grabbing everyone's attention? Well, that's how it is when Buster Boardman comes calling at the *Spectator*.

My desk is on the third floor, way over in the corner near the windows, so I can keep an eye on everything that happens downtown. The stairs are clear on the other side of the room, along the wall next to the Herkimer Hotel. Buster bursts in through the door at the top of the stairs, him and three of his boys. He is wearing a camel sport coat over a pale pink shirt, and all that hair of his is slapped in place with something greasy. He's wearing half a dozen rings and a smile that outshines them all. I swear, for a minute I think he walked right through the wall between our two buildings. I am that surprised to see him.

I am not afraid, mind you. I am not about to let him intimidate me, even if his friends are wearing dark suits that remind me of those striped hornets that buzzed into my father's butcher shop all those years ago.

I recognize Buster right away, but he doesn't know me on sight. He asks one of the copy boys, who points in my direction. That's when the silence moves across the room like a storm cloud blotting out the sun. We only have two reporters, but they look up and stop typing. The advertising salesmen put down their phones. Every head turns to see what Boardman will do next.

He just smiles a little bigger and struts across the room.

"Why, Miss Machinko," he says, offering his hand. "You're much younger and prettier than I imagined. From the sound of some of your editorials, I was expecting an old hag."

He holds out his hand and keeps flashing that big smile, but I make no move to stand up or shake his hand. Would you do business with the devil if he smiled?

"What do you want?" I say. My voice is curt. I don't want anyone to think I am afraid or impressed by his show of friendship.

"My dear," he responds as smooth as butter, "there's no reason to be alarmed. I realize your angry editorials help sell your rag of a paper, and I accept that. They even make me laugh sometimes, don't they, boys?" Buster chuckles and turns to his sober-looking sidekicks, who mirror laughter right on cue. "We know you don't mean any serious threat to us. We're neighbors."

"Our buildings are next door, but the occupants are worlds apart," I say.

Buster snaps his fingers in the direction of an empty chair, and one of his boys slides it next to my desk. Buster sits down and leans across the corner of my desk so I can smell his Old Spice aftershave.

"Perhaps I haven't always been as good a neighbor as I should have," he says in an intimate voice, like he's sharing a secret. "We're doing a little remodeling at the hotel. I should have explained it to you from the beginning. I know you and your reporters have been hearing the jackhammers. I should have come over sooner and told you our plans."

"You mean the casino expansion?" I say.

He just laughs. "Casino? There's no such thing, my dear. You and your reporters can come for a tour at any hour. We are remodeling the hotel rooms, adding bathrooms. People don't want to go down the hall anymore. Everyone wants a private bath attached to the room. All the new hotels are built that way. But this old place is built like a fortress, limestone and cinder block. To make way for plumbing is rather noisy. We're taking out some of the rooms and turning them into bathrooms. That's all, really. Nothing worth newspaper coverage. But I suppose all that noise has been irritating. I don't blame you for retaliating with that foolish editorial speculating about a casino."

Buster laughs again, but his boys aren't smiling.

"I'm afraid the noise may be getting a bit louder this week, and I'm begging your indulgence, madam." Buster reaches for my hand, which I pull away. "We've been working on the fourth and fifth floors, but this week we'll be working on the third floor, just on the other side of that wall," he says, gesturing broadly toward the stairs. "I'm afraid the jackhammer will be shaking your desks over here. You may want to take a few days off. It's going to be very loud."

"Is this your idea of a threat?" I say, rising. "You think you can chase us off with a little noise?"

"On the contrary," he says, standing up to look me in the eye, "I'm just trying to spare you and your reporters a few headaches."

I've had about all of the conniving sweet talk I can take. "You're a slimeball," I say, leaning across my paper-strewn desk. "You can buy off the judges and cops and make up stories about remodeled hotel rooms. Everyone knows the only business you do over there is dice and roulette. Get out of my office, you lying bastard."

Finally, I've chiseled through his fake exterior to his raw and angry heart.

"Listen, you cheap whore," Buster responds, slamming his hands down on my desk as he leans forward. His spittle splatters my face. He doesn't know, and I didn't think to warn him, that the pile of copy paper on my desk is corralled on a metal spindle that easily gets buried under a couple of days' writing. His left hand slaps into the paper. He hits the spike and lets out a surprised howl that has my reporters jumping to their feet. His goons reach inside their jackets for hidden guns. Buster pulls back his hand, but the spike and copy paper are still attached. He spins around howling. Papers flutter to the floor, leaving the metal spike dangling from his palm. One of his men rushes forward, grabs the spike, and pulls it out. Buster squeals even louder as blood spurts all over his camel-hair jacket and natty trousers.

It's not the kind of hurt I want to see. I want Buster in jail, not bleeding on my floor.

"Oh, my God," I exclaim, rushing around my desk. "I'm so sorry."

Two of his men step in my way and one grabs me by the arm. Across the room, I see Matt Shipman, the beefy supervisor in typesetting, heading to my aid. Buster has made such a ruckus that the linotype operators are coming upstairs. Sides are forming for a brawl.

"What the hell is this thing?" says the goon who pulled the spike out of Buster's hand. He rushes toward me, waving the blood-soaked spike. "I ought to ram this down your throat, bitch."

"No, no," Buster says, with regained calm. He pulls the embroidered handkerchief from his pocket and wraps his bloody palm. "You heard the woman. She's sorry. Too bad she has to see blood before she regrets the damage she's done. Some people are like that. Blood's the only language they understand."

Buster lifts his chin and pulls back his shoulders. He has been a vulnerable human for a minute, but that person is gone. "Gentlemen, I believe our business is done here. Good day, Miss Machinko."

Buster turns and heads for the stairs, parting the crowd with the sheer determination of his stride. His men survey the room as though they expect trouble, but no one makes a move except to get out of the way. When the last one has disappeared into the stairwell, I pick up the spike and wipe off the blood.

"Are you OK?" Matt Shipman says, standing by my desk.

"I'm fine, but this spike is a hazard," I say, holding up the sharp spindle. "Can you bend it over so somebody else doesn't get hurt? And do the same with the other spikes in the room."

"Sure," Matt says, taking the spike. He pulls some pliers from his back pocket and makes a crook in the top of the spike so it no longer is a dagger in disguise. He sets his creation on my desk and threads several loose sheets of copy paper over the hook and down the shaft.

"That should do it," he says, returning the pliers to his pocket.

I thank him and he starts to walk away.

"Oh, one more thing," I say. "What do you know about jackhammers?"

Matt looks confused. "They are damn noisy. What else is there to know?"

"Can a jackhammer cut a hole in these granite walls?"

"A jackhammer can punch a hole in Fort Knox."

"Good. I want you to get hold of one. I have an idea for a little remodeling project of my own. I want it to coincide with the noise on the other side of the wall so our 'neighbors' won't notice."

A sudden surge of rock music pierced the early morning haze.

"Jackhammers," Josie thought. She rolled over and pulled a pillow over her head. The radio alarm persisted until she poked her hand out from under the covers, searching for the snooze button. Instead, she knocked over the spike she had retrieved from her late-night tour of the former *Spectator* offices. The green glow of the digital clock glistened off the pointed shaft of the metal spike, its sharp point bent over for safety's sake.

Josie ran a finger over the hook and touched the nail-sharp point. No blood, she thought. Some people only understand blood.

Chapter 17

It was still dark, but Duke was dressed and sitting on the edge of the bed. Sharon was curled into a ball like a kitten with her back to him. He wished he could crawl back under the covers and wrap his body around her again, wake her up with kisses. He wished they could wake up together every morning, like it used to be. But he wanted to leave before Jennifer woke up and found him there. He didn't want an uncomfortable scene, didn't want to give Sharon a reason to say he should never spend the night again.

He touched Sharon's shoulder and kissed her delicate ear. The short hairstyle did make her ears more accessible. She murmured and uncurled from her ball.

"Happy Mother's Day," he whispered.

Sharon mumbled something and stretched beneath the covers.

"I'm leaving now," he whispered. "It was a great evening. Thank you." Duke turned to leave, but she grabbed his arm and mumbled something again. Was she saying "stay"? Duke sat back down on the bed. Her eyes fluttered open a crack.

"Stay a while," she whispered. "I'll fix breakfast and we can talk."

"But Jennifer—"

"She'll probably sleep until noon. She usually does on Sundays." Sharon stretched again and let out a deep, sexy sigh.

Snickerdoodle snot, she's coming on to me, Duke thought. I can't pass this up. I don't want to pass this up. But what if I'm wrong? He hesitated just a second. Sharon opened one eye and looked at him. He kissed her and soon he was slipping out of his jeans and back under the sheets.

It was daylight by the time Duke finally got up to start the coffee and pick up the morning paper that was waiting on the apartment doorstep. That was one advantage of an apartment, Duke thought. He didn't have to go down the driveway half dressed as he did at home. But Duke dressed anyway, in case he bumped into Jennifer. Duke never walked around Sharon's apartment naked like he did when he and Sharon first got married, like he did now that he was living alone again.

It was funny how Jennifer always was on his mind these days. He closed the door to the bathroom, put down the lid when he was finished. Flushed. All for Jennifer. Not Sharon. He'd been subjecting Sharon to his full frontal maleness ever since college. Never saw any need to disguise his raw, no-frills manliness. But even when Jennifer was a little girl, she would squeal if she went into the family bathroom and found the seat up or the bowl unflushed.

"Yuck, Daddy!"

So he started putting down the seat. He wanted Jennifer to think the best of him. He wanted her to expect the best of all men, to never be willing to settle for rude male behavior. Jennifer deserved the best. On this morning, warm with the muskiness of early-morning sex, Duke put his jeans on before retrieving the paper. He was fully dressed, sitting at the breakfast table with his first cup of coffee when Sharon wandered into the kitchen, tying a robe over her naked curves.

Duke smiled. Her relaxed demeanor was more encouraging than any words. She was comfortable with him again. Sharon walked over to the breakfast table, hugged Duke's shoulders and kissed him on the head, just like she used to do. Oh, how much he had missed this simple routine. He had spent the night with Sharon a few times since she had moved out, but he'd never stayed until daylight.

"Anything in the paper about the concert?" Sharon asked as she opened the refrigerator and got out bacon, eggs, bread.

"Let me see. Oh, here's a picture on the local section. Sorry, we're not in it."

"I don't know how they could have missed us. We were practically in his lap. That Becky. When she organizes something, she does it up right, doesn't she? Front-row seats. That was really special."

"I'm glad you enjoyed it."

"So, is she dating Detective Cantrell from the police department, or did he just stop by? They sorta make a cute couple."

"It was a group date, a test run. What did you think of his sister, Linda?"

"Sweet and smart in an unassuming way. It was really surprising some of the things she would say. If you really listen to her, she's got a genius savant quality."

"Yeah, I thought so too. And Tom says she can play piano. I'd like to hear that sometime."

Sharon stripped slices of bacon from the package and laid them into the skillet.

"One egg or two," she asked.

"Two. You gave me such a workout, I'm famished!"

"Shh, I don't want Jennifer knowing all the intimate details!"

"I thought you said she would sleep until noon."

"Well, she doesn't get up until noon, but I wouldn't put it past her to be half awake and listening."

"Great."

Sharon flicked on a radio that was sitting on the counter. "Just in case" she said.

Duke commented on the day's headlines as Sharon fixed the breakfast. He couldn't remember when they'd had such a pleasant, relaxed morning together. Certainly not since she had moved out ten months ago, and not for the last couple of years they were together. After alcohol took over his life, mornings became an ordeal. Sharon would find him asleep in the basement or passed out on the floor somewhere. She would pour coffee down him and push him into the shower, complaining the whole time. Duke never realized until now how much the alcohol had taken away.

"It's been about eight months now, hasn't it?" Sharon said as she placed a plate of bacon and eggs in front of Duke.

"My last drink? Eight months, three days, and ..." Duke looked at his watch as though he could report the exact minute of the final drink. "OK, I don't remember the time," he said with a laugh. "Time used to all run together. But I know the day. It's been more than eight months since I've had a drink."

"That's good, that's really good," Sharon said. "And are you happy being sober? Do you think you can continue? Do you want to continue?"

"What is this? You sound like my counselor."

"I don't want to sound like your counselor. I want to sound like a woman who is concerned about you."

"Concerned? That sounds pretty noncommittal. People are 'concerned' about the high price of gasoline."

"I'm having a hard time with this," Sharon said.

Why did she have to ruin a perfect morning? Duke thought. He should have left before breakfast.

"It's not exactly easy for me," he said, snapping off a piece of bacon. He wasn't so hungry anymore.

"This isn't going the way I had hoped," Sharon said. "I'm trying, I'm really trying. But you are so wary of me."

"Wary? I'm not the one who is wary. Sharon, I don't know how many times I need to say it. I'm willing to do anything, absolutely anything, to win you back. I can't tell you I don't want a drink. I want one every single day. But I am beginning to see that alcohol was robbing me of something I want much more. I want to wake up with you, have quiet little breakfasts together, read the paper together, turn up the radio so our daughter won't hear all our intimate secrets. I want all of that. Not once in a while, but every day."

Sharon was eerily still when Duke finished. "I want all those things too," she whispered.

Duke couldn't believe his ears. "You do?"

"Of course I do. That's what I've been waiting for. I didn't leave you because I didn't love you. I left because I knew you'd never get well if I stayed."

"I know," Duke said, looking down at his plate and examining the pool of yellow seeping from one of his eggs. "I know you are right, Sharon, and I'm grateful. Honestly. I didn't understand at first, but I am beginning to."

Duke reached for Sharon's hand. "No matter what else happens, I want you to know I appreciate what you did. All those years when I was drunk, and then leaving like you did. Thank you."

"You should thank Jennifer. I did it for her," Sharon said, biting her lip. "If it had just been you and me, I probably would have kept on picking you up until you ran a car into a tree someday."

Duke and Sharon stared at each other a minute, holding hands over their cooling eggs.

"I made a Chihuahua-humpin'-a-porcupine mess of our lives, didn't I?" Duke said.

Sharon chuckled at the image, then turned serious. "I failed you too, somehow."

"No, you did—"

"Marriage is a partnership, and both partners need to accept responsibility. You wanted something from me that I wasn't providing, so you turned to booze. I don't know if I was too busy with Jennifer or too out of touch with your work—"

"No, I won't let you blame yourself. I flew into the mountain full throttle."

"And I should have been your copilot changing course."

After another moment of silent hand-holding, Sharon pulled her hands back and began attacking her remaining egg with knife and fork. Duke watched her. This was closer than they'd been in years. He didn't want to let her go again. But he wasn't sure what to say.

"I've been thinking," Sharon said without looking up from her plate. "Maybe it's about time we moved home. Do you think that would work?

"Do I think … sacred succotash, of course it will work. Twirling toadstools. You mean it? Oh, honey, this is what I've dreamed."

Duke jumped out of his chair and pulled Sharon to her feet. "Hurricanes of happiness, this is unbelievable. Let's wake Jennifer and tell her. Let's start packing today. You can move back this weekend."

Duke hugged Sharon and pulled her around the kitchen in an exaggerated waltz.

"I'll buy some steaks for the grill. It's warm enough to cook outside."

"Wait a minute," Sharon said, shaking her head at Duke's wild enthusiasm. "I'm thinking we both need to get used to the idea. We need to think about how things will work. I'm not the same stay-at-home housewife. I'm a teacher now. I have a schedule. I'll need office space in the house. And Jennifer is a teenager. She'll be a senior in high school. She'll need a place to entertain her friends. You've probably sprawled out some since you've had the house to yourself. It's going to be an adjustment for everyone."

"Butterfly burps! We can work out those little things. I'm so glad to have you home again."

"Listen to me. This isn't going to work if you keep hearing only what you want to hear."

Sharon was standing in the middle of the kitchen with her hands on her hips. She was serious. What was she saying? What was he not hearing?

"I think we should take this slow," she said, with a huge sigh. "Let's aim for the end of the month when school gets out. I have this apartment until then. That way you can pick up the house. Get things back in order. We can run it by Jennifer, get her input."

"Oh, Jennifer is cool with it. I know that—"

"Will you listen to me?"

"I'm listening."

"I want this to work out. I really do. But I've got to be a full partner. We both have to be fully committed to the marriage first. Top priority."

"Aye, aye, captain. Top priority."

Chapter 18

Josie had been dreading Monday. She arranged to leave Kevin with Polly before and after school. In her heart, she believed Rudy hadn't done anything wrong, but that was because she didn't dare believe otherwise. She couldn't face the thought that she might have left her son in the care of a sexual predator.

Even if the state didn't close Ranch Rudy, Josie expected most parents would come up with alternative arrangements, just as she had. Josie assigned Becky to stop by the day-care center, check on the turnout, and talk to parents.

"Only three kids showed up," Becky reported. "A preschool boy and his older sister, who was only there a half hour before getting on the school bus, and another toddler boy. Only one of the employees showed up, and Randolph sent her home. He was building a beanbag fort with the two boys when I left, just like everything was fine. But he admitted he was disappointed that nobody showed up today. He said they have forty-five kids on a normal day."

"What does DCFS have to say?" Josie asked, her red pen poised over the page proof on her desk.

"Nothing new," Becky said. "Of course, they won't release the name of the abused child, so there's no way to check on her condition."

Isabel Edison, Josie thought. Rudy had mentioned the name of his accuser, but it didn't seem fair for the newspaper to expose the family to more questions. Josie would keep that knowledge to herself for now.

"What about the parents who dropped their kids off? What did they say?"

"Single dad dropped off the brother and sister. Said he didn't have any relatives to leave them with. Said he was afraid his ex-wife would sue for custody if she found out, so he asked me not to use his name. The mother who dropped off the other little boy, she was great. She said Mr. Randolph runs the best day-care center in town and would never hurt anybody."

"That's good. Use her quote and keep the single dad's name out of it. Keep it short, just a second-day story."

A few minutes before the ten o'clock deadline, Helen, the receptionist, brought Josie a vase full of red roses.

"I'm just dying to know who these are from," Helen said in her fast-paced chatter. "Open the card."

Flowers are not always cause for celebration in a newsroom. Sometimes a plant or arrangement is delivered to thank a reporter for a particularly flattering story. Those gifts elicit moans of disgust because no reporter wants anyone to think a story is ever anything but the unbiased truth. Reporters are not allowed to accept gifts. Most of the time, thank-you flowers will be passed on to someone else, dropped off at the senior center or a hospital room, or used to brighten the dinner table at the local homeless shelter. As Josie removed the envelope from the bouquet, she ran through a mental list of places to take them. Maybe Maggie's room or someplace at the hospital …

"Thanks for a lovely evening. Zach."

Josie's jaw dropped. The beautiful flowers were meant for her. Suddenly they were no longer an awkward obligation but a beautiful gift. She really looked at them for the first time, deep, velvety red roses, full and fragrant, interspersed with delicate white baby's breath and frilly ferns. Josie slipped the card back into the envelope quickly, but there was no hiding the smile on her face.

"So?" Helen badgered. "Who is it? Are we going to keep them?"

"What's the occasion?" Nick said, stopping by Josie's desk.

"Hey, what's the bribe for?" Duke said from the neighboring desk.

"Just a friend," Josie said, picking up the vase. Her desk was too cluttered already, so she placed the vase on the credenza behind her desk, smiling even broader at the fabulous fragrance. She felt very special, like a princess or a movie star. A gentleman friend had sent flowers. That never happened. That hadn't happened since … Josie couldn't remember. Had Kurt ever sent her flowers? Oh, back in college. Valentine's Day. Somehow, she wasn't the kind of woman who normally inspired flowers. But Zach wasn't the type of guy she normally attracted.

"Oh, I get it. It's that guy you're dating. The one you didn't want to name," Duke said, coming over to the credenza to inspect the evidence.

"Josie is dating someone new?" Becky said, joining the growing cluster around Josie's desk.

"A mystery man," Nick said, glancing at the envelope on Josie's desk. "A mystery man who uses Cass Street Floral. Isn't that the shop next to Teasdale Funeral Home? Isn't that one of Teasdale's businesses?"

"Yeah, I think so," Duke said and reached for the envelope. Josie grabbed it first.

"OK, enough," she said, holding the card close to her chest. "If you've finished your deadline stories and you are ready for a break, please go out to the break room so you don't disturb the copy desk. They've got work to do. Duke, you're clear of the morning deadline, so you are free to head on over to St. Joseph, if you're still planning on that trip. And I think I'll go have a banana myself."

Josie headed out of the newsroom to the break area with most of the reporters tagging along. Duke stood at the credenza, smelling the flowers and watching her walk away. He continued to think about Josie and the roses on the two-hour drive to St. Joe. Could she really be dating Zach Teasdale? Didn't she see what a jerk he was? A crook. Duke felt certain Teasdale was involved in some illegal activity, though he wasn't exactly sure what. He was just such a manipulator and so shamelessly wealthy. Josie wasn't stupid or naïve, but she was hopelessly idealistic. She always thought the best of people, avoided stereotypes, even though a lot of stereotypes are based on fact. She really believed in all that innocent-until-proven-guilty stuff.

Without too much trouble, Duke found Anderson and Sons Construction in an industrial park on the south side of St. Joe. An army of yellow earthmovers packed the fenced area behind a small one-story building. Inside he found a secretary/receptionist behind a desk. Two men in hard hats were standing nearby with coffee mugs, but when Duke stepped up to the desk, one of the men said, "Well, we'd better get back at it. Talk to you later, Arlene."

Before the men walked out of earshot, Duke announced, "I'm looking for Mr. Hamilton in personnel." The men stopped.

"We aren't hiring," the woman said. "Sorry."

"Oh, I'm not looking for a job. I just wanted to talk to Mr. Hamilton about a former employee. Blaine Avril. Do you guys remember him?"

"Nobody ever worked here by that name," one of the men said without a second's hesitation. "I'm Bob Anderson, owner. We never had anybody by that name."

Duke was undeterred. "But Mr. Hamilton knew him. I called last week, and he definitely recognized the name."

"Well, maybe he was one of the applicants for the last job," Anderson said. "Dick Hamilton isn't here today. Had a death in the family. Wasn't that funeral today, Arlene? He should be back tomorrow. You can talk to him then."

Anderson and the other man walked away. Arlene rolled a piece of paper into her electric typewriter.

"Well, that's a shame about Mr. Hamilton. He asked me to stop by today," Duke said. "That death in the family. It must have been unexpected."

"Yes, a real shame," Arlene said, looking at Duke. "His sister's husband. He was in the military. Killed in some sort of training exercise in Florida, I think."

"Oh, and the funeral is down there?"

"No. Right here in town. His sister lived here and she had a little baby. She's already been through so much. The baby was born with a cleft palate. And now this. Poor thing."

Blaine Avril had shown Ron Baylor a photo of his wife and an "ugly baby," Duke recalled.

"Yeah, what a shame," Duke said. "Well, I'll try to stop back tomorrow. Are you finished with this newspaper?" Duke picked up the scattered sections of the *Herald-Palladium* that had been tossed on a chair next to the desk.

"Oh, sure, take it," Arlene said, starting to type. "We're finished."

Duke took the paper back to his car. He scanned the obituaries until he found a likely one. "Timothy Norton, 31, died suddenly. Survived by his wife Sara (nee Hamilton) Norton and one-year-old daughter Allison." The obit featured a small flag and said Norton had served as a Navy Seabee.

Of course. The Seabees were the Navy's construction division. That's where he got his training on the big earthmovers. Duke suspected the funeral service would be over by the time he arrived at the church, so he drove directly to the cemetery. A tent set up on the other side of the property had a small cluster of people. A man and a woman in white Navy uniforms were standing at attention by the flag-draped casket. Taps played on a scratchy tape. When the music ended, the two lifted the flag off the casket and folded it in half and half again, like a long, striped tablecloth. Standing at opposite ends of the strip, the man folded over one corner, making a triangle, then rolled the triangle over and over until it was a little star-studded pillow, which he handed to a woman, seated near the casket. She cried uncontrollably, and the man next to her put an arm around her. A woman on the other side held a squirming child.

Duke stood back a distance from the tent. He didn't want to disturb the family. After a few more words and prayers, the family dispersed. Duke waited for his chance. There were hugs, a little muffled laughter, and discussions about eating places and best routes as plans for the next step unfurled. When the widow and the baby were safely tucked into one of the cars, Duke spotted the man who had comforted the widow. He was walking to another car.

"Dick?"

The man stopped and turned. Duke stepped forward and introduced himself.

"I'm the reporter who called the other day."

Dick looked around to be sure they weren't overheard.

"Listen, I don't know anything about it. They said it happened in Miami. I don't know why some paper in Jordan, Illinois, would be asking questions."

"I think you do know," Duke said. "T&T Construction called you from Jordan, and you gave them a reference for Blaine Avril, didn't you?"

"This is not the time."

"I know. And I'm sorry about your brother-in-law. But I think we can help each other. You probably want to know the real story about what happened."

"Mr. Dukakis. All I did was give Tim the reference, like you said, for that fictitious name. He told me not to tell Sara and I didn't. He told her he was going to Florida for a training exercise, and I never told her any different. It wasn't my business. The man's a hero. He works for special forces, and he can't talk about his assignments. I know he was doing something wonderful for his country. We don't need some left-leaning, liberal newspaper dragging his name through the mud. Now, if you'll excuse me, I'm late for lunch."

Dick Hamilton hurried to his car, slammed the door for emphasis, and drove away. Duke looked back at the tented area. Funeral home employees were folding up chairs, and a small tractor was parked nearby to lower the casket and fill the hole.

Dirt mover bites the dust, Duke thought in mock-headline speak.

"Well, Dukakis, you just don't get the message do you?"

Duke turned around to see Fred Wheeler with his balding partner.

"I suppose you'll have to get a taste of your own medicine," Wheeler said.

"Sorry," Duke said. "I don't believe we've met."

"You're damn right we never met," Wheeler said, "and you've never been to St. Joe either."

"St. Joe? You've got me confused with someone else," Duke said, walking away. "I work in Illinois, not Michigan."

Chapter 19

Josie waited until the lunch hour to make personal calls, when the newsroom was quiet and most of the reporters were out. First, she tried Hazelton Manufacturing in Cincinnati. With the hour time difference between Illinois and Ohio, Josie figured the personnel department should just be getting back from lunch. After a couple of transfers, Josie was speaking to the receptionist in advertising.

"Oh, yes, Irwin MacDonald works here, but he isn't around this week. He's in our Chicago office for a meeting. Can I have him call you when he returns next week?"

"Chicago? I'm just forty miles outside Chicago, in Jordan, Illinois, where Irwin used to live. I'm wondering if you might have a number where I could reach him. I'd love to reconnect while he's in the area."

"He usually calls in every day. I could give him your number if you like."

It was a step in the right direction. Josie supplied work and home phone numbers. Next, she called Maggie's hospital room.

"There's not much improvement," Katherine said. "They're about ready to release her. I could take her home, but she would require so much care. I'm thinking maybe a nursing home."

Josie listed some nursing facilities. "The Herkimer has a certain ambiance. It's right downtown. Easy for people to come visit. And whenever I'm downtown on a nice day, I see residents sitting outside, watching all the activity."

Katherine said the hospital staff had recommended the former hotel as well. A physical therapist was available there and would help with Maggie's recovery.

"I really need to get back to California," Katherine said. "I hate to leave Mom like this. I'm not even sure she understands what's happening to her. I just don't know what to do. If Mom doesn't improve in the next month, I think I'll see about bringing her out to California. It would be so much easier to have her close to me."

Josie agreed and assured her that the *Daily News* staff would be sure to visit frequently and keep her up-to-date.

Josie's final lunchtime call was to Zach.

"Hello, madam editor," he said. "Are you off deadline? Published another masterpiece?"

"The flowers are lovely, just lovely," Josie said. "But you really shouldn't have."

"And why not? Did I embarrass you at work? I hope so. I want the whole world to know about us."

Josie felt the slightest twinge of apprehension. Us? she thought. It was a little early after one date and one kiss to be considering this a romance. Certainly not a romance she wanted to share with the whole newsroom. And why was that? Was dating the coroner a conflict of interest for a newspaper editor? Did it mean she couldn't be fair? Maggie had been married to a cop and their union was beneficial to both. Did anyone ever suggest that was a conflict of interest? Josie inhaled the scent of a rose, and her fears evaporated.

"Honestly, they are velvety red, like a dozen little Christmas dresses, and they smell divine. My desk has never smelled so nice."

"Well, I want all those reporters of yours to know the coroner isn't just a source of blood and guts. I have my soft side too."

"And the dinner was wonderful," Josie said. "I should have called you yesterday, but I had to pick up Kevin and do laundry and everything."

"See, you have your maternal side. You're not just keeping the paper running smoothly, you're running a house. And I can proudly say I've seen yet another side of Josie Braun, the sexy, playful side."

Josie's apprehension spiked again. "I think you saw my silly wild-goose-chase side. Thanks for showing me around upstairs at the Red Geranium and putting up with my crazy ideas."

"I love crazy ideas. Did you bring in that spike you found? You can use it to organize the papers on your desk and keep wayward reporters in line."

Josie laughed. "No, the spike has been retired to the back of my closet, where I hope Kevin never finds it."

"Interesting. What other secrets do you have hiding in the back of your closet? Any skeletons the coroner should know about?"

Alarm buttons sounded again. Josie wouldn't ignore them anymore.

"Zach, I need to ask you. Do you think this is a conflict of interest? If we were to continue—"

"I certainly intend to continue," he blurted before she could finish her sentence.

"It's just that when you refer to yourself as the coroner and me as the editor, it sounds like ... I don't know, improper."

"Oh, I'm sorry, I didn't realize—"

"I shouldn't say anything. You've been so nice. But, well, I don't think an editor kissed a coroner the other night. I think we were different people then. I hope we were. Something more than our jobs."

"Guess that's what I like about you," Zach said. "You look right past my titles and my money and still you see something."

"I see a lot."

"Listen, I've got an idea. You said you wanted to see the factory, and I was thinking to set up a tour for next Saturday morning. Kevin might like to see Pop-O coming off the line. I always loved visiting the factory when I was a kid. It's a fairyland. You'll see. Does Saturday morning work for you? We could do lunch afterwards, and I've got a few other surprises. How's that sound? We'll make a family day of it."

The blush that came over Josie's cheeks was almost as red as the roses. Here was a man who not only sent flowers, he recognized the importance of Kevin in Josie's life. Not even Kevin's father could get that right.

"That sounds great. Really great."

"Good. I'll be by about ten, how's that sound?"

"Great."

"Oh, and ... a ... since I'm not the coroner and you're not the editor, it probably won't matter if I share a little gossip I heard this morning about that day-care center guy they arrested."

Josie's mouth went dry. "Yeah?"

"Well, the kid definitely was abused, but the analysis on the semen doesn't correspond with the blood type of the day-care owner, so it had to be somebody else."

"Oh, my God!"

"They were going to interview the kid again. If one of your reporters were to call over there this afternoon, maybe they'll be making another arrest."

"Oh, Zach, thanks for the tip."

"Tip? Just a little gossip between friends."

When Becky entered the homicide division offices later that afternoon, Tom walked around his desk to meet her halfway. "I should have called to thank you for the wonderful concert Saturday night. Linda had such a good time."

"I'm glad you were in," Becky said, taking his outstretched hand in hers and giving a friendly squeeze. "I was down here on something else and just wanted to check in with you. I love your sister. What a sweetheart. She stole everyone's heart."

"She has a way of doing that." Tom pulled out a chair next to his desk, and Becky slipped into it with airy grace.

"So what brings you down to this bastion of bureaucracy?" Tom asked.

"There's been a new arrest in that child molestation case. Tests showed it couldn't be the day-care center owner, so they talked to the kid again and they arrested the mother's boyfriend."

"Yeah, I heard they were looking at him," Tom said. "You can't believe what kids tell you sometimes."

"They told me the kid was afraid of the boyfriend. He threatened to kill her if she told," Becky said, shaking her head. "Somebody suggested the day-care guy, and she thought since he was nice, he wouldn't hurt her, so she said it was him. She just didn't understand how serious it was to lie."

"Poor kid."

"Poor day-care guy. So, how about you? Anything new in the construction murder? Or is that still out of your hands?"

Tom chuckled. "Well, I'm sure you know the body has been picked up by federal agents and I'm not allowed to comment on their investigation."

"Do I hear a 'but' coming?"

"We-e-ll …" He drawled the word with lingering emphasis. "I do need your help with something. There was a disturbance a week ago at the public campground by the Jordan River. A woman who was walking her dog saw three men arguing outside one of the camp trailers. A little later, she thought she heard gunshots coming from that direction. Finally called us. We checked it out and found quite a bit of blood in front of the trailer. She gave us a rough description of one of the men, so I had one of the artists come up with a sketch."

Tom tossed a copy of the drawing across his desk so Becky could see it.

"If the paper could run that, it might give us a handle on what happened."

"I thought you said there were three men, but only one sketch?"

"She only saw one face in the streetlight. The other guys had their backs to her. But she said they were big, broad shouldered. Like football players."

"Wait a minute," Becky said, "didn't this Avril guy have a trailer at the campground? Is there any chance—"

"I think you're catching on," Tom said, grinning from ear to ear. "I promised the feds I wouldn't interfere with their investigation, but I have to follow up on a report of shots fired at a public campground, don't I? And since we found enough blood to believe there might have been a homicide … I may not have a body anymore, but I've got a witness and a sketch. If one of your readers saw something, I might just have myself a couple of suspects."

"But when the feds see the story in the paper, won't you be in trouble?"

"As my Daddy always used to say, it's easier to ask forgiveness than permission," Tom said with a laugh. He sat up and leaned in close.

"Somebody had to roll that body up in a tarp, stuff it in the back of that truck, and then park the truck downtown. That's a lot of opportunity for public exposure. Somebody must have seen something. When people start coming forward, there isn't any way the feds can keep a lid on it anymore."

❀

The news that Rudy Randolph had been cleared of child molestation spread quickly. Soon supporters were knocking on the door at Ranch Rudy. Josie picked up Kevin after school and bought a cheese-pizza peace offering.

When she arrived at the day-care center, she discovered half a dozen other parents had the same idea. It was an impromptu party.

"I knew it, I knew it," said one of the fathers as he gave Rudy a hearty slap on the back. "You can tell a pervert, and I knew you wasn't one of them. I knew it."

"Crystal was so sad when she heard we weren't going to see Rudy anymore," added a mother carrying a bakery cake. "I'm so glad all that mess is behind us now."

The children played and the parents laughed. The crowd grew as the end of the workday came, and more and more families heard the word. Rudy accepted their congratulations, but his mood was subdued. He seemed too tired to cope with people and too polite to tell them to leave. Josie was glad to find him alone in the kitchen when she went in search of napkins.

"It's been a long day, hasn't it?" she said.

"Yeah, I wasn't exactly prepared for a party," he said, wrangling several bottles of juice and a bag of paper cups.

"But you've got to be so relieved."

"Relieved? I knew I was innocent. But it doesn't make the horror go away. A poor little girl has been terribly abused by someone she trusted. There's no party at her house."

"Of course not."

"And look at them," Rudy said, pointing down the hall toward the gathering in the main entry. "Where were they this morning? Where were you? Where was all this support when the chips were down?"

"I'm sorry, Rudy," Josie said, taking one of the bottles of juice that was about to slip from his grasp. "We're all sorry for doubting you. That's why we came, don't you see? We're terribly sorry for everything. For you, for Isabel. We're doing the best we can to make it better."

"Is that what you think? You think you can make it all go away with a piece of cake?"

"Of course not. What do you want from us? We stayed away because we were afraid. We didn't know what else to do. And as soon as it was safe, we came back. What more do you want?"

Rudy shook his head.

"I'm the fool," he said. "I'm the one who thought I was building relationships and respect these past ten years. And today, all day, with just the two little boys here, the house echoed with emptiness. It laughed at me, all day, this empty house. I have nothing here. No respect, no relationships. Nothing."

Rudy set the armload of bottles on the counter and swiped his sleeve across his face. "Excuse me, I can't—" He bolted across the kitchen to the back stairs that led to his living quarters.

"Wait," Josie said, running after him.

He paused at the banister, and she held out one of the paper napkins so he could wipe his eyes.

"This isn't the time to quit," she said. "Remember what you told Kevin two years ago when Kurt moved out? You told him to give his father another chance. Give all of us parents another chance. We believe in you. It's ourselves we were beginning to doubt."

Rudy sank down and sat on the landing. "I'm just so tired. I haven't slept in days."

Josie offered another paper napkin, and Rudy blew his nose.

"Fair enough. But let's go out there and pass around some cups of juice. Give us a chance to toast our tired but faithful child-care worker. Let's make sure everybody knows Ranch Rudy will be open as usual tomorrow morning, and then gently send them out into the night. Grown-ups are just big kids, Rudy. You know exactly how to handle them."

Chapter 20

"So you drove all the way to Michigan, today?" Sharon asked as she set two plates of spaghetti on the table.

"And I'm famished," Duke said, pulling up a chair. "Your invitation couldn't have come at a better time."

"Well, to be honest, I get tired of eating alone and Jennifer's always got something going," Sharon said. "So tell me about the funeral you just stumbled into. Was that for the guy who was found at the sewer construction site?"

"It was the saddest funeral you could imagine," Duke said, twirling a string of spaghetti on his fork. "Here was this young widow crying her eyes out for a man who left her with a kid, and she doesn't even really know how he died. She's thinking he's some military hero who died in a training exercise, when really he got shot in the head for no reason at all. For some crooked sewer contract that probably won't even be investigated anymore."

"So you think he was a federal agent? You think they are doing some undercover investigation of sewer contracts?"

"That's what it looks like to me. The feds love to hire former military."

"Well, maybe the wife is better off thinking he's a military hero. Maybe that's the gift he left her," Sharon said, poking her fork in her lettuce salad and fishing out a ripe olive. "You're not going to destroy that illusion, are you?"

"Not intentionally." Duke stuffed a forkful of spaghetti in his mouth and spaghetti sauce dribbled on his chin. "But I'm not going to let this sewer contract go uninvestigated. The very fact that the feds are interested means something really bad is going down, and I'm going to find out what."

Sharon laughed and handed him a paper napkin. "You know, this is really fun, talking about your day. I feel honored. I suspect you used to talk about these things with your reporter friends or cop cronies. But it's fun to hear what you're working on, what you're thinking."

"And I haven't even told you the biggest news of the day," Duke said, twirling another tangle of pasta onto his fork. "Josie got flowers today."

"Really? From a guy?"

"I don't know for sure, but I suspect it's Zach Teasdale."

"The coroner?"

"Yeah, she won't admit it, but I think she's been dating him."

"Oh, my, he's such a flashy dresser. I thought maybe he was gay."

"Well, he might be. Maybe he's just leading her on. I haven't figured out his devious plot, but I'm sure he's got one."

Sharon laughed. "You make him sound like the villain in an old melodrama."

115

"Can't you just imagine him twirling the ends of his handlebar mustache?" Duke said, wiggling his heavy eyebrows and pretending his mustache was long enough to twist with his fingers.

"Well, I'm happy for Josie. She's been alone since Kurt left."

Duke wasn't about to refute Sharon's assumption. "Maybe, but she could find somebody better than that prissy little twerp."

"Whoa, that's a bit vitriolic, don't you think? He is a little arrogant."

"Arrogant! He's got his deity-defying nose so high in the air he would drown if it started to rain."

"Kurt can be pretty arrogant too," Sharon said. "Maybe that's what appeals to Josie. Everybody has different tastes in men. Just because Josie isn't attracted to raw, virile types like you."

Duke almost choked on his spaghetti.

"Oh, don't pretend you aren't flattered," Sharon said, giving Duke's knee a playful squeeze under the table. "Josie doesn't know what she's missing." He gulped down his pasta and tried to smile.

"Isn't Teasdale a millionaire?" Sharon continued. "That will buy a lot of flowers and dress up a mountain of personality flaws."

"Camel clots. I can't believe you—or a smart woman like Josie—would be seduced by a few flowers."

"Why not? You've seduced me with a lot less."

"I suppose I have," Duke said.

They were silent for a minute, just looking at each other.

"I'm glad you invited me to dinner," Duke said finally. "It's fun to talk to you again and feast on your spaghetti. I swear, if I never eat another takeout pizza, it will be too soon."

"You can cook, silly. You didn't have to eat pizza every night."

"Inferno afirmo, I can cook. But it seems like too much trouble for one."

"I'm usually cooking for one, plus leftovers in the fridge in case Jennifer is still hungry when she gets home. She's got something going every night after school. She's at orchestra practice now. They're playing at the graduation ceremony in a couple of weeks."

Sharon paused for a minute, watching as Duke twirled another forkful. "I told Jennifer yesterday that we might be moving back home."

"Might?" Duke said, pausing his fork midair. "I thought it was a sure thing. I thought—"

"Now, don't go getting your drawers in a knot." Sharon got up to remove her plate from the table. "I just wanted to approach Jennifer as though it was an idea, not carved in stone. So she feels like she can have some input."

"And she's all for it, right?" Duke said, grabbing another slice of garlic bread before Sharon removed the basket.

"Oh, sure. She's happy for us working things out and all. But she thinks she should get a car."

"Iguana guano! Where did that come from?"

Sharon sat back down at the table. "Well, she is driving now, and it would make it easier if she gets a summer job."

"We're raising a blackmailer!"

"I know it seems like that, but she's got a point."

"She may have a point, but she won't have a beaver-logjam car until she can pay for it. Case closed."

"Full partnership. Remember."

Duke expelled a gust of air with an exaggerated sigh. "OK, I'll take it under advisement. You know, I did hear what you were saying the other day, about how the family has changed. I mean you working and Jennifer needing her own space and all."

Duke picked up his plate, scraped the remaining thread of spaghetti into the garbage disposal, rinsed the plate, and opened the dishwasher to find a spot.

"Looks like you've changed too," Sharon said. "I don't remember you ever clearing your own plate and putting it in the dishwasher."

Duke chuckled. "It's amazing what a guy learns living alone." He picked up the pitcher of iced tea and refilled his glass. "Want some?"

Sharon declined and Duke sat down again.

"Anyway, I've been thinking that maybe we move Jennifer's bedroom to the basement room where I used to have my little hideaway. It's got its own bathroom so she'd have more privacy. It's big enough that we could keep the couch and television that's down there, and she could entertain her friends."

"Not boys, not unsupervised," Sharon said.

"Certainly not."

"Might work," Sharon said, tapping a finger on the table. "She'd be close to the washer and dryer. Since we've been living in the apartment, I've made laundry Jennifer's job. It's saved me all the hassle of taking it down to the laundry room and waiting. She does a good job with it. Does her homework while she waits. But it would be handy if her room was right next door to the laundry. She could watch television."

"Or talk on the phone. I've got a phone line down there. I could give her that number, then she'd have a private phone line too. We wouldn't have to wait for her to get out of the bathroom or get off the phone."

"I'm sold," Sharon said. "And I'm sure Jennifer will love it. Especially after we repaint and add some new curtains"

"Mottled money milk! Shoulda seen that coming. Yeah, we can spring for a little decorating. I was thinking we could turn Jennifer's old bedroom into a joint office for both of us."

Sharon arched her eyebrows. "It's not big enough for two offices."

"We could bring up that old kitchen table from the basement. Put it in the middle of the room with two computers, back to back, and we could sit across from each other and talk about our work, like we are now."

"You're full of ideas, aren't you?"

"It's all I've been thinking about since you said you will be coming home in a few weeks."

Sharon reached for Duke's hand.

"We're going to work it out this time," she said. "I'm glad you could come to dinner tonight so I didn't have to eat alone. But now I really do need to get some work done."

"Spaniel splatter," Duke said, jumping to his feet. "I got things to do too. So how is the job? Are you enjoying being back in a classroom?"

"Everything has changed," Sharon said, shaking her head. "I feel like a stranger in a new land. They keep the lesson plans in computers now. Even the tests. Everything is Apple at school and I have this old PC at home. I can't even use the same programs."

"We'll get an Apple," Duke said, pulling Sharon out of her chair and into his arms. "Together, we can do anything."

"You're such a romantic."

Duke pulled her close and dipped her down into a showy, movie-ending kiss.

Chapter 21

Walking into the Bob Evans restaurant, Josie expected she would have no trouble recognizing Irwin MacDonald. She was carrying Tuesday's *Daily News*, hot off the press, just as she had told him she would. He saw the paper under her arm and stood up at the table. He didn't have a cap in his hands like the meek boy in her dream, but he had the same lean stature and slightly apologetic bow to the head.

"Mr. MacDonald," she said, offering her hand. "Sorry, I'm running late. I never can get away at lunchtime."

"Oh, no problem. I've only been here a few minutes myself."

Irwin waited until Josie sat down before he took his seat again.

"I couldn't believe it when I got this message that someone from the *Jordan Daily News* wanted to see me. I lived and worked here for forty years, and no one from the paper ever wanted to interview me. Now I move away and suddenly I'm a celebrity."

"Well, I'm just delighted that you happened to be in town and could spare me a few minutes," Josie said.

"I always stay in Jordan whenever I've got work in Chicago," he said with a shrug. "It just feels like home. And I try to get together with old friends while I'm in the area."

Josie and Irwin chatted about recent changes in the community, including the previous summer's killing spree, as they put in their orders and waited for the food to arrive.

"So what kind of story are you working on?" Irwin asked as he slathered butter on a warm biscuit.

"I'm looking into the disappearance of Zelda Machinko in 1956."

Irwin paused as he chewed a bite of biscuit, then spoke. "Well, I figured you must be doing something from the past if you wanted to talk to me, but that story goes a long way back. I was just a kid."

"I realize that. You were one of the paperboys for the *Spectator*."

He smiled. "You've done your research. But I can't help you much since I was so young. I don't remember much about it."

"I thought maybe you'd have some stories. Everybody who was around then seems to have a story about Zelda," Josie said, as she cut into her steaming chicken pot pie.

"Sorry to disappoint," Irwin said, slicing his smoked sausage. "About the only thing I remember is she was a stickler for counting coins. Had her own method of making little stacks adding up to a dollar. Then you just count the stacks to get the total. I still count coins that way. Taught my kids that way too. Is that the kind of stuff you want?"

Josie smiled, remembering the dream. Somehow she knew that too.

"Yes, that's a great detail," she said, making a note on her pad. "What do you remember about the last time you saw her? Do you know anything about the night she disappeared?"

Irwin shrugged and shook his head. "Sorry."

Josie didn't have any proof that Irwin was lying, just a gut feeling. She could hardly say her dreams told her otherwise. But her dreams had been right so far. She thought of the ledger in the dream, where Zelda recorded the carrier's payment. Josie hadn't been able to find that ledger, but Irwin didn't know that. Bluffing always had been her long suit.

"I found a ledger in the archives," Josie said without looking up. "You're listed as making a payment the day before she disappeared. And the payment is initialed by Zelda, so you must have seen her.

Irwin laid down his knife and fork. "Wow, it's amazing you found those records after all these years."

"Did the police talk to you about her disappearance?"

"No, not at all. That's why I'm surprised there was a record. They must have ignored it back then, thinking paperboys wouldn't know much. And they'd be right."

"But you did see her the night before she disappeared," Josie persisted.

"What makes you think it was night? Did she record the time I made my payment?" Irwin asked, slicing into his meat with gusto. He wasn't confirming Josie's suppositions, but he wasn't denying them either. She forged ahead.

"Well, like I said, Zelda initialed your payment. All the others for that date were initialed by the bookkeeper, so I assumed you came in after the bookkeeper went home. After 5 p.m."

"Assume? You're going to write a story on assumptions?"

"No, I just thought—"

Irwin smiled weakly. "Look, I'm sorry if I can't be any help, but you are asking about something that happened thirty years ago. I was just a kid. How can I remember when I last saw Zelda? I mean, Miss Machinko. We never called her by her first name when she was alive, but after she disappeared she became a legend. People that never met her started calling her by her first name. Even you keep calling her Zelda. I don't want to be part of assumptions and legends, if it's all the same to you."

Josie and Irwin ate in silence for a few minutes.

"I have a confession to make," Josie said. "I'm not writing a story. I'm looking into this for a friend of mine, Maggie Sheffield. She had a stroke, and I thought maybe if I could follow up on this story about her friend, it would help somehow."

"I remember Maggie Sheffield. She was the court reporter," Irwin said. "She had a stroke?"

Josie brought Irwin up to date on Maggie's condition, and they shared memories about stories Maggie had covered over the years.

"You know, it's funny that you should mention Mrs. Sheffield, because I think the first time I ever saw her she was with Miss Machinko. They were friends, like you said. And one year when the Chamber of Commerce had a Christmas ball, I got a job in the cloakroom. I remember Miss Machinko brought orchid corsages for herself and Mrs. Sheffield. I knew about it because it was terribly cold that night, and they wore these big heavy coats. They didn't want the coats to crush their flowers, so Miss Machinko brought the flowers in a box. They pinned them on each other after they took their coats off, just outside the cloakroom."

"Wow, that's a great story," Josie said, making hurried notes in her notebook. "I can't wait to talk to Maggie about that. I'm sure she'll remember. You know, Irwin, it's amazing you remember great details like that, and you don't remember the night Zelda disappeared."

Irwin cleaned up the last few bites on his plate while Josie watched silently. Finally he spoke.

"I remember the night Miss Machinko disappeared, but I wouldn't want anything to run in the paper about it. Can we keep this off the record?"

Josie nodded.

"It was like you said. I dropped off my payment after five o'clock, and Miss Machinko was the only one there. I dropped some money on the floor, and I was under one of the desks picking it up when he came in."

"Who?"

"I don't know who he was. Just a man in a dark suit."

"Dark suit," Josie repeated.

"Yeah, he kind of surprised her, and they tussled a little bit. But it was kind of friendly like. They bantered back and forth. You have to know how Miss Machinko was. She loved to have a battle of wits."

"Could you hear what they were saying?"

"Just snatches of it. Suddenly he grabbed her and kissed her roughly. She slapped him and they left together. He had his arm around her, pushing her, and she seemed to be dragging her feet, but she wasn't really struggling that much. I thought it was just a friendly scuffle until I saw in the paper a few days later that she was missing."

"Why didn't you ever tell anybody about this?"

"I was embarrassed."

"Embarrassed?"

"I was a young teen. Just barely thirteen. To me, Zelda Machinko was a glamorous woman, a movie star. I guess I had a teenage fantasy for her. I told her I was late delivering my payment because of my sister, but the truth is I liked coming into the office late when it was just me and her. Not that she ever knew, unless she saw the bulge in my pants."

Josie was surprised that Irwin was being so frank.

"I've raised two boys, and I've explained to them hundreds of times about those irrational sexual urges teenage boys get. It's natural, and I can joke about it now. But in the '50s, nobody talked about those things. When that man came in and grabbed her, she pushed him and struggled a bit, but to me they were acting out a passionate romance. I saw what I wanted to see, a man gone wild with passion for a woman who plays hard to get, but really loves him. It seemed very sexy to me. If I had thought for a second that she was in trouble, I would have jumped up from under that desk and fought to protect her."

"Maybe she knew that. Maybe she went along to get him away from you so he wouldn't find you and hurt you. Is that possible?"

"I thought of that, years later, when I became a parent. And you're probably right. That's probably exactly why she left with him. At the time, it never occurred to me. I told you, what I saw was a rough romance. He was dark and brooding like Bogie in *Casablanca*. When I saw in the paper that she was missing and they suspected gangsters had kidnapped her and probably killed her, I couldn't come forward. I was there, but I didn't do anything to stop it. He was probably going to rape her, and I had mistaken violence for romance. No wonder I was embarrassed. I'm still embarrassed to admit I could have been so disrespectful of her as a woman. If my wife or daughter ever knew. You see why I can never be associated with this story."

Josie thought for a moment.

"Just one man. That doesn't sound like gangsters. I imagine they come in pairs. Like cops. One man. Maybe your sense of it was right. This man did have a thing for her, and she went along with him, thinking she could get away as soon as she got him out of the office where you were at risk."

"But she kicked off her shoe," he said. "Didn't they say that was supposed to be a sign?"

"I know. Maybe he was one of the gangsters. One of Boardman's men. Maybe it was Boardman. Did you hear anything that might explain who the man was or where he was taking her?"

"Whatever they said, it fit in with my fantasy of sexual play. I don't remember what she called him if she called him by name, but I'm certain of one thing: She knew him."

Chapter 22

Zelda

Christmas makes me schmaltzy. I'm proud to be level-headed, even a little tough most of the time. But once a year I like to believe peace on earth might be possible and calories don't count. That's why I ask Maggie to go with me to the Christmas Ball sponsored by the Chamber of Commerce.

It's at the Herkimer, the finest hotel in town. Well, actually the oldest and the biggest hotel and the only one with a ballroom. The new Holiday Inn has a swimming pool, but no ballroom. Makes sense. People can go swimming every day, and they only have a ball at Christmas. But then we all know how the Herkimer fills its ballroom the rest of the year, don't we?

That's the real reason I'm at this Christmas Ball, a little reconnaissance. Not that I expect the roulette wheel is hiding behind the Christmas tree, but I want to get the lay of the land. See who shows up, who drinks with Boardman, and who seems just a little too comfortable, if you know what I mean.

Maggie's husband, George, is a straight cop. He'd cramp our style. So I convince her to leave him at home to take care of the baby.

"You deserve a night out, a little music, a pretty dress, and lobster. They are serving lobster, the food of kings."

"I don't know," Maggie keeps saying. Sometimes I think the girl doesn't like to have fun.

"I need your help," I say. "If I go alone, all the suits will think I'm fair game, and I don't want to spend the evening fending off advances."

That makes Maggie laugh. "So you think I'll scare them off? You must think I look like a witch."

"Not at all. Everyone knows you're a happily married lady and mother. Maybe some of your respectability will rub off on me."

So she agrees, and I bring orchid corsages for both of us. I've never seen an orchid without a ribbon and a pin attached. They're not like roses or carnations or mums. They don't grow in anybody's garden. They only come in those little white florist boxes. And they last a week or more in the Fridgidare. Every time I open it to get cream for my coffee, there's the orchid smiling at me, singing some exotic song of tropical places I'll never see.

"How about Georgie Porgie? Has he ever given you a corsage?" I ask Maggie as I pin the little lavender blossom to her green velvet dress.

"No, George thinks flowers are a waste of money," Maggie says, crooking her neck to get a whiff of the dainty bloom. "He woos with more solid stuff, like steak dinners."

Maggie takes the second corsage, a white one with bright-gold stamen, and pulls out the pin so she can attach it to my snug red satin number. My dress has tiny spaghetti straps, so Maggie has to work a bit to find a way to anchor the flower without pricking me.

"How about you?" she says. "Has some mystery man ever showered you with flowers?"

"Nope. I wouldn't accept them if he did," I say. "Flowers are just a sneaky form of manipulation. The guy struts around like a cock rooster, looking like a hero, and the poor lady has no choice but to submit. It's all about male domination."

Maggie finally attaches my corsage and stands back, shaking her head. "You see the worst in everything."

"That's because everything men do is to keep control, like George sticking you with a baby. You can't go anywhere anymore. Does he ever tell the police chief he can't work late because he has a baby at home? Of course not. And does he cancel his weekly poker game to stay home with the baby? Of course not."

My point made, I strut off to join the party. Maggie scampers after me.

"George didn't stick me with anything," she says. "I wanted a family. The family is the very foundation of our society."

That stops me in my tracks. "Exactly! Our male-dominated society."

A waiter passes by with a tray of champagne glasses and I snag two.

"Here, let's drink to feminine wiles. At least for tonight we can be in charge."

We clink glasses and each take a sip.

"The problem is you don't understand the difference between love and domination," Maggie says.

"Funny, I was just going to say the same thing about you."

"Domination is using fear or threats to take control of another person," Maggie says.

"And love is when a person willingly concedes control to another," I say, walking away.

We drift apart for a while. Maggie is talking with her coworkers from the *Daily News* or friends from the police department. I have my associates too. I make the rounds. No matter who I talk to, I never listen. I'm always thinking, What's he up to? Or watching to see what's going on across the room. Before dinner is served, we go to our marked places at the media table. Maggie is seated next to me, but we act like we barely know each other, talking mostly to everyone else.

The lobster is divine.

"You know, someday when I'm rich, I'm going to wear orchids every day and eat lobster at every meal," I say loud enough for the whole table to hear.

"You'll never be rich writing for a newspaper," one of the *Spectator* reporters says. All the others agree. While our tablemates are laughing about the financial challenges of our chosen profession, Maggie leans over and whispers to me, "Is he here?"

"Who?" I whisper back without looking at her.

"The man of your dreams."

I smile. "Of course he is."

"Anyone I might know?"

"Maggie, that's my secret."

"What secret?" the *Herald* reporter says. "What exposé are you working on now, Zelda Machinko?"

"You'll have to wait and read about it in the *Spectator*," I say.

As soon as the dessert dishes are picked up, the band begins to play. The others wander away from the table to dance or get another drink. Suddenly, Humphrey Bogart is standing there in a white tuxedo jacket. We dance away, pausing only briefly to look back at Maggie. She's gray-headed and wrinkled, bent over in a wheelchair. She's wearing a hospital gown and a dried-up corsage.

Josie bolted upright. Her bedroom was dark and it took a few seconds to get her bearings. Maggie from the past; Maggie in the present. The glory days of an old hotel now serving as a nursing home. A missing editor; a mystery lover. And orchids.

Josie looked at the digital clock. Four thirteen. She lay back and rolled to one side. What did it all mean?

Chapter 23

The witness wasted no time picking Ron Baylor out of the lineup.

"Number three," she said as soon as the men faced forward. "No question. He's the one I saw standing in front of the trailer."

"A setup," his lawyer said. "There are only two big guys in the line, and they're both suspects. Either one she picks, you cops win. Means nothing."

But Tom was smiling. Running the sketch in the newspaper had been a huge success. Several anonymous tipsters had named construction worker Ron Baylor as matching the description, and several more named his buddy Herbert Flatt. The two did have similar builds and worked together, so it wasn't too surprising that tipsters might confuse the two. Tom placed both of them in the lineup, along with four city employees as big and beefy as he could find. But Baylor's attorney was right. None were quite as big and rugged looking as Baylor and Flatt.

Police had picked up the men at the construction site, and company owner Terry Tate had sent attorneys over so quickly that Tom hadn't been able to get much out of either man. Baylor insisted he had never been to Blaine Avril's trailer in the small Riverside Campground. He insisted he'd never been to the campground in the entire thirty-two years of his life.

But Tom had an ace up his sleeve.

"Do you recognize this?" Tom said, tossing a wallet-size flip-pack of photographs onto the gray metal table. Baylor barely glanced at it.

"Nope," he said, his standard answer to all questions.

"Pick it up. Look a little closer," Tom said. "Have you seen this before?"

"Nope," Baylor repeated without touching the photos.

"If you don't have anything else," the attorney said, closing his briefcase and preparing to leave the interview room.

"Wait, he hasn't looked at the pictures," Tom said. "Several people have told us Mr. Baylor bragged about Avril showing him a photo of an 'ugly baby.' I'm just wondering if he can pick out that photo."

Baylor shrugged. "Guys show off photos all the time. I don't remember what they looked like or who showed them to me. Jeez."

"Just take a look," Tom said, holding out the photo pack until Baylor accepted it. "Several people remembered you saying Avril showed you a picture of his wife and baby. Could this be the photo he showed you?"

Baylor looked at the first photo and tossed the packet back on the table. "Maybe."

"Do you remember commenting on the 'ugly baby'?"

"What if I did? Is that a crime?"

"No. The comment isn't a crime, but it might be a motive," Tom said. "If Avril heard you call his baby ugly, he might have jumped you. Might have started a fight. Is that what happened?"

"A fight? Are you crazy? I didn't have no fight with this Avril character."

Curiosity was getting the better of Baylor. He picked up the packet. "Yeah. This is the picture. Look at that baby. Did you ever see such an ugly puss?"

Baylor held up the packet so his attorney could see the photo.

"What does this have to do with anything?" the attorney said. "The child is obviously deformed."

"Yes, the child has a cleft lip and palate," Tom said. "It's a fairly common deformity. One in about every 700 births. But it's repairable. This little girl will be cute enough to be prom queen when she grows up."

"That's all very interesting," the attorney replied, "but it doesn't have anything to do with my client."

"Is that the photo you said Blaine Avril showed you?" Tom asked.

"Yeah," Baylor said. "That's the photo."

"And where did you see this photo?"

"Hell, I don't know. At the bar, I guess."

"And based on this photo, you told several people that Avril had an ugly baby."

"Yeah, I did. It's the truth."

"Do you know when you saw this photo?"

"Hell, no."

"Avril was on the project a little over a week. Did you see it the first time you met him?"

"Yeah, maybe so."

"But nobody else we've talked to ever saw the photo. Why did Avril show it to you and nobody else?"

"How should I know?"

"But this is definitely the photo you saw."

Baylor picked up the photo pack and looked again. "Yeah, it was this photo, all right. Man, that's an ugly baby."

"And you are saying you saw the photo in Avril's wallet."

"That's what I've said a hundred times."

Baylor tossed the packet back on the table and Tom picked it up.

"Do you think maybe you saw this picture at Avril's trailer, at the campground?"

"No, because I never went to the trailer."

"That's funny, because this is Avril's wallet," Tom said, tossing a small leather tri-fold onto the table. "He didn't have *any* photos in it. It doesn't even have a place to put photos. This photo packet is from my wallet," Tom added, flipping to pictures of his sister and other relatives.

Tom pulled out the photo of Avril's wife and baby and laid it on the table. "This is a copy of an eight-by-ten photograph we found in a frame at the trailer. It was hanging just inside the door. You couldn't have missed it when you went out there to kill Avril."

"I didn't—"

"You did. That's the only way you could have seen this photograph. The only way you could have known about the ugly baby. Avril never showed the photo to the other workers. No one else here ever saw it. Only you, because you were in his trailer."

"I never went to the trailer," Baylor repeated, glaring at Tom.

The attorney stood up. "If that's the best you can do to put my client at the scene of a reported confrontation, then I think you've wasted enough of my time. Come on, Mr. Baylor, we're leaving."

The attorney and Baylor headed for the door. As soon as they left, Fred Wheeler and his partner from the Justice Department stepped into the room. Wheeler closed the door.

"What the hell do you think you're doing? You're going to blow this whole case."

"I'm blowing the case?" Tom said. "I'm the only one who's doing anything to nab a couple of killers."

"Yeah, sure. Even if you can build a case against Baylor and Flatt, they're just the tip of the iceberg," Wheeler said. "They're just following orders."

"I agree. Avril, or whatever his name is, was investigating something much bigger. But I can't just let a couple of killers run loose. They get by with this, they'll kill again. If I turn up the pressure, maybe they'll cut a deal, hand us Tate or whoever gave the orders."

Wheeler shook his head. "They don't know who gave the orders. Don't you realize this is bigger than Tate and his piddly construction company? Do you know how many road construction contracts are awarded in Illinois every year? How much money is skimmed off the top before the first shovel hits the dirt? There's every reason to believe this network extends beyond Illinois, maybe even beyond the United States."

"Well, if Baylor and Flatt and Tate are so 'piddly,' then it won't hurt your case none if I put them behind bars for killing a guy in a campground," Tom said. "He was one of your agents. Don't you care about that?"

"Yeah, I care. But the job comes with risks," Wheeler said. "I'm trying to preserve as much of this operation as I can. We were making progress."

"But his cover was blown."

"Not necessarily. The agent screwed up. Got himself killed. They figured out he was spying on them, but they probably think he was from another construction company. That's all part of the plan. It's a setback, but it's not checkmate."

"Checkmate? This is just some high-stakes game to you? Fine. Go ahead. Investigate world corruption. I don't care. But when the corrupters start shedding blood in my town, I'm not going to pretend it didn't happen."

Chapter 24

Tom had been looking forward to Friday evening. He had promised to take his sister to Charley's Piano Bar, where they would show off some of the four-hand melodies they practiced at home. He had invited Becky— he wouldn't dare pass up an opportunity to impress Becky. To insure Becky would come, he'd also invited Duke and Sharon.

"What should we do first, what should we do first?" Linda said excitedly. "What do you want to hear? I can play anything."

"Well, not anything," Tom said, taking a long pull from his beer.

Duke and Sharon exchanged glances. They weren't sure what to expect. Was Linda a prodigy as she claimed or would they need to applaud politely when she picked out a few notes and missed a few more?

Becky tried to be encouraging. "Do you know chopsticks?"

"Yeah, let's do chopsticks," Linda said, sitting down at the piano. With two chubby fingers, she started picking out the simple beginning of the familiar tune.

"Nah, that can get old," Tom said, joining his sister on the piano bench. "Let's do something nice and slow to begin with."

"The Goetz 'Sonata,'" Linda said. "That's slow."

"Yes, let's start with that." Tom looked down to check that his foot was on the right pedal. Becky, Duke, and Sharon brought their drinks and leaned against the baby grand.

"Ready?" Tom asked.

"Ready," Linda replied.

Tom started out the somber melody, with Linda adding a note or two with one hand. Slowly, mournfully the piano sighed as Tom swayed and Linda followed suit. As the intensity built, Linda added both hands to the keys, and the melody trilled down the ivories as if all four hands were expressions of the same body. Soon, everyone in the bar was gathered around the piano, applauding.

Linda stood and bowed formally. Tom just smiled.

"Can you do more? Can you really do more?" Becky asked.

"Sure," Tom said. "You wanted to hear chopsticks. We have our own version."

"Let me start! Let me start!" Linda said, taking her seat again.

"No, the bass starts," Tom said, starting a slow, steady beat.

"Oh, yeah," Linda said, nodding her head in time with her brother's bass beat while she awaited her signal. Suddenly she started playing the two-finger melody from before, then expanded it until once again all four hands were dancing across the keys together. The crowd, as they say, went wild.

For their finale, they played a boogie-woogie, getting up from the bench and dancing around each other to take turns at the keyboard. The whole bar applauded. Linda couldn't stop bowing. When the bartender offered her a drink on the house, she said she'd prefer hers in a plastic cup. She ordered a chocolate malt with extra ice cream.

"She's really very talented," Becky said.

"Yeah, she's got the knack," Tom said. It was the first time he and Becky had been able to chat one-on-one all night. "Hey, you got some time Sunday? Mom would like to meet you. She said to bring you by for dinner after church. Maybe Linda will play one of her solo numbers."

"Your mom wants to meet me?" Becky said, biting her lip. "Ah, I don't know.... Yeah, I guess. That sounds nice. What can I bring?"

"Dessert. Linda adores sweets."

When Linda finished her shake, she returned to the piano bench. Sharon and Becky joined her for basic lessons in chopsticks. At a nearby table, Duke sipped his coffee while Tom guzzled his second beer of the evening as if piano playing was as strenuous as a three-legged race.

"It's been quite a week," Duke said.

"Yep," Tom agreed.

"So what about Baylor and Flatt? Do they look good for Avril's murder?"

"They did it. No question. Proving it is going to be tough, but I think I can do it if the feds don't get in the way."

"Which they will."

"You know, that's what I thought too, but something's screwy," Tom said, finishing his beer and raising his hand to order another. "The chief hasn't called me in and told me to stay clear. Instead, he's been meeting with the coroner and the mayor. I don't know what they've been plotting."

"Divine defecation! The mayor too?" Duke said, twisting his lips in a puzzled pose. "I figured the coroner was in on it, but I didn't suspect the chief and the mayor."

"What do you mean, 'in on it'?" Tom asked.

"Think about it. If the feds are investigating a local sewer contract, it has to be because the local authorities are breaking the law somehow."

"Good God. How do we prove that?"

"I don't know. Who ya gonna trust?"

Duke wanted a beer in the worst way, especially when the waitress set another bottle in front of Tom with droplets of sweat cascading down the side. If Duke drank another cup of coffee, he wouldn't sleep for a week. Suddenly, Sharon was at his side holding out a tall frosted glass of tonic water with a lime twist on the top.

"I thought you might like a drink," she said.

Duke took the glass and started sipping right away. She was an angel and a mind reader.

"Remember, you guys, no fair talking business," Sharon said.

"Never," Tom said. "How 'bout them Cubs?"

Sharon shook her head and walked away. As soon as she was out of earshot, the conversation returned to business.

"I've been looking into the ownership of the Herkimer and the Red Geranium," Duke said. "I'm not sure if it's related to the sewer contract, but I suspect some of the same people are involved."

"In real estate? What are you thinking?"

"Well, both buildings were pretty much abandoned before they were purchased five years ago. County records show the county sold the Herk for $77,000 in back taxes. And even though no building permit was issued for any restoration, the county turned around a year later and started renting the same building at $140,000 a year."

"Good grief. Why would they pay more than the sales price just to rent it?"

"Because it's a federally funded program, and the outrage is buried in paperwork," Duke said, playing with the straw in his drink.

"So who owns it?"

"That's the snag. It's held in a blind trust, and the law says they don't have to reveal the principals. But I know one thing. The coroner is on the board of Herkimer House."

"That seems logical. Guess a lot of people die in a nursing home," Tom said, setting down his empty bottle.

"Yep, wouldn't raise an eyebrow."

"You know, I've been thinking that Baylor and Flatt really blew it," Tom said, leaning back. "If the coroner is involved, like you say, and they wanted to get rid of a nosy federal investigator, why didn't he just fall victim to an accident on the job site? If they hadn't put a bullet in his head, the coroner's inquiry could have glossed right over it. No one would have been the wiser. And why did they bring the body downtown to the construction site where it was sure to be connected to the project? If they had left him in the campground, he would have just been some guy passing through. We may never have made the connection. If Tate ordered these guys to get rid of the problem, he must be really pissed because the whole thing points at Tate now."

"T-Rex Tootsie Rolls! I hear what you're saying," Duke exclaimed. "Baylor and Flatt are probably in a truckload of turds from Tate and our control-freak coroner. You're thinking the bungling boys may be agreeable to a little police protection?"

"Could be, if I can ever talk to them without Tate's legal team running interference," Tom said.

"Well, the police may need to read 'em their rights, but I don't," Duke said, holding a hand up for a high five from Tom.

Chapter 25

Zach arrived Saturday morning with a sack full of treats for Chippie and Buttons.

"How did you know we had dogs?" Josie asked.

Zach shrugged and looked at Kevin. "Every boy's gotta have a dog, am I right?"

Kevin laughed, took the bag of treats, and used them to show off Chippie's repertoire of dog tricks—sit, shake, roll over. Buttons took his bone and ran under the dining room table to chew it. Zach said he could teach Chippie a new trick. He gave the sit command, and when the golden retriever was sitting at attention, he placed the treat on his snout. He held a finger on the dog's nose and kept repeating the command, "Wait." Zach pulled his hand away and said "OK." Chippie snapped and the treat fell to the floor.

"Nope, you can't have the treat yet," Zach said, snatching the bone from the floor. He repeated the process three more times before Chippie caught the bone in his mouth before it fell to the floor. Everyone cheered.

"Now you have to work on getting him to wait for his treat even when you take your hand off his nose," Zach said. "He needs to wait just because you say so. This may take a few days. We'll try again when we get back. Is everybody ready to go? Did you brush your teeth?"

Josie and Kevin exchanged glances and then nodded.

"Good. There's a story behind that question," Zach said as he led Josie and Kevin to his gold Mercedes in the driveway. "My father was a dentist. He always asked if we'd brushed our teeth before we went anywhere."

"A dentist? Oh, yuck," Kevin said.

"Kevin, that's not nice," Josie chided.

"Oh, that's OK," Zach said. "Nobody likes the dentist. I think most people would rather face a robber with a gun than a dentist with a drill."

"Any day," Kevin said, climbing in the back seat and buckling his seat belt. Zach closed Kevin's door and opened the front door for Josie.

"Is Mr. Zach a dentist too?" Kevin asked as Zach was walking around the car.

"No, honey, he's a …" Josie was at a loss to describe "coroner" to her son. "Kevin asked if you're a dentist," she said as Zach took his place behind the steering wheel. "How should I describe your career?"

"I'm the candy man," Zach said without skipping a beat. "Remember that song in *Willie Wonka and the Chocolate Factory*? Well, that's where we're going today. It's not a chocolate factory. It's even better. It's a bubble gum factory, and it's all mine," Zach said, rubbing his hands together and making googly eyes.

Kevin laughed with delight.

Zach continued talking animatedly on the hour drive to the Pop-O bubble gum plant.

"Like I said, Dad was a dentist, and he thought it was terrible that people chewed sugary gum. It's very bad for your teeth. So he invented a sugarless gum. And to make it even more fun, he made sugarless bubble gum."

"Does it still taste good?" Kevin asked.

"Oh, the best. You'll get to taste it and see."

Zach made the factory's story sound like a fairy tale. His father, the faithful dentist, kept creating different recipes in the kitchen, trying to come up with a tasty gum with no sugar. Zach described the whole family sitting around the kitchen table trying to blow bubbles, testing the elasticity of various recipes.

"But it takes lots of money to build a factory, and my dad didn't have that much money. My grandpa gave him some money to build his first factory and buy enough ingredients to make a batch of gum big enough for all the kids in Chicago. Last year Pop-O sold a billion dollars' worth of gum all over the world.

"My mother—that's grandpa's little girl—always called her father Pop-O. That was sort of her slang for Daddy-o, which all the beatnik people said in those days. Anyway, people think the gum is named Pop-O because the bubbles pop, but it's really named after my grandpa."

When Zach's car pulled into the curving driveway, the factory didn't look exciting from the outside. It was a large one-story building in an industrial park. It looked like it could be an assembly plant for dryer controls or a warehouse full of car parts. There was no movie-land gingerbread structure, just a big white sign with the green Pop-O logo. The reception area and offices were routine, not much different than the *Daily News* office. Josie was afraid Zach's tales of fantasy had been overstated.

Then a man in a white coat walked in. A man in a white coat with a net over his hair and powdered sugar on his nose.

"Paul here is going to show us around," Zach said. He gave Paul a hearty pat on the back, and a white cloud of dust rose like steam from a boiling pot.

"First, everyone needs to put these on," Zach said, handing out white coats and hair nets. "It's a little messy inside."

Kevin received a special "junior taster" coat that was just his size. Zach also passed out blue paper covers for their shoes.

"Ready?" Paul said with a mischievous smile. He took them down a hall, opened a door, and everything changed. The cloud of white powder that puffed off Paul's clothes when he walked suddenly filled the air. Through the sugary haze, Josie could see a collection of factory machines. One was a mechanical arm stirring a giant vat. Another extruded pink ropes of gum. Another chopped the ropes into one-inch pieces with a methodical thud. The chunks of gum fell onto a belt that moved through another machine that wrapped bright-green paper around each piece. The little green packages were funneled into boxes, which were stamped and sealed and stacked. Just like car parts. Or dryer controls. A factory, just like any other factory. Except all the machines were covered in a cloud of what looked like powdered sugar.

"It's actually a starch," Paul said, shouting to be heard over the whir of machinery. "We have to use lots of it to keep the product from gumming up the works." He chuckled at his pun, but Josie and Kevin were too enthralled by the spectacle to pay much attention. At one end of the line, a mountain of raw gum stood taller than the man who shoveled the concoction like pink coal into the jaws of the machinery.

The room smelled like grape Kool-Aid, sweet and fruity. As they walked beside the machinery, the river of pink chunks of gum kept flowing—logs, snapped into chunks and wrapped—again and again and again.

Eventually Zach thanked Paul and escorted his guests through a door at the other end of the room. This was a laboratory, just like Josie remembered from high school chemistry, with long black counters and beakers of shiny amber liquid.

"Mitch will show us what happens here," Zach said, pointing to another man in white coat, minus the sugar coating. Mitch wasn't as cheerful as Paul. Speaking softly, barely above a whisper, he talked about chemicals with long names and reactions and bonds and tensile strength and other terms Josie couldn't understand.

"So I have set up a test," he said, pointing to a counter with four black stools lined up. In front of each was a little glass petri dish with a carefully measured chunk of pink gum. It appeared to be the very same gum that was being shaped and cut and wrapped next door. The lab, however, offered none of the whimsy of the factory.

"Now if you will take a seat, we will each test a different batch—A, B, C, and D. Just take the gum like this and chew for exactly two minutes."

Mitch put one of the pink chunks in his mouth, and Kevin quickly obeyed. Josie and Zach laughed a little before they complied.

"We must time this exactly if we want measurable results," Mitch said between smacks of his mouthful of gum.

"I am assuming everyone knows how to blow a bubble, but just in case, I will elaborate. Once the gum has been chewed for two minutes to obtain optimum uniformity, use your tongue to flatten your portion against the back of your teeth, and then use your tongue to poke it through the space between your upper and lower teeth—"

"We know, we know," Kevin said and started to press a little pink gum between his lips.

"No, the two minutes are not up yet," Mitch said, consulting his watch. "We will be going for the biggest, long-lasting bubble. Blips that pop don't count."

Mitch watched his timepiece. "OK ... get ready ... set ... blow."

Not surprisingly, Kevin was the first to achieve a bubble, followed closely by Zach. Mitch and Josie weren't far behind, but Josie's burst first, mostly because she couldn't help laughing at three adults blowing bubbles. Zach's burst soon after Josie's. Mitch seemed to have the best control, growing his bubble slowly, but Kevin's was the biggest. Kevin and Mitch each held out, but Kevin was the winner with the longest lasting and biggest bubble.

"Batch C," Mitch said, making a note on his pad. "That's a consistent winner."

"You mean my gum was better?" Kevin asked. "I thought I was just a better blower."

"Well, that too," Mitch said, allowing the smallest smile.

"You mean you test bubble gum for a living?" Josie asked, spitting her wad into a tissue. "Do you have some sort of degree to do this kind of work?"

"A doctorate in chemistry," Mitch said without a glimmer of a smile.

❀

When they reached the car, Zach and Josie burst out laughing.

"Remember, chew for exactly two minutes," Zach said in Mitch's nasal tone.

"For optimum uniformity," Josie added, and they laughed some more.

"Oh, I wish I had had a camera," Josie said. "Mitch looked so ridiculously serious with his white coat and stopwatch and diploma on the wall. And you, Mr. Coroner. The next election, when your photo is plastered all over town, I'm going to come around with a marker and draw a big pink bubble in your mouth."

Zach laughed. "Hey, it's better than adding a mustache. I'll tell my campaign manager. Maybe that would be a good attention getter."

Kevin arrived at the car a little behind the adults, carrying his reward: a box of 100 pieces of Pop-O bubble gum. When he tried to open the door to the back seat, the box slipped from his hands and spilled all over the pavement, scattering little green-wrapped bundles.

"Stupid car," Kevin huffed in frustration and kicked at the back tire.

"Kevin!" Josie exclaimed, stepping out of the front seat. "Don't blame the car. Now tell Mr. Teasdale you are sorry."

"I'm not sorry," Kevin said, stomping his feet and smashing some of the gum bundles. "I was the best blower. I blew the best bubble. And that doctor man said it was because it was better gum. He was just jealous because my bubble was bigger."

"Kevin, this isn't like you," Josie said, placing a calming hand on her son's shoulder. He pulled away and continued stomping on the scattered pieces of gum.

"Well, that's a new use for Pop-O gum," Zach said as he came around from the other side of the car and watched Kevin's tantrum.

"I'm so sorry," Josie said. She was on her knees picking up pieces of gum.

Zach picked up the half-empty box and handed it to Kevin. "Here, you can use this to collect the pieces that didn't get stepped on."

Kevin scowled but took the box. He didn't make any effort to pick up the gum. Josie put a handful into the box and reached under the car to pick up some more.

"Don't bother," Zach said, putting a hand on Josie's shoulder. "Kevin can decide how much of his gum he wants to pick up, and I'll ask the custodian to sweep up the rest after we pull out." Zach held out a hand to help Josie to her feet, and she took it.

"I'm so sorry for the mess," she said.

"Why? You didn't make it," Zach said. Then looking at Kevin, he added, "Accidents happen."

Zach motioned to Josie to sit in the front seat and he closed the car door.

"Look, Kevin, some of the pieces scattered all the way to the front of the car," Zach said, pointing to some pieces on the ground. "Do you think maybe this is better gum because it fell the farthest?"

Kevin looked at Zach as if he wondered what he meant, but the boy headed to the front of the car and picked up those pieces of gum and walked back.

"Let me help you with this car door. It's pretty heavy," Zach said, opening the back door. "You know, when your hands are full and you've got a heavy car door to open, it's OK to ask for help."

Kevin set his half-full box of gum on the rear seat and got down on his knees to pick up the gum that was under the car.

"Would you like me to move the car? That might make it easier," Zach said.

"Yes, please," Kevin replied in a meek voice.

Zach drove the car forward a few feet, revealing a treasure trove of gum. Kevin gathered the pieces like Easter eggs and brought them by handfuls to his box in the back seat.

Zach and Josie sat in the front seat, not saying a word as Kevin gathered the pieces of gum, smashed and unsmashed, and put them into his box.

"You are handling this very well," Josie whispered. "Where did you learn your parenting skills?"

"Handling children isn't much different than handling employees," Zach said, giving Josie a little smile. "You should know that."

After a minute or so, Zach got out and walked around the car. "Here, let me help you with that heavy car door."

"I picked up all the pieces," Kevin said proudly. "You don't need to call the custodian."

Josie looked back as Zach helped his young passenger connect his seat belt.

"That's very good, Kevin," Josie said, patting his knee. "I'm proud of you."

"My grandpa used to say, when you lose your temper, you lose. Everybody has accidents, but if you let it make you mad, it just gets worse," Zach said, closing Kevin's car door.

Zach got back in the car and turned toward Kevin. "You know, Kevin, I'm an expert in control. Your mom will tell you I'm a control freak. I want to control what the newspaper says about me and the cases I handle for the county even though it's not my job to control the newspaper." Zach looked over at Josie and she smiled.

"I learned a lot about control from my grandpa, who ran lots of businesses but never raised his voice. He would say, if you want to control big things, like a bubble gum factory or a newspaper, you have to first control yourself. And really, that's all you can control. You can't control other people. Like Doctor Mitch. You can't control how he runs his test or what he thinks about the results. You can only control your reaction. In the end, what you think is all that matters. If you know that you blew a bigger bubble because you are a better blower, you don't need Doctor Mitch to tell you so. You just have to believe in yourself.

"Sometimes it does matter what other people think. You can't just tell yourself you are the best speller in school. You have to prove it. You have to study, and you have to do well on the spelling tests. But the only way to do that is by controlling yourself. There's no other secret. You can become anything you want, from a champion soccer player to a prize-winning scientist, just by controlling yourself. And you know what? When you are in control of yourself, other people will notice. They will ask for your advice and your help. Before you know it, they will do what you ask. It may seem like you are controlling other people, but you are only controlling yourself."

"I know," Kevin said with a whine.

"If you want to learn self-control, you can start with little things like the tone of your voice," Zach said as he turned the key in the ignition.

"Tone?" Kevin asked. "What's that?"

"It's like blowing a bubble," Zach said, winking at Josie. "You have to chew your words carefully and then send them out gently or they will pop."

"Oh, I get it," Kevin said. "Like the way Mom can say my name, and sometimes it sounds like a fluffy blanket, and sometimes it sounds like an ax chopping down a tree.

"Kevin!" Josie exclaimed.

Zach looked at Kevin and the pair said in unison: "An ax."

Zach pulled out of the parking place and headed toward the highway.

"OK, Kevin," he said, "you get control over where we go to lunch."

"McDonald's!" Kevin shouted.

Zach smiled. "I figured as much. There's one close by, on the way to our afternoon stop at Brookfield Zoo."

Zach pulled into the nearby McDonald's and directed Josie and Kevin to the party room with its playground of colorful plastic balls. A few smaller kids were playing, and Kevin stayed back.

"Go ahead," Zach said.

"He's a little shy sometimes," Josie said.

"It's for little kids," Kevin said, taking a seat at a table.

"Oh, I see. You are too old for the balls. Well, you two have a seat and I'll go pick up the food. What does everyone want?"

They placed their orders and Zach was gone only a minute when Ronald McDonald burst into the room. All the children gathered around as the orange-wigged clown made little balloon animals and handed them out to the youngsters.

"How about you, young man?" the clown asked. "Don't you want a wiener dog?" He twisted red and blue balloons together and handed the dog to Kevin, who smiled ear to ear.

"You know, you look big enough to play cards," Ronald McDonald said, waving one hand over Kevin's head and magically pulling a card out of his hair. He handed Kevin the card and then pulled another and another and another from his hair.

"How many is that?" the clown asked, handing them to Kevin.

"Four," he responded, holding them up in one hand as Zach returned with a tray of food.

"Oh, here's the rest of the deck," the clown said, waving his hand over Zach's head and coming up with a fist full of cards. "Count them, there should be fifty-two." The clown moved to another table and pulled a nickel out of a girl's ear.

"Did you see what he did?" Kevin asked Josie.

"Are all the cards there?" Zach asked.

Kevin counted cards as Zach set the meals before them on the table. Josie was almost as excited as Kevin to see her son having so much fun.

"There's only forty-eight," Kevin announced.

"Well, that's enough for most games," Josie said. "You'd better eat your Happy Meal."

Kevin opened the box and inside were the missing four cards.

"How did he do that?" Kevin asked.

"Magicians have a lot of self-control," Zach said.

Ronald McDonald left a few minutes later, and Kevin calmed down enough to eat most of his burger and fries before running off to play with the other children in the jumble of multi-colored balls.

"Strange that Ronald McDonald would show up just as we got here," Josie said, sipping her Coke. "I thought he only came to birthday parties."

"And special occasions," Zach said, taking a sip of coffee.

"How many surprises do you have up that sleeve of yours?"

Zach smiled. "As many as it takes."

The next surprise was a private tour of the animal hospital at Brookfield Zoo, where Kevin got to see newly born snow leopard cubs. He was able to offer a bottle of milk to a young monkey and pet a velvety stingray floating in a plastic pool. By the time they returned to Jordan, Kevin was asleep in the back seat. When they pulled into the driveway, a car pulled in behind them and Bill and Chuck, Zach's assistants, got out.

"Did you have a nice time?" Bill asked.

"Looks like the little one is down for the count," Chuck added. "Want me to carry him inside?"

Josie knew that none of this was coincidence.

"Zach?" she said, spinning around.

"Oh, my! Sounds like an ax just missed my head," Zach said, with an elaborate ducking motion. "I've been taking control of too much again, haven't I? But wouldn't it be nice if Bill and Chuck took Kevin inside, maybe called out for a pizza if he's hungry. They could watch a little TV with him. And you and I could go have a nice grown-up dinner someplace."

Josie shook her head. "I swear, Zach Teasdale."

"Well, that was a little softer, maybe a rubber mallet."

"Have these guys been following us all day?"

"No. I called when we were leaving Brookfield and gave them an ETA."

"We've been waiting down the street about ten minutes, ma'am," Bill said.

Kevin stirred. "Mom?"

"I'm right here, Kevin."

The boy emerged from the car, rubbing his eyes.

"Well, look who's up and ready for a game of cards," Chuck said, waving a hand over Kevin's head and pulling a handful of cards out of his hair.

"Hey!" Kevin said.

"Ooops! Forgot to mention that Chuck sometimes moonlights as a clown magician with orange hair," Zach said.

"I thought you said they weren't following us," Josie said in her best sharpened ax voice.

"Well, not all day," Zach said.

"Yeah, we were waiting for you to arrive at McDonald's, and then we came back to Jordan," Bill said.

"I just don't know what to think," Josie said, shaking her head.

"Aw, come on," Zach said, nudging her gently. "I'll bet Chuck has several card games he can play with Kevin while they wait for a pizza to arrive. And Bill is real good at dog tricks. I'll bet he can help Kevin teach Chippie a new trick or two tonight while you and I go off for a nice quiet evening. He might even teach Buttons a couple of easy tricks. What do you say, Kevin? Does that sound like fun?"

Kevin fingered the latest batch of cards. "I guess so. Did you get these out of the car?" he said, turning to Chuck. "Are these the same ones from Ronald McDonald or are these different ones?"

"I don't know, let's count them and see," Chuck said, unloading Kevin's haul of prizes from the back seat.

"If you'll give me your key, ma'am, we'll head indoors and let the dogs out," Bill said. "They must be bursting at the seams. And I'll make sure the young man is in bed by whatever hour you say."

"Thanks, Bill," Josie said, pulling the key out of her purse and placing it in his hand. She turned to her son, who was busy counting cards with Chuck. "You behave, now."

"Sure, Mom," he said without looking up.

In an instant, Josie and Zach were on their way again.

"You are a whirlwind, Zach. I feel like I've been swept up by a tornado."

"Is that the same as being swept off your feet?" Zach asked, with a big smile.

"Perhaps. But I don't like the feeling."

"I know. It's all about control. We're both control freaks."

"I guess we are."

"How about we call a control truce?"

"OK. How does that work?"

"Well, I was planning on the Seafood House for dinner. They have great lobster. But I'll leave that choice up to you. We can go wherever you want, from health food salads at One Planet to your favorite pizza joint."

Josie was silent for a few seconds. "Lobster sounds good."

"OK. Seafood House it is."

"How did you do that? Let me make the choice knowing it would be the choice you had planned already?"

"Just like I knew Kevin would pick McDonald's for lunch. Anticipating what people want is good business."

The lobster dinner was every bit as good as Zach had predicted. As they nibbled away in the darkened restaurant, Zach told more stories about his father, who died when Zach was in college. Zach said his grandparents were gone too, and his mother usually stayed with his sister in Florida. "So I'm all alone."

"Alone with a football team of attendants."

"True. There are ten bedrooms at the compound, and most of them are in use with aides, housekeeper, and gardener. But in the main house, where I live, there's just one bedroom, a big master suite with a king-size bed that's empty most of the time. I usually fall asleep on the sofa if I sleep at all."

"Oh, come on. I've seen photos of you at social events, and there's always a pretty little thing on your arm."

"You hit the nail on the head. A pretty little thing. A puff of perfume and hairspray. Needless to say, I bulldoze right over most women. It's boring."

"So why do you do that?"

"Bulldoze?"

"Yeah. If you are such an expert in control, why don't you control your urge to run everything and nurture a woman so she can blossom?" Josie said, spearing a bite of lobster and dipping it in butter.

"Will you teach me how?" Zach said, running his chunk of lobster into the butter pot right next to Josie's.

"I suppose we could both learn something about nurturing each other," she said. The conversation seemed too heavy, so she changed the subject. "This lobster is just divine. The food of kings. I heard that somewhere."

Josie remembered where she had heard it. Her dream. Zelda said she wanted to live on lobster. Josie ran another chunk through the melted butter, and she had to agree.

"Would you like to visit the compound after we finish dinner?" Zach said, holding his wine glass up for a toast. "I can serve you an excellent cheesecake for dessert."

"And check out that big, empty bed? I'm not sure I'm ready for that," Josie said, clicking her glass against his. "Besides, I noticed on the dessert menu they have cheesecake here, with fresh raspberries."

Zach smiled. "Now I've done it. I've gone and told you one of my secret loves. When you know what someone loves, it gives you a way to control him."

"Me? Control you?"

He chuckled again. "OK. You're right. We can order cheesecake right here, where there isn't any pressure."

The two shared a small piece of cheesecake and more wine as they talked about their work and families.

"Maggie was moved into Herkimer House today," Josie said. "She's probably not going to get much better. She's in a wheelchair, and she can't talk very well. She just grunts. But she seems to recognize us. Katherine returned to California. I promised her we would check in on Maggie."

"I can have Bill stop in every afternoon, read her the newspaper, if you think that would help."

"Zach."

"Too controlling?"

"A little. I know you mean well, but your reach is scary sometimes."

"I'm not trying to be scary, but I do have several people on the payroll who have time to spare. I'm always looking for projects for them. What's the difference if I volunteer my time or theirs?"

"That's what's scary about it. An individual's time is limited, so the impact is minimal. But your time—extended through your staff—is … limitless."

"But if I'm doing good for the community, how is that wrong? If my money and my power scare you, I don't know how I can prevent that. I am who I am."

Zach paused as the waitress removed the dessert plate and refilled the wine glasses.

"How about you? How did you become a control freak?" he asked, looking into Josie's eyes.

She laughed. "You wouldn't have called me that a few years ago. When Martin Jameson died and I became city editor, I was completely overwhelmed. My marriage fell apart at the same time, and I had no control whatsoever. I still regret that I let Kurt just walk away. Marriage is a lifetime commitment. It would have been better for Kevin if Kurt and I would have worked things out."

"You'd rather be with that pompous ass than me?"

Josie smiled, and then looked down into her glass as the smile faded away. "I believe in marriage. I never wanted to be a single mother."

"If he was intent on leaving, you couldn't stop him. You don't control others."

"Maybe not," Josie said, looking up to meet Zach's eyes. "But it's like you told Kevin. You only control yourself, but if you have yourself in control, it affects the way others respond. I allowed Kurt to walk out. If I had responded differently, perhaps he would have stayed."

Josie took a sip of wine. "Everything changed for me last summer at the pottery shop."

"I read about your escape from the killer," Zach said, reaching for her hand. "That must have been awful."

"Beyond words," Josie said, looking into her wine glass again. "But it changed me. There's no way I could have fought off a deranged killer. I survived by the grace of some power far beyond me, I know that. But I also know that I survived because I took control. I refused to become his victim. And now that same attitude spills over into everything I do. I used to let Hammond walk all over me. Now I stand up to him. He doesn't need a lapdog. He needs a strong counterpoint. It's my job to provide that. And it's the same with the reporters. I still try to nurture and encourage them, but I won't accept less than their best. I wouldn't be a good boss of I did."

"I can tell," Zach said, leaning closer. "I know you think I'm just trying to impress you, but I really can see a difference in the paper because of your leadership. We all have an effect in this world. The sum total of good and bad forces stays pretty balanced, and the world keeps spinning. But sometimes the influence of one person is enough to knock it off kilter. Like Hitler. His hatred was so pervasive that it knocked the whole world off its axis for a while. If evil can have an effect like that, it stands to reason that goodness can be just as earth changing."

A slow smile lit up Josie's face.

"Oh, Mr. Teasdale. Sometimes you say the most amazing things." She turned her head slightly to the left. He responded with a slight tilt in the opposite direction. Each one edged forward slightly until their lips touched, lightly at first and then with growing force and passion.

They continued sitting there, locked in an embrace across the corner of the table. They spoke in hushed whispers, punctuated by occasional kisses, until the lights came up and the waitress was running a vacuum through the dining room.

"I think they are trying to tell us they are closing," Josie said. "It's after ten."

They drove to Josie's house and said goodbyes in the car in the driveway.

"No pressure," Zach said as he reached across the seat to kiss her.

"No pressure," Josie breathed as she kissed him back. Once again, the physical attraction was strong. Even in the confines of the car, they seemed to lock into an easy embrace. Zach dug his fingers into Josie's short blond hair, held her face in his two hands, and kissed her with such passion that she felt once again sucked into the vortex of a whirlwind. His lips pressed against her ear, her neck, her shoulder. She knew she was losing what little control she had.

Zach stopped kissing and just held her.

"This no-pressure thing isn't working," he said.

"I know," Josie replied.

"I'd better go."

"Yes, I should go in."

Zach got out just as Bill and Chuck emerged from the house. They exchanged a few muffled words with Zach, got into their car, and drove away, giving Josie a friendly wave. It all felt very much like a well-run machine, Josie thought. Not the randomness of a whirlwind, but the precision of a factory. Attendants show up to entertain, babysit, chauffeur. Whatever the boss needs. This could get addictive.

Zach opened the car door, and Josie rose into another embrace.

"Thank you. It's been a wonderful day," she whispered between kisses. "Thank you for inviting Kevin. I'm afraid you've made a friend for life."

"I hope so," Zach said, "because I'm pretty fond of his mother."

Josie watched from the porch as Zach returned to his car and drove away. Inside, she found Kevin asleep in his bed with Chippie and Buttons curled together in the nearby dog bed.

"Oh, Lord," Josie prayed as she kneeled beside Kevin's bed. "Thank you for my beautiful son. Help him to grow into a beautiful man with good self-control. And thank you for Zach. He's such an amazing man. Help me to let go of my urge to control things. Help me to remember that you're in charge. Guide me in the way that you would have me to go."

Chapter 26

Becky arrived at Tom Cantrell's west side ranch house about 1 p.m. on Sunday, carrying a plate of iced brownies.

She was nervous about meeting Tom's mother. Her own mother was a drug addict she hadn't seen since childhood. She didn't even know if her mother was alive. Becky had no idea who her father was. Her grandparents, Haitian immigrants, had served as her parents, along with a bevy of aunties. Her grandmother, who died a few years ago, was the powerhouse of the family. Although they worshiped in a noisy Church of God, Grandma also kept a little altar in her bedroom, remnants of some island spiritualism. Friends in the Cabrini Green housing project, where Becky grew up, often asked Manna, as she was called, to do a "spell" for them, to make a baby or take an unwanted pregnancy away or conjure up the money to pay the rent.

Becky had long fantasized about what it would be like to grow up in a normal family with a real mother, father, brothers, and sisters instead of a revolving mixture of live-in relatives whose exact relationship wasn't clear. A normal American nuclear family with 2.3 kids and a wood-paneled station wagon.

At least Tom had this nice suburban home. Probably three bedrooms. Attached garage. It looked normal. And he had Linda, a devoted sister who looked retarded at first glance but was actually pretty extraordinary, Becky thought. Duke had told Becky that Tom's father, Tom Cantrell Sr., also had been a Jordan city cop. The very first African American on the force, back in 1960. But he had been killed on duty, a high-speed chase that ended in a fiery crash, when Tom Jr. was a boy.

Becky imagined what Tom's mother must be like. A strong woman who had survived the death of her husband and managed to raise a pair of very special children. A religious woman who invited guests over after church on Sunday. Becky imagined her singing in the choir; Tom and Linda must have learned their love of music from her. She probably wore one of those big-brimmed, colorful hats that were the Sunday tradition in so many African-American homes. Becky imagined she'd be a great cook. She was hoping she'd get to taste some of the soul food she enjoyed at the projects: pig's feet, chittlin's, greens, and cornbread.

She was a little intimidated that this woman wanted to meet her. She and Tom were not even officially dating, but he must have mentioned her to his mother. And she cared enough about her son's friends to want to meet them. Becky liked her already. She had stewed about what dessert to bring. She could have tried something fancier, such as a layer cake or a fruit pie, but she worried that her limited cooking skills might be found wanting. She made good brownies—rich and moist—and she was fairly sure Linda would love a sweet she could hold in her hand. Becky decided to dress them up a little with icing and a sprinkle of crushed peppermint candy, something to make them worthy of Sunday dinner and a big flowered hat if Tom's mother was wearing hers.

Becky wore a simple cotton dress with a little cardigan against the chilly spring weather. It was from the conservative end of her closet, respectable but not pretentious. Appropriate for a business interview, but not as stuffy as a suit.

Linda answered the door and quickly snatched the plate of brownies. With barely a hello, Linda ran off with the plate. "Mom," she bellowed. "May I have a brownie?"

The house smelled wonderful, and Becky tried to imagine what was cooking.

"Pot roast," Tom said, as he came around the corner and caught Becky sniffing the air. "Mom always fixes pot roast on Sundays so it can cook while we're at church. She's the choir director."

I knew it, Becky thought, glancing around the living room to see if there was a flowered hat tossed somewhere. "Well, I hate to rush her when she's had such a busy morning."

"She fixes the pot roast every week, whether we have company or not. But we usually have company. Mom's pretty traditional that way. And she makes enough homemade rolls every Sunday that we eat them all week."

"Homemade rolls? When she's running off to church in the morning?"

"She's got this do-ahead recipe that rises in the fridge overnight. Makes a great breakfast on Monday morning."

Becky heard the click of high heels and turned. Walking toward her was a graceful blonde woman wearing a pink suit.

"You must be Becky. I've heard so much about you," the woman said, striding across the living room with an outstretched hand. "I'm Carolyn Cantrell."

Becky shook the hand, nodded, and smiled, but she was confused. Who was this person? She was white, for Pete's sake. Tom and Linda were light skinned but clearly African American. This woman looked more like Dutch American or Swedish American or good ol' British American. She couldn't possibly be Tom and Linda's mother, could she?

"Tommy, that bulb is flickering in the kitchen light fixture. It's driving me mad. Can you get a ladder and change it, please?"

"It's the ballast, Mom. Once it warms up, it will be OK."

Becky smiled weakly. Mom, he said. This was Tom's mother. Certainly not the mother Becky had been imagining. Suddenly Becky's absent drug-addicted mother and her spooky spirit-chanting grandmother seemed so much more normal than this sterile, bland "white" mother.

148

"Come hear me play piano," Linda said, barging into the room. "I have a song I can play all by myself."

"After dinner," Carolyn said. "Give our guest a chance to relax first. Dinner will be ready in a few minutes," she continued, smiling sweetly at Becky. "I'm making some cheese sauce for the broccoli. Do you like broccoli? And I just put the rolls in the oven. Linda, you can help by putting ice in the glasses. What would you like to drink, Becky?"

Becky stood with open mouth, unable to speak.

"We have tea or lemonade, if you prefer," Carolyn said as she turned and headed back into the kitchen. "Or you can have water, with or without lemon."

Becky looked at Tom, still speechless.

"Sorry, no spirits in this house. Mom's a teetotaler," Tom whispered. "But she makes a mean lemonade. I'd recommend it."

"Lemonade," Becky said, finally finding her voice.

"Me too," Tom said.

"You can pour, dear," Carolyn said from the kitchen. Tom headed to the refrigerator and snagged a large cut-glass pitcher of lemonade with slices of fruit floating on top. He followed Linda around the table as she used tongs to place two ice cubes in each glass. Carolyn carried in the platter of beef surrounded by potatoes and carrots as the oven timer signaled that the rolls were ready.

"You can sit over here," Tom said, pulling out a chair on the far side of the round oak table as his mother came back in with a basket of hot rolls. Becky slipped into her place. Linda and Tom each reached out a hand to her and Becky realized the family held hands for grace.

"Thank you, heavenly father for this glorious day," Carolyn prayed. "Thank you for our guest Becky. Bless her as she goes about her work this week. And thank you, father, for this food. Bless it to the nourishment of our bodies. Amen."

"Bland blessing too," Becky thought. She was angry with herself for feeling this way. She was a guest in this home. Why did such details matter? She had lots of white friends. She worked with white people every day and liked them very much. She'd inherited a farm from Ben, an amusing old white man who had sort of adopted her last summer. She had all white neighbors, and she was learning to love them and fit into their close-knit farm community. But she had so misjudged Tom's family. A white mother just wasn't what she had been expecting.

"Becky?" Tom was holding out the plate of meat and potatoes.

"Oh, sorry," Becky said, taking the dish.

"Mom was asking how long you've been at the *Daily News*."

"Oh, ah, three years. It was my first job out of college. I went to Northwestern on a scholarship."

"Oh, Northwestern. That's quite a good school. Expensive though. You were lucky to get financial aid," Carolyn said. "I'm afraid Tom here went to the junior college. It was about all I could afford. And I teach music there. It was convenient."

"There's nothing wrong with the junior college," Tom said. "They got a good criminal justice program. You learn most stuff on the job anyway. Nobody can teach you how to be a cop. You just gotta be out there. Dad didn't do no college at all."

"I go to workshop three days a week," Linda said, eager to add her qualifications. "Tuesday and Thursday afternoon and Wednesday morning. I pack boxes. I'm the fastest packer in the workshop. Except Bob Smally, and he cheats sometimes."

"It's a great program, sponsored by United Foods," Carolyn explained.

"Oh, I know," Becky said as she poured a generous coating of gravy over her meat and potatoes. "I did a story on the program a couple of years ago at Christmas time. Maybe Linda was in the group the day I visited."

"I was there! I was there!" Linda shouted. "I go every Tuesday and Thursday afternoon and every Wednesday morning. Except when it's a holiday. No workshop on holidays."

"How did you decide you wanted to be a journalist?" Carolyn asked. "Are your parents in the media too?"

Becky didn't usually talk about herself or her family situation. But with gentle, innocent questions, Carolyn opened it all up: the story of Becky's mother's drug addiction, her grandparents' escape from Haiti. Life in the projects.

"So much in the world isn't fair," Becky said as she finished the last of her dinner. "I guess I went into journalism to do my part to expose injustice, to make things right."

"That sounds like the reason I became a cop," Tom said. "But it seems childish now. Sometimes I don't feel like I can make a difference. I feel like we're just scraping the surface. Slapping another coat of paint on the problem but never replacing the rotten wood underneath."

"Oh, Tom, it can't be that bad," Carolyn said, patting her son's hand. "We have to believe we're making a difference. Otherwise we'd all give up, wouldn't we?"

"Tommy says never give up," Linda said, filling her plate with more potatoes. "Just keep trying, he says. I can learn to play the piano, he says. That's what Tommy tells me. And he's right, aren't you, Tommy? I can play anything."

Becky giggled. "I bet you can, Linda. I bet you can."

"Now?" Linda said suddenly with her mouth full.

"In a little bit after dinner," Carolyn said, smiling and handing her daughter a paper napkin.

Linda was the last to finish eating, stuffing the final bites into her mouth as the rest of the table watched.

"Take your time," Tom said. "We've got all afternoon."

But Linda wasn't to be dissuaded. Once the thought of playing the piano had entered her mind, eating dinner was just in the way.

"You don't need to eat all your potatoes if you've had enough," Carolyn whispered.

"I'm finished," Linda announced. "I'm going to play a song all by myself." She jumped up from the table and headed to the living room. She paused and turned to look back at her mother. "May I be excused?"

Carolyn smiled and stood. "Of course, dear. We're all ready to hear you play."

Linda played a Gershwin tune, "I Got Rhythm." The steady beat seemed to be part of what carried her along, Becky thought. The beat controlled the impetuous outbursts of her normal conversation and pulled her through her gaps in understanding. Music, especially music with a strong beat, seemed to connect the dots for Linda.

As the chorus came round again, Carolyn started singing along and raised her hand for the others to join in. Becky was surprised at Tom's rich voice and enjoyed this impromptu entertainment.

"I know another," Linda said when the song was over, and soon was playing "April Showers." Carolyn led a sing-along again.

The impromptu factor was fading fast. Becky was feeling a desperate need to escape all this forced frivolity. When the song ended, she said, "Anyone ready for dessert?"

"Brownies!" Linda said, jumping up from the piano.

Becky made an excuse to leave right after the brownies were passed around. Tom seemed disappointed, but Becky said she had some work to do. Then she drove to the office just because she didn't want to go back to her big old farmhouse at the end of a dirt road with nothing but white neighbors as far as she could see. What was she doing? She didn't want to think about it. She would look at the computer at work. She would think about notes for stories. Anything to forget the way Tom's mother made her feel.

But the office wasn't dark. Nick was at his computer.

"Gotta get things organized for the Memorial Day weekend," he said, not even looking up from his keyboard. "It's only a week away. I hate holidays. Everybody gets an extra day off, but the paper doesn't take a day off. It comes out every day, even holidays. Gotta do that extra work sometime. What are you doing here?"

"The same," Becky said. "I need to get organized."

The room was quiet except for the clacking of keys as Nick edited some advance copy for the holiday weekend. Becky turned on her computer, but she just stared at the bright-green letters on the dark screen. Finally, Nick stopped what he was doing and rolled his chair over beside her desk.

"Hey, what's up? Something wrong?"

"No."

"Didn't you have dinner at Cantrell's house today? How'd that go?"

"Fine."

"You don't sound fine. So I take it the relationship is not moving up to the next level?"

"I don't want to talk about it."

Nick looked at Becky. She turned away and pretended to be consulting a dictionary. He got up, went to his desk, and ripped his *Sports Illustrated* swimsuit calendar off the wall. He rolled it up and stuffed it in the waste can.

Becky looked at him, confused. "Why'd you do that?"

"Peace offering," Nick said, reclaiming the chair next to her desk. "Something's wrong and you don't want to talk to me, so I thought if I made a gesture of friendship, maybe you'd do the same."

"You're being silly. The calendar doesn't have anything to do with what's bothering me."

"I know. But I don't want a couple of sexy pictures to get in the way of you trusting me. What's up with Cantrell?"

"It's not him."

"I'm sure Duke would respond with some creative expletive, but I'll just say, that's a crock of shit."

"Nick, I feel really stupid. Did you know Tom's mother is white?"

Nick shrugged. "No, never thought about it."

"Me neither. I mean, he's light skinned, but so are a lot of African Americans. I just assumed—"

"Wait a minute. Are you saying you're in this blue funk because Cantrell isn't black enough for you? Because he's got a white mama? Girl, you're a racist!"

"I am not. I've dated white men. I'm just surprised, that's all. Dinner at their house is like Betty Crocker. The woman went to Julliard. Can you believe it? She's WASP through and through."

"You are. You're a racist. I never would have believed it."

"I'm not a racist," Becky said, standing. "How can I explain this to you? OK, in sports terms. What's your favorite baseball team?"

"Cubbies, of course."

"Even if they're not having a very good season?"

"They never have a good season, but they're the Cubs. They're my team."

"Well, why not the White Sox? They're from Chicago too."

"The Sox are OK. I follow them. I follow all the teams. But it's not the same. The Cubs are my team."

"Well, this is my team," Becky said, patting her chest with her open hand. "I like White Sox, folks like you and Josie and Duke. I'll cheer for you. But Black is my team." She patted her chest again for emphasis. "It's who I am."

"And you feel like Cantrell has crossed over to the wrong team?"

"I just feel like there's a disconnect in our experiences."

Nick shook his head. He rolled his chair back to his desk and started typing again. Then he stopped.

"I gotta tell you, I'm not buyin' it. You're a racist. Plain and simple."

Becky dropped her head into her hands and started to cry. "I know. You fight against something your whole life, and then you look in the mirror and see it staring back at you. How did this happen to me? I know it is stupid, but it's the way I feel."

Nick wheeled his chair over to hers.

"Welcome to the real world," he said. "Many of us are disgusted to confront our own racist feelings. But it's a start."

Chapter 27

"This trick is called the four aces," Kevin said as he placed a deck of cards on the rolling tray table in front of Maggie's wheelchair. "I learned it from my friend Chuck."

Kevin glanced at his mother for approval, and she nodded. "Kevin wants to show you his new magic trick. Is that OK?"

Maggie looked from Josie to Kevin and back to Josie. Her expression was a sort of frightened grimace. She looked lost. Maggie's room in the Herkimer was fairly nice and welcoming. Katherine had hung some family photographs on the wall, and Josie thought she recognized the bedspread from Maggie's house. Even the nightstand and bedside lamp looked familiar. But Josie wasn't sure if Maggie recognized anyone or anything. She just looked at them with that plaintive fear.

As in all the rooms on the third floor, there were two single beds. A little woman named Irene was lying in the second bed, but she was so quiet, Josie forgot she was there.

"First we need to make four piles," Kevin said as he split the deck of cards in half and then went back and split each of the two stacks in half again.

"Now we take the first pile and put three cards from the top on the bottom." He picked up one of the card stacks and smoothly slid one card after another to the bottom. "Then we deal one card from the top onto each pile."

The routine movements seemed to intrigue Maggie. She watched Kevin closely as he repeated the procedure for each stack—move the first three cards to the bottom, then deal one card to the top of each pile.

"Now all I need to do is say the magic word—abracadabra." Kevin waved his hands over the four stacks of cards. One by one he turned over the top card on each stack. "And as you can see, the four aces come to the top."

Maggie slapped her hand up and down on the table several times, her best attempt at applause, Josie guessed.

"Isn't that a great trick?" Josie said, patting Kevin on the back. "You did a very nice job. Yesterday Kevin got to see how bubble gum is made. Why don't you tell Maggie all about it?"

As Kevin carefully replaced his deck of cards in its box, he replayed the previous day's adventures for Maggie, who seemed interested in his animated storytelling. Josie figured the exchange was good for both of them. Kevin needed to see people coping with physical challenges, and Maggie needed to surround herself with enthusiasm and energy.

"That's quite a story, young man. Have you ever thought about becoming a reporter?" Duke said, walking in with an African violet plant. Before long, Kevin was dealing out the cards again, showing his trick to

Duke. Gary, the nursing assistant, came in near the end of the trick. He was a young, skinny black man who didn't look much over twenty. Josie had heard him humming a tune as he walked from room to room, taking temperatures and blood pressures.

"Hey, that's cool. How do you do that?" Gary asked as he inserted a thermometer under Maggie's tongue.

Kevin repeated the trick for Gary.

"Cool, man," Gary said. "Hey, you want to do rounds with me, show your trick to the other residents? Nobody likes to see the thermometer man come, but they'll get a kick out of you."

With Josie's approval, Kevin headed out on his first magic tour, leaving Josie and Duke to visit with Maggie.

"Do you understand any of this, Maggie, girl?" Duke asked. "If you know who I am, give me a sign."

Maggie raised one hand a few inches.

"Great. I'm glad you can understand us. Is there anything you want?"

Again Maggie gently slapped the table.

"OK. We'll have to play charades here. Slap once for yes. Do you understand?"

A gentle tap on the table.

"Are you hungry or thirsty? Do you want something special to eat?"

No response.

"Are you cold? Do you need a sweater or a blanket?"

No response.

"This sounds like an impossible task," Josie said. "We could be here all night."

"That's it. Do you want to go home?"

Maggie tapped the table vigorously.

"Now listen, old girl," Duke said, kneeling to look Maggie in the eye. "I'm sure Katherine and the doctors already explained to you that you can't go home yet. You need to get better first. Do you understand?"

Maggie gave a faint rap on the table.

"Good, at least we know you understand," Duke said.

"We're going to keep coming to visit you," Josie added. "We won't leave you alone. We'll help you get better."

Maggie made another faint rap on the table.

"Every day," Josie said. "Someone will be here every day. We'll make a schedule, OK?"

"Now doesn't that sound just like Peter Pan?" Duke said, throwing an arm over Josie's shoulders. "She's even got your recuperation organized as a team effort."

"And why not?" Josie said, with hands on hips. "Maggie is part of our team."

The older woman's fingers rapped the table gently.

"Oh, I see how it is," Duke said, bending close to Maggie's face. "This stroke is an elaborate undercover scheme, isn't it? It's part of your disguise to investigate the county home at Herkimer House. You're the Nelly Bly of the *Jordan Daily News*. You'll probably win a Pulitzer for this one."

Maggie seemed enthralled at Duke's words, mystified and amazed all at once. Her eyes were big and her mouth open. Josie laughed.

"Yeah, Maggie, you're our inside person at the Herkimer. Keep your eyes open for any news stories. Can you do that?"

Maggie's head dropped a little, almost in a nod, as her fingers faintly tapped the table.

"Well, we shouldn't get you too tired. I'm going to go in search of my magician son before he makes somebody disappear," Josie said. "I'll let you and Duke visit for a while."

Kevin the Magnificent was acing his way around the third floor. Josie stood at a safe distance to observe. She was proud of how easily Kevin interacted with the elderly residents, all strangers. Each time he finished his trick, he carefully gathered his cards into the pre-planned order and tucked them into the box so they would be ready if someone else wanted to see the trick. And just about the time he finished, someone would invite him to come over.

Josie admired the architecture of the old hotel. The floor was covered with a new neutral linoleum, but the walls featured the deeply curved moldings of a fancy old building. Every door was big and heavy, shaped in the traditional six-panel design with long, skinny filigree metal plates behind the oblong door knobs. The hardware was brass, Josie figured, but time had turned all the hinges and knobs black. Above each door was a transom window, and the high ceilings gave every room a little bit of majesty.

"He's quite a performer," Duke said, joining Josie as she watched her son.

"He is enjoying himself, isn't he?" Josie said without taking her eyes off Kevin. "Have you figured it out yet?"

"The trick? He's pretty protective of the way he puts his cards away, so I'm guessing there's some counting going on."

"Easier than that. The aces come to the top because they start out on top," Josie said. "That's all there is to it."

"Sounds like a lesson in life," Duke said. "Those who start out on top tend to stay there."

Josie chuckled. "Speaking of those at the top. Any luck figuring out who owns this building?"

"Nope, it's still hidden in that blind trust. But it makes a pretty neat nursing facility, doesn't it?"

"I know. I stopped in the cafeteria on my way up. It's the old ballroom on the second floor. It's seen better days, I'm sure, but it still has a sense of grandeur. The ceiling has all the old plaster work. Big gold chandeliers hang down from the center of each elaborate design. Across the front of the room there are little alcoves with shell-design molding. Probably they used to have sculptures in them. Someone stuck vases of silk flowers in there, but they still look nice."

"Yeah, I did the tour too and stopped by the second floor. Then I went up and checked out the fourth floor. The nurse told me the fourth and fifth floors are private rooms for people who are ambulatory. Each door has its own door decoration, like it's a little neighborhood. The residents are the folks who have been neighbors in Jordan all these years. The third floor is for folks in wheelchairs or confined to bed, but they're all from Maggie's generation. Her cronies."

"I know. Look at the man Kevin is doing the trick for now. Isn't that Abe Hendrix? The guy who used to own Hendrix Hardware?"

"Yep, and down the hall I passed Daniel Pasternak. He was with the Jordan Police Department for years. Maggie is bound to know him. She's going to feel right at home when she starts getting around."

"Pasternak. That sounds familiar."

"He retired before you came. But he handled a lot of big cases over the years. Oh, I know. He investigated Zelda. Maybe you met him in your dreams."

Josie ignored Duke's wisecrack. She remembered why she recognized the name. Pasternak was the detective holding the red shoe in the newspaper clipping.

"I know you think my dreams are silly," Josie said, "but I met with Irwin MacDonald the other day, and the story he tells of Zelda's last night is just like my dream. Things I couldn't have known any other way."

Duke shook his head. "Gnat scat. There's got to be a logical explanation. You read it somewhere."

"MacDonald told me Zelda left with someone she knew. A lover perhaps. They could have run away or maybe her boyfriend killed her. A crime of passion. Buster Boardman may not be involved at all."

"Kitty crumpets! What about the shoe? You think after a couple of stupid dreams you know better than years of investigation?"

"When you go with your gut, I don't pooh-pooh it," Josie said. "You kept saying there was something screwy about the Blaine Avril ID, and you were right. Your gut told you there was something wrong with the rental contract on this building, and it appears you are right about that too. You know, we keep thinking the story is who owns this building, who is profiting. But maybe we don't need to hold the story for that. Maybe the story is that the law allows such a situation to exist and protects the identity of the owner.

Explain the situation to some of our local state legislators. They're always running for reelection. They aren't going to defend a law that is protecting people who scam the government. We may not be able to get to the bottom of this, but with a little pressure, I'll bet the legislature can."

"We'll have to watch the timing of any story about the Herkimer," Duke whispered. "Tom Cantrell is about to charge a couple guys with the Avril murder, and I suspect the sewer contract and the rental scam are related somehow."

"All the better. If you are right, the legislative pressure may push that federal investigator Wheeler to start cooperating."

"That would be a dream come true."

"You haven't talked to Sharon yet."

"Galloping grasshoppers, things are going great with Sharon. She's moving back home at the end of the month. I don't want to throw a wrench in the works."

"She's moving back? Oh, Duke, that's fantastic. Really."

Kevin came up to his mother, beaming.

"I need to learn another trick, Mom. They want me to come back and do more. They love me."

Chapter 28

Zelda

What do you think, kiddo? With this blonde wig and slinky dress, don't I look like Marilyn Monroe? Bet you didn't know I had cleavage under my business suit.

Matt Shipman from typesetting is going with me on our first test run of the secret passage into the Herkimer. Remember when Boardman's crew was making all that noise remodeling the hotel? Well Matt did a little jackhammering of his own. Our buildings are close enough to kiss. He chiseled right through the granite of one into the concrete block of the other. He had some help from a buddy on Boardman's crew so we could put the opening into a closet, where it wouldn't be noticed.

It's all part of my plan to check out what really goes on at the Herkimer. I can't exactly walk in the front door. Even with this disguise, I might be recognized on the street, especially so close to the *Spectator* offices. And I'm not sure what gauntlet Boardman has set up in the lobby to keep out undesirables. He's got to be protecting himself from snoopy lawmen and deadbeat gambling addicts who can't pay their debts.

Matt's a big guy and smart enough to keep his mouth shut. There's no romance between us, you understand, but I feel safe with him. I need a strong arm to lean on if I'm going to play the dumb, defenseless dame. I figure as long as I keep my trap shut, the disguise will work. If I start running off at the mouth, I'm liable to get myself in real trouble.

When we emerge from the closet on the third floor of the hotel, we're feeling our way, not so much because the hall is dimly lit but because we don't know where we're going. Up until now my editorial accusations of illegal gambling at the Herkimer have been all supposition. I'm not sure if we'll find individual poker games tucked into smoky hotel suites or a line of one-armed bandits in the basement. I only know the cars parked behind the hotel every night are not for guests renting rooms.

We follow the noise down to the second floor, where we're both amazed to step into a flashy, full-fledged casino. The ballroom is filled with poker tables, roulette, blackjack. A row of slot machines covers up all that sexy nude sculpture they got stuffed in the little alcoves in the front. Las Vegas comes to Jordan. It's bright as daylight, with those giant chandeliers turned up to full power. I wonder that I never noticed all that light outside. Then I realize the ballroom doesn't have any windows. It's tucked in behind the tile mural on the front of the building.

The room is packed with people. Many of them are faces I recognize, city council members, school board members. Abe Hendrix from the hardware store. They are laying down their chips, betting, and cheering when they win. Not one of them seems to be worried about the police showing up or seeing some rat like me.

There are many faces I don't recognize. People who must have come out from Chicago. Maybe even Indiana and Wisconsin. Matt stops at the cashier's desk in the corner and exchanges $500 for chips. It's enough to sit in at the blackjack table. I am at his elbow, standing there like the encouraging wife or lady friend. All the time my eyes are searching the room for details I can use. Where does all this equipment come from? How is it hidden when the ballroom is used for other events? I'm examining the roulette table when I notice this distinguished man betting on red. He's the handsome kind of guy who can make a gal forget all the warnings Mama gave ya. He's smooth, not flashy. He bets quietly and celebrates in silence, like he expects to win. He's got on this white coat and a narrow tie, the kind cowboys wear, but he doesn't look like a cowboy. More like a foreign dignitary. Mysterious. Suddenly he looks up and smiles at me. He knows I'm putty in his hands.

It's a strange thing about wearing a disguise. I'm trying to look like a cheap floozie, and it's affecting the way I think. Instead of turning away like a wise woman playing hard to get, I am licking my lips. Begging him, tempting him. Next thing you know, I kind of wander away from Matt, just to see the guy a little better. I'm standing there at the other end of the roulette table. Just watching him, the quiet way he chooses his bets and then sweeps in his chips if his number's called. I'm so hypnotized by the guy that I don't notice one of the dealers in those short black coats is eyeing me. He comes up right next to me and says in a loud voice. "Can I help you, ma'am? Do you want to place a bet?"

I panic and look around for Matt, but he's left the blackjack table. He's probably looking for me. The dealer takes my elbow kind of rough, like he thinks I'm a prostitute, and he says, "What are you doing here? This room is for invited guests."

"The lady's with me," says a deep, melodious voice. It's that gorgeous hunk from the other end of the table.

"Sorry, sir," the dealer says, backing away. "I didn't see you two come in. Sorry, ma'am."

I continue to watch from my post at the other end of the table. My handsome friend gives me looks, like he is silently asking my approval for his betting choices. I nod a few times, then play around with telegraphing different choices. When he's about to bet red, I hold up my little black purse to my cheek. He gets the message and switches to black. He nods when the choice wins, and I give my purse a kiss. I swear it's the blonde wig. I've become some playful, flighty girl without a serious thought in her head. And I like it.

We continue these charades for several plays, talking without saying a word. Finally, the gentleman gathers up his chips and heads to my end of the table. I know this is dangerous. I know my whole cover can be blown if I say the wrong thing. But I can't move. I simply can't take my eyes off this man who is coming my way. I know if he asks, I would run away with him to Casablanca. He threads his way through the crowd of onlookers. Just as he gets about halfway, there is a ruckus at one of the poker tables. An ugly scene. Name calling. Fists flying. The crowd becomes electric, everyone moving at once. In the confusion, I lose sight of my Romeo.

A couple of bouncers drag away Sid Collins, the guy who runs Sid's Standard gas station. He's kicking and screaming. I figure more goons are heading upstairs, and my cover may be blown if I hang around any longer. I spot Matt over by the door. He nods to me. He opens the door and we're out in the hall. Without speaking, we turn away from the ruckus where the goons are stuffing a reluctant Sid into an elevator. If anyone sees us, they will think we are headed to the restrooms at the other end of the hall. We duck into the stairs and run up to the third floor. In a flash, as if by magic, we're in the *Spectator* office.

I kick off the shoes, yank off the wig. I'm anxious to be myself again, a woman I can trust. I can't wait to go to the restroom, slip out of the dress and into a sensible sweater and skirt. It scares me, this other side of me. This flirtatious woman. I've been a tease before but always making it clear that I was in control. If a man comes on to me, he knows it will be a battle of equals. But this silly blonde, she's so needy, so eager. I don't know who she is.

I start making notes at my typewriter. I've got some names. Lots of names. Bet poor Sid will have a tale to tell. I don't have to interview people. I'm getting plenty of details for a great exposé. I could write my story after one night, but I think I'll go back a couple more times. I don't think I even need Matt. Might be easier to make my getaway alone.

And I've got see if my Roulette Romeo returns.

Chapter 29

When Josie arrived at the newspaper office on Monday morning, the door to Hammond's office was closed and the blinds drawn. It was unusual, but Josie didn't worry about what it meant. Maybe the cleaning people closed up the room over the weekend. Hammond wasn't an active part of the deadline, so no one missed him watching over them from his glass castle at the south end of the newsroom.

When he called Josie's desk a little after eight o'clock, she was surprised.

"I'd like you and Mr. Dukakis to step into my office, please," he said in his most brusque, officious tone.

Mr. Dukakis? Ham never used courtesy titles. He was putting on a show for someone in his office. Duke was on the phone. Josie grabbed a notebook and stood next to Duke. She placed her open hand on the notebook where he was taking notes. He looked up long enough to shake his head and wave her away. She kept her hand on his notebook.

"Well, listen, I really appreciate the information. Let me see what I can do about that. I've gotta go now. Deadline, you know. Yes, sir, I will. I'll get back to you this afternoon. Thanks for calling." Duke placed the receiver in the cradle and looked up at his impatient editor. "Buffalo bowling balls, what's so important that you have to interrupt a phone interview?"

"Hammond wants to see us in his office, now." Josie walked quickly toward Hammond's office. Duke caught up to her just as she reached the door.

"Any idea why?"

"Your guess is as good as mine." She rapped on the door and turned the knob as soon as she heard Ham say, "Yes." The managing editor was standing behind his desk, motioning to his guest, Fred Wheeler. Wheeler had a smug smile on his face as he rose when Josie and Duke came in.

"Close the door. Have a seat. I believe you know Mr. Wheeler."

"Never met him in my life," Duke said, dropping into one of the four wine-colored club chairs lined up in front of Ham's desk. The chair was on casters, and Duke landed with such force that the chair rolled back a few inches. He slouched into the chair with his feet out and his head tucked down, like a sulky teen. He pushed his chair back away from the others until it hit the wall. He clearly wanted no part of this discussion.

Josie took exactly the opposite tact. She smiled brightly and marched up to Wheeler with her hand extended. "I don't believe we've been introduced. I'm Josie Braun, city editor."

Wheeler's smile curled a little tighter. He grunted an unintelligible response as he shook Josie's hand. Wheeler and Hammond remained standing until Josie seated herself in the chair next to Wheeler.

"Mr. Wheeler tells me the Justice Department is in the middle of an investigation in Jordan," Hammond said. Mr. Wheeler asks our cooperation in withholding any information about the recent death of a Mr. Avril. I have assured him that it is the policy of the *Daily News* to cooperate fully with investigators at the local and federal level. Any problem with that, Josie?"

"Of course not, we're delighted to cooperate," Josie said, smiling toward the guest. "Can you give us a little more information about the parameters of this investigation? The man originally identified as Blaine Avril was on the construction crew for the sewer project. Is that the area you are investigating? Sewer contracts? Or is it T&T Construction? We need to have some idea what exactly is included in your request."

"I'm not at liberty to get into any specifics," Wheeler said, giving Hammond a conspiratorial nod. "Just stop doing stories about the body that was found at the sewer construction site."

"Oh, you mean Timothy Norton, 31, a former Navy Seabee from Michigan," Josie said. Hammond seemed surprised by the details Josie listed. "I'm sorry, Ham, I didn't have a chance to brief you on all the information Duke has uncovered. Norton was an undercover agent, evidently. We have confirmed identification, but we have been withholding publication at Wheeler's request. Is that all you want, Mr. Wheeler? If so, we've already done as you asked."

"Like hell you have," Wheeler shouted loud enough to be heard beyond the closed door. "You ran an artist's sketch asking for tipsters. You had no business doing that."

Josie sat quietly for a moment, allowing Wheeler's outburst to fizzle.

"Local police asked us to run that sketch related to a shooting at a campground, nowhere near the sewer construction site. Since you won't tell us anything about what you're investigating, how were we supposed to know the two incidents were connected?"

"That prick Cantrell knew exactly what he was doing," Wheeler said, leaning forward so he practically spit in Josie's face. "He knew the connection, and Dukakis here knew it too. You purposely smeared it all over the paper in defiance of my request."

"Becky Judd did the piece about the campground shooting," Josie said, keeping her voice calm. "As Hammond says, we want to cooperate, but you must outline for us the scope of your investigation so we have some idea exactly what might be sensitive."

Hammond smiled and shrugged his shoulders. "I think our city editor has a valid point, Mr. Wheeler. Cooperation is a two-way street."

"The Justice Department doesn't negotiate with newspapers," Wheeler said, standing up.

"Oh, what do you call it when you show up asking for favors?" Duke said, barely lifting his head to look at the others in the room.

"Fine, do it your way," Wheeler said, heading for the door. "But don't expect any answers from me when this goes down."

"Don't worry, I never expected much from you anyway," Duke mumbled.

Hammond stood behind his desk. "Mr. Wheeler, let's not get hasty. I'm sure if we discuss this calmly, we can come to a mutually beneficial compromise."

"Fat chance," Wheeler said, and slammed the door.

"That didn't go well," Hammond said. He sat down, opened his desk drawer, and took out his nail clippers. "I don't like to be threatened. I'm willing to cooperate, but that man just has no sense of fair play. He tells me the two of you have been involved romantically."

"He told you?" Josie exclaimed, glancing at Duke.

"That son of a lady labrador."

"This is no time for your silly jokes," Josie said.

"Seems like the perfect time," Duke added with a shrug. "We need a laugh."

Josie shook her head. "It was a brief indiscretion, sir. Last summer. It's over. It will have no effect on our ability to work together, I assure you."

"I don't give a rat's ass or whatever creative curse you'd prefer," Hammond said, slowly clipping each fingernail. "As long as your personal life doesn't interfere with your job, I don't care if you're kissing frogs looking for Prince Charming."

"How come the feds are spying on the newspaper staff, that's what I want to know," Duke said, rolling his chair up in front of Hammond's desk. Hammond dropped the clipper in his open drawer, closed the drawer, and folded his hands in the middle of the deskpad calendar.

"It doesn't matter," Hammond said. "It's the same with politicians. The dirt always comes to the surface. It's going to slap you in the face, and it's going to embarrass the paper. Just so you know. It's coming."

"Iguana guano!" Duke snorted and crossed his arms.

"I have an idea," Josie said, sitting up with renewed determination. "There's another story Duke's been working on that might be related. He has uncovered some irregularities in the county's contract with Herkimer House. The rental rate for the property seems much more than the value of the property, but the ownership of the property is hidden in a blind trust."

"Interesting," Hammond said. "But how is that related to the Avril murder?"

"We're not sure," Duke said. "But it seems too much of a coincidence that Avril was working for T&T Construction, and they have office space in the Herkimer."

"You think T&T Construction is behind this blind trust?"

"Possibly," Duke said. "The records of a private company aren't public information like the county contract for the nursing home, but when I visited their office right after the murder, the secretary was talking about maintenance problems in the building. She seemed to think Zach Teasdale was her best bet to get repairs."

"Zach?" Josie exclaimed.

"Yeah, he's on the board of the Herkimer. Maybe that's the connection," Duke said.

"Maybe," Josie mumbled.

"I don't know," Hammond said. "I don't think the feds would have an undercover agent working on a sewer project just because the county is paying too much rent."

"These are just little pieces floating on the surface, but they indicate a submerged iceberg of corruption," Duke said. His eyes glistened as he laid out the facts for Hammond. "We know the county is over paying, and maybe the city's sewer contract also is inflated. Maybe the Justice Department was called in because of suspected corruption in Cade County and the city of Jordan at the highest levels."

"Well, that is interesting," Hammond said, rubbing his chin. "We can hardly ignore that."

"Exactly," Josie said. "But we need your help. Illinois law protects this blind trust. Only the state legislature can change that. Perhaps if you talk to a couple of the state legislators—"

"William Stiles. We golf at the same club. I'll call him right away," Hammond said, making a note on the calendar pad.

"We don't want to show our whole hand," Duke warned. "Only mention the rental contract. We'll stay clear of any connection to the Avril murder. I'll do a story about how much the nursing home is costing the county, whether the rental rate can be justified, and—"

Nick barged into the room after giving a quick rap on the door. "Thought you'd want to know. It sounds like they dug up another body at the sewer construction site."

"What in the endless incinerator is going on?" Duke said, jumping up and following Nick out of the Hammond's office.

"Send a photographer too. Where's Page?" Josie added, following close behind.

Hammond remained at his desk, his hands folded neatly. He had the perplexed look of an organized man whose orderly morning had just been turned topsy-turvy. Breaking news always was too rude for him.

❈

Duke jumped into Page's rusty brown van for the quick ride two blocks down Jackson to the construction site. On his own, Duke would have walked because parking was such a problem in the area, but Stanley "Page" Pajenewski, the paper's giant six-foot-seven photographer, was used to parking his old van in any open spot. Sidewalk. Loading zone. Someone's driveway. It didn't matter to Page. He put his van as close as possible to the action so he wouldn't have far to carry the big canvas shoulder bag that held his cameras and lenses. And if he needed more lights or reflective panels to improve exposure, they'd be close at hand in the back of his van.

He pulled around the orange and white barricade that announced "Road Closed." He parked in the dirt beside a police car. Ringed with orange and white barrels, the torn-up roadway was crawling with policemen—more than double the number who responded just a couple of weeks before when a body was found in a nearby truck. The construction landscape had changed quite a bit in those weeks, Duke noticed. The trench down the center of the former roadway was deeper now, with mounds of excavated dirt, sand, and gravel piled along one side of the road and huge concrete pipe sections, like segments of some giant prehistoric worm, lined up along the other side.

Duke and Page got out of the van and headed toward the cluster of police and construction workers near a yellow front-end loader at the center of the sandy sea.

"You can't come in here," ordered a uniformed policewoman, who stepped in front of Page with her arms outstretched.

"We're from the *Daily News*," Duke said, pushing forward.

"Sorry, no one is allowed in. Orders."

"OK," Page said, reaching in his bag for the telephoto lens. He attached it to his camera, lifted the camera to his face, and instantly had a close-up shot of Tom Cantrell and Fred Wheeler going head to head next to the huge earthmover. Page wandered off to one side, always staying just beyond the ring of policemen stationed around the construction site. Duke remained with the police woman.

"What have they got up there?" he asked. "A body?"

"Can't say," the woman said without looking at Duke.

"I'd like to get a comment from Cantrell for today's paper," Duke said. "Could you ask him to speak to me outside the perimeter?"

"Can't leave my post. Stay back," she said curtly.

"I know, but can't you talk to him on your radio? I've got a deadline."

"The detective is busy," she said. "He'll make an announcement when he's ready."

"Peacock piddle. Can't you give me some idea what happened? Did somebody get killed on the job? Or did they just find the body when they arrived this morning?"

The woman looked at Duke, stone-faced.

"OK. Sure. Orders. I know. Have a nice day."

Following Page's circle around the scene, Duke headed off looking for a more talkative cop. He could see a mixture of uniformed city cops; the Department of Justice contingent in their dress suits, buzz cuts, and ear pieces; construction workers in jeans and yellow hard hats. He could pick out Tate near the center, in a confrontation with Wheeler and Cantrell. They were shouting loud enough to be heard over the low rumble of the engine in one of the earthmovers.

"I don't give a damn about your schedule," Wheeler said.

Tate responded with something about "time is money."

Off to one side, away from the police perimeter, Duke could see Ron Baylor and Herbie Flatt leaning against the cab of a yellow excavator, the shovel bent over like the long neck of some metallic monster lapping up water from the trench. The men were smoking cigarettes, taking advantage of this break in the action.

"Hi, guys," Duke said, coming up to join the construction workers. "Always something, ain't it? What did they dig up today?"

"Another body," Herbie said, raising his eyebrows playfully.

"A skeleton, stupid," Ron clarified. "They won't be trying to blame this one on us."

"Bones? Really?" Duke said, making a note on his pad. "Who dug them up?"

"Smitty. Earl Smith," Herbie said, looking at the notebook to see what Duke was writing. "That's him over there, having coffee at the site trailer."

"Gee, thanks, guys. That helps a lot," Duke said. "So what about that other body? Avril? I hear the cops have been talking to you two."

"We can't talk about it," Baylor said, tossing his cigarette butt on the sandy ground and snuffing it swiftly with a twist of his boot.

"I know, but if you change your mind." Duke held out a card.

Baylor thrust out his palm, stuffing the card against Duke's chest.

"We won't change our minds," he said and walked away. Flatt flicked his cigarette into the sand and followed Baylor toward the construction area. Duke headed to the trailer to talk to Smitty. He was older than the other machine operators, probably in his forties. Short and stocky, he sipped coffee from a paper cup. When Duke asked about his discovery, he didn't answer right away.

"It was kind of spooky," he said in a quiet voice. "We were starting on the next section, and I'd just scooped up the first load of dirt. I saw something underneath, like a face looking up at me. I got down from the cab for a closer look, and I could see there was a skull down there, still buried in the ground."

"So did your shovel break up the skeleton?"

"No, I don't think so. We stopped digging and called the cops right away. The evidence techs got down in the hole and were digging around it. Looked like it was all there as far as I could tell."

Smitty told Duke he had joined the project from Bloomington, a hundred miles south of Jordan.

"I don't usually like to work this far from home because it costs too much to live in a hotel, but Tate called me and said one of his dozer dudes was leaving. He didn't want a machine sitting idle, so he made me a good offer. But I don't know. It's like this project is cursed or something."

"What do you mean?"

"Well, my first day on the job was the day they found that guy who'd been shot and stuffed in his truck. Now this."

"Gopher golf balls, that's spooky all right," Duke said, making careful notes of everything Smitty had said. "So Tate called you when? The day before? And you just dropped everything?"

"Not exactly. He called me over the weekend as I recall. Wanted me to show up on Monday. But I had another obligation, so I couldn't get here until Tuesday, the day they found that guy's body." Smitty shuddered, crushed his paper cup and tossed it into the plastic garbage bin. "Just a little too much excitement for this old digger."

Smitty excused himself and headed toward the big green Porta-Potty at the edge of the site. Duke headed back toward the hole where the body was found. He spotted Coroner Zach Teasdale bending over, looking into the trench in front of the loader. As usual, Teasdale was wearing a nicely tailored suit. He probably had on some fancy Italian shoes, Duke thought. He imagined Teasdale hated getting his fine things dirty. But he didn't have to come to the scene. Teasdale's title was an elected job, an administrator. He didn't declare people dead. Medical examiners did that. But he usually showed up at crime scenes. He seemed to like being in the center of activity. And Duke figured he got some perverse thrill from the gory details. That's why he seemed such an unlikely match for Josie. It wasn't his prissy clothes, although he cared much more about fashion than their tomboy city editor. No, it was more his taste for the macabre that Duke thought was so at odds with optimistic Josie. What did she see in him? Teasdale reminded Duke of a snazzy Count Dracula seducing the innocent maiden.

But Teasdale enjoyed publicity, so when Duke could catch his eye, he waved him over. Soon the coroner was outside the police perimeter, making a statement.

"Well, this is probably not a big headline for today's paper," Teasdale said with a smile. "This body has been buried a long time, probably at least thirty years. She was found beneath the roadbed, so it seems logical she was buried before the road was built."

"You said 'she.' Is it the remains of a woman?" Duke asked.

"Judging by the size and shape of the skull, I would say yes. Smaller than most men. Probably a woman, but that will be up to the forensic specialists to determine. We'll be calling in the state lab on this one. Carbon dating isn't something my office does."

"Did you see any signs of foul play?"

"There again, we'll rely on the experts to tell us for sure, but I did notice a gash in the skull. Probably she was hit in the head."

A minute later, Duke spotted Tom Cantrell heading to his city-issued beige Taurus.

"Leavin' so soon, Detective?" Duke shouted.

Tom paused and shook his head. "We got to stop meeting like this."

"I don't know what either of us is doing here," Duke said. "Sounds like this body is yesterday's news."

"Yeah, doesn't sound like a homicide investigation, especially now that Teasdale is calling in the state forensics team," Tom said, opening his car door. "You hoofin' it? Hop in."

Duke slid into the passenger's side. "I did stumble upon something you'd be interested in. The guy who dug up the skeleton, Smitty."

"Yeah, I talked to him. The guy from Bloomington."

"Yep, well he mentioned that his first day on the job was two weeks ago, the day we found Avril's body."

"So?"

"Well, he said Tate had called him a coupla days earlier to fill in for someone who was leaving. Sounds like Tate hired a replacement for Avril a few days before the body was found."

"Zelda!" Josie exclaimed when Duke told her about the skeleton. "It's got to be Zelda."

"Rubber ducky dung! What makes you think that?"

"Maggie's stories," Josie replied, following Duke to his computer. "A lady named Pearl Zaenger reported seeing someone bury something at the construction site when the road was being built. It was right at the end of her little dirt road. I figure when they paved Pearl Street, they named it after the lady who lived there for so many years. The mysterious bundle was buried at Pearl and Jackson."

It was almost ten o'clock, so Duke typed a quick brief for the first edition, as Josie chattered.

"Pearl didn't come forward until years later. After her husband died. Maggie tried to get them to dig up the road, but the city council wouldn't approve it. Robert Kennedy even came to town to look into Zelda's death as counsel to the Senate's committee on racketeering."

"Robert Kennedy? I never knew that. Hey, Hoss!" Duke yelled to the chubby news editor sitting in the center of a U-shaped desk. "I sent that brief over, and I'll get started on the story for final."

"I'll get the clips on Zelda," Josie said, heading toward the newspaper's morgue.

"Ah, come on, Peter Pan. Give it a rest," Duke said, following after her. "I'm not going to suggest the body they uncovered is Zelda Machinko unless one of the cops says so."

"We can't leave it out," Josie said, stopping halfway across the newsroom. "She's a local legend."

"I'll see if Cantrell is back in his office."

"Sis, do you have—"

"The clips don't go back that far," the curly-haired librarian said as she stood in the doorway to the room that housed the clip files. She spent her days in silence, sitting alone, cutting up newspapers and filing the stories. But she always kept her ears peeled to newsroom conversations. She often responded before being asked. "We got rid of everything before 1960. I don't have room for everything."

"How about microfilm?"

"No," Duke said, grabbing Josie's arm. "I don't have time to mess with some blinkin' blurry microfilm."

Josie smiled patiently. "Make your calls. Sis and I will find enough details to make a mention of Zelda's connection to the site."

Sis returned into her cave of files with Josie following behind. Sis opened a shallow drawer filled with small boxes of film. She ran a finger over the labels.

"Date?"

"Well, the story about Zelda's disappearance ran June 13, 1956, I believe. The story about Pearl Zaenger was later, 1958 I think."

Sis picked out a box and headed to the microfilm machine in the corner. As she flicked on the light and began threading the film, Josie thought how the contraption was like a giant microscope, with the film running under the light across a small glass platform similar to the way a slide of bacteria is placed under a microscope. The microfilm pages were projected onto the table below.

Sis turned a crank on the side to whir past page after page of newspaper advertisements and stories. She slowed when she saw the black index slide for June and turned the crank slower until she reached June 13. Although the image was a little burry and dark, Josie recognized the story about Zelda's disappearance.

"Great, that's what we need. Can you print out a copy?"

Duke was just hanging up the phone when Josie returned to his desk carrying a copy of the 1956 story. "Detective Cantrell said they haven't found any clothes that would help identify the remains. He doesn't want to speculate one way or the other about whether this could be Zelda Machinko, but he said your theory is interesting. Get this. He said Wheeler is all over it. He's calling in a special team to strain the soil, looking for evidence. This could halt the sewer project for weeks. Tate is going ballistic.

"That's odd," Josie said. "You know Wheeler. He always thinks the world should revolve around his purpose. Why is he taking time out to investigate a death that clearly predates the sewer project?"

"You forgot that Wheeler's primary purpose is intimidation. I'm just surprised he's suddenly so public about the Justice Department being involved. I mean, why act like 'we never had this conversation' and then show up at a crime scene and get into a public fight with Tate?"

"Unless, this was the purpose all along," Josie exclaimed.

"What?"

"Finding Zelda. What if the whole purpose of the undercover guy and everything was to be there if the body was uncovered? What if there is no city corruption like we thought? They knew this sewer project was going to dig up that road, and they were betting the body would be there."

"Dalmatian dollops! This is the federal government we're talking about. If they'd wanted the street dug up, they would have done it years ago."

"Would they? You know how it is. You have to have enough evidence to get a court order, and they didn't have enough evidence. But if a sewer project comes along, and the road is going to get dug up anyway—"

"They waited twenty-nine years for this? I don't think so," Duke said, shaking his head. "Besides, what could they possibly expect to find? Even if there's something down there that proves Boardman did it, he's been dead for twenty-some years. Machinko was declared legally dead back in the sixties. Anybody who might have benefited from her assets is long dead too. What would be the point?"

"I don't know, but I've got a feeling these bones may be more important than we thought."

Chapter 30

Zach called just after lunch.

"Well, madam editor," he said, "aren't you proud of yourself? You've got a nice page-one story about the remains that were unearthed this morning, and we haven't even got them out of the ground yet. I see you even managed to connect it to the ever-popular legend of Zelda Machinko. Congratulations."

"Are you being facetious?" Josie asked.

"Me? Not at all. I'm always amazed how fast the newspaper—any newspaper—responds to breaking news. I can barely brush the dust off my shoes, and you've already got a story written, edited, pasted up, printed, delivered … I don't know how many steps are involved. Pretty amazing. So congratulations."

"Why do I think you're laughing at me?"

"Laughing?"

"You don't believe it's really Zelda, do you?"

Zach paused. "Are you asking Zach, the handsome, lonely bachelor who's hoping you'll save another Saturday night for him? Or Teasdale, that know-it-all coroner?"

"The coroner," Josie said without hesitation.

"Well, if you want an official answer, it's too early to tell. We'll have to wait for the team from Springfield, but so far we have found nothing to tie these bones to any missing person. We've found no clothes, no purse or shoes or jewelry. The whole site seems a little too clean to me. I mean clean of evidence. It's got enough dirt flying around to gag an elephant."

"Too clean? What do you mean?"

"Are you actually taking notes on this?"

Josie was, but she said nothing. Zach continued.

"In the dozen years I've been coroner, we haven't uncovered any remains that had been underground this long. But a couple of times people have found bodies that were buried a decade or more. Remember that hiker who came across some bones in the woods and it turned out to be little Kelly Sanders, that kid who never came home from school? Well, that grave wasn't very deep, so you would think there would be more decomposition. Still we found stuff from her backpack. The bones we found today were way down there. About ten feet below grade. Down with the bedrock. And there was no stuff. None of the trappings of society. That's odd to me. Not even a cross on a chain. Nothing."

"But it's exactly where Pearl Zaenger said she saw someone bury something all those years ago," Josie said. "It's gotta be Zelda."

"I agree it's a strange coincidence. And it makes for a great story. Your readers are going to love it."

"But you're not really looking into the Zelda connection?"

"We're open to any connection. I'd like to think our objective is the same as yours. To find the truth."

Touché. Josie was letting her personal desires overcome her objectivity. Big mistake.

"I'm sorry," she said. "I've just been so immersed in this old story, I guess I lost my perspective. You're right. It's too early to jump to any conclusions."

"Oh, I'm jumping to conclusions, all right. I concluded Saturday night that our relationship has just begun. I had a wonderful time, and I can't wait to do it again and jump to an even better conclusion."

Josie smiled. "Thanks. I had a wonderful time too. And Kevin was ecstatic. He shared the card trick Chuck taught him with the residents at Herkimer House. He's already talking about learning more tricks."

"That can be arranged," Zach said. "Is midweek all right? I can have Chuck stop by Wednesday to give Kevin a class in card tricks while we check out the restaurant of your choice. See, I didn't even suggest a cuisine. I'm leaving you in complete control."

"Wednesday? I don't know. I go to work so early. I'm afraid I'm not much of a partier during the week."

"I'll get you home early, I promise. What's Kevin's bedtime? Nine? I'll have you home in time to kiss him good night. It's just I don't want to wait until Saturday to see you."

"I'd like to see you too."

"It's settled then. A midweek liaison. Not a full date. Just a little snack to tide us over until the weekend."

Josie was still floating when her workday ended. Part of it was the exhilarating possibility that a thirty-year mystery was about to be solved. Somehow, against all odds, they would uncover something that would identify the body as Zelda. That wouldn't necessarily answer who killed her, but it would reopen the case.

The other source of Josie's euphoria was Zach. A funny, caring community leader who liked her. Really liked her. Liked what she liked. A fair newspaper. A strong community. Responsible kids. He was respectful of her career and her status as a single mother. He was a good example for Kevin. He was smart and cultured, and yet he was reserved. And he treated her like a queen. Divorce had left her leery of men. She had decided she didn't need a man in her life. She would get her satisfaction from her work and making a home with Kevin. But having a man's attention made her skin glow. It was as if she had been awakened from the fog she had been in. Suddenly she was alive.

She was humming when she arrived at Ranch Rudy. Although it was well before the six p.m. closing time, Kevin was the only child there.

"Where is everybody?" she asked. "Is everyone taking off early for Memorial Day weekend?"

Rudy didn't pause as he bustled about the room, stacking chairs on tables so he could sweep the floor.

"I still haven't recovered from the arrest setback," he said. "Some families came back, but not enough. We used to have forty-five kids. We're down to twelve regulars now."

"Oh, no. That can't be," Josie said as she helped to stack chairs. "Don't they realize you were cleared of all charges?"

"I know, but I suppose some people got scared. They're afraid of a day-care center run by a man. I had to give notice to most of the staff today. After the end of the month, it's just going to be me and one assistant."

"Oh, Rudy, don't give up. You'll build it back up again. The kids love you."

Rudy stopped and stood in the center of the room, looking at all the empty chairs and tables. "I don't think so. This doesn't feel like love."

"We just need to get the word out. How about the summer program? That's always packed with a waiting list."

"Not this year. The school-year kids will be back plus three other applicants."

"Only fifteen? I can't believe it," Josie said as she grabbed Kevin's backpack. "Listen, parents need child care in the summer. Why don't we make up some fliers and distribute them at the schools? I'll talk to the other parents. I'm sure they'd be willing to help pass them out to their friends. And we could hit the parking lots and put fliers on the windshields. I'll come up with something."

"You don't have to do that," Rudy said, running his hands through his hair.

"Yeah, I think I do. I should have had faith in you. I let you down. I owe you my support now. And so do the other parents."

Josie warmed up some leftover homemade vegetable soup and served it with crusty chunks of French bread and slices of Havarti cheese. After dinner, she and Kevin went to Herkimer House armed with oatmeal cookies and two copies of the *Jordan Daily News*. Kevin brought along his Ouija board.

"Are you going to tell Maggie's fortune?"

"No, silly," Kevin said. "I don't believe that stuff. But she can use the letters to point out words. She can use it to talk to us."

Kevin set the board up on Maggie's tray table. He asked some simple questions which she answered by pointing to "yes" or "no" in the corners of the board. He asked her to spell her name using the letters clustered in the center of the board. Maggie went along with the game, using a shaky finger to point to the letters. But Josie was in a hurry to share the latest news. After a few minutes of Kevin's game, Josie spread the front page of the paper on top of the Ouija board.

"You'll never believe what happened today," she said. "Remember the sewer project? Well this morning they uncovered some bones deep below the road bed. The bones were very near the intersection of Jackson and Pearl streets."

Maggie's eyes were wide as she stared at Josie. Was that excitement Josie saw? Disbelief?

"I know," Josie said, patting Maggie's hand. "I know from reading your stories that's where Pearl Zaenger saw something being dumped the night Zelda disappeared. Zach Teasdale said it is too early to identify the remains. They haven't found any clothing or other clues."

Josie was bubbling with excitement, but she wasn't sure Maggie understood. She hadn't seen any signs of joy on Maggie's face since the stroke. The way her face sagged on one side, pulling down her mouth into a permanent, lopsided frown, didn't help.

"Here, Kevin is going to read the story to you," Josie said, pulling up a chair for the boy next to Maggie's wheelchair. She gave the second copy of the paper to Kevin, and he started reading, stumbling on long words but mostly reading smoothly. He'd had a lot of practice. Josie had him read front-page stories to her as she was cooking dinner, and then they would discuss the news. As the third-grader read, Josie noted a look of interest in Maggie's eyes, entertainment perhaps. She probably longed for grandchildren. She always seemed to seek out the youngsters at any of the family events for *Daily News* employees. Josie always thought of her as the grandma type, even though neither of her children had married or brought home children.

It wasn't a long story, and when Kevin finished, Maggie brushed the paper aside. She started pointing to the letters on the Ouija board. Kevin and Josie stared at the board as Maggie spelled out a name: Z-E-L-D-A.

Josie squeezed Maggie's hand. "I know. It's exciting, isn't it?" Josie said. "Oh, we missed you so much today in the office, Maggie. We needed your expertise on this story. Duke and I had to look it up on microfilm. They don't have the clips in the library anymore, and I didn't have time to run home and get your collection. I'll bring your clips into the office tomorrow so we'll have them ready for the next story. It may be a week or more before they have something to pinpoint the date of the bones. I wish you could tell us where to turn next."

The left side of Maggie's face seemed to be trying to smile, but it only made the right side seem more distorted. Josie looked down at Kevin, who had turned to the comic section of the newspaper.

"Great idea, Kevin. Why don't you read the comics out loud while I find that baggie of cookies we brought?"

As Kevin read, Josie put one of the cookies in Maggie's left hand to see if she could raise her hand to her mouth. She made an effort and the cookie finally found her lips. Her mouth barely opened, but she was able to break off a bite and mash it with her teeth. It was hard to see such a basic act require so much concentration.

"Oh, good, you got her to eat something," Gary said as he walked into the room, his arms full of sheets.

"Is it time to change beds?" Josie asked.

"This one needs it," the nursing assistant said, stacking the sheets at the end of Irene's bed. Maggie's roommate was so quiet that Josie often forgot she was there. Her eyes were open, but she didn't really seem awake.

"Lady Irene gets pretty messy being in bed all day," Gary said, as he pulled a curtain between the beds. Behind the curtain, Gary bustled about changing Irene's sheets and talking to her as he worked. Josie thought it was odd that he kept talking to someone who couldn't respond, but Gary seemed adept at one-sided conversations. She heard him talking about the lovely May weather and Irene's pretty white hair. He asked about the nightgown selection and then answered his own question. "Let's use the blue one, OK? It's so pretty."

In a few minutes, he emerged from behind the curtain with an armload of soiled linen, which he stuffed into a hamper. After washing his hands at a sink along the wall, he opened the curtain and proceeded to check Irene's temperature.

"Do you really think she understands what you're saying?" Josie asked.

"I'm not sure, but she knows I'm talking to her," Gary said. "Talking to people makes them feel special, doesn't it, Lady Irene? And she never complains."

As he continued his work, Gary began humming a tune. When he pulled up the retaining bar on the side of the bed, he finished by singing the words: "Goodnight Irene, goodnight Irene. I'll see you in my dreams."

He changed his focus to Maggie, who was finishing her oatmeal cookie.

"It's really good that you got Maggie to feed herself," he said. "I've got fourteen patients on the floor, so I can't spend much time feeding them. We take them downstairs to the cafeteria, but even with eight around a table, I can only get in a few bites here, a few bites there. Some of the aides use a huge syringe filled with all the food blended together into a paste. It's faster, but not very nice. It makes my heart hurt to see them use it. So you keep on trying to feed yourself, Miss Maggie. OK?"

Gary checked Maggie's temperature and blood pressure. When he finished, he told Josie she would have to leave so he could get Maggie ready for bed.

"Oh, I'm sorry," Josie said, rising to go. "It's not even eight o'clock. I didn't realize—"

"Don't worry, sweetie. You didn't do anything wrong. Most of these folks are anxious to get into bed as soon as dinner is over. But it takes a while for me to make the rounds."

Josie and Kevin said a hurried goodbye. Josie left a newspaper with the Ouija board on Maggie's tray and tucked the second newspaper under her arm. When they left Maggie's room, she steered her son down the hall to Daniel Pasternak's room. The former police detective had a bushy white mustache and only the faintest fuzz of white hair, with big tortoise-shell glasses perched on his large hooked nose. Wearing red plaid pajamas, he was sitting up in bed watching television. A white-haired woman that Josie presumed was his wife was sitting in a chair knitting.

"Mr. Pasternak," Josie said, standing in the doorway. "May we come in?"

"Oh, my, it's the magician. Did you come to do another trick for me?"

Kevin blushed and looked up at his mother for the right answer.

"Sorry, no magic today. But I did bring you a newspaper," Josie said, holding out the paper. "Let me introduce myself. I'm Josie Braun, city editor at the *Daily News*. I understand you are the detective who investigated the disappearance of Zelda Machinko."

"Of the hundreds of cases I investigated in forty-two years, why is that the only one anybody remembers?" Pasternak said, taking the paper Josie offered.

"And you must be Mrs. Pasternak," Josie said, offering her hand to the woman who stood up and smiled.

"Why, yes, I am," she said. "He's right, you know. Everyone remembers that case and none of the others."

"I just thought you might be interested in a story in today's paper. We're in the midst of a sewer project that has torn up Jackson Street."

"Oh, we know about that," Mrs. Pasternak said. "It's on the news all the time, and everybody is complaining."

"Well, this morning one of the bulldozers uncovered some bones that had evidently been there ever since that road was built thirty years ago," Josie said.

"Twenty-nine years, you mean," the former policeman said. "You're saying they finally dug up Zelda Machinko?" Pasternak squinted at the newsprint. "Is that what this here story says?"

177

"Well, it's definitely a possibility," Josie said. "The bones were near the intersection with Pearl Street."

"Boy, howdy. That rings a bell, don't it?" Pasternak said. "Finally dug her up. Well, every crime has its day. All your sins will be made known. Yep, that would be Zelda, all right. 'Bout time. Finally get to close the book. Yes, sir. I'll rest in peace now."

"I thought you'd be interested."

"I was just tellin' the cap'n the other day that we should reopen that case," the old cop continued.

"The captain?" Josie looked at Mrs. Pasternak, who was chewing her lip.

"Yep, that was a strange one. Left a shoe behind. Did you know that?"

"Yes, I know."

"Well, thanks for your report, girlie. What do I owe ya?"

"Owe me? Oh, you don't owe anything for the paper, sir. I just brought it by."

"I used to get the *Spectator*. They stopped publishing that, you know, coupla years ago."

"Quite a few," Josie said, glancing at Mrs. Pasternak, who shook her head silently.

"Good paper, that *Spectator*. But that crazy editor, Zelda Machinko, she's gonna get herself killed one of these days. You know that?"

"Yes," Josie said, shaking her head sadly. "I know."

Kevin had been watching the baseball game. "Come on, Kevin. Time to go," Josie said as she headed for the door. Mrs. Pasternak followed them into the hall."

"It comes and goes," she said. "The problem is, he sounds so strong. You can't get him to understand that he's saying crazy things."

"I'm sorry," Josie said. "I was hoping maybe he could help us out if they do identify the body, but I guess I'd better just let the subject drop."

"Oh, no, please come back and visit. I'm sure he loves talking about it. Of course, it's hard to believe what he says. He does have a box of files from the case at home. He's got all his files on the Ping-Pong table. You're welcome to come by anytime, if that would help."

Chapter 31

After work, Duke parked outside Mel's Bar and watched the happy-hour customers come and go. He needed to talk to Herbie Flatt, and he assumed the construction team would be at their usual haunt, even though work on the sewer project had been halted. Duke needed to catch Flatt alone, away from his pushy buddy and Terry Tate's watchful eye.

Dusk had settled on the alley behind the bar when Duke recognized the twin broad-shouldered shapes of Baylor and Flatt coming out of the bar. They were laughing, not seeming too concerned with the police inquiry. Baylor turned to his right and quickly jumped into a dirty black pickup truck. Flatt continued walking straight ahead. He picked out a beer can on the edge of the pavement and dribbled it down the alley in front of him with short, controlled kicks. When he neared the end of the lot, he delivered the scoring blow, sending the can into the shadows. Duke was waiting there with his experienced goalie save. He returned the can with a swift kick, sending it right into Flatt's chest.

"Hey," Flatt exclaimed. "I didn't see you there."

"Obviously," Duke responded, stepping into the glow of a streetlight.

"Oh, you're that newspaper guy. I told ya. My lawyer says I can't talk to you."

"Your lawyer? He's not working for you. He's working for Tate. His job is to make sure you don't do or say anything that will hurt his client."

"Whatever. I'm still not talking to you," Flatt said, turning away and opening the door of a fairly clean silver pickup.

"I understand. Tate's the boss," Duke said, rushing to be heard before Flatt closed the truck door. Duke stood next to the truck, and Flatt rolled down the window.

"Listen, Tate's a good boss, OK?"

"If you say so," Duke said, with a shrug. "But I'm figuring he's pretty pissed right now. One of his employees gets murdered, and then cops start questioning two more employees. It's gotta be unwelcome attention. And now his whole project gets detained by a second body right in the middle of the street."

"He can't blame us for that one. That body's been down there longer than I've been alive."

"But he blames you for the first one, doesn't he?"

"What? I don't know what you're talking about."

"I'm talking about your boss. He's the one who told you and Baylor to get rid of that snoop from Michigan. You do the best you can, and now he blames you guys for screwing up everything. It's not your fault. You were just trying to please the boss, right?"

"One last time, I didn't have anything to do with the guy who was killed," Flatt said as he turned the key in the ignition.

"I know, but if Tate got rid of one problem employee, what's to stop him from getting rid of you two?" Flatt turned to look at Duke, who tossed his business card through the open window. "I can protect you."

"You? Flabby ol' man," Flatt said with a laugh.

"Ever hear of that saying, 'The pen is mightier than the sword?' Once the paper writes a story that Tate ordered the murder, he won't ever be able to bother you again."

Flatt shook his head and stomped on the gas, sending gravel flying as the truck sped down the alley.

❀

Within fifteen minutes, Duke was ringing the buzzer at Sharon's apartment building. It was after eight, and he was afraid she wouldn't want a visitor, but he had put this off as long as he could. He had to talk to her before Wheeler did.

"Yes?" Sharon's voice sounded hesitant through the apartment security speaker.

"Hi, just me," Duke said, trying to sound as cheery as possible. "Ready to take a break from grading papers?"

The buzzer to unlock the door sounded and Duke walked in. Sharon met him at the doorway of her second-floor apartment, wrapped in her terry robe.

"You timed that just right, mister," she said. "How did you know English term papers were due today?"

"You said something about it the other day. How much you were dreading it."

"And you remembered?"

"Of course, I remembered. And I know what will pick up your evening. Chocolate." Duke held up a bag of half-priced, chocolate Easter eggs wrapped in brightly colored foil.

"Perfect," Sharon said, grabbing the bag of chocolates and offering Duke a welcome hug. He held her a little tighter, enjoying this moment of warmth. He didn't want to do anything to lose this.

"Come on in," Sharon said, gesturing toward the sofa. "Can I get you something to drink?"

"Don't ask," Duke said, taking long strides into the living room and dropping onto the flowered couch.

"Well, I've had two Cokes since dinner," Sharon said. "I needed the infusion of energy. I've also got root beer. I could add a scoop of ice cream and make it a float."

"A root beer float? I haven't had one of those in years. Why not?"

"It's one of the benefits of having kids," Sharon said, tossing the bag of chocolate onto the table as she headed into the kitchen. "You get to do all that kid stuff again. Root beer floats are Jennifer's current obsession."

Duke followed Sharon into the kitchen. "Speaking of our lovely daughter—"

"Orchestra practice. She'll be home about ten," Sharon said, pulling a half-gallon of vanilla ice cream from the freezer. Duke came up behind Sharon and kissed her neck as she scooped ice cream into two glasses.

"Don't get any ideas," she said, shaking a spoon in Duke's direction. "I may look like I'm ready for bed, but I've got lots of work to do."

"I know," Duke said, backing away. "So, are these essays as bad as you feared?"

"Research papers," Sharon said, as she poured the foaming brown liquid into each glass. She waited for the foam to subside and then added a little more. "An essay can be all personal opinion. These papers must quote at least five sources and be properly footnoted."

"Ah, yes, footnotes," Duke said, accepting the glass Sharon offered. "Found any future writers for the *Daily News*?"

"I've found that a dozen declarative sentences in a row do not a point make," Sharon said. She took a sip of her float. "I know they are only eighth graders, but logic and drawing conclusions is beyond most of them. Even my best students make horrid mistakes. Every paper misuses words. The wrong form of to, two, or too. Or your for you're. And it's instead of its. Don't get me started on its."

"I've been thinking that next week I'll do a session on imposters. That's what I'm going to call them, words that sound like another word, but show up in the wrong place in sentences. I think if I make it fun enough, maybe dress up in a trench coat and talk about disguises and spies and such, maybe they will listen. And more importantly, maybe they will remember."

Duke smiled. "You must be a very good teacher."

"Or not," Sharon said, taking a seat at the table. On the other end of the woodgrain laminate oval was a stack of ungraded research papers. "I must say that the availability of computers and printers has made the papers much neater. Remember when we went to school, typing the papers at an old typewriter and using white correction fluid on all the mistakes?"

"Turtle curdle. I didn't make mistakes," Duke said as he sat down in the chair next to Sharon.

"So, how about your day?"

"You won't believe it. They found another body at the sewer project."

"I saw the story in the paper. But it doesn't sound like a recent murder. Gosh, it may not even be a murder. Maybe it's an old graveyard."

"And then, of course, maybe it's Zelda Machinko."

"You think so?"

"No, but Josie does. Did I tell you she dreams that Zelda is talking to her? Telling her story."

"You're kidding!" Sharon giggled at the thought, but stopped when Duke shot her a serious look. "Oh, dear. You're serious. You think she's having a nervous breakdown or something?"

"Something," Duke said with a shrug.

"Well, she has been under a lot of stress this year."

Duke looked down at his glass. It was the perfect opening to tell Sharon about Wheeler coming to the office, but Duke couldn't find the words. He could write a spellbinding story about a school board meeting, but he couldn't find any words to describe what he and Josie had done last summer.

"One of your cop friends came to visit me at school today," Sharon said, stirring the ice cream into the frothy brown liquid with her straw.

"A cop came to see you?" Duke repeated.

"Yeah, somebody named Fred Wheeler. He was with some bald guy who never said a thing."

"Wheeler came to see you at school?" There was no getting out of this now. Duke's mind was racing.

"Yeah. What's his problem anyway? It might have been his idea of a practical joke, but I didn't think it was very funny. And I told him so."

"What did he say?"

"Oh, some cock-and-bull story about you having an affair last summer. He was real cagey about it, tried to make it some big mystery for me to guess. And I must admit he had me going for a while. You and I have been going through a rough patch, so I can see how one of your sick-in-the-head cop friends might think it would be fun to make up a story and get me all mad at you. But he blew the whole thing when he said you were having an affair with Josie. Josie! Can you believe it? If he had said anyone else, I might have had some doubts about you. But Josie's my friend. And you're not her type at all. We were just talking about that the other night, weren't we? How she seems to fall for guys that are kinda prissy. The type of guys you can't stand, like that fancy-pants coroner."

"Clydesdale cogwheels. This is getting deep," Duke exclaimed, with wide-eyed horror.

"I know." Sharon laughed. "Now that I'm retelling it, I guess it is kind of funny. But at the time, all I could think was this guy could spread this rumor to people who didn't know how ridiculous it was. Jennifer could hear some ugly talk like that, and it would be devastating. I lit into him like a mother lion, claws and all. I let him know in no uncertain terms that his storytelling wasn't funny and wouldn't be tolerated. I told him Senator Connie Davis was a personal friend, my sorority sister, and if his ridiculous rumor spread any further, she would get him fired so fast he would think FBI stood for Failed Basic Inglish."

"Oh, I wish I could have seen that," Duke said, laughing and shaking his head. "I never knew Connie Davis was a friend of yours."

"Haven't you been listening? This wasn't a battle of truths. This was a contest of whoppers. I can tell 'em with the best of them." Sharon made a huge slurping sound as she sucked the final drops of root beer through her straw. Duke watched her with overflowing love and fear. There it was. The horrible truth was right there on the table between them. He would never have a better opportunity to clear this up. And Sharon was in such a good mood, he halfway thought he might be able to get away with telling her. He reached out and took her hands in his.

"Honey, I want you to know how very much I love you. I know I screwed up—"

"No, don't dwell on the drinking," she said, squeezing his hands. "It's behind us. We're going to be stronger for it. As long as you stay sober, I'll fight off anything and anybody who tries to tear us apart.

Chapter 32

Zelda

My casino story is the talk of the town.

I describe it all. The row of craps tables and the five poker tables. Even the slot machines in front of the naked statues. I credit some "secret source in the Boardman gambling empire," but there's enough detail so anyone who's been up there knows it's the truth.

Even Judge Springer chuckles and shakes his head when he sees me at the courthouse. He's too smart to say anything incriminating, but I can tell from the look in his eye that he's read my story. He knows it's a true description because he's been there too.

Abe Hendrix calls me, threatening to sue.

"What's this about a certain hardware store owner being at this secret casino?" he says, sputtering like a Model T because he's so mad he can hardly talk. "Mine is the only locally owned hardware store in town. And I'm a law-abiding citizen. I would never visit such an unholy place. You'll be hearing from my attorney. You and this secret source."

One flaw in my description turns out rather funny. I mention that "a curly-haired board member for Jordan Public Schools had such a good run at blackjack that the district should look to the casino to finance its shortfall." Well, Hazel Akerman calls me, screeching into the phone that her hair isn't naturally curly. She gets it permed every three months at Cynthia's Salon.

"I think the secret source was referring to a male board member," I say, trying not to laugh into the phone. "Yes, I'm quite sure the source said, 'HE had a good run.'"

"Oh," she says, and then "Oh" again when she realizes the secret source must have been describing board president Timothy O'Neal. He's got a bright-red curly top like a clown. She hangs up, and I'm not sure if she's mad because she thought the story had placed her at an illegal activity or because it implied her coiffure came from inferior "natural" curls instead of her high-priced salon.

But it isn't all fun and games. Journalism never is. A couple of days after the first story runs, I go by Sid's Standard to visit Sid Collins. I figure maybe he can give me the inside track. And there he is, behind the counter, in a wheelchair. The goons busted up both his legs. Of course, he says a jack slipped and a car fell on him in the shop. But I know. And he knows I know. I owe it to him to expose these scum. Illegal gambling doesn't just put money in Buster's pocket. It puts poor slobs like Sid in wheelchairs.

So I don my blonde wig and another slinky dress and head back to the casino. I leave Matt behind this time. I don't tell him or anyone else where

I'm going. I worry a little because I'm kinda partial to my shapely legs just the way they are.

Then I see him. The Roulette Romeo. And I am drawn to him like a moth to a flame. Sure, I want to reconnect with him, but I need him too. I need to hide beside him. He's part of my cover. I walk up behind him and whisper in his ear.

"Red is hot tonight."

He turns, sees me, and smiles. He switches his bet from black to red and loses. He's still smiling.

"I thought you were one of those apparitions from another plane," he whispers. "Something you can see but not hear. I thought I'd never see you again."

"I was waiting for you to be ready," I say, ducking my head slightly and looking up at him through my eyelashes. It's a trick every little girl knows, the shy flirt. I haven't used it in years. I've always thought a woman ought to look you in the eye if she wants to be treated equal. Blame the wig. I'm thinking like a blonde now.

He puts an arm around my waist and pulls me in. I submit a little but not completely and look away. He returns to his game, consulting me now and then. Making comments. Laughing at mine. It's a relaxed, playful banter. Non-threatening. I brush against his shoulder, feel the warmth of his body standing next to mine. When he looks at me, I can feel my cheeks blush.

But I'm still working. My eyes are scanning the room looking for familiar faces. I'm listening to the conversations. Making mental notes. I pay close attention to the employees, the bouncers, the big guys at the door. I watch for confrontations. I notice a little discussion at one of the blackjack tables. This guy in a tux, that Romeo calls the pit boss, is talking to one of the dealers, and before you know it, a pair of goons is pulling him out the door. The pit boss takes over his table.

"Must have been cheating," Romeo whispers.

"The dealer?" I ask softly. "But isn't he an employee?"

"Yeah, but when an employee cheats, that means the boss loses. And bosses don't like to lose," Romeo explains.

By the way Romeo's eyes dance, I suspect my smile is sending messages of unlimited possibilities. I don't know what makes me do it, but I tuck my hand under his elbow and hold on like I'm counting on him to guide me through this maze. I saw my mother do it a hundred times. She was from the old country and had very strict ideas about what was proper behavior for a woman. But this was a gesture she used with men she barely knew. The cop on the beat or the milk man—Mama would take his elbow when she asked for help. She wasn't a frail woman. She took the stairs two at a time to her dying day. But she knew most men like to be in charge. They want to fix things. She knew just how to get the fixes she wanted.

The gesture works on Romeo. He pats my hand and smiles. "Why don't we take a break? Get a drink at the bar."

I hold on to his arm as he heads across the room.

"I'm Al. Alphonse Baker. What's your name?"

"Marilyn," I say, because it's the first thing that pops into my head. Seems to go with the wig.

There's only one stool left at the bar and he motions for me to take it. He orders a whiskey straight for himself and gets me the requested whiskey sour. Then he leans against the bar to talk to me, creating a wall between me and the guy at the next stool.

"So where's that guy you were with last time?"

"My brother? Oh, he couldn't make it tonight."

"Brother, huh? You don't see solo women in places like this unless they're working."

"I'm not solo," I say, touching his hand.

"You don't seem like much of a gambler, and you don't seem like a whore, so what are you doing here?"

"Looking for you."

"You're not going to tell me, are you?"

"I just told you," I say with a playful giggle. "So what are you doing here, Mr. Baker? Don't you have respect for the law?"

He laughs and takes a swig from his glass. "Do I respect the law? That's a good one. I am a lawyer. But I guess attorneys have less respect for the law than just about anybody, because they know how it can be twisted and squeezed into anything you want."

He proceeds to tell me about his job in Chicago. He's a corporate attorney, works on mergers and acquisitions. "Legal robbery," he calls it and orders another whiskey.

"A casino like this may be technically illegal, but it's all up to the whim of the legislature," he says. "How long will it be before Chicago is just another Las Vegas? It's what people want."

"But like you say, it's dangerous." I play with the straw in my drink. I'm afraid if I look at him, he'll see I have no patience with these scofflaws.

"Come on, bring your drink. I want to try the craps table," he says, offering me his elbow. I tuck my hand in, squeezing his strong bicep and feeling totally at ease. As he guides me out of the crowded, darkened bar area into the flashy brightness of the gaming area, I notice Buster is headed our way. Before I can excuse myself to the powder room, Buster raises his hand in salute.

"Baker! How are you? Having fun?"

"Always," Al says, extending his hand.

The two men chortle their masculine greetings while I sidle a little closer to Al, trying to hide behind his protective shoulder.

"And who's this lovely little thing?" Buster asks.

"My lady," Al says. "Lyn, this is the Mr. Boardman I told you about. He runs the hotel."

"Pleased to meet you," I say, keeping my head down and looking up through a veil of eyelashes and blonde hair.

"Well, you two have a good time and let me know if you need anything," Boardman says, squeezing my bare arm. He turns to talk with another guest behind me. As soon as the other guest speaks, I realize it's one of the city council members.

"What's this? I see you've made the paper," the councilman says. "I was afraid nobody would come tonight. Afraid you might get busted."

Boardman responds with something about the newspaper exposé being "good publicity" before Al escorts me out of earshot.

"You don't like Boardman, do you?" Al whispers.

"What do you mean?"

"I thought you were going to squeeze my arm off."

"Oh, sorry," I say, nodding into his shoulder playfully. "I heard he's a gangster."

"You don't have to be afraid of him. He wants his customers to be happy."

"Tell that to Sid Collins," I say with more bitterness than my blonde head could hold. Al looks at me with soft eyes that encourage me to go on. "Remember that ruckus last week at the poker tables? Sid's the one they dragged out of here. Boardman's goons broke both his legs."

"Sorry. A friend?"

"No, a local businessman."

"So you're local then?"

I stop in the middle of the room, pulling my hand away from Al. I am revealing too much about myself.

"Back there, why did you introduce me as Lyn?"

"Because it's more believable than Marilyn," Al says, taking my hand and tucking it back inside the crook of his elbow.

"Is he a friend of yours?"

"Boardman? He's nobody's friend. It's all business to him."

So that's how we begin. I return every night to observe the operations from the safety of Al's elbow, and at some point I excuse myself to go to the powder room and disappear through my safety hatch. Al knows I'm not really Lyn, or Marilyn, but he never asks more. He talks about work and the stupid people he works with. He says a little about his projects, but they are too complicated for me to sort out from the sketchy details. I just listen to the frustration he can't share with anyone else. But mostly we play casino games and laugh. He helps me understand house rules. When there's a ruckus or someone is escorted away, he helps me understand what's happening.

In a few days, I've got a half-a-dozen examples of people being roughed up and intimidated by Boardman's goons. Lyn gathers the tips at night, and one of the *Spectator* reporters follows up the next day. I know it's not a good idea for me to show up at the casino the day after a story breaks, so I tell Al I'm going to be out of town for a few days visiting my mother.

The second casino story raises the stakes. We lay out the details of what illegal gambling means for Cade County. It means a man from Evanston in the hospital, a couple from Naperville run off the road. I include Sid's injuries, without his name, since he continues to claim it was a work-related accident. That dealer they escorted out? He never comes back, and my story suggests he may be the body they found in an incinerated car.

I follow with an editorial about government complicity in this travesty, how elected officials are sitting at the gaming tables and police are ignoring everything.

"This can't be true," says one caller after another. "Our police would not be ignoring this."

"Unsubstantiated claims," says a small item in the *Daily News*. That newspaper is so beholden to its advertisers that it's part of the cover-up.

After three days, I can't wait any longer to see Al. I drive into Evanston to buy a new slinky dress and some tantalizing perfume. I curl my wig so it will be extra bouncy. I'm expecting him at the roulette table. He isn't there. I don't want to look as lost as I feel, scanning the poker tables on one side and the blackjack tables on the other. Where is he? I'm standing there, watching a short, bald man lose three times in a row, when Boardman and a trio of goons burst through the door. Buster stops to shake a few hands, but he's not the same jovial huckster who was bragging about publicity just a week earlier. I slip through the crowd, hoping to hide from view.

Suddenly, there's Boardman and his buddies.

"What are you doing back here?" he says. "This is no place for a beautiful woman all alone."

"I was just looking for an easy route to the powder room," I say, looking down and turning away from him.

"Don't I know you?" he says, grabbing my arm.

"We've been here a few times," I say, brushing my free hand across my face as if flicking away a stray strand of hair.

"Well, then you know the powder room is on the other side. What are you really doing here?"

"There you are!" Al's deep voice is the most glorious sound on earth. I lunge forward and grab him like a life preserver in a stormy sea. Boardman and his buddies laugh.

"You don't want to lose this one," Boardman says. "I think she needs a tether."

"Yeah, she's got a terrible sense of direction," Al says, kissing my forehead. "She can get lost going to the fridge for a beer."

The men laugh at my expense and I let them. Being a dumb blonde is the oldest female defense strategy.

"I was beginning to think you weren't here," I say as soon as we are far enough from Boardman. "I was afraid something might have happened to you."

"Don't believe everything you read in the papers," Al says, playfully running a finger down my nose. "I've been here every night waiting for you to get tired of your mother or whoever you went to see."

"Well, I'm back," I say. "What did I miss? Any big jackpots?"

"No, I'm an unlucky loser without you."

I take his elbow and let him steer us back to the roulette table. I don't know what it is about this man. I feel like I can follow him anywhere, and yet I know practically nothing about him. I'm not an ingenue. I'm used to relying on myself, being in charge. But Lyn needs this man, and he has accepted responsibility for her. He didn't have to. She's promised no favors in return, and he hasn't asked. He seems happy with the moments they share.

And so we return to our game, Lyn and Al, making quips, betting red and black. Winning. Losing. Laughing. Then suddenly one of the goons is grabbing the roulette wheel off the table. The dealer is passing out little paper sacks.

"Grab your chips and go down the stairs," the dealer says. "The police will be coming soon, and they'll be blocking the entrances. You need to get out now."

There's a dull confusion for a half a minute, as we comprehend what we've been told. Then everyone grabs their chips and stuffs them into the sacks. There's shouting and shoving as the dealer yanks the felt cloth off the table. Chairs are knocked over. People running.

The cashiers and the money are gone. Down the stairs, I assume.

"Come on," Al says, grabbing my hand and heading for the door. The stairs are packed. I break away from him in the crowd and head up instead of down. I can't be caught here. If I get arrested, my disguise will be blown. Al follows me up the stairs. I can't dare to show him my secret passage. Think.

When we emerge from the stairway door, I pull him aside.

"We can hide in a closet up here. They won't check this floor." I figure we'll wait in the closet, and I'll only reveal the secret passage if it becomes necessary.

"I've got a better idea," he says, holding up a room key.

As I hear police cars pulling up out front, Al leads me to a room down the hall, inserts the key, and turns the knob. Voilà. We're inside in an instant.

"You rented a room? Did you know there was going to be a raid?"

"Nope, that was unexpected. But it worked better than what I'd planned," Al says, smiling broadly as he backs me against the wall. Just that quick, we are in a passionate clutch. I'm not sure who is kissing whom. It's more of a kissing avalanche with lips landing everywhere.

Chapter 33

The next morning, after deadline, Josie sent Becky and Mack to the "dig," as the sewer construction site had become known. In the twenty-four hours since the bones were discovered, the construction site had been transformed into a science lab. A team from Springfield had arrived to exhume the bones. Zach had arranged for a *Daily News* reporter and photographer to have limited access. It was no longer a bloody crime scene or even a city sewer project. It had become an opportunity for the state to show off its forensic expertise. Suddenly publicity was welcome.

Josie figured dapper Mack would have more patience than Page with the tedious governmental restrictions for shooting photographs of the site. And Becky was more receptive than Duke to the possibility that these were the remains of a community legend. Besides, Duke was busy working on his story about the county's contract with Herkimer House.

The yellow earthmoving fleet was parked at one end of the site, and a train of huge concrete cylinders of sewer pipe lined the edge of the former road. In between, the blue-gray Illinois earth had been transformed into a science lab. A white tent had been erected over the excavation. Although the bones had survived thirty years of the elements, good scientific procedure dictated no further exposure. Sun could be more destructive than rain, site manager Joe Humboldt told Becky. She was ushered to the observation platform, a reinforced area at road level that overlooked the diggers working the excavation below. The trio of folding chairs on the fenced platform reminded Becky of the observation area high above a hospital operating room.

There were six workers in the pit, which was strung with spotlights and dotted with numbered, color-coded flags marking the location of every speck. One of the workers was a photographer, capturing close-up pictures of the position of each bone as it was uncovered by other workers wielding tiny brushes.

Becky couldn't help but notice how small and helpless the bones seemed, lying in the soil. The skeleton wasn't stretched out in a prone position. It was curled in more of a crouch or fetal position, with the skull on top, looking up. "Had this woman been buried alive?" Becky wondered.

Two of the workers, both women who seemed to be about college age, carefully coordinated lifting the skull out of the dirt. As one held on to the rounded top of the skull, the other kept her hand just underneath. Still, Becky gasped involuntarily when the jaw bone separated and fell into the ready hands of the second scientist. The skull was placed into a box to be taken back to the lab for closer inspection, but not before Humboldt posed with it for Mack's picture. Becky peeked over Mack's shoulder at the bony face.

Without thinking, she touched her own facial bones for comparison. The skull in the box was definitely smaller. Becky knew she was taller and bigger boned than most women. This skull was more like the size of Josie or even smaller. Interesting to think that Zelda was a small woman, since she had become such a huge legend. Somehow, Becky thought her bones would be bigger. More powerful.

"We won't know anything for sure until we examine the bones in a lab," Humboldt told Becky as he placed the box in his van. "We'll take this and the mandible and teeth back to the lab and run tests while the others work on the dig. In a day or two, we should have a statement for you."

Humboldt told Becky the bones would be packaged in eighteen to twenty carefully labeled boxes. The sewer construction would be halted for at least two more days.

After Humboldt drove away and Mack headed back to the office, Becky returned to the observation area to watch the continuing excavation. It was as if they were digging with spoons. Progress was almost non-existent.

"So what do you think?" Tom said as he took a chair next to Becky. "Is this the craziest thing you ever saw?"

"Pretty crazy. What are they expecting to find? Fingerprints?"

Tom laughed. "Worm tracks is more likely."

"I can't believe this is the city's idea. It seems like overkill," Becky said.

"Oh, it is. This is all Wheeler's idea. I liked it better when the feds were incognito. Ever since they came out of hiding, it's been a feeding frenzy. Tate and his lawyers are petitioning the court to make the forensic guys truck out as much dirt as they want and play scientist someplace else, someplace away from the city's project."

Becky was making notes.

"I'm not the source on any of this," Tom said.

"Oh, I know," Becky said. "The delay is not police business. How about that other case? Is the Avril murder investigation on hold?"

"Just between us sewer flies, I think that's Wheeler's plan. Make this a big enough stink that we'll forget the original turd in the pond. But I'm still pursuing a couple of leads. Bad thing is, with the project halted and all the distractions, I'm afraid Baylor and Flatt are just going to slip right out of town."

"They'd be fools to stick around."

"Oh, great. You're on their side."

"No, I'm just saying you're right to be concerned."

Tom turned to Becky with a big smile. "Did I hear you correctly? Did you say I was right about something?"

"Some things," Becky said, not looking at him.

"I wonder if it would be too presumptuous of me to ask if we might have dinner sometime. Just the two of us. A real date."

"Are you complaining our relationship is progressing too slowly?" Becky said, turning to smile at him.

"Well, sometimes I feel like you're using one of them little brushes to dig me out of the dirt." He pointed at the workers in the pit below.

"And you'd like to call in an excavator."

"Something like that. But I'd be happy with a romantic rendezvous. Maybe dinner at the Red Geranium."

※

While Becky and Tom negotiated the slippery slope of a fledgling romance, Duke and Josie were meeting in the conference room at the *Daily News* discussing the Herkimer story.

"I've got the county land transfer records that show the Herkimer was purchased for back taxes, $77,000, in 1981. A year later, 1982, the county board approved opening a retirement home with nursing care. They agreed to pay almost double the sales price, $140,000, in annual rent. I think it's significant that this action came fairly soon after Congress approved the Boren Amendment in 1980. That ruling significantly increased the minimum payments from Medicaid. It's an effort to increase the quality of nursing homes, but there's really no federal oversight to determine whether the facilities meet quality and safety standards. It's up to the states to set payment rates and police the quality."

"So you're saying this amendment opened the door for nursing homes to reap a profit at government expense?"

"Possibly."

"So in these board meetings, who represented the owner of the Herkimer?" Josie asked.

"I've looked in the clips, and there's no indication that anyone spoke on behalf of the NBT Trust that owns the building. The owner isn't mentioned. A couple of county board members proposed the idea as a good use for a vacant building. It seemed like a win-win. Improve downtown and meet the needs of a growing population of senior citizens. It wasn't like the owner of the property was trying to sell the county on the idea. It was the board's idea."

"Who reported on these meetings?"

"Maggie."

"Should have guessed. She probably knew exactly what NBT Trust stands for. Maybe one of us should ask her.... Is it possible whoever purchased the old hotel spent a lot of money bringing it up to code?"

"Maybe, but they did so under the table. No building permits were filed. At least I haven't found them." Duke shuffled through his papers. "I did find this safety inspection that was required by Medicare, and it showed some electrical upgrades were required. Presumably they were completed to Big

Gov's satisfaction. I tried to sort through the county budget for that year and there is an item in there for electrical upgrades, but it's not specific what county properties were involved. It's possible the county paid to get this building up to code before moving in."

"How about the county administrator, Bob Wise? What's he say?"

"I've got an appointment with him this afternoon. I've put in a Freedom of Information request for all financial records, inspections, and safety reports, but they have up to twenty days to respond."

"It's going to take a while to gather everything we need. But with all the developments at the sewer project, we wouldn't have room for the Herkimer story this week anyway," Josie said. "I guess the real question is whether the county is getting its money's worth."

"Yep, that's what I'll be asking Wise. Medicare payments cover a lot of the expense, especially for those residents requiring nursing care. The others, on the fourth and fifth floors, are mostly private pay. I talked to Rosemary Hintz of Gerontology Associates. They're the Herk's management company. She's the eternal optimist. Always says the Herk is in great shape. She gave me a copy of the prospectus they give new tenants. It shows annual budget figures, but I don't know how accurate it is. It's doctored up to show only those figures they want to brag about. I suppose if the county isn't losing money on the operation, maybe it doesn't matter that the rent seems higher than it should be. Maybe it doesn't matter that somebody is making money hand over fist and we've got no idea who."

Josie stared at Duke and then she started laughing.

"You almost had me there for a second," she said. "You know, maybe the rental rate isn't the only thing out of line. If there's not much oversight from Medicare, maybe there are other scams going on, charging for procedures that don't happen, charging for more clients than they have, or collecting for clients who are deceased."

"I'm hoping the financial records I've asked for under FOIA will expose irregularities like that if they exist," Duke said. "And since we have reporters over there every day visiting Maggie, we have lots of opportunity to spot any safety concerns, such as patients who are being unreasonably restrained or exits that are blocked."

"Great idea. I'll mention that to all the reporters. So is there anything you've come across that ties the trust to T&T Construction or the sewer contract?"

"Only an address and a date," Duke said, pulling another sheet of paper out of his folder. "T&T Construction was incorporated in 1981, the same year it moved into the office on the first floor of the Herk. Could be a coincidence that the office space became available right after the trust bought the building. I can't tie it to NBT Trust, but I did figure out why the feds are investigating."

"You did?"

"Yeah, I got to thinking about other sewer contracts that caused a stink, and I remembered that one in Naperville, back in 1980. Cityscape Engineering."

"Oh, yeah. They got sued for installing a shoddy sewer system in a new subdivision up there."

"That's the one. Well, I looked up some of the old clips, and guess who is quoted as the chief engineer of Cityscape Engineering? Terrence Tate."

"You're kidding!"

"Would I feed you bison biscuits? No sin is ever buried deep enough as long as newspapers have morgues," Duke said, leaning his chair back on two legs and crossing his arms. "Cityscape closed up right after the lawsuit, and Tate opened a new company. Maybe he had enough ill-gotten gain to start NBT Trust. The feds must have had him on their radar and put an undercover guy on the job to document whether the local work was up to specs."

"Did Wheeler confirm that?"

"Now you're feasting on fantasy. I haven't run this by Wheeler yet, but I will. As long as the bones have put the brakes on the bulldozers, he's got some time to investigate the pipe that's been laid, make a case for any problems they spot. He just needs to find cause to subpoena the records. Then that story's going to break like icicles dropping from the roof during spring thaw."

"Well, you're making good progress," Josie said and stood up to leave.

"Hold on a sec, I need to talk to you about something. Wheeler went to see Sharon yesterday at school."

"Oh, no," Josie said, dropping back into her chair. "What happened? What did she say?"

Duke started laughing. "It's the craziest thing. He told her about you and me, and she won't believe him. She has complete faith in you as her friend and a little less faith in me as her loving husband. I'm afraid she might have left claw marks on Wheeler."

Josie laughed. "See, you should have trusted Sharon in the first place. She's going to fight for her man. Hooray for her."

Duke shook his head. "I don't know. I think it is optimistic to think this problem is just going to go away."

"Maybe it will. Hammond took it pretty well, I thought."

"Josie, I know we joke about our little 'mistake,' but I don't want to move on to the next phase of our lives and pretend last summer was a typo to be erased."

"You're the one who decided to go back to your wife."

"Only after going through addiction counseling to please you."

They stared at each other for a moment, then Duke spoke. "Before we move on, I want to say that I am happy for what happened between us last summer. We made a real connection. It changed us. We're gonna always have something special between us."

Josie smiled. "You're right. I'm happy about the special bond we have. I count on you in ways you may never know."

Duke reached for Josie's hand. "Good, because I feel like I need to talk to you about something else. I'm worried about you and this foolish obsession with Zelda."

Josie yanked her hand away. "You won't be calling it a foolish obsession tomorrow or the next day when they identify the bones."

"Crapochinos! You know it's not going to be that easy. Even if the skeleton is from that era, what are the chances they'll ever have a positive ID? It's been too long. Even your buddy Teasdale said there weren't any clothes or shoes remaining. Everything has rotted away."

"OK, so the mystery lives on, unsolved. That's OK with me."

"It's more than your notion that this body is Zelda. You told me yourself she talks to you in your dreams. Do you know how crazy that is? I'm serious. I think you may be having a nervous breakdown. You need to talk to someone."

"Duke, I can't believe you are being so narrow-minded about this," Josie said, shaking her head. "You know that reality isn't confined to things you can see, like this table and these four walls. After all the stories you've done about people, you know that all this physical stuff is temporary. What's real is love and faith and truth. Those are the things that matter, the things that last."

"What in Faust's house are you talking about? That doesn't mean someone who died thirty years ago can talk to you in your dreams. That isn't reality."

"Who's to say? We both know there's no way I should have survived a deadly encounter with Malcolm Jones. But I did. There was this moment when he had me backed up against the wall, no way out. And somehow I managed to slip behind a shelf unit, out of his reach. I don't know how. It was impossible. But I did it. I don't know how or why Zelda Machinko is talking to me. But she is. When a miracle happens, only a fool would ignore it."

"These dreams are not miracles, Josie. You said yourself they are all mixed up with people from the past and present."

She laughed. "Lately, they're like a romance novel. Zelda's in love, and I can't wait to go to bed at night to see what's going to happen next."

Duke shook his head. "Don't you see? You're dreaming about your life, not Zelda's. You've got this thing going on with Teasdale, and you're projecting your romance into Zelda's life. That doesn't mean she had any romantic entanglements. It's not some message from the grave she's trying to tell you."

Josie smiled. "Duke! I do believe you are jealous of Zach!"

"Walrus whoppers! If I was going to be jealous, it wouldn't be of fancy-pants Zach Teasdale. In fact, he's the reason Sharon figured you and I could never have been an item. Anyone who would date la-di-da Teasdale would never be interested in a real man like me."

"Sharon would never say something like that. She's a lot more open-minded than her my-way-or-the-highway husband."

"Listen to me. You'd better be careful about getting into a relationship with Teasdale. What are you going to do if it turns out he's the one behind this blind trust?"

Josie threw her hands up in exasperation. "What are you talking about? Where does this come from? Do you have any proof for what you just said?"

"No, I don't have proof, but I have this gut feeling."

"Oh, you're allowed gut feelings, but I'd better not have dreams."

"My gut feeling is based on facts. I told you, Tate's secretary said she copies Teasdale on all the company's correspondence. Teasdale is the one she went to when she wanted to complain about the air conditioner. He's connected to this in some way. You'll see."

"No, you'll see. He's a wise and wonderful man. He's a good businessman who gets things done. That's why people go to him. You'll see."

❋

"If there's a story here, Mr. Dukakis, it's a success story," county administrator Bob Wise said as he sorted through the papers on his desk. "I don't seem to have the figures right at hand, but Herkimer House is a model facility. County residents receive quality care at a reasonable price. This annual rental concern you mention, like I say, I don't have the figures, but the facility rental is part of the operating budget which is covered by the fees charged."

"I have the figures," Duke said, tossing another piece of paper onto Wise's cluttered desk. "The building was purchased for $77,000 in 1981 and annual rental is $140,000. Almost double the cost of the building."

"Well, now you see, there's the problem. This sales price you mention. That's the back taxes owed to the county, not the actual value of the property. And of course the rental rate is not related to the sales price in any way. An acceptable rental rate is based on similar square footage rates in the area."

"Similar to what? The opulent marble halls of the old Fox Theater down the street? That building dates from the same era as the Herkimer. It's a venue for Broadway tours and is occasionally rented out for weddings and parties. Is that a comparable rental? Or perhaps you compared the peeling plaster of the Herkimer to office space in the new chrome-and-glass office complex that just went up downtown. There's no other aging hotel to compare it to. No other nursing home in the area."

"Exactly. Exactly," Wise said. "There was a need. And if the county were to build a facility in the suburbs ... well, this is just a much more economical solution. I'm sure you agree."

Duke shook his head. "I just wonder, if the county wanted to open a nursing home anyway, why didn't the county assume ownership of the Herkimer for back taxes? Then there'd be no annual rent payment."

"Own the facility? Oh, no," Wise said, stuffing papers into a manila folder. "The county cannot be tying up capital in more buildings. The cost of maintenance and insurance. Oh, no. Private ownership is much better for the county. Rental payments are more liquid and figure into the cost of service, unlike capital investments. It helps to balance the budget to have clearly defined annual income and expenses, not long-term obligations. Have I answered your questions?"

Duke tried not to laugh. If there was an answer in the administrator's ramblings, Duke couldn't translate it. "Just to clarify, sir. You are saying that $140,000 is a reasonable annual rental for the Herkimer."

"Oh, yes, I'd say so, if that's the negotiated rate. I can't put my finger on the figures, but the Herkimer is consistently operating in the black."

"But if, as you say, sir, it's not in the county's interest to own the facility, why is the county involved at all? If a home can operate in the black on the compensation supplied by Medicare, why doesn't NBT Trust operate the home privately? Why involve the county?

"Well, of course, there is a small amount of tax support. I don't have the percentage at my fingertips—

"I know," Duke said, shaking his head. "I'm sure you've seen my FOIA request for documents. I'm hoping you can supply those promptly so I'll have accurate figures for my story, just how much it's costing taxpayers."

"I'll look it over. You know we have a month—"

"Twenty days."

"Twenty business days. Four weeks."

"Fine. But the sooner the better."

"I'll look into it."

Duke could hardly wait to step out of the county building into fresh air. The mumbo-jumbo of government thinking was clouding his brain. The clock atop the city hall building across the street was chiming three o'clock. Just in time for his appointment with Mayor Hatch.

Duke crossed to the old limestone building. It was about the same era as the Herkimer, but the details seemed newer: the wide steps to the raised entrance, the shiny brass plates on the big wooden door, the bright fluorescent lighting in the entryway.

Roy Hatch was a rambling man, not just in his penchant for storytelling, but in his inability to sit still when he talked. He walked around his office continuously, like a six-year-old on a sugar high.

"Just got off the phone with Senator Davis. Her office is getting almost as many calls as we are," he said, pacing back and forth behind his large polished desk. "I assume the paper is getting the calls too. We can't allow this delay in the sewer project. Jackson Street is part of the state highway system. We can't detour people onto Adams forever. And there is federal funding involved in this project. If we miss the completion date, there will be fines."

"What can the city do?" Duke asked, spinning around to keep an eye on the moving mayor.

"Well, we'll be supporting Tate's petition to get this delay lifted. Tate's already moving his crew farther west down the street to the next part of the project. It will mean closing another block of Jackson before this block is open, but we don't have a choice at this point."

"How did Tate end up with this job, anyway? He wasn't the low bidder."

"Didn't we have this discussion before? I talked to one of your reporters about this. The lowest bid isn't always the best bid. The council felt it was better to keep the work in Cade County. Hire local. That helps the economy."

"But surely you know Tate's background. He was involved in that sewer scandal in Naperville."

"What? No. That wasn't his project. That was Cityscape, as I recall."

"And Tate was chief engineer for Cityscape."

"Well, yes, I knew that. But he wasn't named in the suit. You can't blame every worker for decisions others made. No, Tate has been great to work with on this sewer project. And he would get it done on time if it weren't for these infernal delays."

"What about Fred Wheeler and the Justice Department? Why are they involved in this sewer project?"

"Oh, that's got nothing to do with us. Something to do with the man who was killed or the bones that were found or both. Nothing to do with our project. Nothing at all."

"Are you sure, sir? Are you sure the feds aren't here to investigate the city's involvement in misappropriation of federal funding on this sewer deal?"

The mayor had been looking out the window. He spun around. "What? I can't believe you'd ask such a question, Dukakis!"

"I'm just giving you an opportunity to defend the city's reputation before the feds lob their accusations."

"Oh, well, I see." The mayor took a seat behind his desk and considered his words. He drummed his fingers on the desktop.

"The city of Jordan is privileged to have a dedicated council and staff of civic-minded individuals who invest their time and money in the future of this community. No one in this city's government is benefiting financially from this sewer project. The benefits to the council members are the same as those to the community: A better infrastructure to sustain the city's growth into the next century."

Duke jotted down the mayor's words. He could almost hear the applause.

✽

After he left city hall, Duke walked down the street to the office of T&T Construction. As soon as he stepped in, he could hear Tate blustering on the phone at his small wooden desk.

"I got two dozen men making mud pies here. We're closing down the next block tomorrow. We got a deadline to meet. We can't wait for some forensic team to play name that bone."

Margaret looked at Duke and shrugged. "Can I help you?"

"No, I'll wait for Mr. Tate," Duke said, picking up a Komatsu flier and looking at glossy photos of the latest earthmoving machines. Tate's bluster was winding down, and after about five minutes he walked over and stood in front of Duke.

"OK. What do you want?" he said, making no pretense at politeness.

"I'm Ormand Dukakis from the *Daily News*—"

"I remember who you are. What do you want now?"

"Well, it sounds like you've found a way around the delay. I guess that's good news."

"I don't know if the public's gonna see it that way. The detour is going to start a block earlier. That's a bunch of businesses people won't be able to get to. We'll be moving as fast as we can to get the road opened up again. That's about all I can tell you."

"We'll all be anxious to see the job get finished. About the murder—"

"Sorry. My attorney says we can't discuss that. If that's all …" Tate picked up a hard hat and headed out the door.

"I'm just wondering about the federal investigation," Duke said, following after Tate.

"I don't know anything about that," Tate said. "You'll have to ask them."

"But I'm wondering if the man who was murdered was working for the feds."

"I'm glad to hear he was working for somebody because he sure wasn't doing much work for me." Tate opened the door to a white van in the parking lot with "T&T Construction" printed in big red letters on the side.

Duke rushed after Tate. "Is that why you hired Earl Smith to replace Avril two days before the body was found?"

Tate paused. "Listen. I told you, on advice of my attorney, I'm not discussing the murder of Blaine Avril, which means I'm not discussing some rumored federal investigation or who may or may not have been hired to replace Avril."

"I'm just trying to give you the opportunity to tell your side of the story!" Duke hollered as Tate slammed the van door and pulled out of his parking place.

To finish his afternoon, Duke rode the elevator to the third floor of Herkimer House. He kept an eye open for anything that might indicate the Herkimer was not being properly run. Cracks in the plaster. Dirt in the corners. A man belted into his wheelchair. Was that a reasonable protection for the resident or a sign of abuse? In Maggie's room, he noticed the smell of urine coming from her roommate's bed. When had it been changed?

He slid a chair next to Maggie and sat down.

"I've had a rough day, girl. How about you?"

Maggie nodded her head slightly, although Duke wasn't sure if she was drowsy or trying to agree with him. Duke rattled on about his interviews with Bob Wise and Roy Hatch, civic leaders Maggie knew well. He complained about a county administrator who never has the figures to back up his statements. Maggie seemed to be nodding in understanding. Duke talked about the mayor doing laps during interviews, and Maggie made an "oh-oh-oh" sound that Duke figured was her attempt to laugh.

Duke saw the Ouija board leaning against the nightstand and placed it on Maggie's lap.

"I'm working on a story about the Herkimer, and I thought maybe you could help. We are trying to figure out who owns it. Do you know who owns Herkimer House?"

Maggie looked at Duke and then the board. She moved her finger to point to "B-O-A-R-D-M-A-N."

"Boardman? No, he used to own it, years ago. But he died," Duke said. "It's held by a trust, NBT. Do you know what that is?"

Maggie pointed to the letters again. "B-O-A-R ..."

"Boardman? The Boardman family? The Boardman family is behind the trust?"

Maggie pointed to "Yes."

Chapter 34

Zach Teasdale was standing in front of Josie's desk when she looked up. It was about eight in the morning, right in the middle of the deadline rush. No time for romantic repartee.

"Oh! Where did you come from?" Josie blurted.

"The coroner's office," Zach said with a faint smile. "Good morning, madam editor. I wonder if we might go into your conference room for a minute."

Josie glanced around the room. Nick and Becky were on their phones and didn't seem to see the coroner standing there. Duke, however, was staring at them, recording every word for his instant recall.

"Should I bring a reporter?" Josie said, rising to her feet.

"Let me give you an update, and then you can decide," Zach said, stepping back so Josie could lead the way. Once the door to the glassed-in room was closed, Zach took a seat at the table opposite Josie.

"I hope you don't mind me dropping in like this on deadline. I could have just called, but I know what I have to say will be disappointing, so I thought I should deliver the message in person."

"Disappointing? If you are canceling tonight's dinner, a call would have been sufficient," Josie said. She was irritated that he might let their personal relationship interfere with the morning deadline.

"Oh, no," Zach said, raising a hand in protest. "This is business." He paused a second to let her ire fade.

"The bones that were found under Jackson Street are not Zelda Machinko." He paused again, his words hanging like a gray cloud in the room.

"Who is it?" Josie asked.

"Well," Zach said, chuckling a little, "I don't exactly have her name, but the tech team has confirmed these remains are of archaeological interest. Our lady friend lived between 200 and 300 years ago, before the white settlement of this area. They found a stone hatchet head, probably the murder weapon."

"Oh, wow!" Josie exclaimed. "How big a deal is this? Are archaeologists going to be coming from all over the world?"

"Probably not," Zach said, "but certainly from around the state. To be honest, I sort of suspected these bones were pretty old, but I didn't want to burst your bubble until we knew for sure."

"I appreciate your concern, Zach, but I'm not made of glass."

"I know that."

"So what will this mean for the sewer project?"

"The forensics team is turning it over to a group of archaeologists. They'll be in court later today to ask for an indefinite hold on the sewer project so the entire area can be examined by certified archaeologists. State law backs up their request."

"Indefinite hold? On Jackson Street? People aren't going to like that. And what about the economic impact on those businesses, the traffic?"

Zach shrugged. "You know, you're taking this a lot better than I thought you would."

"I don't think I'm taking it very well. I'm just as irritated as everyone else about the traffic detours and the parking problems this sewer project has caused. Now you're telling me everything probably will be put on hold. We expected the road to get back to normal in a month or so. Now it sounds like Jackson will be torn up all summer. Oh, wow, this is a big story. Not to mention the possible archaeological interest. I don't know anything about the Indians who used to live in this area. I'll have to get Becky looking into that."

Zach laughed. "I guess I don't know you as well as I thought I did. I thought you would be upset that this isn't the answer to the Zelda Machinko mystery."

"Of course I'm disappointed," Josie said with a shrug. "But I have to accept the facts. Like you said, we both have the same goal: to find the truth. And this truth offers lots of possibilities. If you'll excuse me, I need to get the reporters going on this story for today's paper. Can you talk to Becky on the record? I'll send her in."

"Sure," Zach said, rising as Josie headed for the door. "We're still on for tonight?"

"Sure."

In a flash, Josie was briefing Becky on the latest development. Then she stopped by Hoss's desk to discuss A1 placement and jump space. There were several side issues involved, and she wanted to touch on as many as possible in the first-day story. It was too late to increase the size of the paper, but Hoss could look at his lineup of stories and choose some that could hold.

Josie asked Duke to call the city manager to discuss the traffic and parking problems if the project was delayed indefinitely. She also asked him to get an updated comment from Terry Tate, since the original comment was from Tate's reaction to a two-day delay, not this proposed indefinite delay.

She arranged to have another reporter cover the archaeologist's presentation in court that afternoon. The pieces of the puzzle came together before the deadline at ten, with Mack's magnificent photo of the sad, cracked skull played large on A1.

Josie joined Hoss as he headed to the back shop. When production was running tight, there was no time to pull proofs. All proofreading would have to be done while the stories were being pasted up.

Josie watched as columns of type spewed from the typesetting machine. Ron, the supervisor of the back shop, snatched strips from the little chrome basket and fed them through the rollers of the waxing machine without pausing his jovial banter with the other members of the paste-up crew. Josie never ceased to be amazed at how efficiently these men worked, slicing the sheets with a surgeon's skill, right next to the copy, but seldom nicking a letter. Yet they chattered while they worked, talking about weather or sports or politics. Mostly they teased each other, constant putdowns about extra pounds or thinning hair. They never seemed to read the words in their hands, even the inch-tall headline type. Murders, fires, sewer projects. It was all the same to them.

Hoss and Josie used turquoise markers to note necessary changes on the pages. The light turquoise color allowed some flexibility because that color wouldn't register when the page was photographed for the offset process.

As news editor, Hoss was responsible for making the puzzle pieces fit. The paste-up crew placed the stories on the page according to his penciled layout and lopped off any lines that didn't fit. If a story made sense without those remaining lines, Hoss made sure the final paragraph ended with proper punctuation.

But if the excess lines were too important to cut, Hoss read back through the story looking for other lines to cut to attain the desired story length. He looked for "widows"—one word alone on a line at the end of the paragraph. Sometimes that word could be cut, saving a whole line in the story length. During this rereading, sometimes the editors would find a misspelled word in the copy. Those masterful paste-up guys would carve one letter out of the leftover type, paste it on top to correct the error, and then run a rubber roller over everything to make sure it stayed. When all the stories had been cut to fit, and corrections made, Josie or Hoss scrawled a quick, turquoise "OK" in the corner of the page.

It was a demanding process when the clock was ticking away the remaining seconds until the pages needed to be released. The pages still needed to go through the plate-making process and those plates placed on the press. The work required such close cooperation between all the people involved that it intensified the sense of accomplishment when the job was done.

Josie returned to the newsroom. Before long she felt the faint vibration in the floor that meant the presses were running. She sighed. She'd be seeing papers soon. And it was a good paper. She was proud of the work the staff had done on deadline. The town would be talking tonight about the continuing delay of the sewer project. Some also would be interested in the former Indian village in their midst. But she didn't feel happy and satisfied. She was devastated.

Josie headed to the ladies' room, closed the stall door, and cried. Was Duke right? Was she having a nervous breakdown? She had responded to Zach's news the way she thought a city editor should. It was like second nature now. Whatever happened in her world, she saw the story potential, broke it down into elements, and began assigning people. She lived by the clock. She got the job done.

Inside she ached for every murder victim, every family that lost their home to fire. But she had never been as invested in a story as she was in the legend of Zelda Machinko. It had become her personal quest. She had been so sure the skeleton was the answer. It seemed to be the reason for everything, for her dreams, for Maggie's stroke. Finding the body made everything fit together. Now nothing made sense. None of it meant anything. Duke was right. She was losing her hold on reality. Maybe he was right about Zach too. Maybe Zach wasn't the Prince Charming she envisioned. Maybe she was just lonely, grasping at love in any guise.

She needed to make an appointment with a counselor. Someone had given her one of those brochures last summer about counseling for victims of crime. At the time it seemed as silly as that brochure they gave her about spotting sex abuse in children. But she had put it away in one of her files at home. She would find that. She would make an appointment.

But if she really was going crazy, could she continue to run the newsroom? Could she maintain the respect of the reporters? Oh, she needed this job. Not just to support her son, but to give her purpose. This was her identity. She couldn't lose that. She yanked off a wad of toilet paper and blew her nose. Then she pulled off another handful and ran the tissue under her eyes. She looked at the smudge of black mascara on the tissue, wadded it up, and threw it in the toilet. She pushed the lever and watched as the tissue wads disappeared. Then she took a deep breath, opened the stall door, and went back into the world.

❄

For dinner that evening, Zach and Josie opted for something light from Healthy Planet. Josie had a large salad of spring greens with chick peas, almonds, and a rainbow of chopped peppers. Zach ate black beans and rice with carrot sticks cut like crinkle fries. The restaurant seemed to be a mutual decision, but Zach was monopolizing the conversation. Working with the state's forensic team, and now a team of archaeologists, was a treasure trove of stories. The tales spilled out nonstop as if Zach had been storing them up, waiting to see Josie to release them. She listened, trying to decide if this behavior revealed Zach's narcissism or if it was really kind of sweet that he wanted to share so much of his daily life with her. It would never occur to Josie to tell Zach about every detail of her day, such as repeating the banter from the back shop or her frustration dealing with reporter access to the project negotiations in court. She found herself pulling away from the conversation, trying to look at Zach objectively. Weighing everything he said.

"Is something wrong?" Zach asked suddenly.

"No, the salad was delicious. I'm just not hungry," she said, pushing the plate away.

"I didn't mean the food. You haven't said two words all evening. Are you angry with me for stopping by your office today? I didn't mean to embarrass you."

"I know. It was fine, really. Thoughtful. I appreciate that you stopped by."

"Then what is it? You seem a million miles away."

"Sorry. I'm just not feeling in a party mood, I guess. Middle of the week. Tired."

"I think we know each other well enough now that every meeting doesn't need to be a party. We're both tired. It's good to share the ups and downs. I feel like I can tell you anything. You can tell me your problems too. I'm a good listener."

Josie smiled faintly but didn't say anything.

Zach stopped the waitress and asked for two cups of Jasmine tea.

"Have you ever had the tea here?" he asked when the waitress returned with a small white porcelain pot and two mugs. "Very nice and fresh. I think you'll like it."

He filled the two mugs and handed one to Josie. Then he sat silently, watching her. Finally she decided to break down and talk.

"I'm sorry. I guess I'm just disappointed about the way the story on the bones turned out. I really did want it to be Zelda."

Zach smiled. "I can understand that. It would have made a great story."

"It's more than that," Josie said, running a finger around the top of the mug. "It makes me doubt my judgment. A journalist gets a sense about how the world works, who to trust. Alarm bells should go off when something doesn't add up. You've got to know whether to believe what people tell you. It's a critical skill. And I really thought this one added up. I really thought—"

Josie's voice broke. She didn't trust herself to continue.

"It's OK," Zach said, patting her hand. "That's why we call in the experts, because gut feelings are wrong sometimes. Everyone makes mistakes."

Josie shook her head. "But I need to make good judgments. People are counting on me."

"I know exactly what you mean. People count on the coroner to make good judgments too. Of course, I usually trust the medical experts, but my judgment comes into play. I understand the pressure."

Zach refilled each mug from the pot, and they sipped in silence for a minute.

"What do you think about dreams?" Josie asked.

Zach smiled. "Dreams? That sounds like a great change of topic. Tell me what your dreams are. Do you want to run the *Daily News* forever or do you want to move up to the *New York Times* or the *Washington Post?*"

Josie shook her head. "Not those kind of dreams.... Sometimes at night I dream about Zelda Machinko. It seems like she's talking to me. Trying to tell me something. Do you think that sounds crazy?"

"Whoa, you mean like you're clairvoyant? A gypsy fortune teller?"

"Well, I never thought I was before. I can't make a bell gong just by looking at it, but I've always thought such things are possible. I believe the mind has all sorts of abilities we never tap. What do you think?"

"Yeah, sure, it's possible. Anything is possible. What kinds of things does she tell you?"

"Oh, you know, about the night she disappeared. And there's this guy, a boyfriend."

"A boyfriend? Oh, now that's the kind of dreams I can understand. I usually dream about women. I guess all men dream about sex. So, are Zelda and her boyfriend, you know, intimate?"

"Huh? No. I mean, not yet."

"Hmm. But you think there's hope for him?"

Zach was smiling so sweetly that Josie started laughing. "Yes, I think there's hope for him."

"Good, because I was going to suggest that we take a little trip this weekend. It's the holiday weekend, and I remember you said Kevin was going someplace with his dad. I thought we could get away from the coroner's office and the newspaper deadline. Get away from our titles and just be ourselves."

Josie smiled. "That's very romantic, but I don't think I'm ready—"

"I think you are," Zach said, smiling confidently. "I've seen the way you operate, madam editor. You weigh the options, you make decisions. You're not wishy-washy. We're not the kind of people who need to pretend we've gotten caught up in the moment. We're capable of making a thoughtful choice. I've decided I want this relationship to move up to the next level, and I think that's what you want too."

"I don't know—"

"You do know. You know exactly what you want in a man, don't you?"

"Well, I—"

"Come on, admit it. You are feeling this same attraction that I feel. Isn't that right?"

"Well, yes, but—"

"But the newspaper. But the conflict with my job. But your son. I won't listen to anymore buts. That's why I want to take you away from all of that. I want it to be just you and me. Then we can relate on the most basic level.

Once we build the basic human bond, all the rest of this stuff can be worked out."

"Where would we go?"

"What does it matter? I don't want you to go away with me just because I can fly you to my own private island in the Bahamas or take you to a mountain retreat or enjoy the lights of Broadway from a penthouse suite. I want you to say you will go away with me because you want to be with me. I want you to say you have decided to take a chance on me, to move up to the next level of commitment and intimacy. Will you do that, Josie?"

"You have got to be the most persuasive man I have ever met. Yes, Zach Teasdale, I will go away with you, even if we end up in a tent in the woods. I've got to see what happens next."

Chapter 35

Zelda

I'm OK. Really. It's just this dang mascara. Gets all over my face when I cry. Mind if I smoke? It's about the only thing that helps.

Needless to say, this isn't going the way I planned. The raid results in a couple of arrests and a slap on the wrist for Boardman. It's all a setup. He says he allows the local Catholic Church to run innocent games of chance in the ballroom occasionally without securing the proper charity permit. The photo in the *Daily News* shows a priest and two nuns climbing into the back of the paddy wagon. It makes the cops look like fools raiding a church event that is raising money for missions in Africa. My stories become a dinner-time joke. And the real casino at the Herkimer is back in business the next day.

You'd think I'd just let it go, but I can't. Gambling isn't the only illegal activity at the casino. There are prostitutes and drug sales as well. It's just going to take a lot more watching and listening to get enough facts for my reporters to follow up.

And besides, I have this thing for Al.

This thing. You'd think I'd know better at my age. But I have to see him. Have to. I stumble through my days in the office waiting for my nights in his arms. Two or three nights a week he rents a room at the Herkimer. Some nights we never even make it to the casino.

Now you are probably wondering how I can maintain such an intimate relationship without flipping my blonde wig, so to speak. Well, that silly thing doesn't last thirty minutes. That first night, the night of the raid, I rip off that wig before I unhook my stockings. Once a man sees your girdle, there aren't any more secrets.

Besides, I want to know Al completely and be known completely. Isn't that what making love is? You unzip your dress and open up your heart. Who would want to show a man every ripple of fat on her thighs if she can't trust him with her highest ambitions and deepest fears?

So I tell Al that I'm involved in the stories that have been appearing in the paper. At first, I only admit to being one of the "sources," but I am so proud of the stories the *Spectator* is printing that I soon take full credit as the paper's editor, Zelda Machinko.

Al also "comes clean." He is a lawyer for a Chicago law firm and specializes in corporate law, just as he had told me before. But Boardman is one of his clients.

"I'm involved up to my natty little bolo tie," he tells me one night as we are nestled together in our hotel room.

Between us we probably have enough information to get some serious charges filed against Boardman, but we'd have to go to the feds. Clearly some of the local cops are involved. I'm not willing to publicly acknowledge my spying campaign. I may need to go undercover again sometime. Al doesn't want to turn on his client. Even if he didn't lose his license, who would want to hire an attorney who runs to the feds when a client is skirting the law? So I remain the quiet airhead blonde at Al's elbow, almost invisible. I talk to prostitutes in the ladies' room trying to glean a little information about that arm of the Boardman empire and keep my ears peeled for any mention of drug connections.

Then Sid Collins turns up dead, garroted in his own garage. They didn't even try to hide the body or cover it up with a fire.

"It's probably a message to somebody, a warning," Al says as we're sitting up in bed, puffing on cigarettes after a sweaty session of lovemaking.

Who is Boardman warning? Another gambler who hasn't paid his debts? Another cheating dealer? Or has Boardman figured out that Collins is the "unidentified local businessman" mentioned in my stories? I visited Collins personally. Did I reveal something that could blow my cover?

A few minutes later, Al's in the shower and I'm dressing. As I step into my tall red heels, it hits me. The shoes. I've been wearing the same shoes in the office and in the casino. Did someone notice? Boardman? Collins? I scan my memory. Did anyone make a comment about my shoes? One of the prostitutes? Yes, I'm sure one of the women in the restroom made a comment. But she never would have had the opportunity to see me wearing the shoes as Zelda Machinko. Or would she?

I tell Al maybe Sid's death is a warning to me.

"You can't go back into the casino," he says. "Get out of here as quickly as you can. If someone asks about Lyn, I'll tell them we had a fight. I'll say I found out you've been screwing some guy in St. Louis."

"But if they suspect that Lyn is the leak, then they will suspect you too," I protest.

"Probably, but I'll think of something. I'll stop coming to the casino, tell them the boss has me working on a big case in the city."

"Can't you just get out of town?" I ask.

"Which town?" Al says, shaking his head. "Jordan? Chicago? The mob is everywhere. If I go to New York or St. Louis, they'll be waiting for me. If the mob wants you dead, you're dead. Our only hope is that you are wrong. Maybe Boardman hasn't made the connection between Lyn and Zelda."

"And if he has, then they'll kill you too!" I bury my head in Al's chest and blubber like a poor defenseless blonde. If I could dig deep within myself, maybe I could find a scrap of Zelda's fearlessness, but Zelda seems completely lost to me whenever Al's around. Zelda can be brave because she never loved like this. She never was this happy. She never had anything to lose. But now I know love, and I know I'm going to lose it.

"It's better if we don't try to contact each other," I say, pulling away from Al. "Even if they don't know about the Lyn connection, they know how to find Zelda. She's right next door."

"But you can't keep doing these stories. They definitely will kill you."

"If I stop doing the stories, I might as well be dead. Boardman will have won."

"Some gambles are worth losing," Al says, holding me tight. "How will I contact you when the coast is clear?"

"Clear?" I squeal. "Don't you see there's no way out? No hope. They are going to kill me. There's nowhere I can run, no cops who will protect me. My only hope is that you will be safe. Please, don't come back here. Don't contact me. Promise me."

"I can't make a promise like that."

"You're all I have. Please, promise me that you will leave this casino tonight and never look back. When they get me, it will be in all the papers. You'll know. And until then, I'll be reading the *Tribune* every day, hoping I don't see anything about a missing attorney."

"But eventually—"

"No, my love. We will never, ever see each other again. I'm dead. But if you survive, a little bit of me will survive. Promise me."

❄

So that's how we left it, kiddo. Damn these fancy Italian shoes. Damn, damn, damn. I know that's what tipped them off. They're my signature, like great big red fingerprints.

Give me another cigarette. Oh, that tastes good. Why is it Boardman can be mixed up in all this murder and mayhem, and he comes through it unscathed? Wearing his fancy suit, livin' in his big brick house. Not a scared bone in his body. His son grows up to work for the New York Stock Exchange and his daughter marries doctor or dentist. Livin' like respectable folks. He comes home at night and watches television. And what about Sid and Sid's family? They pay the price. Like my Papa. And now me. This is going to cost me my life. There's no getting around it. Boardman is gonna get me. I'll tell you what. When he does, I'll kick off one of my fancy shoes as a sign that it was him. Then you'll know for sure. I want you to do lots of stories in the paper. Keep hounding the cops. Don't let me die in vain. I'm counting on you, kiddo. Make sure Boardman pays.

Chapter 36

Friday evening, after Kevin left with his father for the Memorial Day weekend, Josie opened the cardboard box she had picked up at Daniel Pasternak's house.

"Take them all," his wife had said, pointing to the files in their basement. "I don't have any use for them, and Danny will never be back to normal. You'll be doing me a favor. I'll just have to haul them all out to the trash."

Josie chose only the box marked with a big "Z" in green marker. Mrs. Pasternak said that was the former detective's mark for papers relating to Zelda Machinko.

"I'll bet he hasn't looked at any of those boxes in a dozen years," Mrs. Pasternak had said as she followed Josie down the sidewalk to her car. "Hope you don't find any rats in there. But don't say I didn't warn you. Might want to keep a can of bug spray handy."

Josie used an old rag to brush off the dust and cobwebs before she lifted a handful of files out of the box and spread them on her kitchen table. As she munched a tuna sandwich, she glanced through the forms, mostly typewritten translations of interviews, smudged and faded, hard to read. Every now and then she would come across something interesting, a name she recognized, like Mr. Hendrix, who used to run the hardware store, or interviews conducted by Maggie's late husband, George Sheffield.

Most of the pages, however, only repeated what Josie already knew. She hadn't made it halfway through the box when Chippie whimpered to go out. Two hours had passed. It was getting dark. She went out and stood on the patio for a minute, refreshed by the cool breeze and the sound of crickets chirping in the grass.

"A bunch of junk," Josie thought as she followed Chippie and Buttons back into the kitchen. "I'll never get through this whole box."

Instead, she should start packing. She was leaving with Zach in the morning, destination unknown. Just away. Together. Bring a swimsuit, he had said. And a nice dress for dinner. But other than that, Josie was on her own. It was going to be an adventure, possibly the beginning of a great love affair. Possibly a horrible mistake. She was putting off the packing until the last minute because the whole idea frightened her. And yet it was all she could think about.

She gathered the papers on the kitchen table and put them back into their green folders. She was trying to maintain the order, though she wasn't sure exactly what order the folders had been in. Most had lost their plastic labels. She picked up the dozen or so folders to return them to the cardboard box, but the files didn't want to drop back into the space from which they'd come. Something had fallen underneath the files, something from the loose papers stuffed in the back. Josie pressed the folders back, reached in her hand, and felt along the bottom of the box.

Hope I don't find a rat, she thought.

Instead her fingers felt a more familiar shape. A shoe. She pulled it out and held it up. Unbelievable! A red high-heeled shoe!

Josie ran down the hall to her bedroom, where she had stashed Maggie's suitcase of clippings. She threw the case on the bed, slid the brass latches with her thumbs, and the case popped open. On top of all the clippings was an identical red shoe.

Josie held the shoes side by side and then switched sides. The dusty one from Pasternak's box was the right foot of the pair, she realized. The one from Maggie's case, shiny from Josie rubbing it so often in recent weeks, was for the left foot.

Josie was panting. What did this mean? She had always assumed Maggie had received her red shoe from the police after they were no longer pursuing the case. She figured George had brought it home. But Pasternak had never closed the case. He'd never given up any of the evidence. He kept the red shoe that was found on the loading dock, the one Zelda kicked off when she was taken. That had to be the right shoe, Josie repeated to herself as she held up the dusty one.

But how did Maggie get the mate? Josie reached for the shiny left shoe and rubbed her fingers across its silky, paisley-embossed fabric. According to the legend, Zelda had kicked off one shoe as a sign. The other shoe, presumably, stayed on Zelda's foot. So how did Maggie get it? Did this mean Zelda didn't disappear? Or did it mean that after she disappeared, Maggie made up the story about the shoe? The shoe that was found on the dock wasn't kicked off in a life-threatening struggle; it was placed there. Calmly. Methodically. Zelda, or possibly Maggie, had planted it as a clue. Then Maggie's stories in the newspaper had created the legend.

But why? Why?

There was only one logical reason. To frame Boardman for Zelda's disappearance.

But that couldn't be. Maggie couldn't possibly have taken part in such an elaborate ruse. Zelda, perhaps. Josie was willing to believe that devious Zelda, in her zeal to make Boardman pay for other crimes, might have faked her own kidnapping and murder. Zelda had tried in vain to bring attention to Boardman's crimes. The *Spectator* headlined the murder of Sid Collins and the disappearance of some underworld casino dealer, but the *Daily News* and the *Chicago Tribune* had ignored those crimes. It wasn't until a lady newspaper editor disappeared and Maggie started telling her story in the *Daily News* that the whole country listened.

But surely, Maggie didn't knowingly make up all those stories. Surely, she must have believed that Zelda had disappeared. She must have been convinced of Boardman's guilt. Maggie was a journalist who honored truth above all. Didn't she?

But if she had the other shoe all this time, she knew. Maggie knew the truth.

Without thinking it through, Josie dropped the shoes into a brown paper grocery sack and jumped into her car. She had to talk to Maggie. Even though it was late. Even though Maggie couldn't talk. She needed answers.

She drove downtown and parked across the street from the Herkimer. It was dark now, with the streetlights creating an eerie pinkish glow around the old buildings. The Red Geranium was still open. Josie could hear a couple laughing as they came out of the restaurant and headed to their car. The Herkimer looked closed. Josie punched in the daytime code she had memorized, and the front door opened. The lobby was dark, with only a small desk lamp glowing at the empty reception desk. Josie slipped into the elevator and emerged on the third floor. The halls were quiet without the usual clutter of wheelchairs and lost residents eager for some attention. Everyone must be in bed already.

Josie found Maggie's door open. The room was dark except for a glow coming from the television. Maggie's bed was cranked up into a sitting position, and she seemed to be watching the action on the screen.

"Oh, good, you're still awake," Josie said, flicking on the overhead light switch. If the light disturbed Irene in the other bed, she didn't show it. She remained in the same position as always, staring off into space without any expression.

"I need to talk to you," Josie said as she dumped the contents of the paper sack onto Maggie's bed. "See these shoes? These are Zelda's shoes. Do you remember?"

Maggie's eyes were wide open. She worked her mouth, but no sound came out. Josie spied the Ouija board on the nightstand and laid it on Maggie's lap.

"This is the shoe that was in the suitcase at your house," Josie said, placing the left shoe on the board. "And tonight I found this shoe in an evidence box I got from Daniel Pasternak."

Maggie moaned.

"Yeah, big problem," Josie said, tapping the right shoe on the board. "This is the shoe that the police had. This is the shoe that was found on the loading dock."

Josie picked up the left shoe with her other hand. "Where did this shoe come from, Maggie? How did you get this shoe?"

Maggie made her "oooo" sound.

"Spell it, Maggie. How did you get this shoe?"

Maggie's finger pointed to the Z.

"Zelda. Zelda gave it to you."

Maggie pointed to the "yes" in the corner of the board.

Josie held up the two shoes. "Did Zelda give you both shoes? Did you plant one on the dock? Did you make up the whole story?"

Maggie looked at Josie like she didn't understand the question.

"Maggie, did you make up the whole story about Zelda kicking off a shoe? Is it all a lie?"

Maggie's hand slowly found the "yes."

"Damn it, Maggie! How could you do something like this?"

Maggie reached out a finger, moving to the "B-O-A—."

"Boardman," Josie said.

Maggie's finger slid to "K-I-L—."

"Boardman killed somebody. Zelda. He killed Zelda."

Maggie worked her finger on the board again, pointing to M-A-N-Y.

"Boardman killed many. I know. But that's up to the cops. It's no excuse to make up a story. It violates everything newspapers stand for."

"O-N-L-Y-W-A-Y," Maggie spelled out quickly. "B-A-D-C-O-P-S."

"Did George know what you were doing?"

Maggie's finger moved to the "yes."

"Of course he did. You were working together on it, weren't you? But what good did it do? Boardman never was arrested. Never convicted of anything."

Maggie pulled her hand back into her lap, and one corner of her mouth lifted as though she was trying to smile.

"He died. Killed by other gangsters. His cronies."

Josie looked at the distorted smile firmly planted on Maggie's face. It was the proudest, most satisfied look Maggie had managed since her stroke. Josie realized what was making her smile.

"Boardman's cronies turned on him because he was a liability. His reputation was bringing too much attention to their rackets. They had to get rid of him because of all the publicity."

Everything seemed to be buzzing around in Josie's head. Maggie, Josie's perfect example of the journalist's eternal search for truth, was the opposite. She had used the power of the press to perpetrate a lie. A lie that became a legend. A lie that destroyed at least two lives. Josie put her hands over her ears to block out the deafening roar. It was crashing down on her. Everything she believed in. What was that awful buzzing sound? Was she going insane?

No. The sound was real. It was an alarm. A fire alarm.

"What is this?" Josie asked. "Some sort of drill?"

She stuck her head into the hall.

Gary, the nursing assistant, was rushing toward her. "What are you doing here? Where's that alarm coming from?"

"I don't know," Josie said. "Is it a drill?"

"Stupid time to have a drill," Gary said, grabbing a wall phone. He tried several numbers before he got an answer from one of the nurses on another floor. "I don't know what it is," Gary said. "Any smoke up there? Can we confirm whether this is the real thing?"

Some of the more ambulatory residents were getting out of bed, coming into the hall.

"Put on a robe, Mr. Hendrix," Gary said to a man wearing only disposable underwear. He handed the receiver to Josie as he tried to steer Hendrix into his room. "Keep calling the main desk," Gary said over his shoulder. "Try to get confirmation. I'm going to put some of the walking wounded on the elevator and get them out of here."

"But what about the ones who can't walk? How will we get them out?" Josie said, standing with the receiver in one hand.

Gary disappeared into a room and returned with a robe wrapped around Hendrix. Daniel Pasternak was standing in his doorway.

"Come on, guys. I'm going to take you two downstairs." Gary corralled the two men toward the elevator and pushed the button. "Can't get Thelma to answer the phone. She's probably running around trying to figure what set off the alarm."

Gary slapped the button again. "Dang it. The elevator's been turned off. The alarm must have shut it off automatically."

Gary put an arm around each man's waist and hurried them toward the stairs. "Call the alarm company," he yelled to Josie. "Tell them we need to have the elevator turned back on. There must be some sort of override."

Josie saw a list of typed numbers taped to the wall beside the phone. She ran a finger down the list, looking for the alarm company. About the time she found the number, Gary opened the door to the stairwell, and the first whiff of smoke entered the hall. The stairwell was full of residents from the fourth and fifth floors, chattering as they worked their way down the stairs.

"Excuse me, ladies," Gary said, pushing Hendrix and Pasternak into the stairwell. "Will you ladies please keep an eye on these two guys? Keep them with the residents' group in the parking lot. Don't let them wander off."

Two women linked their arms around Pasternak and a third took Hendrix's elbow.

"But you aren't my Sophie," Hendrix complained. "Where's my Sophie?"

"Just follow these ladies outside to the parking lot. Sophie is coming," Gary said.

A recording answered at the alarm company. Josie slammed down the phone and returned to Maggie's room.

"Come on, Maggie. We need to get you into your wheelchair." The chair was folded along the wall. Josie unfolded it and rolled it next to the bed.

"Here, put your arm around my neck, and I'll lift you into the chair." Just as Josie was lifting Maggie, the lights flickered and went out. Several of the residents squealed like children afraid of the dark. Even at night, the Herkimer was never dark. Light always filtered into the rooms from the hall. But now the room was so dark Josie could barely see Maggie. She felt for the handles of the wheelchair and pulled Maggie into the hall. In the hall, Josie bumped into two more residents in chairs. She could hear Gary talking to a woman with a walker, but she couldn't see them.

"Adeline, I think you can make it down the stairs," he said, trying to guide the woman toward the stairs. "Damn the elevator. I don't think we can get all these chairs down the stairs."

A nurse carrying an extra flashlight emerged from the stairwell.

"I can manage one of these chairs on the stairs," she said, handing Gary the flashlight and steering one of the chairs into the stairwell.

The beam from the flashlight was diffused through a haze of smoke. The light bounced off the faces of half a dozen people in wheelchairs lining the hall, coughing, crying, calling for help. Josie knelt beside Maggie.

"Maggie, do you know how to get to Zelda's escape hatch? Do you know where the secret door is?"

In the glimmer from the flashlight, Josie could make out Maggie's finger pointing down the hall. Josie rolled her in that direction. The hall was dark, with only a faint light coming from Gary's flashlight as he brought each resident into the hall. Josie clanged Maggie's chair into a supply cart she didn't see. She pushed on. When they reached the door to the stairwell, it was slightly ajar. They could hear the echo of panicky voices as the residents made their way down the stairs. Flickers of flashlights seeped through the opening. Maggie thrust out an arm in the direction of a closet door across the hall. Josie opened the door and felt inside. She rolled a mop bucket into the hall and worked her way into the closet. She banged her fists on the walls. Solid plaster-on-lathe construction. But the back wall sounded hollow, as if it was made of plywood. Josie banged harder. She struck close to the edges, looking for a hinge or latch. Then she pounded the other side. Suddenly the wall trembled and swung open.

Fresh, clean air poured in through the opening. But the passage was so dark that Josie couldn't discern a floor. It appeared to be an open shaft. She got down on her knees in the closet and reached her hand through the opening to assure herself there was a floor on the other side. When she felt a solid floor, Josie turned around, grabbed Maggie's wheelchair, and headed into the inky blackness. It was so dark that she pushed Maggie into a wall she couldn't see. They edged along the wall. It was like walking through a house of horrors, unable to see what slimy creatures might jump out at any moment. The passage turned and in the distance, Josie could see windows, stripes of gray light across the wooden floor.

"I know this room," she told Maggie. "There's a light and an elevator."

No sooner had she said the words than she ran into a string hanging from a bulb. Josie pulled the string, and the light glowed. The restaurant building still had power. Josie pushed the button on the elevator, and it roared to life.

"The elevator is coming," she said to Maggie. "I'm going to get another passenger. I'll be right back. Don't worry. Don't be afraid."

Josie ran back into the blackness, hitting walls, feeling her way, following the smell of smoke. She grabbed the first wheelchair she came to. "This way," she hollered to Gary. "The elevator is working next door."

She pushed the chair into the closet, out the back side, and into the blackness. It was like crossing into Narnia through the back of a wardrobe. The darkness was so deep, it fooled the senses. Josie just had to believe there still was a floor beneath her feet and she wasn't stepping off the end of the earth. This time she didn't hit the wall. When she reached the elevator, Maggie had managed to move her chair into the opening.

"Good girl," Josie said, wheeling in the second chair.

"Miss Maggie? Where are you?" Gary's voice echoed over the sound of coughing.

"We're here," Josie responded, running back into the darkness. She followed the sound of coughing, the smell of smoke, until she could see a wheelchair resident with Gary's glowing flashlight in her lap.

"What is this place?" Gary asked.

"A secret passage into the building next door. I'll take this one the rest of the way. You go back and get another."

Josie handed Gary his flashlight and wheeled the third resident into the elevator. She pulled the rope to close the gate and turned the knob to select the floor. The elevator jerked and moved. When the elevator reached the ground floor, one of the kitchen helpers was waiting.

"What's going on? Where did you come from?"

"The Herkimer is on fire," Josie said. "You take these residents outside to the parking lot. I'll go back for the rest."

Josie pushed the chairs off the elevator and returned to the third floor, where Gary had assembled three more. Josie wheeled them into the elevator as Gary arrived with the fourth.

"Is this all?" Josie asked.

"I'm … going back … for Lady Irene," Gary said coughing between words.

"I'll send these down and go with you," Josie said, pulling the rope to close the gate and turning the knob to start the elevator.

Gary handed Josie a damp washcloth. "Cover your mouth. It's really bad in there."

By the time Josie and Gary returned to the closet in the Herkimer, it was filled with heavy smoke. They couldn't breathe. They crawled along the floor trying to get a little air. In Maggie's room, they took opposite ends of the sheet on Irene's bed and lifted her. Her eyes were open, and she was sputtering. Not coughing fully, but affected by the smoke.

"Save your breath, dear lady," Gary said as he wiped a damp cloth across her face and then laid it lightly over her mouth and nose.

Hunched over, Gary dragged the sheet as Josie crawled along on her knees, moving chair and table legs out of the way and trying to protect Irene's head with her hand. The smoke made Josie's eyes water so much that she kept them closed and felt for obstructions. Behind them, they could hear firefighters coming up the stairs. A firefighter came out of the stairwell just before they got to the closet.

"We've got the last resident from three!" Gary yelled to the fireman. "Check four and five!"

As Gary and Josie stumbled through the secret passage, dragging Irene on the sheet, the smoke thinned and oxygen seemed to rush into Josie's lungs. She was able to stand again. She picked up her end of the sheet, and they carried Irene the last few steps through the darkness of the Red Geranium's third floor. The freight elevator was just arriving, and one of the dishwashers emerged when the gate opened.

"Any more?" he asked, as Josie and Gary staggered into the elevator. They lowered Irene onto the safety of the elevator floor. Josie fell back against the cage of the elevator, gasping for air. Gary doubled over coughing.

"Gee, she don't look so good," the dishwasher said, bending over Irene.

"She always looks that way," Josie said between gasps of air.

But Gary fell to his knees and grabbed Irene's wrist. Then he reached up to search for a pulse in her neck.

"Damn!" he hissed. "Damn, damn, damn. She's not breathing."

Gary bent over and puffed into Irene's mouth, then he positioned his arms over the center of her chest and started the rhythmic percussions of CPR.

"Get this elevator moving," Josie said to the dishwasher, who quickly complied. As soon as they were on the first floor, firemen and paramedics rushed into the elevator to take over. Josie and Gary backed out of the space.

"She's not going to make it," Gary said. "Lady Irene is dead."

❋

Once outside, Gary found his charges in the parking lot, all except two who had been transported to the hospital for smoke inhalation. Josie found Maggie and wrapped her arms around her.

"We made it! We made it!" Josie cried.

Maggie mumbled a word that sounded like "How?"

Josie pulled back, unable to believe her ears. Maggie had spoken.

"Did you just ask me how we made it?"

"How?" Maggie repeated.

Josie was on her knees now, looking into Maggie's face. Firemen, paramedics, and bystanders were bustling around, but it seemed in that instant that there were just the two of them. The light in the parking lot was bright enough for them to see each other clearly, and a bubble of cool night air seemed to enclose them.

"How did I know about the secret passage? Zelda told me. In my dreams." Josie laid her head on Maggie's lap. "I know it sounds crazy, but she's been telling me everything. About the paperboy. And Sid Collins' death. And Al. I don't know what's true and what's fantasy." Maggie's fingers brushed Josie's hair. Josie lifted her head and looked into Maggie's face. "But the secret passage was true. I didn't imagine that."

Josie still had her head in Maggie's lap when Becky found them. She was the reporter on duty that Friday night.

"Should have known Maggie would find some way to be the first on the scene," Becky said with a laugh. "If she can't get to the news, the news comes to her."

Josie stood up and explained that she had been visiting Maggie when the alarm went off.

"I know you. You didn't trust Maggie to cover it on her own," Becky teased.

Gary walked over with a fireman.

"This is the woman who got us out," Gary told the fireman. "The elevator was off. We couldn't have gotten all these wheelchairs down the stairs in time. Somehow, she knew about a hidden door into the neighboring building."

The fireman turned to Josie. "I never knew about a link between these buildings. How did you know?"

Josie's mouth was dry. She couldn't say Zelda Machinko told her in a dream. She couldn't say Zelda built the secret passage to spy on Buster Boardman. But thanks to her crazy dreams, she had escaped that burning hotel and was breathing the cool night air. Becky had her pen poised to record Josie's answer. Josie glanced at Maggie and her distorted half-smile.

"It was Maggie," Josie said. "She told me once that when the Herkimer was a hotel, there was a passage between the two buildings. It was in the back of a closet. I asked her where and she pointed. She saved us. Maggie saved us."

Chapter 37

The sewer construction area was dark and abandoned when Duke arrived about three in the morning. He replayed the late-night call in his mind.

"If you want the full story, meet us at the sewer project. Twenty minutes."

The caller sounded like Herbie, but he hung up before Duke could ask. Twenty minutes hadn't given him much time to sort out his options. He had pulled on his jeans and grabbed a notebook. He didn't even wash his face or stop for a cup of coffee. And he didn't call the cops.

He figured Herbie and Ron had set the fire at T&T Construction, a convenient little blaze to destroy company records before they could be subpoenaed by Wheeler and the Justice Department. Maybe the fire was supposed to be confined to the first-floor office. Surely they didn't intend to set the whole building ablaze. But several elderly residents had been hospitalized, and Duke knew at least one woman was dead. Another screwup by the bungling big-bod boys. The cops would be looking for them. Wheeler's team probably would be too.

The hotel fire was under control, Duke knew, but the air still smelled of smoke. Even several miles from downtown at the sewer construction site, the odor was sharp, like a fall evening after a day of leaf burning. Duke parked his turquoise Pontiac at the corner of Jackson and Pearl, about where Blaine Avril's truck was found a month earlier. He sat in the car a minute, hoping to see some sign of activity, but there were no lights at the site trailer, no sound from any of the earthmovers. The white tent at the archaeological dig flapped in the breeze like a flag of surrender.

Duke got out of his car and walked down to the site. He followed the giant snake-like train of concrete pipe sections that lined the north side of Jackson Street. He was walking east, toward the trailer, when he heard a voice.

"Psst. In here."

He paused and looked inside one of the five-foot cylinders. Nothing. Beside it stood a shorter upright section. A manhole. Duke cocked his head to look inside and found Herbie.

"Come on. Follow me," Herbie said, hefting himself out of the concrete case and lowering himself down into the trench below. Rich Illinois prairie soil formed the inky-black walls in the trench. The pungent earthy odor made the site seem safe, peaceful. Duke followed as Herbie ran along the trench for a hundred yards or so. They climbed back up onto the roadbed, where a faded Komatsu excavator stood with its boom lifted high like the neck of gigantic swan.

Duke could see a man in the large cab. The tinted fiberglass door opened, and Ron looked down at them.

221

"I'd invite you in, but it's pretty much a one-man castle," Ron said. He had a beer in one hand and a cigarette in the other, with rock music booming from the radio.

"Turn that crap down so we can talk!" Herbie shouted.

"Just talk louder!" Ron shouted back as he turned the volume down a little. Herbie sat on one of the treads and motioned for Duke to do the same.

"Listen, guys. This is cutting into my dream time," Duke said as he leaned against the tread, his feet still firmly on the ground. "If you've got a story to tell, I'm listening."

"It was your idea," Ron said, motioning to Herbie with his cigarette.

"Yeah, well, I'm beginning to think you were right. Tate is setting us up."

"Setting you up?" Duke repeated.

"Yeah, like tonight. He told us to stop by the main office downtown. Pick up some files."

"And burn the rest," Ron said. "Except the cap he gave us wasn't no little incinerator like he said. It exploded in a gush and almost caught us inside. He was trying to kill us."

"I don't know if he meant to kill us, but it sure wasn't a small, slow fire like he said it would be," Herbie added. "He said to hit the fire alarm first so they'd have time to start evacuating the building. He said all those people leaving would make the perfect cover for us. Wait three minutes, he says, and light the fuse. That's what we did."

"Yeah, but scaredy-cat here was halfway out the door before I lit it," Ron said.

"Good thing I was, or we would have been blown up. I was able to grab you and get gone."

"OK, you set the fire on orders from Tate," Duke said, making notes in his notebook. "You got any proof to implicate him? This cap or whatever he gave you. You got anything with his name or his fingerprints?"

"Don't you believe us?" Herbie said, punching Duke's shoulder.

Duke flinched. "*I* believe you. It's just I'm wondering if you got some proof. The police are going to need some proof."

"Hell, no, we don't have proof," Ron said, swinging down from the cab. "Everything got burned up, including the files we were supposed to save."

"What files were those?" Duke asked.

"I don't know. Annual budget. Articles of incorporation. That sort of stuff," Ron said.

"Articles of incorporation?"

"Yeah, stupid legal stuff. Deeds and stuff."

"Deeds?"

"Listen. They burned up. OK?" Herbie said.

"But if you're right. If Tate didn't intend for you to survive, then why did he ask you to save some files?" Duke asked.

"See, I told you," Herbie said, shoving Ron. "He didn't mean to kill us. It was just an accident."

"It weren't no accident," Ron said, knocking Herbie's head into the side of the cab.

Herbie lunged off his perch on the tread and punched Ron. Soon the two were rolling in the dirt, fighting. Duke reached up into the cab, grabbed a cold beer from the three remaining, shook it well, and popped the tab in the direction of the fighters.

"Buzzard butts, break it up!" Duke shouted as the cold beer sprayed over the men. "We gotta figure out your defense. The cops are after you, and so is Tate."

Ron pulled back, shaking off the beer that had soaked his T-shirt. Herbie looked up from the ground, and Ron helped him to his feet.

"Tell me about the shooting of Blaine Avril. Was that Tate's idea too?"

"Hell, no," Ron said, reaching up into the cab for another beer. "We went over there, yeah, 'cause Tate wanted us to rough up the mole and bring him back for questioning. We didn't even have a gun."

"We don't need guns," Herbie said, holding up his fists.

"Bastard pulls a gun on us. That's what happened," Ron said, taking a swig of beer.

"And I took it away from him," Herbie said, inflating his chest proudly.

"You took it away?" Duke said. "He was a former Navy Seabee who knew how to handle guns, so that's a pretty good trick if you got his weapon away from him."

"Well, I'm a former Marine. I could have been special ops," Herbie said.

"Not with all your time in the brig," Ron said. "But he did get the gun away from him."

"Yeah, I keep it with me now," Herbie said, pulling a gun out of his waistband.

"That was his gun? That's the one you used to shoot Avril in the head?" Duke asked.

"No," Ron and Herbie said in unison.

"All I did was bind his hands with electrician's tape so he wouldn't try any more tricks," Ron said, downing the last of his beer.

"He was a slippery mole, that one," Herbie added.

"Mole? Why do you keep calling Avril a mole?" Duke asked.

"Because he was spying on us, trying to sabotage our project," Herbie said.

"Spying?"

"Yeah, taking pictures. Measuring pipe. Poking in the files," Ron said. "He was a mole from Anderson or one of those contractors in Michigan. We

223

beat out Anderson for this job, and he was trying to cause trouble. Get us thrown off the job."

"Tate cuts corners," Herbie said. "He uses a lower grade of pipe than the specs call for. Means the sewer will fall apart in thirty or forty years instead of being tight for a hundred or more. But none of the city council members will be around in forty years, so what do they care? By the time it starts leaking, this contract will be long forgotten."

"Is that what you think?" Duke asked. "You think Avril was spying for another company? You think that's why he was killed?"

"Listen, I'm not sure why he was killed. But I'm sure he was a mole," Ron said, slapping Duke on the back.

"Listen, you briar burper! What do you mean you don't know why he was killed?" Duke asked.

"That's what we been trying to tell you," Herbie said, reaching for the last beer in the cab. "We didn't shoot Avril. It was some sniper."

"A sniper?"

"Yeah, we were just having a nice little conversation with him, like we are talking with you now," Ron said.

"And *kapow!* A shot comes from the trees. High-power blast to the back of the head, practically blew his head off," Herbie added, popping the top on the beer.

"Who was the sniper?" Duke asked.

"Hell, how do we know? We were too busy ducking for cover," Ron said.

"Let me get this straight. You went over there to rough him up, he pulls a gun, you take it away, and then some unknown sniper shoots him," Duke said.

"That's about it," Herbie said, taking a sip of beer.

"So how did he end up in the back of his truck?"

"We figured somebody might have seen us there, heard the shots, so we rolled him up in a tarp and put him in the back of his truck," Herbie explained. "I didn't want him bleeding all over my new truck."

"I drove his truck down here," Ron said. "I figured we could dig a hole during the course of the day's construction work, and that night, after everybody left, drop him in. Nobody would be the wiser."

"Did you tell Tate what happened?"

"Hell, yes," Ron said. "He was good with it. We just didn't count on the mole bleeding so much that it would be leaking out of that rusted truck bed."

"So you didn't kill the guy, but you were going to bury the body. I gotta tell you, guys. Nobody is going to buy a story like that. Not the cops, not the judge, not the jury."

"It's the truth," Ron said, swinging up into the cab of his excavator.

"Swear to God," Herbie said, holding up his beer like the Statue of Liberty's torch. Just as he did, a gunshot punctured the can about where Ron had been standing only a second before. Duke and Herbie fell to the ground and scrambled behind the treads while Ron pulled the door closed on the cab.

"Flying frog farts. What's going on?" Duke asked.

The sniper's back," Herbie said, pointing toward the white tent. On the observation platform stood a solitary figure with a huge gun resting on the railing. The next shot pierced the cab of the excavator.

"Ron?" Herbie yelled, sticking his head above the treads. Another shot pinged off the metal of the machine, and Duke yanked Herbie back behind the treads.

"He might have got him," Herbie said, pulling out the handgun. "That bastard might have shot Ron. We've gotta help him."

"There's nothing we can do as long as that guy's got a bigger gun," Duke said.

"But my bud could be wounded, bleeding."

The engine of the excavator roared to life, ready proof that Ron was still breathing. Herbie smiled, and then his eyes got wide.

"Holy shit," he yelled as he scrambled from beneath the huge machine. "Move!"

Duke and Herbie pawed their way across the dirt and dropped down into the trench as bullets zinged past them. The boom of the excavator swung around and reached out toward the white tent. The shooter ran across the observation deck and dove into the tent area as the jaws gobbled up the deck like a Godzilla rampage. The boom followed the running shooter, snatching up the canvas of the white tent like a dainty handkerchief.

"Atta boy, Ron. Go get him!" Herbie cheered.

The shooter disappeared for an instant, then Duke heard him clatter down the metal steps and saw him drop behind the row of cement pipe. Several police cars with lights flashing and sirens wailing were converging on the scene. Someone must have reported the gunfire. The excavator nosed a piece of pipe, and it rolled into the trench.

"Thanks, buddy!" Herbie yelled, waving his gun toward the shadowy cab. "Ron's giving us some cover. Come on."

Herbie ran along the trench toward the pipe, with Duke following close behind. Duke could see the dark outline of a head and gun peeking over the rim of concrete pipe. A shot rang out and Herbie fell. Duke leaped over Herbie and dove into the concrete cylinder in the trench.

Crouched in the cold, damp pipe, Duke couldn't see the sniper or the police, but he could hear the rumbling excavator crashing through the site. He could only imagine the damage the monster machine was doing. Herbie stirred and sat up.

"In here," Duke said, reaching out a hand. Herbie stumbled into the pipe as another shot whizzed by. His shoulder was bleeding.

"This is the police. Put down your weapons and come out with your hands up," said a voice over a bullhorn.

"That means us," Duke said to Herbie.

Instead a shot came from the direction of the excavator, and police responded with a barrage of bullets.

"Damn, the cops think we're shooting at them," Herbie said, holding his pistol at the ready.

Another shot came from the general direction of the excavator, and again police returned fire. The excavator turned, rumbling slowly toward the police cars. Herbie crawled to the edge of the pipe and stood up just enough to see over the rim of the trench. The long boom of the excavator swung into the intersection, dropping a load of dirt and debris onto a police car as the officers ran for cover. Then the boom dropped, slamming into the hood of the car, shattering the windshield and setting off a squealing alarm.

"Holy shit. He's done it now," Herbie said, pulling back inside the pipe. More shots zinged overhead. Herbie stuck his head up and shot at a policeman crouched in the shadows.

"What are you doing?" Duke asked.

"They're shooting at us," Herbie said.

"But you need to put your gun down and your hands up. You'll never win against all those cops."

Moments of silence passed like hours. Then Duke saw some movement in the shadows. Police officers in riot gear were surrounding the excavator.

"No, no!" Herbie yelled, standing up suddenly. His gun was pointed at the policemen. An officer swiveled and shot Herbie in the face. The door of the cab swung open. "Bastards!" Ron yelled. At least three officers shot him, and his body pitched out of the cab, falling face first into the dirt.

Duke remained crouched inside the pipe.

"Freeze!" an officer yelled as he turned his weapon on Duke.

"I don't have a gun," Duke stammered, his arms raised over his head as much as possible in the confines of the pipe. "I'm a reporter."

"Dukakis? I might have known," Wheeler said, as he turned a flashlight into the pipe. "Anyone else in there?"

"No, just me," Duke replied.

Wheeler reached out a hand. Duke accepted the assistance to get out of the pipe and rise to his feet.

"Did you get the sniper?" Duke asked.

Wheeler laughed. "You don't usually call a guy in a rampaging excavator a sniper."

"No, I mean the guy over there by the tent. Before the police cars arrived."

"The tent is gone, gobbled up by the motorized monster," Wheeler said.

"That's where the shooter was. That's why Baylor got into his excavator and tore up the tent. He was chasing the shooter."

"Yeah, well your buddy Baylor tore up some police cars too with that monster machine of his."

"Because you were shooting at him. He was unarmed."

"Wait a minute, Dukakis. It was a righteous kill. Baylor was armed with a monster machine and your buddy on the ground there still has a pistol in his mitt."

"But you heard the shots. They were from a rifle. The sniper got away."

Duke looked down at Herbie's lifeless body. Police photographers were setting up lights and taking pictures.

"His shoulder. The sniper shot him in the shoulder before the police arrived. If you take the slug from the shoulder, it'll be different than the police slug."

"We'll look into it," Wheeler said, walking away.

"Then you believe me?"

Wheeler chuckled and shook his head. "Listen, Dukakis. I know you have a hard time accepting that I'm one of the good guys, but we've known all along that there was somebody else involved besides these two goons."

"Tate," Duke said, following Wheeler as he walked toward the police cars. "Tate told them to set the fire tonight. And Tate sent them after Avril."

"Already sent someone to pick him up," Wheeler responded.

"So you think Tate hired the sniper too?" Duke asked. "To clean up the mess?"

Wheeler paused. "Listen, Dukakis. I'm not talking to you about what I think or don't think. I'm sending you down to the local police station to get a cup of coffee and make your statement. Then I want you to go home. Get some sleep. And stay out of my hair."

Chapter 38

"So that's how we left it, kiddo. I'll never see Al again. Damn these fancy Italian shoes. They're gonna cost me my life and my love. How is it Boardman can be behind all these murders and live like a king? He's got that great big brick house and a fancy car. His son can grow up to be a respectable stock broker in New York and his daughter can marry a doctor or a dentist. He goes home every night and watches television, just like normal folks. What about Sid and his family? They pay the price. Just like my Papa. And now me. I'm gonna lose my life over this. Promise you'll make him pay. When I'm gone, it will be up to you to tell the story so I won't die in vain. Promise me."

Josie sat up and shook her head. Every time she fell asleep, she kept seeing the same scene over and over. Zelda puffing on a cigarette, whining about Boardman and the shoes. Smoke encircled her, making the dream scene hazy, like the horrible smoke-choked hall in the Herkimer.

Josie used to enjoy the dreams. She used to be eager to imagine Zelda's love affair, to cheer on her journalistic pursuit of evil. Now she wanted to forget Zelda. All these years, Maggie had been lying about the shoe. Maybe Zelda really was kidnapped, but the shoe was window dressing. A trick to sell the story. If Josie didn't expose Maggie's lie, she was a part of it. Yet, as much as she hated the thought of lying, she knew there was no way she could expose Maggie. Not now. Not as she neared the end of her life. How could Josie tarnish her career? Her memory?

Josie wrestled with the blanket and threw it off. She should have taken a sleeping pill to blot out the fire. Lady Irene's lifeless face. Maggie's pleading eyes. The dreams. She got up and padded down the dark hallway to the kitchen. In the dim light of the open refrigerator door she poured a little milk into a cup and sipped it. The milk would calm her restless stomach and help her to sleep without the grogginess of a pill.

When the doorbell rang, Josie was surprised to see it was light. She pulled on her robe and answered the door. Zach burst in with his arms outstretched.

"Oh, thank God, you're all right. They told me about the fire last night, but I didn't know until this morning that you were there. I can't believe it," he said, grabbing her in a hug. "I was reading the story in the paper this morning, and I couldn't believe how you helped everyone escape. You're a hero."

Josie fell into Zach's arms. Escape. Escape. She needed to escape the dreams. The memory of the fire. He kissed her and smoothed her hair.

"Come on. Get dressed. I've got the jet all ready to take us away. You need to get away."

Yes. Josie wanted to get away. Forget it all. Leave it behind. Fly off to whatever extravagant rendezvous Zach had planned. But she pulled away from him.

"No, I can't go. I'm sorry." Josie turned away from Zach. "The story. I need …"

Zach followed her across the room, and when she paused, he placed his hands firmly on her shoulders.

"Let your staff take care of that," he whispered in her ear. "You've done enough. You need a break to clear your head. You'll see everything in a new light when you get back."

Yes, Josie thought. Zach was right. Getting away for a few days would refresh her perspective. But it would complicate things too. Going away with Zach might liberate her from the past problems, but she would be pulled into a new intimacy. An exciting but frightening new world.

"I'm sorry. After last night, I just can't leave," Josie said, searching Zach's face for understanding. "I need to check in at the office this morning. Make sure everything's on track."

Zach caressed her cheek.

"OK," he said after a brief pause. "I understand your nose for news is picking up a new scent. We can postpone the flight a few hours. I should really stop by the coroner's office anyway. I didn't want to mention it until we were safely in the air, but there was a shootout early this morning."

"A shootout?"

"Yeah. Police shot the guys who started the fire.

"Oh, my gosh. I'd better call the office."

"Don't worry, madam editor. The *Daily News* is on the story. Our friend Dukakis was right in the middle of it."

"Duke?"

"He's all right. I heard him on the radio on the way over here. He's a regular cowboy."

"I need to get down to the office."

"I understand. Why don't you give me your suitcase. Then we can load up the plane, and you can meet us at the airport, say about two this afternoon. That will give us time to get to Florida for a late dinner."

"I didn't get packed last night. The fire—"

"Oh, don't worry. I'll have Bill pick up a few things for you. It's not going to be a fashion extravaganza anyway. I just want you. You and me. Alone. Away. We need it."

"I don't know—"

229

Zach pulled her into his arms. "Josie, I'm trying to be patient and understanding. I want us to work this out. I believe we can have something very special together. But there always will be another news story getting in the way. You have to choose to put us ahead of your job. I learned that a long time ago. I have to be willing to make a choice for the things I want. And I want you."

"That's sweet, Zach, but—"

Zach placed a finger on her lips to hush further excuses.

"The plane will be ready to go at two o'clock from the industrial hangar. If you choose to give us a chance, you'll be there. If you're not there, we'll fly away without you. I'll walk the moonlit beach alone tonight. It's your choice. But I won't wait forever."

❀

Within an hour, Josie was at her desk listening to Duke regale the reporters with his tale of the shootout at "OK Trench." Duke stomped around the newsroom with one arm hanging over his head trying to impersonate the rampaging excavator. He peppered the story with exaggerations and commentary that kept his audience laughing. Josie knew he was joking to hide his fear and horror at seeing two men shot to death. She also knew his bravado wasn't that different from the foolish cockiness that had gotten Flatt and Baylor killed.

Josie, on the other hand, said little about the fire at the Herkimer. If someone asked, she'd simply hang her head and say she'd rather not think about it. She was afraid if she talked about it, someone would ask what she was doing visiting Maggie so late at night. She was afraid someone would find out about Maggie's lie.

Josie thought it was ironic that both she and Duke seemed to have become the thing they despised. While Duke was spouting a masculine masquerade, Josie was learning to live with a lie.

"If these two nimwits had just put their hands up and surrendered, they'd be alive today," Duke said. "But no. They have to jump up and shout something stupid, scare the cops, and get shot for their stupidity. You don't argue with an assault weapon."

"So, who was the sniper?" Josie asked. "Did they ever catch him?"

"No, but they arrested Tate. He'll probably spill all," Duke said.

Josie was working with Hoss and Duke to plan the Sunday stories when the guard ushered Fred Wheeler into the newsroom.

"Dukakis, a moment of your time, please," Wheeler said, jerking his thumb toward the conference room.

"Who does he think he is?" Josie said as Wheeler proceeded to move into the conference room as if he owned the place.

"I'm not going to tell him he has to leave," the guard said. "He's armed and so are his buddies outside."

"He said please," Duke said with a shrug. "That's downright polite for him."

Duke headed into the conference room, and Josie was right behind him. Wheeler didn't question her presence.

"I hear you filed a Freedom of Information request for financial information about Herkimer House. What's that about?"

"Well, it seems like a moot point now," Duke said, offering a chair to Josie and then taking a seat next to her. "Sounds like the Herkimer is too damaged to reopen."

"Exactly. This fire destroyed records we were about to confiscate from T&T Construction. But it may have destroyed the records you were requesting too. Were these documents stored at the Herkimer House or the county office?"

"I don't know, but I doubt I'll see them now," Duke said.

"Probably not," Wheeler agreed. "Sounds a little too convenient."

Duke explained the high rent being paid for the Herkimer and the ownership being cloaked in a trust. "So you're thinking NBT Trust could be connected to this fire?" Duke asked. He knew Wheeler probably wouldn't respond.

"For the record, this case is closed," Wheeler said, leaning back in his chair. "Terry Tate confessed to everything. He admitted using substandard pipe on the project and ordering a fire to cover up the records. He even said he was the mystery sniper who killed our agent Timothy Norton, alias Blaine Avril, and started the shootout last night. He's supplied the rifle he said he used, and I have no doubt it will match the slugs."

"But you don't think he did it?"

Wheeler smiled. "Doesn't matter. He's a pawn. Somebody else is moving the pieces. Off the record, there's an influence network that's arranging road and bridge contracts in Illinois. They've got the influence to get the contracts, get the federal funds, and then skim off the profits. But we can't catch them at it. Tate was a red flag because he's been involved with the network before. When he got this contract, we thought maybe we could trap him, get him to rat on the network. But it looks like somebody is making it worth his while to go to jail. They're probably taking care of his family, putting his kid through college, while he sits behind bars. Not a bad deal. Worth it to him, anyway. I don't think he's going to change his story, so we're going to accept that confession and close the case."

"So why did you ask me about the Herkimer investigation?"

"Off the record? It sounds like the same network. It's operating the same way. Nothing overtly illegal, but lots of red flags. And lots of government money slipping through fingers."

Duke and Josie exchanged glances.

"We've approached state senator William Stiles," Josie said. "He'll be introducing legislation in the next session to require that all principals must be identified for any entity doing business with a government body in Illinois. If it passes, that will keep a blind trust like NBT from entering into contracts with any city or county."

"That might help," Wheeler said. "Listen. We're leaving town today, actually leaving the state."

"And this conversation never happened," Duke said.

"No, you can quote me on anything about the official closing of this case. Ignore all the off-the-record stuff about the network since we can't prove any of that." Wheeler threw a couple of business cards on the table. "Keep in touch. Let me know if you spot any red flags, and we'll come back."

After Wheeler left, Josie worked with Duke, Becky, and Hoss to finalize story plans for Sunday. Once the plan was in motion, she disappeared into the newspaper morgue. Something from the dreams was nagging at her, so she sat down at the microfilm reader and became lost in the world of the 1950s. She zipped through headlines and advertisements and photographs.

Becky had done a story on the fire for Saturday's paper. For Sunday, she was working on a follow-up about where the displaced residents were living. Some had moved into other nursing facilities; some were staying with family members. Maggie had temporarily returned to the hospital. Katherine was flying in from California and planned to stay long enough to pack up her mother's household. Some things would be sold or given away. The rest would be sent to California, where Maggie would make her new home with her daughter.

Becky was surprised when she looked up, and the guard was escorting Tom Cantrell into the newsroom.

"Look who I found at the back door," the guard said.

"Uh, oh," Duke said. "You're the second cop to make a house call today. That's never a good sign."

Becky just smiled.

"Actually, I'm celebrating," Tom said. "Wheeler and his creepy band of suits-with-hearing-aids piled into their snazzy black cars today and left town."

"Yeah, he was our first visitor. Had to stop by and say goodbye," Duke said.

"Well, can't say I'm sorry to see them go," Tom said as he sauntered over to Becky's desk.

"I'm almost finished," Becky whispered.

"Take your time. I just got antsy waiting in the car," Tom said.

"Uh, oh. Saturday night date?" Duke asked. "You two need a chaperone?"

Becky and Tom exchanged glances.

"Nah, I think we'll rough it on our own," Tom said. "She's going to let me get a look at this mysterious farmhouse she inherited."

"It will be more than just a look. Tom volunteered to help me till a garden patch this afternoon, and I promised him grilled burgers."

"Sounds like a fair trade," Duke said.

Josie burst out of the darkened library and into the brightly lit newsroom. She glanced at the clock.

"Oh, my gosh, it's almost two," she said, rushing for the door.

"Alice in Wonderland?" Tom asked. "Late for a very important date?"

"Actually, that was Peter Pan," Duke said. "Time is a crocodile snapping at her heels."

❈

When Josie pulled up to the industrial hangar at Jordan's small municipal airport, Zach's little white jet was out in front, the engines roaring. Zach emerged from the plane, came down the short stairs, and met her on the tarmac.

"I knew you'd come," he said, reaching for her with both arms.

She held him back. "No, I'm not going. I just wanted you to know that I know."

"What? I can't hear. What are you saying?" Zach waved toward the cockpit, and the engines were silenced. "Now what's this about no, no, no?"

"I said I wanted you to know that I know," Josie repeated. "I know about your mother and Boardman and NBT Trust. I know all about your grandfather. You tell cute stories about Pop-O, the bubble gum namesake. But you neglect to mention he's Buster Boardman, the gangster. You tell my son his sage advice about controlling your temper, but you never tell him that your grandfather controlled all the petty criminals in this county in the 1950s."

"Josie, I think there's been some misunderstanding."

"I don't think so," Josie said, handing Zach a printout from the microfilm. The smudged, gray picture was blurry, but Zach quickly recognized his parents' wedding photo.

"Your mother was Nancy Boardman, Buster's daughter. She married Donald Teasdale, a dentist and the son of the local mortician. I hate to think what kind of business arrangement Grandpa Boardman had with Grandpa Teasdale. But the son, Donald, was your dad. He moved his family up to Naperville and started a bubble gum factory with Grandpa's money. Your mom became Mrs. Teasdale, the dentist's wife. Nobody ever mentioned her maiden name again. Long after Grandpa Boardman was killed and forgotten, you moved back to Cade County as Mr. Teasdale, heir to the local funeral home. Nobody ever made the connection to Boardman."

"You're being ridiculous."

"Do you deny it?"

"Did I ask you who your grandfather was? Do you think I would judge you by his reputation?"

"My dad's father was a bus driver and mom's father was a farmer. My dad was a welder. None of them went to college. And the closest they ever came to gangsters was reading about them in the newspaper."

"Well, maybe the newspapers don't tell the truth about gangsters," Zach said. "I described my grandfather to you accurately. He was a mild, quiet man. Very controlled. Wise."

"Maybe so, but you knew I was doing research on Zelda Machinko. Yet you never said anything in Boardman's defense. You never said she was wrong about him. You never said he was misrepresented in the newspaper."

"And if I had, you wouldn't have believed me. That isn't the point. The point is, you are judging me for something my grandfather might have done. It's in the past."

"Is it? What is NBT Trust? Isn't that the trust for your mother, Nancy Boardman Teasdale? And aren't you the principal in that trust? She probably inherited the Herkimer, and the taxes piled up while it was sitting vacant. So you bought it back for the taxes and then turned around and leased it to the county for more than it's worth. The same county in which you serve as coroner. If nothing else, it's a conflict of interest for you to serve on the board of a facility that is paying rent to you."

"That's all conjecture."

"Yes, but you won't deny it. What else does NBT Trust own? This airplane? T&T Construction? Did you use your influence to get that sewer contract? How much is it inflated above the real cost of construction? That's why the feds were investigating. That's why the records for the Herkimer and the construction company had to be destroyed. Did you order that fire to destroy the records? A fire that almost killed me? A fire that did kill one woman."

"Irene Miller was near death anyway. It was just a matter of time."

"Will you listen to yourself? You're justifying the fire. You did order it, didn't you?"

"This is crazy talk. Your ordeal last night has muddled your mind. I'll get Bill to take you home. Call a doctor. You need a sedative."

Until that moment, Josie hadn't noticed that she was surrounded. Chuck and Bill had come out of the hanger and were standing behind her. Bill stepped forward and took her by the elbow. Josie shrugged him off.

"No, I'm not going anywhere with him or you. What are you going to do, make me disappear like Zelda Machinko?"

Bill took Josie's arm again and held firm while she kicked and screamed. Zach shook his head and laughed.

"Let her go," he said. "You've really gone off the deep end, Josie. I don't know why you think you are being threatened. I wouldn't hurt you."

Zach put a hand on each side of Josie's face, pulling her lips to his. She stubbornly pulled away. Zach held her tight, their faces inches apart.

"It's a shame," he whispered. "We could have been something great together. I wanted to share it all with you."

"Who do you think I am that I would want to share in your power plays?"

"Power is everything. It's the only thing. If you want to change the world, Josie, you have to have power. I can give you that."

"It's not worth selling my soul."

Zach stepped back, pulled himself a little straighter, and held out a hand in a formal farewell. Josie made no move to shake it.

"Well, I'm going to be late for dinner in Boca Raton," he said. "Sorry you won't be joining me."

With that, Zach turned and went up the steps into the plane. Bill and Chuck followed as the engines roared to life.

Chapter 39

Josie beat on the door with both fists. It was after midnight, but she couldn't sleep. How could anyone sleep? The whole world was upside down.

Maggie, who had devoted her life to honest reporting and covering the justice system, had been telling a humongous lie for almost thirty years. Zach, who had seemed so compassionate and understanding, was just using Josie. And it wasn't only her heart at stake. He was manipulating the entire community, winning their trust with good deeds while he was stealing from the government. The Herkimer and the inflated sewer project were just a hint of Zach's deceit, Josie realized. His entire realm of worldwide businesses was under suspicion.

Josie pushed the doorbell button repeatedly and stood on tiptoe to look in the small window in the front door. Duke's house was dark. Maybe he was staying over at Sharon's. Josie knew they were getting back together, and she was happy for them. But right now, she wanted to talk to Duke.

She probably should have told him about the NBT Trust earlier. But after she confronted Zach, all she'd wanted to do was cry. The fact that the county coroner was a crook was nothing compared with her humiliation. She'd loved him. Trusted him. Almost committed to him. All she could think of was the "what ifs." What if she had gone off with him this weekend and they had become lovers? What if he continued to treat her like a queen, to fill her every need and desire? What if he had continued to shower Kevin with attention? What if they had married and become a family, with all the conveniences, all the opportunities his money could buy? What if they had had children together, with dreams of providing the best educations for them? And what if she didn't discover his underworld ties until much later, after she was more invested in Zach's life? Would she have accepted his world as "just business"? Would she have looked the other way at hints of arson and murder? Would she sell her soul for a better life? Wouldn't anyone if the price was great enough?

Josie pounded on the door a few more times. She was ready to give up and leave when a small light came on in the living room and the door opened a crack.

"Josie? What in the fertile firmament?"

"Duke, I have to talk to you. I know who's behind the NBT Trust, and you were right. It is Zach. Oh, Duke, what are we going to do?"

Duke stepped back and opened the door into the darkened living room. A small night-light provided a soft golden glow, just enough to make out the outlines of the furniture but fading into blackness around the edges.

"What's this about the trust?"

"Nancy Boardman Teasdale. NBT," Josie said, stepping into the room. "She's Zach's mother and the daughter of Buster Boardman. Yeah, that Boardman. Zach's grandfather was a gangster."

"Pachyderm pack-a-dung! Where'd you get that?"

"The morgue. The wedding announcement was on microfilm. Newspapers record all if you just take the time to look," Josie said, plopping onto the sofa.

"So this Nancy inherited Boardman's holdings, or at least some of them, and that fell to Teasdale to manage," Duke said, taking a seat next to Josie.

"Yes, and when I confronted him with it, he didn't deny it."

"He admitted to being behind NBT Trust?"

"No, but it was clear. Oh, my God! He's probably behind everything: the fire, Avril's murder, the inflated sewer contract, the county's overpriced contract for the Herkimer, and who knows what else. Maybe he even hired the sniper that started the shootout at the sewer project. One of his all-purpose security guards, no doubt. And how about his business dealings in South America? What is that? Drugs? And the crazy thing is he thinks he's entitled. He thinks he has the right to decide what is best for the community. He thinks taking a bigger slice of the governmental pie is OK because he is somehow better qualified to say how that money should be spent. He does whatever he wants, snuffs out anyone who gets in the way, and then smiles and shakes your hand like he did you a favor."

Duke laughed. "I forgot how vicious you can be."

"Oh, and I haven't told you the worst part."

"You're pregnant."

"Oh, my God. Thank goodness we hadn't consummated the relationship. No, it's worse than that."

"What could be worse than carrying a little Zach inside? It's enough to give a person morning-noon-and-night sickness."

"Duke, are you listening to me? It's something else entirely. It's Maggie."

"She's a little old to be pregnant."

"Duke! Will you listen? She lied about Zelda kicking off a shoe. She made up the whole story to sell papers."

"You're kidding me. Maggie?"

"She had some crazy notion that it was justified to put pressure on Boardman. And I guess it worked. I suppose the story about him being behind the disappearance of a lady newspaper editor was so big that it led to his demise. He went from being a shady union organizer to a creep who kills women. Fine, upstanding women."

"So what did happen to Zelda?"

"Who knows? Maybe he killed her and buried her under Jackson Street, and maybe she just ran away with her boyfriend."

"How did you find out that Maggie made up the story about the shoe?"

"Oh, it doesn't matter. The point is good people like Maggie are going over to the dark side just to get some justice. Does that make any sense? Is the system really so bad that the only way to make it work is to lie? What happened to truth, justice, and the American way?"

"You're mixing *Superman* and *Star Wars*. Definitely a mixed metaphor."

"I don't know who to trust anymore. I'm obviously a horrible judge of men. I always fall for jerks—"

"Hey," Duke said, puffing his chest out in a show of indignation.

"And I can't even tell when a reporter is lying. That's the crux of my job, isn't it? I need to smell a skunk, and I blew it completely. Good God. I even imagined Zelda's spirit was talking to me. I am going crazy."

Josie turned her face into the sofa cushion and started bawling. Duke stroked her back.

"Oh, come on. Everybody was fooled by Maggie's shoe story. It's a great legend. No one would have guessed—"

"But you guessed that Zach was crooked, and I didn't see it at all," Josie said, turning her head onto Duke's shoulder. "It's like the whole world is off track. An innocent man like Rudy Randolph is destroyed by a false accusation, and somebody like Zach can get away with anything. Doesn't it seem like something is off-kilter? Like Atlas is hobbling around with one shoe off?"

Duke chuckled. "Don't worry. It will all get back on track. Rudy will survive because he's determined enough to keep trying. And Zach will get caught because he's arrogant enough to keep lying. Good folks just can't stop being good, and the bad guys can't stop being bad."

Suddenly the living room's overhead light came on. Duke jumped to his feet. Sharon was standing in the doorway.

"Duke, what are you doing? What's Josie doing here?"

"A development in a story. She came by to tell me," Duke stammered as Josie wiped her eyes and tried to regain her composure.

"In the middle of the night?" Sharon exclaimed. "And you answered the door in your underwear?"

Duke looked down at his white jockey shorts and then gave Josie an embarrassed glance.

"That's how I sleep," Duke mumbled. "Excuse me. I'll put on some jeans."

As Duke rushed out of the room, Josie rose to her feet.

"I'm sorry, Sharon. I didn't realize you were here."

"That's pretty obvious," Sharon replied. "We're in the middle of moving back in."

"Jennifer is here too?"

"Yeah. We thought we could be a nice little family again. I didn't realize Duke's job included late-night visits from the boss."

"I said I'm sorry to wake you. I'm glad you're back, really. I wouldn't have knocked so late if I had realized—"

"That's what's so strange," Sharon said, stepping forward to confront Josie face-to-face. "You came over here in the middle of the night expecting to find Duke alone. I come in and find you two in an embrace on the sofa in a dark room, and he doesn't even have any clothes on."

Duke rushed back into the living room, pulling on a white T-shirt over his jeans. He rushed to his wife and put a calming hand on her shoulder.

"Come on, Sharon, don't get carried away," he said in a low, soothing voice. "Josie went through that fire Friday night, and then her relationship with Zach fell apart tonight. She needed a friend, that's all."

"Oh, my God! How could I have been so stupid?" Sharon said, pulling away from Duke's touch. "That Wheeler guy tried to tell me, and I wouldn't believe it. You are having an affair with her, aren't you?"

"No!" Josie and Duke protested in unison.

"Oh, my God! Look how you fawn over each other. How long has this been going on?"

"It's not what you think," Duke said, reaching for Sharon again.

"There isn't anything going on between us," Josie said.

Duke looked to Josie and then his wife. He shook his head.

"Please, Sharon, I tried to tell you."

Sharon gasped and put a hand over her mouth.

"It was last summer," Duke continued, looking down at his feet. "You had left me, and I was drinking a lot. We were dealing with that serial killer and working all hours. One thing led to another."

Sharon let out a wounded yelp and put her hands over her eyes.

"It was only a week, less than a week," Josie said.

"A week?" Sharon yelled. "You slut! I thought you were my friend."

"I am your friend!" Josie yelled back. "You left your husband. Did you think he was gonna become a monk?"

Sharon lunged at Josie, clawing at her face. Josie squealed and fought her off.

"Come on, ladies," Duke said, trying to pull them apart.

"This isn't a college dorm where you can rifle your roommate's closet the minute her back is turned," Sharon hissed in Josie's face.

"And a husband isn't some rumpled blouse you can cast off when it goes out of style," Josie responded.

"Wait a minute!" Duke said. "I don't appreciate being compared to a fashion accessory."

"Stay out of this," Sharon said, shoving Duke away.

"You never should have left him when he needed you," Josie said.

"You don't have any idea what you're talking about!" Sharon shouted. "I did what I had to do."

"And we did what we had to do in the moment. It wasn't planned."

Duke tried to step in again. "Wait, Josie, don't—"

"Stay out of it," Josie repeated, holding up a hand to Duke. "This is between me and Sharon."

"Stop telling my husband what to do. You're not his boss in this house."

"And neither are you. You've got control issues, Sharon. You want to run his life."

"How did this conversation get to be about me? You're the one who slept with someone else's husband. Maybe *you* should have a little more control."

"And maybe you should accept a little responsibility for what happened. We apologized. We nipped it in the bud, and we haven't done anything improper since that week last summer."

"Oh, and that's supposed to make everything OK?"

"It's not OK. We know we made a mistake. But we corrected it the best we could. Can't you just forgive and forget?"

Sharon burst into laughter. "Forget? I'll never forget. But I'm not going to let you destroy my marriage. Duke was a drunk then. I've forgiven lots of things in the past. But I'll never forgive you. You betrayed me. Get out of my house. Get out!"

"I can accept that," Josie said, heading for the door. "I don't need your forgiveness. Sorry about interrupting your first night home."

Josie threw open the front door just in time to see Duke's car pulling out of the driveway and speeding down the road. Sharon rushed to the doorway, yelling Duke's name. The women stood side by side and watched his taillights disappear.

"Where's he going?" Sharon mumbled.

"You've got to stop him," Josie said. "He's upset. He may go to a bar. He may think he's lost you already."

"You don't know my husband," Sharon said, storming back into the house.

"Maybe not," Josie conceded, following her. "But I think he's under a lot of pressure right now. He gave up booze for you. If he thinks he's lost you—"

"It's his choice. He has to choose not to drink. He has to accept that responsibility. I can't keep covering for him."

"I'm not asking you to cover anything. But he needs to know you still love him. Believe me, if he thinks he's lost you, he could do anything."

"I can't go running after him every time he gets his feelings hurt. He needs to claim sobriety for himself, not for me."

"If you don't go after him, I will," Josie said, heading out the door. She jumped into her car and backed out of the driveway. As she started to pull forward, she saw a figure running across her headlights. She stopped, and Sharon opened the passenger door.

"I'm going with you. Maybe if he sees us together ... maybe if we tell him we've worked it out and it's all forgiven ..."

Josie paused to take this in, then turned her attention to the road.

"I thought I'd go by Mel's," Josie said. "That's where he used to go after work. Any other bars you would suggest?"

"The Rusty Tug on Black Road. That's the closest to the house. That's where he'll be."

The women didn't find Duke's car at either bar or at any of the other watering holes they checked. If he wanted to drink alone, he might have picked up a bottle at a package store and gone anywhere. They drove past the *Daily News*, thinking he might have sought out a familiar parking lot. They also went to Sharon's old apartment. Duke had a key, and they had access through the end of the month. Duke wasn't at any of the places.

They decided to return home, thinking Duke might have returned. On the way, they spotted a turquoise Pontiac in the parking lot at Denny's, one of the few restaurants open at this hour. They pulled in beside it and rushed inside. In a back booth they found Duke and Rudy Randolph chatting over coffee. Sharon slid in next to Duke and gave him a peck on the cheek as if nothing had happened.

"We've been looking everywhere for you," she said.

"I had no idea you two knew each other," Josie added, sitting next to Rudy.

Duke and Rudy exchanged glances. Then Duke turned to his wife. "This is Rudy, my sponsor with AA. Rudy, this is my wife, Sharon."

Rudy looked alarmed. "Duke, I don't know if we should—"

"No, really. I'd better come clean," Duke said. "I don't want somebody spreading rumors that we're having a gay liaison."

"Heavens, no," Rudy said.

"I was feeling a little vulnerable," Duke said. "I wanted a drink in the worst way. But I called Rudy instead, and he suggested this place."

"I'm glad," Sharon said. "Great to meet you, Rudy."

"Well, you ladies look like you ... ah ... survived," Duke said.

"We're working on a truce," Sharon said, scowling at Josie.

Josie leaned forward and spoke in a whisper. "Maybe I shouldn't mention this, Sharon. But you're still wearing your nightgown."

"This old thing," Sharon said, looking down at the lace-trimmed pink shift. "It's the latest fashion. If Cyndi Lauper can go around with her bra on top of her blouse, I can wear my nightie to Denny's. It is night, after all."

Chapter 40

At the church service Sunday morning, Josie prayed with a grateful heart.

"Thank you, Lord, for bringing us safely through the fire. I know now that you revealed that secret passage to me for a purpose. I don't understand how dreams work, but I know you are taking care of us."

She also asked for a new beginning. As she had many times before, she asked to be forgiven for her affair with Duke, and she asked for the Lord's help in healing Sharon's hurt. She asked for help to forgive Maggie for breaking the cardinal rule of journalism. She prayed that Maggie would find forgiveness as well and live out her last days secure in God's grace.

"It was so long ago, Father. I don't see any reason why I should tell anyone about Maggie's falsehood. It's almost as if she made a choice to twist the truth so justice could prevail. But I know that isn't right. Help me to understand."

She asked for an open mind where Zach was concerned.

"Help me not to rush to judgment, Lord. It's so easy now to blame him for everything. Help me not to imagine fault where there is none. But open my eyes to reality. Don't allow me to be blinded by meaningless gestures of kindness. Help me to lead my staff to be alert for injustice in all guises. Guide us in our search for truth."

After church, she stopped by Ranch Rudy where Rudy had sketched a chalk outline of the United States in the parking lot. He had lined up little cans of paint in a variety of bright colors. A small brush was standing up in each can.

"It's for the summer camp," he said, tapping a brush on the edge of the yellow paint. "We'll teach the kids the names of the states and the capitals. And we'll use it for games. It's a little bit of work, but it will get a lot of use."

"Has the enrollment improved?"

"So far we've got twenty-one. Enough for a good summer camp, but not enough to continue into the fall. I'm going to put the house on the market. Maybe move to another town. I'll never be able to run a profitable day care in this town."

"That's so unfair. Why is it that some people can manipulate the system and get away with it? And someone like you, who didn't do anything wrong, ends up getting punished?"

"Life isn't fair. You've just got to accept that," Rudy said as he bent over to outline the state of Florida with a sunny yellow paint.

"It was good to run into you last night. To see you in a whole different role."

"Not so different. I'm a listener. I listen to kids during the day."

"But I had no idea you were involved with AA."

"Duke shouldn't have told you."

"Well, I'm sorry if it breaks some sort of confidence. But I'm glad to know that about you. I see you as more than just a funny guy who takes care of kids. You have other interests."

"Naturally, I have other interests."

"I'm scared to ask what all Duke has told you about me."

Rudy looked up and smiled. "We never use names when we discuss problems."

Josie picked up the brush in the red paint can. "Is this OK to outline New York state? The Big Apple?"

"Sure."

Josie knelt down and painted a red brush stroke along the chalk outline of New York. "This is really a fun idea. It's too bad you'll only use it for the summer. Are you sure you aren't opening in the fall?"

"I'm sure. Parents need to know well in advance so they can make other arrangements."

"Where will you go? Back to Vermont?"

"No, I don't think so." Rudy switched to the bright-orange paint to outline Georgia.

"Did you ever think of moving into another career, something other than child care?" Josie asked as she finished the New York shape.

"Sure. I could try for a teaching certificate. I always thought I'd be an English teacher in a high school, but after my daughter died ... " Rudy's voice trailed off.

"What color for Vermont?" Josie asked.

"Green. The Green Mountain Boys."

"Right. Green Mountain," she said, reaching for the brush in the green paint. She stroked the brush along the outline of the small state next to New York. "I remembered in our research that you were studying creative writing at the University of Vermont. Would you be interested in a job as a reporter for the *Daily News*?"

Rudy looked at Josie with a quizzical expression. "Where does this come from?"

"Well, I have an opening," Josie said, not looking up from her painting. "Our court reporter, Maggie Sheffield, won't be returning to work. She's moving to California. I'll be looking for another writer. The job won't necessarily be covering courts, but it could be. We try to match the interest and experience of each writer to the beat assignment, but it's good to expand into new areas as well. You'd be a natural for covering education, writing about kids and families."

Josie finished the outline of Vermont and looked up. Rudy was staring at her with his mouth open.

"Are you serious? I never thought about writing for publication in anything beyond a literary magazine."

Josie smiled. "Well, reporting isn't exactly creative writing. A little creativity can make a boring subject interesting, but you've got to stick with the facts. The goal is to fade into the background so the subjects can tell their story. We want readers to see the people they are reading about, not the writer. We need good listeners."

Rudy agreed to submit an application and writing samples. Josie said she would set up an interview appointment with Hammond. After outlining New Hampshire, Massachusetts, and Maine, Josie left Rudy to finish his task.

Josie's next stop was Maggie's house. Katherine was sorting knickknacks and dishes into two stacks: mementos she wanted to take to California and those that would be sold at an estate sale. The collection for the sale was spread over the dining room table, while only a handful went into the California box.

Maggie was in her wheelchair in the sunroom off the living room. She seemed relaxed and almost smiling. She was stroking Buttons, who was curled on her lap. Katherine had decided to keep the dog as a companion for her mother.

"Don't you two make the perfect picture," Josie said, kneeling beside Maggie's chair and letting Buttons lick her fingers.

"J-J-Jo," Maggie stammered slowly.

"You're talking!" Josie exclaimed.

"Just a few words," Katherine said. "She still has a lot of trouble, but it's a start. At least she can say more than 'oh, oh, oh.' What do you think about this tea set? If you see anything you want, help yourself."

Katherine returned to the china cabinet, leaving Josie and Maggie alone on the porch.

"I'm going to miss you so much, Maggie. These past few weeks … I feel like we've become so close."

"S-s-s-so r-r-r-ry," Maggie managed.

"I know. I'm sorry too for all the things I said. I wasn't there when you were dealing with Boardman. It's not my place to judge the decision you made."

Maggie reached her hand out to touch Josie's face. That's when Josie noticed the orchid corsage pinned to Maggie's shoulder.

"What a lovely flower!"

"Oh, that's from Alpha and Omega," Katherine said, coming out on the porch. "You just missed them. They heard about the fire and flew up here from Florida to check on Mom."

"Alpha and Omega?" Josie repeated.

"Some friends of Mom's from a long time ago," Katherine explained. "They send Christmas cards every year, but this is the first time I got to meet them."

Alpha and Omega? Josie thought. A to Z. Al and Zelda. Could it be?

"How old are these people?" Josie asked.

"Oh, I don't know. Mom's age or a little older, I guess," Katherine said, picking up a little vase from a table on the porch. Maggie stroked a purple petal of her orchid. When she looked at Josie, her eyes were dancing with delight.

"You know, Alpha and Omega are the cutest people," Katherine continued as she picked up another figurine. "They live on their own little island in the Florida Keys. Alpha is a lobster fisherman, and Omega grows orchids. Isn't that just the ideal life?"

"Someday I'll eat nothing but lobster and wear orchids every day."

That's what Zelda said in the dream.

When Katherine returned to the living room, Josie whispered to Maggie, "Is it her?"

Maggie nodded and her lips struggled to form the word.

"Z-Z-Z-Zel-d-da."

1) Duke says the people of Jordan have the "right to know" how and why Blaine Avril was murdered. (p. 55) Do you think the public has a right to information about crimes? Do you think the wife of Blaine Avril/Timothy Norton has a right to know how her husband died, or is it better for her to believe he died in a military exercise? Does Duke's wife have the "right to know" about his affair during their separation?

2) Rudy says parents who are late picking up their children from the day-care center are undermining the bond of trust between parent and child and caregiver. (p. 14) Do you agree? Do you think the parents respond fairly when Rudy is accused of abusing a child in his care? After he is cleared of charges, Rudy's business continues to suffer. Who is to blame? The child who lied? The media that reported the arrest? The aggressive intervention of Family Services?

3) Becky wants to keep her relationship with Detective Tom Cantrell "strictly professional," (p.38) but what happens when Duke shares some details of Cantrell's life outside the job? Can you think of other instances when Duke's interaction with sources is not "strictly professional?" Do you think Duke's relationships with sources help or hinder his effectiveness as a reporter?

4) Zelda says "Neutral is journalism jargon for ignorance." (p.21) Do you think newspapers should remain "neutral" on the stories they report? Or should the paper take sides based on the facts they uncover? Zelda is determined to expose illegal activity such as gambling which others seem willing to overlook. Is that the job of the media?

5) When Buster Boardman puts a spike through his hand, he says "blood's the only language (some people) understand." (p.97) Does Boardman's statement justify the necessity of violence? How does Zelda react to his injury?

6) Josie's dreams offer supernatural insight. Do you think that's possible or do you agree with Duke that people can only dream what they already know?

7) Why did Sharon leave Duke? Did her action cause Duke to give up drinking or were other factors at play? Should Sharon accept some of the responsibility for Duke's extramarital affair?

8) Zach Teasdale says his grandfather taught him that "when you lose your temper, you lose." (p. 139) Does he follow his grandfather's advice? How does Zach's personal self-control affect others? Does it give him power? Does Josie keep her temper under control?

9) Josie says bluffing is her long suit. (p. 120) How does she get information from Irwin MacDonald by bluffing? Does she use bluffing to get information from anyone else?

10) Duke calls Ron Baylor and Herbie Flatt "the bungling big-bod boys." (p. 221) What are some of the mistakes they made? They end up dead and Terry Tate goes to jail—do you think justice is served? Wheeler believes someone has made it worthwhile for Tate to go to jail by paying for his son's education. (p.231) This implies that someone wealthy is responsible. Who might that be?